Mary Louise Booth, Edouard Laboulaye

Laboulaye's Fairy Book

Fairy Tales of all Nations

Mary Louise Booth, Edouard Laboulaye

Laboulaye's Fairy Book
Fairy Tales of all Nations

ISBN/EAN: 9783337137649

Printed in Europe, USA, Canada, Australia, Japan

Cover: Foto ©Andreas Hilbeck / pixelio.de

More available books at **www.hansebooks.com**

LABOULAYE'S FAIRY BOOK.

FAIRY TALES OF ALL *NATIONS.*

By ÉDOUARD LABOULAYE,

MEMBER OF THE INSTITUTE OF FRANCE.

TRANSLATED BY MARY L. BOOTH,

Translator of "Martin's History of France," &c., &c.

With Engravings.

NEW YORK:

HARPER & BROTHERS, PUBLISHERS,

FRANKLIN SQUARE.

1870.

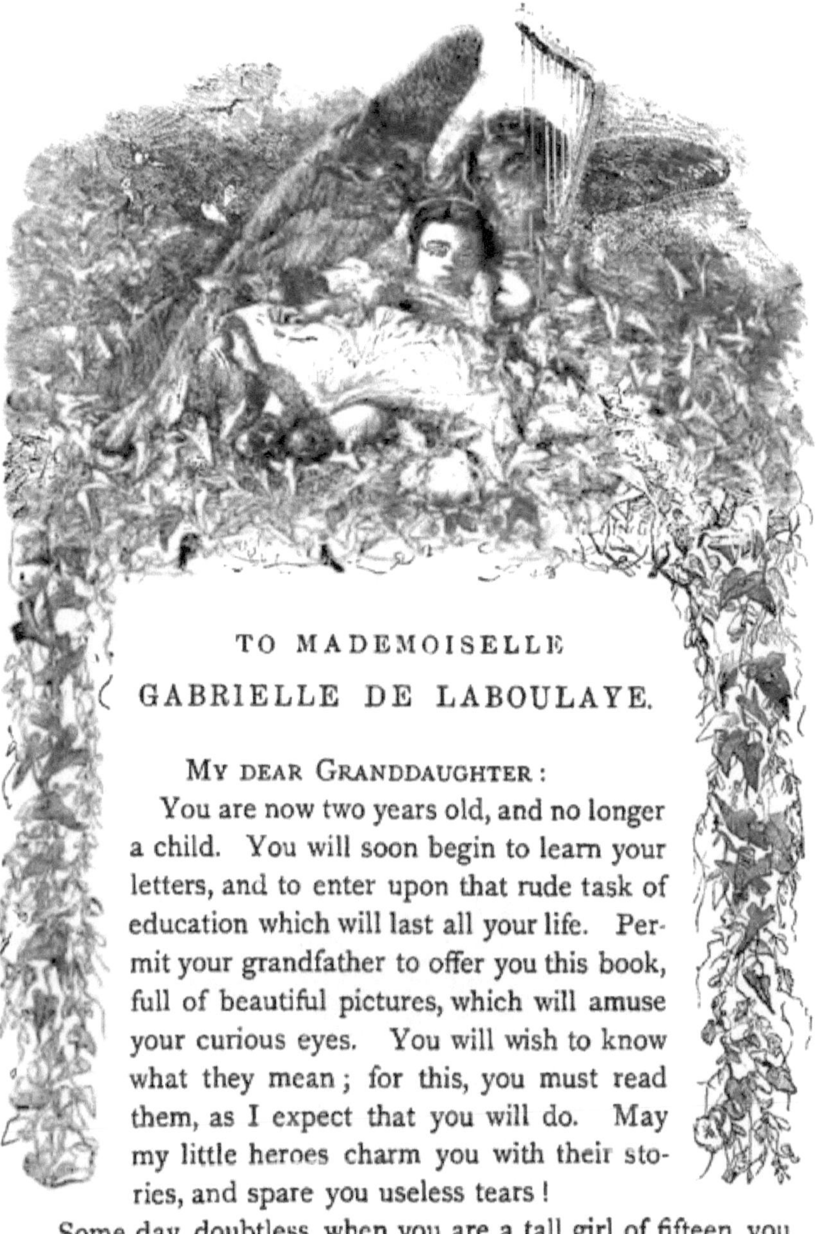

TO MADEMOISELLE
GABRIELLE DE LABOULAYE.

My dear Granddaughter:

You are now two years old, and no longer
a child. You will soon begin to learn your
letters, and to enter upon that rude task of
education which will last all your life. Permit your grandfather to offer you this book,
full of beautiful pictures, which will amuse
your curious eyes. You will wish to know
what they mean; for this, you must read
them, as I expect that you will do. May
my little heroes charm you with their stories, and spare you useless tears !

Some day, doubtless, when you are a tall girl of fifteen, you
will throw aside this book with your doll, and perhaps even
wonder how your grandfather, with his gray beard, could have

had so little sense as to waste his time on such trifles. Be not too severe, my dear Gabrielle ; grant me five or six years' indulgence. If God spares your life, you, too, will have children, and grandchildren perhaps ; and experience will teach you only too quickly that the truest and sweetest things in life are not those which we see, but those of which we dream. Then, in repeating my tales to the young folks whom I shall never see, you will remember him who loved you when you were little ; and perhaps you will find pleasure in talking to them of the old man who delighted in trying to amuse children, while they will listen with sparkling eyes, and be proud of their great-grandfather. I desire no other fame ; this immortality suffices me.

With these words, I respectfully lay at your feet my Fairy Book, and subscribe myself, with a hearty kiss,

Your Old Grandfather.

AUTHOR'S PREFACE.

to my young friends in america:

Dear Children,—When you are large, and are studying the glorious history of your country, you will be told that on the other side of the Atlantic there is an old country by the name of France. You will also be told that almost a hundred years ago, when your grandfathers were fighting for their independence, it was in France that they found sympathizing hearts and devoted hands. It was from France that the friend of Washington came, the brave and noble La Fayette—a name which also belongs to the history of the United States.

Years have passed, and nothing has disturbed the friendship of a century's growth between America and France—that friendship which you, my children, I am sure, will preserve. And it is in order to keep up this mutual affection that I send you these tales, which have amused your young friends in France, and which I hope will amuse you also. He who writes them is not a stranger to your fathers and mothers; he was heart and soul with them in the trials which they have nobly passed through. To-day he would esteem himself happy could he make you laugh or dry up your tears; and nothing would touch him more than sometimes to think that over yonder, on the other side of the ocean, there were young gentlemen and charming young ladies who forgot the hours in listening to the tales of their friend, the old Frenchman,

Édouard Laboulaye.

TRANSLATOR'S PREFACE.

PROMPTED in part by the desire to please a certain Prince Charming of my acquaintance, I have amused the leisure of an arduous undertaking by collecting the exquisite tales which M. Laboulaye has been in the habit for some years past of scattering through various books and journals, and which can not fail to delight both young and old by their sparkling wit and richness of fancy. The brilliant author of "Paris in America" needs no introduction to American readers. One of the first humorists, as well as one of the first judicial writers of France, it is his favorite recreation to amuse children with tales wherein the grotesque veils a keen and subtle satire rarely equaled. The style is inimitable, and the fancies are not surpassed even by those of the famed Hans Christian Andersen.

The selection now offered to the American public was first submitted to the approval of the author, who has kindly signified his full approbation of it, and furnished a preface written expressly for this edition. "The composition of the volume is excellent," he says, "and I shall take great pleasure in seeing myself in an American dress. I am especially delighted that Abdallah finds a place in the collection. This little volume cost me more than a year's study. There is not a detail in it that is not borrowed from some narrative of Eastern travel, and I read the Koran through twice (a wearisome task) in order to extract therefrom a morality that might put Christians to the blush, though practiced by Arabs. My granddaughter, who is now five years old, and is going to learn English, is very proud to think that her name will be known in America."

The dedication to Mademoiselle Gabrielle de Laboulaye, the author's granddaughter, here alluded to, is that prefixed to the *Contes Bleus*, an elegant volume published some three years since, and from which several of these tales are taken. It was at first designed to omit Abdallah, which forms a separate volume in the original. I am happy to have been able to embrace this beautiful story of Oriental life in the volume which I offer to the perusal of my young American friends, persuaded that the name of the illustrious author will thereby become a household word among them, as it is already among their parents, and as it will be in history.

MARY L. BOOTH.

CONTENTS.

FAIRY BOOK.

PERLINO.

A NEAPOLITAN TALE.

I.

VIOLET.

MANY years ago there lived at Pæstum a merchant by the name of Beppo, who was as good as bread, as sweet as honey, and as rich as the sea. He was a widower, and had but one daughter, whom he loved like his right hand. Violet, for that was the name of this beloved child, was as fair as a lily, and as blooming as a rose. She had long black tresses, eyes as blue as the sky, cheeks as velvety as a butterfly's wing, and lips like a twin cherry. Add to this the wit of a demon, the grace of a seraph, the figure of Venus, and the fingers of a fairy, and you will understand that neither young nor old could help loving her at first sight.

When Violet was fifteen years old, Beppo began to think about marrying her. "The orange-tree," thought he, "brings forth its flower without knowing who will gather it, and the father watches over his daughter for long years like the apple of his eye, only that a stranger may rob him of his treasure some fine day without even saying " thank you." Where shall

I find a husband worthy of my Violet? No matter, she is rich enough to choose whom she likes. She is so beautiful and witty that she would tame a tiger should she undertake it."

The good Beppo often tried to talk to his daughter of marriage, but he might as well have flung his words to the wind. No sooner had he touched this chord than Violet cast down her eyes and complained of headache ; upon which her poor father, more troubled than a monk that loses his memory in the midst of his sermon, directly changed the conversation, and took from his pocket some gift that he always had in store— a ring, a bracelet, or a gold thimble, whereupon Violet kissed him, and the sun returned after the shower.

One day, however, when Beppo, more prudent than usual, had begun where he generally ended, and Violet held in her hands a necklace so beautiful that it was impossible for her to be sulky, the good man returned to the attack. "Oh, love and joy of my heart, staff of my old age, and crown of my gray hairs !" said he, caressing her, "shall I never see you married? Do you not feel that I am growing old ? My gray beard tells me every day that it is time to choose you a protector. Why don't you do like other women? do you not see that they are all dying to marry? What is a husband?—a bird in a cage, that sings whatever tune you please. If your poor mother was living, she would tell you that she never shed tears on account of not having her way ; she was always queen and empress at home. I dared not breathe before her any more than before you, and I can not console myself for my freedom."

"Father," said Violet, playfully chucking him under the chin, "you are the master, and it is for you to command. Dispose of my hand—make your own choice. I will marry when you like and whom you like ; I only ask one thing."

"Be it what it may, I will grant it," cried Beppo, charmed at an obedience to which he was not accustomed.

"Well, father, all that I desire is that my husband shall not look like a dog."

"What a childish idea!" exclaimed Beppo, radiant with joy. "Men are right in saying that beauty and folly go together. If you did not resemble your mother, could you be guilty of such absurdities! Do you believe that a man of sense like me—do you believe that the richest merchant in Pæstum would be stupid enough to accept a son-in-law with a dog's face? Be easy; I will choose for you, or, rather, you shall choose the handsomest and most amiable of men. Were he a prince, I am rich enough to buy him for you."

A few days after, Beppo gave a great dinner, to which he invited all the flower of the youth for twenty leagues around. The repast was magnificent; the guests ate much and drank more; every one was at his ease, and spoke from the fullness of his heart. When dessert was served, Beppo withdrew to a corner of the room, and, taking Violet on his lap, whispered to her, "My dear child, look at that handsome, blue-eyed young man, with his hair parted in the middle? Do you think that a woman would be unhappy with such a cherub?"

"Don't think of it, my dear father!" said Violet, laughing; "he looks exactly like a greyhound."

"It is true," cried Beppo, "he really does look like a greyhound. Where were my eyes that I did not see it? But that fine-looking captain, with his cropped head, stiff cravat, prominent chest, and protruding eyes—there is a man! What do you say to him?"

"Father, he looks like a bull-dog; I should always be afraid that he would bite me."

"It is true, he does look something like a bull-dog," replied Beppo, sighing. "We will say no more about him. Perhaps you would prefer a graver and more mature person. If women knew how to choose, they would never take a husband less than forty years old.　Under that age, they find nothing but fops who suffer themselves to be adored ; it is not till after forty that a man is really ripe to love and obey.　What do you say to that counselor of law, who talks so well, and who likes so well to hear himself talk?　What matters his gray hairs ! gray hair is wiser than black."

"Father, you are not keeping your word.　You see very well that with his red eyes, and his white curls hanging over his ears, he looks like a poodle."

It was the same with all the guests ; not one escaped Violet's tongue.　One, who sighed timidly, resembled a Barbary dog ; another, with long black hair and caressing eyes, had the face of a spaniel.　No one was spared.　It is said, indeed, that every man looks like a dog when you put your hand under the nose, hiding the mouth and chin.

"Violet has too much wit," thought Beppo ; "I shall never do any thing with her by reasoning."　Upon this, he pretended to fall into a rage, called her ungrateful, hard-hearted, and foolish, and ended by threatening to put her into a convent for the rest of her days.　Violet began to cry ; he fell upon his knees, asked her pardon, and promised never more to speak to her of any thing that she did not like.　The next morning he rose, after passing a sleepless night, kissed his daughter, thanked her for not having swollen eyes, and waited for the wind that turns the weathercocks to blow toward his house.　This time he was not wrong.　With women more things happen in an hour than with men in ten years ; and the saying, "I will never travel this road," was not made for

II.

BIRTH AND BETROTHAL OF PERLINO.

ONE day, when there was a festival in the suburbs of the town, Beppo asked his daughter what he should bring her.

"Father," said she, "if you love me, buy me half a ton of white sugar, and the same quantity of blanched almonds, five or six bottles of scented water, a little musk and amber, forty pearls, two sapphires, and a handful of garnets and rubies; bring me also twenty skeins of gold thread, ten yards of green velvet, and a piece of cherry-colored silk; and, above all things, don't forget a silver trough and trowel."

. The merchant was greatly astonished; but he had been too good a husband not to know that with women the shortest way is not to reason, but to obey, and he returned home at night with his mule heavily laden.

Violet ordered all her gifts to be carried to her chamber; then shut herself up, and set about making a paste with the sugar and almonds, which she moistened with the rose and jasmine water. She kneaded the paste in the trough, and moulded it with her silver trowel, like a potter or a sculptor, into the most beautiful young man that ever was seen. She made his hair of the gold thread, his eyes of the sapphires, his teeth of the pearls, and his tongue and lips of the garnets and rubies; after which she dressed him in the silk and velvet, and christened him Perlino, because he was as fair and rosy as the mother-of-pearl.

When she had finished her masterpiece, and stood it on the table, Violet clapped her hands, and began to dance about Perlino. She sang him the most tender airs, addressed to him the sweetest words, and blew him kisses that would have warmed a heart of stone, but all in vain—the doll did not stir. Violet was beginning to cry for spite, when all at once she recollected that she had a fairy for a godmother. What godmother, above all when she is a fairy, ever rejects the first prayer of her godchild? Violet prayed so long and earnestly that her godmother heard her two hundred leagues off, and took pity on her. She blew with her lips—it is all that fairies need to do to work a miracle—when lo! Perlino opened first one eye and then the other, turned his head to the right and left, and yawned in the most natural manner imaginable; then, while Violet wept and laughed for joy, he began to walk slowly, and with mincing steps, across the table.

More delighted than if she had won the kingdom of France in a lottery, Violet caught Perlino in her arms, kissed him on both cheeks, and sang,

> " Perlino, my darling, my treasure, my pride,
> Now let us dance, and I'll be thy bride ;
> Now let us dance, now let us sing,
> I will be queen, thou shalt be king.
> Now we are both in the spring-time of life,
> Light of my eyes, I'll be thy wife,
>   To dance and to play
>   Through the long day ;
> This will be life, joyous and gay :
> And if my wish thou dost ever obey,
>   The gods will not be
>   More happy than we."

Beppo, who was taking an account of his goods for the second time, dissatisfied at having made only a million of dollars in a year, heard the noise overhead. "Upon my word," he exclaimed, "there is something strange up stairs ; it sounds as if some one were quarreling."

He mounted the stairs, and, pushing open the door, saw the most beautiful sight in the world. Opposite his daughter, flushed with pleasure, stood Cupid in person—Cupid, dressed in silk and velvet. With both hands clasped in those of his little mistress, Perlino was skipping and dancing, as if he were never to stop.

As soon as Violet perceived her father, she made a low bow, and, presenting to him her beloved, said, "My lord and

father, you wish to see me married. To obey and please you, I have chosen a husband according to my own heart."

"You have done well, my child," replied Beppo, who read the mystery; "all women ought to follow your example. I know of more than one that would cut off one of their fingers, and not the little one either, to manufacture a husband according to their heart, all made of sugar and orange-flower water. Give them your secret, and you will dry up many tears. For two thousand years they have been complaining, and for two thousand years longer they will complain of being misunderstood and sacrificed." Saying this, he embraced his daughter, and asked for two days to make ready for the wedding. No less time was needed to invite all their friends round about, and to prepare a dinner which would not be unworthy of the richest merchant of Pæstum.

III.

THE ABDUCTION OF PERLINO.

To see so novel a marriage, every one came from the whole country round; rich and poor, young and old, friends and foes, all wished to know Perlino. Unhappily, there never is a wedding without the devil meddles with it, and Violet's godmother had not foreseen what would happen.

Among the invited guests there was a personage of considerable importance—a countess of the neighborhood, by the name of the Lady of the Chinking Guineas. She was as wicked and as old as Satan; her skin was yellow and wrinkled, her eyes haggard, her cheeks hollow, her nose hooked, and her chin pointed; but she was rich, so rich that every one bowed down to her as she passed, and disputed the honor of kissing her hand. Beppo bent to the ground, and seated her at his right hand, happy and proud to present his daughter and son-in-law to a lady who, having more than a hundred millions, did him the favor to eat his dinner.

During the whole meal the Lady of the Chinking Guineas did nothing but gaze at Perlino. Her heart was burning with envy. The countess lived in a castle worthy of the fairies, with walls of gold and pavements of silver. In this castle there was a gallery in which all the curiosities of the world were assembled—a clock that always struck the hour desired; an elixir that cured gout and headache; a philter that changed sorrow to joy; an arrow of love; the shade of Scipio; the heart of a coquette; the religion of a doctor; a stuffed siren; three horns of a unicorn; the conscience of a courtier; the politeness of a man newly enriched; and the hippogriff of Orlando—all things that never had been and never would be seen any where else. But this treasure lacked one gem—this cherub of a Perlino.

Before dessert arrived the lady had resolved to gain possession of him. She was very avaricious; but what she desired she must have at once, no matter at what price. She bought all that was to be sold, and even that which was not for sale; all the rest she stole, quite certain that the laws were only made for the poor. "From an ignorant doctor, a stubborn mule, and a wicked woman, good Lord, deliver us!" says the proverb. No sooner had they risen from the table than she drew near Perlino, who, born only three days before, had not yet opened his eyes to the wickedness of the world, and told him of all the beauty and riches in the Palace of the Chinking Guineas. "Come with me, my dear little friend," said she, "and I will give you whatever place you like in my palace. Choose; would you rather be a page dressed in gold, a chamberlain with a diamond key suspended about your neck, or a door-keeper with a silver halberd and a great gold breast-plate that will make you more brilliant than the sun? Speak but a word, and all is yours."

The poor innocent was dazzled ; but, however short a time he had breathed his native air, he was already a Neapolitan, that is, the reverse of stupid.

"Madam," answered he, ingenuously, "to work is the trade of oxen ; there is nothing so healthful as repose. I should like a profession in which there was nothing to do and a great deal to gain, like the canons of St. Januarius."

"What !" said the Lady of the Chinking Guineas, "at your age, would you already be an idler ?"

"Yes, and twice over," interrupted Perlino, "so as to earn double wages."

"That makes no difference," returned the countess ; "in the mean time, come, and I will show you my carriage, my English coachman, and my six gray horses." She drew him toward the door. "And Violet ?" said Perlino, faintly. "Violet is following us," replied the lady, dragging on the imprudent boy, who suffered her to lead him. Once in the yard, she showed him her beautiful horses, which were pawing the ground and shaking their nets of red silk hung with golden bells ; then persuaded him to enter the carriage to try the cushions, and look at himself in the mirrors. Suddenly she shut the door, the coachman cracked his whip, and off they went at full gallop toward the Castle of the Chinking Guineas.

Violet meanwhile was gracefully receiving the congratulations of the assembly. Astonished at not seeing her betrothed, who had clung to her like her shadow, she ran through all the rooms without finding him ; then climbed to the top of the house to see if he had not gone there to breathe the fresh air, but all in vain. In the distance she perceived a cloud of dust, and a coach with six horses going at full gallop toward the mountain. There was no more doubt ; it was carrying off Perlino. At the sight Violet felt her heart sink within her. Without thinking that she was bareheaded and

in bridal attire, with lace dress and satin shoes, she rushed
from her father's house and ran after the carriage, shouting
Perlino's name, and stretching out her arms. She might as
well have cried to the winds. The ungrateful boy was wholly
absorbed in the honeyed words of his new mistress. He was
playing with the rings on her fingers, and dreaming already
that the next morning he should awaken a prince. Alas!
there are older ones than he that are no wiser. When do
men learn that at home goodness and beauty are worth more
than riches? When it is too late, and they no longer have
strength to break the chains that they have put on their own
hands.

IV.

NIGHT AND DAY.

Poor Violet ran all day long after Perlino ; ditches, brooks,
thickets, briers, thorns, nothing stopped her. He who suffers
for love feels no pain. When evening came she found herself in a dark forest, overpowered with fatigue and half dead
with hunger, her hands and feet covered with blood. Seized
with terror, she looked round her ; a thousand faces seemed
to glare threateningly from the darkness. She threw herself
trembling at the foot of a tree, calling on Perlino, in a low
voice, to bid him a last farewell.

As she held her breath, so frightened that she dared not
move, she heard the trees about her talking together. It is
the privilege of innocence to understand all the creatures of
God. "Neighbor," said a carob-tree to a hollow olive-tree,
"that young girl is very imprudent to lie on the ground. In
an hour the wolves will quit their den, and if they spare her,
the morning dew and cold will give her a fever from which
she will never recover. Why doesn't she climb among my

branches?   She could sleep there in peace, and I would willingly give her some of my pods to recruit her exhausted
strength."

"You are right, neighbor," answered the olive-tree.   "The
child would do still better if, before going to sleep, she should
put her hand into my trunk, where the bagpipe and clothes
of a piper are hidden.   A goat-skin is not to be despised as a
protection from the cold night air ; and a lace dress and satin
shoes are a light costume for a girl to roam the world in."

Violet was reassured when she had found the coarse jacket,
goat-skin cloak, pointed hat, and bagpipe of the piper.   She
bravely climbed the carob-tree, ate its sugared fruit, drank
the evening dew, and, wrapping herself up warmly, lay down
among the branches as well as she could.   The tree clasped
its paternal arms about her, the wood-pigeons left their nests
to cover her with leaves, the wind rocked her like an infant,
and she fell asleep thinking of her beloved.

On waking the next morning she was filled with terror.
The weather was calm and beautiful, but in the silence of the
woods the poor child felt her solitude more deeply than ever.
Every thing was living and loving around her ; and who
thought of the poor forsaken one?   She began to sing in order to call to her aid all that passed by without looking at
her ; but the wind swept on murmuring, the bee set out in
search of his booty, the swallows chased the flies high in the
air, the birds chirped and sang to each other in the foliage,
and no one troubled himself about Violet.   She descended
from the tree with a sigh, and marched straight forward, trust-
ing to her heart to find Perlino.

V.

THE THREE FRIENDS.

A TORRENT fell from the mountain, the bed of which was partly dried up. Violet followed this road. The red laurels were already springing from the water, their branches covered with flowers. Violet plunged among the verdure, followed by the butterflies, fluttering around her as around a lily shaken by the wind. She walked faster than an exile returning home; but the heat was intense, and before noon she was forced to stop.

On approaching a pool of water to cool her burning feet, she saw a drowning bee. She extended her tiny foot, and the insect climbed on it. Once dry, the bee remained for some time motionless as if to regain breath; then it shook its damp wings, and, passing over its whole body its foot softer than silk, it dried and polished itself, and, taking flight, buzzed around her who had saved its life.

"Violet," it said, "you have not obliged an ingrate. I know where you are going; let me go with you. When I am tired, I will rest on your head. If ever you are in need of me, only say

> "'Nebuchadnezzar, hark and behold,
> The peace of the heart is better than gold,'

and perhaps I can serve you."

"Ah!" said Violet, "I never can say '*Nebuchadnezzar.*'"

"What do you want?" asked the bee.

"Nothing, nothing," replied Violet; "I shall not need you till I reach Perlino."

She set out again on the way with a lighter heart. In a few minutes she heard a faint cry; it was a white mouse that had been wounded by a hedgehog, and had escaped its enemy, covered with blood, and half dead. Violet took pity on the poor animal. Notwithstanding her haste, she stopped to wash its wounds, and to give it one of the carob-pods which she had kept for her breakfast.

"Violet," said the mouse, "you have not obliged an ingrate. I know where you are going. Put me into your pocket with the rest of your carob-pods. If ever you are in need of me, only say

> "'Tricche verlacche,
>   Coat of gold and heart of a lackey,'

and perhaps I can serve you."

Violet slipped the mouse into her pocket, that it might nibble there at its ease, and continued to ascend the torrent. Toward dusk she approached the mountain, when suddenly a squirrel fell at her feet, pursued by a frightful screech-owl. Violet was not timid. She struck the owl with her bagpipe, and put it to flight, then picked up the squirrel, which was more stunned than hurt by its fall, and brought it to life by dint of care.

"Violet," said the squirrel, "you have not obliged an ingrate. I know where you are going. Put me on your shoulder, and pick some nuts for me, that I may not let my teeth grow long for want of something to do. If ever you are in need of me, only say

> "'Patita, Patite,
>   Look well and you'll see,'

and perhaps I can serve you."

Violet was somewhat astonished at these three encounters. She relied little on this gratitude in words; what could such weak friends do for her? "No matter," thought she, "it is always right to do good; let what will happen, I have had pity on the unfortunate." At this moment the moon came out from a cloud, and its pale light fell on the old Castle of the Chinking Guineas.

VI.

THE CASTLE OF THE CHINKING GUINEAS.

THE sight of the castle was not calculated to reassure her. On the top of a mountain, which was nothing but a mass of crumbling rocks, she saw battlements of gold, turrets of silver, and roofs of sapphire and ruby, surrounded with great ditches full of greenish water, and defended by draw-bridges, portcullises, parapets, enormous bars, and loopholes from which protruded the throats of cannon, and all the paraphernalia of war and murder. The beautiful palace was nothing but a prison. Violet painfully climbed a winding path, and finally reached a narrow passage, which led to an iron door furnished with a huge lock. She called without receiving an answer; then pulled a bell, upon which a jailer appeared, blacker and uglier than Cerberus.

"Begone, beggar!" he cried, "or I will knock you down. There is no lodging for the poor here. In the Castle of.the Chinking Guineas we give alms only to those that do not need them."

Poor Violet turned away weeping. "Courage!" said the squirrel, cracking a nut; "play your bagpipe."

"I never played in my life," answered Violet.

"The more reason for doing so," replied the squirrel. "So long as you have not tried to do a thing, you don't know whether you can do it or not. Blow!"

Violet began to blow with all her might, moving her fingers and singing in the instrument, when behold! the pipes filled, and played a tarantella that would have caused the dead to dance. At the sound the squirrel leaped to the ground, and

the mouse did not stay behind.   They skipped and danced like true Neapolitans, while the bee buzzed and whirled around them.   It was a sight well worth paying for.

At the sound of this sweet music the black shutters of the castle were quickly seen to open.   The Lady of the Chinking Guineas had her maids of honor, who were not sorry to look out from time to time to see whether the flies always buzzed the same way. It was in vain not to be curious ; it was not every day that they heard a tarantella played by such a handsome shepherd as Violet.

"Boy," cried one, " come this way !"

"No," called another, " come on my side." And they all smiled on him, but the door remained shut.

, "Ladies," said Violet, taking off her hat, " be as good as you are beautiful. I have been overtaken by night in the mountain, and have neither lodging nor supper. Give me a corner in the stable and a crust of bread, and I and my little dancers will amuse you all the evening."

The regulations were strict in the Castle of the Chinking Guineas. There was such fear of robbers that no one was admitted after dusk. The ladies knew this well ; but in an honest household there is always a hangman's rope to be found. One end was thrown out of the window ; in an instant Violet was hoisted into a large chamber, with all her menagerie, and there she was forced to blow, and sing, and dance for long hours without being permitted to open her mouth to ask after Perlino. No matter, she was happy in feeling herself under the same roof with him, and it seemed to·her that at this moment the heart of her beloved must be beating like her own. The innocent child believed that it was only necessary to love in order to be loved. Her dreams that night were sweet ones.

VII.

NEBUCHADNEZZAR.

EARLY the next morning, Violet, who had slept in the barn, clambered on the roof and looked about her ; but her eyes wandered in vain in all directions ; she saw nothing but grated towers and solitary gardens. She burst into tears, in

spite of all the efforts of her three little friends to comfort
her.

In the court-yard, all paved with silver, she found the maids
of honor seated in a circle, spinning gold and silver flax on
their distaffs. "Begone!" they exclaimed, as soon as they
saw her; "if the countess should see your rags, she would
turn us all out of doors. Begone! vile piper, and never return; unless, indeed, you should become a prince or a banker."

"Oh, do not send me away so soon, fair ladies," replied
Violet; "let me wait on you; I will be so good and so obedient that you will never regret having let me stay."

The first maid of honor, a tall, thin, wrinkled, yellow, and
sharp-featured woman, rose, and, for her sole answer, motioned
the little shepherd to the door, and called the jailer, who advanced, frowning and brandishing his pike.

"I am lost!" exclaimed the poor girl; "I shall never more
see my Perlino!"

"Violet!" said the squirrel, gravely, "gold is tried in the
furnace, and friends in misfortune."

"You are right," exclaimed Violet.

> "'Nebuchadnezzar, hark and behold,
> The peace of the heart is better than gold!'"

The bee instantly flew in the air, and behold! a beautiful
crystal coach, with ruby shafts and emerald wheels, suddenly
appeared in the court-yard. The equipage was drawn by four
black dogs the size of rats. Four large beetles, dressed as
jockeys, guided the tiny steeds with a light hand. At the
back of the carriage, luxuriously reclining on cushions of blue
satin, was stretched a young woodpecker, dressed in a little
rose-colored bonnet, and a heavy brocade robe, so full that it
fell over the wheels. The lady held a fan in one hand, and
a smelling-bottle, and a handkerchief embroidered with her
arms and trimmed with broad lace, in the other. By her side,

half buried under the silken folds, was an owl, with languid air, listless eye, and bald head, and so old that his beak lapped like a pair of dislocated scissors. They were a new-married couple who were making their wedding-calls—a fashionable establishment, such as the Lady of the Chinking Guineas adored.

At the sight of this masterpiece, a cry of admiration and joy awakened all the echoes of the palace. The jailer let fall his pike with astonishment, while the ladies ran after the carriage and four spaniels, which set off at full gallop as if they were carrying the king in person. The strange noise disturbed the Lady of the Chinking Guineas, who was in constant fear of being robbed. She ran thither furious, resolved to turn all her maids of honor out of doors. She paid to be respected, and was determined to have the worth of her money. But when she perceived the equipage—when the owl saluted her with a sign of his beak, and the woodpecker waved her handkerchief three times with charming nonchalance, the lady's anger vanished in smoke.

"I must have this!" cried she. "What is the price of it?"

The countess's voice frightened Violet, but the love of Perlino gave her courage. She replied that, poor as she was, she loved her fancy better than all the gold in the world, and that she prized her carriage, and would not sell it for the Castle of the Chinking Guineas.

"Oh, the foolish vanity of beggars!" muttered the lady. "Truly, none but the rich have a holy respect for gold, and are ready to do any thing for a dollar. I must have this carriage," added she, in a threatening tone; "cost what it may, I will have it."

"Madam," said Violet, greatly excited, "it is true that I will not sell it, but I shall be happy to offer it to your ladyship as a gift if you will grant me one favor."

"It will be dear," thought the countess. "Speak!" said she to Violet; "what do you want?"

"Madam," replied Violet, trembling, "it is said that you have a museum in which all the curiosities of the world are collected. Show them to me; if there is any thing there more wonderful than this carriage, my treasure is yours."

For her sole answer, the Lady of the Chinking Guineas shrugged her shoulders, and led Violet to a great gallery, the like of which had never been seen. She showed her all her riches—a star fallen from heaven; a necklace made of a moonbeam, plaited in three strands; black lilies; green roses; an eternal love; fire that did not burn, and many other curiosities; but she did not show the only thing that would have moved Violet—Perlino was not there.

The countess vainly sought admiration and astonishment in the eyes of the little shepherd; she read nothing there but indifference. "Well," said she, "all these marvels are far more wonderful than your four puppies; the carriage is mine.'

"No, madam," said Violet; "all these things are dead, and my curiosities are living. You can not compare sticks and stones to my owl and woodpecker—personages so real and natural that it seems as if you had just met them in the street. Art is nothing compared with life."

"Is that all?" said the countess. "I will show you a little man made of sugar and almond-paste, who sings like a nightingale, and reasons like a professor."

"Perlino!" cried Violet.

"Ah!" said the Lady of the Chinking Guineas, "my maids of honor have been chattering." She looked at the piper with the instinct of fear. "On reflection," she added, "I do not want your child's toys—begone!"

"Madam," said Violet, trembling, "let me speak to this miracle of a Perlino, and take the carriage.'

"No," said the countess, "begone! and take your animals with you."

"Only let me see Perlino."

"No, no!" replied the lady.

"Only let me sleep a night at his door," resumed Violet, in tears. "See what a jewel you are refusing!" she added, bending on one knee, and offering the carriage to the Lady of the Chinking Guineas.

At the sight the countess hesitated, then smiled; in an instant she had found the means of deceiving Violet and obtaining what she coveted for nothing. "It is a bargain," said she, seizing the carriage; "you shall sleep to-night at Perlino's door, and shall even see him; but I forbid you to speak to him."

The evening come, the Lady of the Chinking Guineas sent for Perlino to sup with her. When she had made him eat and drink heartily, which was an easy thing with a youth of a yielding disposition, she poured out some excellent wine into a gilt cup, and, taking a crystal box from her pocket, took from it a reddish powder, which she threw into the wine. "Drink this, my child," said she to Perlino, "and tell me how you like it."

Perlino, who did whatever he was bid, swallowed the liquor at a single draught.

"Pah!" cried he, "this drink is detestable; it smells of blood and wine; it is poison!"

"Foolish fellow!" replied the countess, "it is potable gold; whoever has drunk it once will drink it always. Take another glass," she added; "you will find it better than the first."

The lady was right. Scarcely had the child emptied the cup, when he was seized with a raging thirst. "More! more!" he cried. He would not quit the table; and, to persuade him to go to bed, the countess was obliged to make him a great paper cornet of this marvelous powder, which he put carefully into his pocket as a remedy for all evils.

Poor Perlino! it was indeed a poison, and the most terrible of poisons, that he had taken. Whoever drinks potable gold feels his heart frozen the instant the liquid enters his stomach. He neither knows nor loves any thing thenceforth, neither father, nor mother, nor wife, nor children, nor friends, nor country; he thinks only of himself, and wishes to drink, and would drink all the gold and blood of the world without quenching a thirst that nothing could satisfy.

Meanwhile, what was Violet doing? The time seemed as long to her as a day without bread to the poor. As soon as night put on her black mask to open the starry ball, Violet ran to Perlino's door, quite sure that on seeing her he would throw himself into her arms. How her heart beat when she heard him coming up the stairs! and what was her sorrow when the ingrate passed by without even looking at her!

The door closed and double locked, and the key taken out, Violet threw herself on a mat that had been given her through pity, and, bursting into tears, covered her face with her hands to stifle her sobs. She did not dare to complain for fear of being driven away; but when the hour came in which the stars alone had their eyes open, she scratched gently on the door, and sang to Perlino in a low voice,

> "Dost thou hear me, Perlino?
> 'Tis I who would free thee:
> Open quickly to me,
> Lest I die ere I see thee.
> I tremble, I shiver, I sigh,
> Since thou, love, no longer art nigh.
> Night or day,
> Since thou art away,
> I no more am glad or gay."

Alas! it was in vain. Nothing stirred in the room. Perlino was snoring, and dreaming only of his gold dust. The hours dragged slowly along, bringing no hope. But, however long and painful the night, the morning was still sadder. The Lady of the Chinking Guineas appeared at daybreak. "Are you satisfied, handsome piper?" said she, with a malicious smile. "The carriage is paid for at your own price."

"May you have such contentment all the days of your life!" murmured poor Violet. "I have passed such a wretched night that I shall not soon forget it."

VIII.

TRICCHE VERLACCHE.

VIOLET retired sadly. Her hopes were vanished, and nothing was left for her but to return to her father's house, and forget him who no longer loved her. She crossed the court-yard, followed by the maids of honor jeering at her simplicity. On reaching the gate, she turned to take a last look. Seeing herself alone, she burst into tears, and hid her face in her hands.

"Begone, beggar!" cried the jailer, seizing her by the collar, and shaking her with an air of importance.

"Begone!" said Violet; "never!

> "'Tricche Verlacche,
> Coat of gold and heart of a lackey,'"

cried she.

And behold! the mouse sprang at the jailer's face, and bit it till it bled; then an immense bird-cage, as large as a Chinese pavilion, rose up before the gate. The bars were of silver, and the seed-cups of diamonds, with pearls for hemp-seed, and guineas, strung on ribbons of all colors, for cuttle-fish. In this magnificent cage, on a swinging ladder that turned with the wind, hopped and twittered thousands of birds of all sizes and countries—humming-birds, parrots, cardinal-birds, linnets, canaries, and every other species. All this feathered world was warbling the same song, each in his jargon. Violet, who understood the language of birds as well as that of plants, translated it for the benefit of the maids of honor, who were greatly astonished to find such rare prudence among canaries. The chorus ran as follows:

> " Freedom is folly,
>   Hurrah for the cage !
>   Whoever is sage
> Will come hither to stay,
> To eat, and to drink, and be jolly,
> Where, for all these delights,
>   He has only to pay
>   By warbling a lay.
> Freedom is folly,
>   Hurrah for the cage !"

A deep silence followed these joyful cries. Then an old red and green parrot, with a grave and serious air, raised one claw, and, swinging on his perch, sang in a nasal tone, or rather croaked, this solo:

> "The nightingale in his black vest,
> Who never comes out of his nest
> Till the sun has gone down in the west,
> To sing to his mistress the moon,
> Is s fellow unpleasant to see.
> He is proud as a king, though he lives
> Like a beggar, yet still he believes
> No bird is so happy as he.
> Then his voice—what a bore !
>   We should, *entre nous*,
>   Without more ado,
>   Hang all such fools who
> Good fortune refuse to adore."

And all the birds, ravished with his eloquence, began to whistle in shrill tones,

> " Freedom is folly,
>   Hurrah for the cage !"

As the maids of honor were crowding round the magic bird-cage, the Lady of the Chinking Guineas appeared, and it may be believed that she was not the last to covet this marvel. "Child," said she to the piper, "will you sell me this cage at the same price as the carriage?"

"Willingly, madam," answered Violet, who had no other desire.

"It is a bargain," said the lady. "None but beggars would be guilty of such follies."

The night did not differ from the preceding one. Perlino, drunk with the potable gold, entered his chamber without even raising his eyes; and Violet threw herself on her mat, more wretched than ever. She sang as on the first night, and shed tears that would have melted a heart of stone, but all in vain. Perlino slept like a dethroned king, and the sobs of his mistress lulled him like the murmurs of the winds and waves. Toward midnight, Violet's three friends, grieved at her sorrow, held council. "It is not natural that he should sleep in this way," said the squirrel. "We must go in and wake him," said the mouse. "But how shall we get in?" said the bee, who had been vainly seeking a crack in the wall. "That is my business," said the mouse. And he quickly gnawed a little hole in the door large enough for the bee to glide into the room where Perlino lay asleep on his back, snoring. Angry at this calmness, the bee stung him on the lip; he sighed, and struck his cheek a blow, but did not wake.

"He has been put to sleep," said the bee, returning. "There is magic in it. What shall we do?"

"Wait!" said the mouse, who had not let his teeth rust. "It is my turn to go into the room. I will awaken him, should I eat his heart out."

"No, no," said Violet, "I will not have my Perlino hurt."

The mouse was already in the room. To jump on the bed,

and creep under the coverlid was play for the cousin of the rats. He went straight to Perlino's breast, but before making a hole in it he listened. The heart did not beat; there was no more doubt—Perlino was enchanted.

Just as the mouse brought back this news, day broke, and the lady appeared, smiling maliciously. Violet, furious at having been played with, gnawed her fingers in anger. She nevertheless made a low courtesy to the countess, saying to herself, "To-morrow I will have my revenge."

IX.

PATITA, PATITE.

THIS time Violet went down to the court-yard with more courage; her hope had revived. As on the day before, she found the maids of honor there still spinning on their distaffs. "Come, handsome piper," they cried, laughing, "what have you to show us now?"

"Something that will please you, fair ladies," answered Violet.

> "'Patita, Patite,
> Look well and you'll see.'"

The squirrel threw one of his nuts on the ground, and a puppet-show instantly appeared. The curtain rose. The scene represented a court of justice. At the upper end of the room, on a throne hung with red velvet spangled with stars, sat the judge, a huge cat of respectable appearance, notwithstanding a few crumbs of cheese that remained on his long whiskers. Buried in contemplation, with his hands crossed under his long sleeves and his eyes closed, you would have thought him sleeping, if justice ever slumbered in the kingdom of cats.

On the side was a wooden bench, on which were chained

three mice, whose teeth had been filed and ears cut off by way of precaution. They were suspected, which at Naples means convicted, of having looked too closely at a rind of musty bacon. Opposite the culprits was a canopy of black cloth, on which was inscribed, in letters of gold, the sentence of the great poet and magician Virgil,

"CRUSH THE MICE, BUT SPARE THE CATS."

Under the canopy stood the public prosecutor, a weasel with a receding forehead, red eyes, and pointed tongue, who, with one hand on his heart, was eloquently demanding that the law should condemn the mice to the gallows. His words flowed like a silvery fountain; he prayed for the death of these wretched little animals in so tender and pathetic a voice that one became indignant at their obduracy. They seemed wholly lacking in their duty in not themselves offering their guilty heads to calm the feelings and dry the tears of this excellent weasel, whose voice was choked with such emotion.

When the prosecutor had finished his touching speech, a young rat, scarcely weaned, rose to defend the culprits. He had just adjusted his spectacles, taken off his cap, and turned down his sleeves, when the cat, through respect for free defense and for the interest of the accused, forbade him to speak; after which, in a solemn voice, Master Grimalkin soundly rated the accused, witnesses, society, heaven, earth, and rats. Then, putting on his cap, he pronounced an avenging sentence, condemning these guilty animals to be hung and flayed on the spot, their goods to be confiscated, their memory to be branded, and themselves to pay the costs of the suit; imprisonment for debt being limited, however, to five years, as it was necessary to be humane even to villains.

The farce played, the curtain fell.

"How natural it is!" cried the Lady of the Chinking Guineas. " It is the justice of cats copied to the life. Shepherd or sorcerer, whatever you may be, sell me your star chamber."

" At the same price, madam," answered Violet.

" You shall sleep here to-night," returned the countess.

" Yes, madam," replied Violet ; adding to herself, " May you repay me for all the harm you have done me !"

While the comedy was being played in the court-yard, the squirrel had not wasted his time. By dint of climbing over the roofs, he had finally discovered Perlino eating figs in the garden. From the roof it was an easy matter to leap to a tree, and from the tree to a thicket, until he at length reach- ed Perlino, who was playing morra with his shadow, a sure way of always winning. To play morra, one player holds up one or more fingers, and the other bets at the same instant how many he will hold up.

" My friend," said the squirrel, " solitude has its charms ; but you do not look as if playing alone amused you much ; suppose we have a game together."

" Bah !" said Perlino, " your fingers are too short, and you are nothing but an animal."

" Short fingers are not always a fault," replied the squirrel ; " I have seen more than one man hung whose only crime was that of having them too long ; and if I am an animal, Master Perlino, at least I am a wide-awake animal. That is better than having so much wit and sleeping like a dormouse. If happiness ever knocks at my door in the night, at least I shall be up to let it in."

" Speak clearly," said Perlino. " Something strange has been the matter with me for the last two days. My head is heavy and my heart sorrowful, and I have horrible dreams. What is the reason ?"

" Guess !" said the squirrel. " Do not drink and you will not sleep ; do not sleep and you will see many things. A word to the wise is sufficient." Saying this, he sprang on a branch and disappeared.

Since Perlino had lived in retirement, reason had come to him. Nothing makes one so wicked as being dull in company; nothing makes him so wise as being dull alone. At supper he studied the face and smile of the Lady of the Chinking Guineas. He seemed as gay as usual, but every time that she gave him the cup of forgetfulness, he went to the window, pretending to admire the beauty of the evening, and threw the gold into the garden, where it fell, it is said, on some white beetles that were burrowing in the ground, and from that time the cockchafers were golden.

X.

THE RECOGNITION.

ON entering his room, Perlino noticed the piper looking at him mournfully, but he did not stop for any questions, such was his haste to be alone to see whether happiness would knock at his door, and in what form it would come. His anxiety was not of long duration. He was not yet in bed when he heard Violet's sweet and plaintive voice, reminding him, in the most tender terms, how she had moulded and made him with her own hands; how it was to her prayers that he owed his life; how, notwithstanding, he had suffered himself to be seduced and carried off; and how she had pursued him with such toil and pains. Violet also told him, in still more touching accents, how she had watched for the last two nights at his door, and, to obtain this favor, had given away treasures worthy of a king without obtaining a single word from him; and how this night was the end of her hopes and life.

On listening to these words, which pierced his soul, it seemed to Perlino that he had awakened from a dream, and that a cloud fell from his eyes. He opened the door, and softly called Violet, who threw herself into his arms weeping. He attempted to speak, but she stopped him. We always believe those we love, and there are moments when we are too happy for any thing but tears.

"Let us go," said Perlino; "let us quit this hateful dungeon."

"To go is not so easy, Master Perlino," answered the squirrel; "the Lady of the Chinking Guineas does not willingly let go of what she has in her clutches. We have exhausted all our gifts in awakening you, and to save you a miracle is needed."

"Perhaps I have a means," said Perlino, whose wit grew as the sap rises in the trees in spring-time.

He took the cornet which contained the magic powder, and made his way to the stable, followed by Violet and the three friends, saddled the best horse, and, walking softly, reached the gate where the jailer was sleeping, his keys in his belt. At the sound of footsteps the man awoke and started up. Before he had time to open his mouth, Perlino poured the potable gold down his throat, at the risk of suffocating him; but, instead of complaining, he began to smile, and fell back in his chair, closing his eyes, and stretching out his hands for more. To seize the bunch of keys, open the gate, shut it again, triple lock it, and throw the keys of perdition into the ditch to imprison covetousness forever, was the work of an instant. Unhappily, Perlino forgot the keyhole, which left room enough for it to escape, and invade the human heart anew.

At length they were free and on the road homeward, both mounted on the same horse, Perlino in front and Violet behind. She wound her arm round the neck of her beloved,

and clasped him to her, to be sure that his heart was still beating. Perlino continually turned his head to see the face of his dear Violet, and to behold that smile which he was in constant fear of losing. Fear and prudence were forgotten ; and if the squirrel had not more than once caught the reins to keep the horse from stumbling or going astray, who knows but the travelers would still be on the road?

I leave you to imagine the joy of Beppo at recovering his daughter and son-in-law. He seemed the youngest of the household. He laughed all day long without knowing why, and wished to dance with every body. He lost his senses to such a degree that he doubled the salaries of his clerks and settled a pension on his cashier, who had served him only thirty-six years. Nothing blinds us like happiness. The wedding was magnificent, but this time they took care to try their friends. The bees came from twenty leagues round, bringing a beautiful cake of honey, and the ball ended with a tarentella of mice and a schottisch of squirrels, which was long talked of in Pæstum. When the sun drove away the guests, Violet and Perlino kept on dancing, and nothing could stop them. Beppo, who was wiser, made a fine speech to show them that they were no longer children, and that people do not marry for amusement. They threw themselves into his arms, laughing. A father's heart is always weak; he took them by the hand, and danced with them till evening.

YVON AND FINETTE.

A TALE OF BRITTANY.

I.

ONCE upon a time there lived in Brittany a noble lord, who was called the Baron Kerver. His manor-house was the most beautiful in the province. It was a great Gothic castle, with a groined roof and walls, covered with carving, that looked at a distance like a vine climbing over an arbor. On the first floor six stained glass balcony windows looked out on each side toward the rising and the setting sun. In the morning, when the baron, mounted on his dun mare, went forth into the forest, followed by his tall greyhounds, he saw at each window one of his daughters, with prayer-book in hand, praying for the house of Kerver, and who, with their fair curls, blue eyes, and clasped hands, might have been taken for six Madonnas in an azure niche. At evening, when the sun declined and the baron returned homeward, after riding round his domains, he perceived from afar, in the windows looking toward the west, six sons, with dark locks and eagle gaze, the hope and pride of the family, that might have been taken for six sculptured knights at the portal of a church. For ten leagues round, all who wished to quote a happy father and a powerful lord named the Baron Kerver.

The castle had but twelve windows, and the baron had thirteen children. The last, the one that had no place, was a handsome boy of sixteen, by the name of Yvon. As usual, he was the best beloved. In the morning, at his departure, and

at evening, on his return, the baron always found Yvon waiting on the threshold to embrace him. With his hair falling
to his waist, his graceful figure, his willful air, and his bold

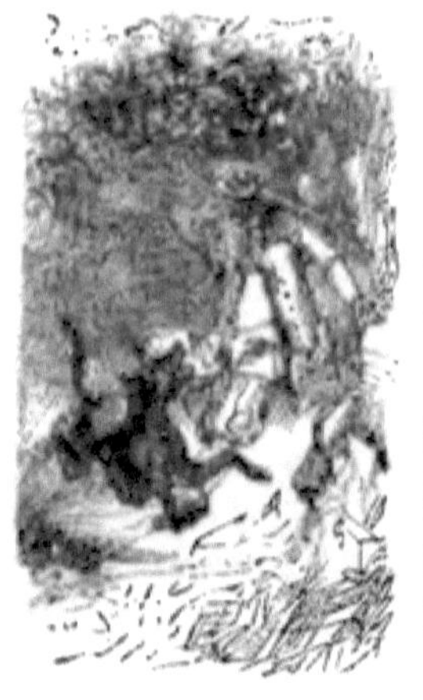

bearing, Yvon was beloved by all the Bretons. At twelve years of age he had
bravely attacked and killed a wolf with
an axe, which had won him the name of
Fearless. He deserved the title, for never was there a bolder heart.

One day, when the baron had staid at
home, and was amusing himself by breaking a lance with his squire, Yvon entered
the armory in a traveling dress, and,
bending one knee to the ground,

"My lord and father," said he to the
baron, "I come to ask your blessing. The house of Kerver is rich in knights, and has no need of a child; it is time
for me to go to seek my fortune. I wish to go to distant
countries to try my strength, and to make myself a name."

"You are right, Fearless," replied the baron, more moved
than he wished to appear. "I will not keep you back; I have
no right to do so; but you are very young, my child; perhaps
it would be better for you to stay another year with us."

"I am sixteen, my father; at that age you had already
fought one of the proudest lords of the country. I have not
forgotten that our arms are a unicorn ripping up a lion, and
our motto Onward! I do not wish the Kervers to blush for
their last child."

Yvon received his father's blessing, shook hands with his
brothers, embraced his sisters, bid adieu to all the weeping
vassals, and set out with a light heart.

Nothing stopped him on his way. A river appeared, he
swam it; a mountain, he climbed it; a forest, he made his

way through it with the sun for a guide. *On—the Kerver!* he cried, whenever he met with an obstacle, and went straight forward in spite of every thing.

For three years he had been roaming over the world in search of adventures, sometimes conquering, sometimes conquered, always bold and gay, when he received an offer to go to fight the heathen of Norway. To kill unbelievers and to conquer a kingdom was a double pleasure. Yvon enlisted twelve brave comrades, freighted a ship, and hoisted from the main-mast a blue standard, with the unicorn and motto of the Kervers.

The sea was calm, the wind fair, and the night serene. Yvon, stretched on the deck, watched the stars, and sought the one which cast its trembling light on his father's castle. All at once the vessel struck upon a rock; a terrible crash was heard; the sails fell like tinder; and an enormous wave burst over the deck, and swept away every thing upon it.

"*On—the Kerver!*" cried Yvon, as soon as his head appeared above the water; and he began to swim as tranquilly as if he had been bathing in the lake of the old castle. Happily the moon was rising. Yvon saw, at a little distance, a black speck among the silvery waves—it was land. He approached it, not without difficulty, and finally succeeded in gaining a foothold. Dripping wet, exhausted with fatigue, and out of breath, he dragged himself on the sand; then, without more anxiety, said his prayers, and went to sleep.

II.

In the morning, on awaking, Yvon tried to discover in what country he had been cast. He saw in the distance a house as large as a church, with windows fifty feet in height. He walked a whole day before reaching it, and at last found him-

self in front of an immense door, with a knocker so heavy that
it was impossible for a man to lift it.

Yvon took a great stone and began to knock. "Come in,"
cried a voice, that sounded like the roar of a bull. At the
same instant the door opened, and the little Breton found
himself in the presence of a giant not less than forty feet in
height.

"What is your name, and what do you want here?" said the
giant, taking up Yvon between his thumb and finger, and lifting him from the ground so as to see him better.

"My name is Fearless, and I am seeking my fortune,"

answered Yvon, looking at the monster with an air of defiance.

"Well, brave Fearless, your fortune is made," said the giant, in a mocking tone. "I am in need of a servant, and I will give you the place. You ·can go to work directly. This is the time for leading my sheep to the pasture ; you may clean the stable while I am gone. I shall give you nothing else to do," added he, bursting into a laugh. "You see that I am a good master. Do your task, and, above all things, don't prowl about the house, or it will cost you your life."

"Certainly I have a good master ; the work is not hard," thought Yvon, when the giant was gone. "I have plenty of time to sweep the stable. What shall I do meanwhile to amuse myself? Shall I look about the house? Since I am forbidden to do so, it must be because there is something to see."

He entered the first room, and saw a large fireplace, in which a great pot was hanging, suspended from a hook.· The pot was boiling, but there was no fire on the hearth.

"What does this mean?" thought Yvon ;·"there is some mystery here." He cut off a lock of his hair, dipped it into the pot, and took it out all coated with copper.

"Oh, oh !" cried he, "this is a new kind of soup ; any body that swallows it must have an iron-clad stomach."

He went into the next room ; there also a pot was suspended from a hook, and boiling without fire. Yvon dipped a lock of hair into it, and took it out all coated with silver.

"The broth is not so rich as this in the Kerver kitchen," thought he, "but it may have a better taste."

Upon this, he entered the third room. There also a pot was suspended from a hook, and boiling without fire. Yvon dipped a lock of hair into it, and took it out all coated with gold.   It shone so brightly that it might have been mistaken for a sunbeam.

"Good!" cried he.   "In our country the old women have a saying, 'Every thing gets worse and worse;' here it is just the contrary, every thing gets better and better.   What shall I find in the fourth room, I wonder—diamond soup?"

He pushed open the door, and saw something rarer than precious stones.   This was a young woman of such marvelous beauty that Yvon, dazzled, fell on his knees at the sight.

"Unfortunate youth!" cried she, in a trembling voice, "what are you doing here?"

"I belong to the house," answered Yvon; "the giant took me into his service this morning."

"His service!" repeated the young girl.   "May Heaven preserve you from it!"

"Why so?" said Yvon.   "I have a good master; the work is not hard.   The stable once swept, my task is finished."

"Yes, and how will you set to work to sweep it?" said the lady.   "If you sweep it in the usual way, for every forkfull of dung that you throw out of the door, ten will come in at the window.   But I will tell you what to do.   Turn the fork and sweep with the handle, and the dung will instantly fly out of itself."

"I will obey," said Yvon; upon which he sat down by the young girl and began to talk with her.   She was the daughter of a fairy, whom the wretched giant had made his slave. Friendship soon springs up between companions in misfortune.   Before the end of the day, Finette (for that was the lady's name) and Yvon had already promised to belong to each other, if they could escape from their abominable master.   The difficulty was to find the means.

Time passes quickly in this kind of talk.   Evening was approaching, when Finette sent away her new friend, advising him to sweep the stable before the giant came home.

Yvon took down the fork, and attempted to use it as he had seen it done at his father's castle. He soon had enough of it. In less than a second, there was so much dung in the stable that the poor boy knew not which way to turn. He did as Finette had bid him; he turned the fork and swept with the handle, when behold! in the twinkling of an eye, the stable was as clean as if no cattle had ever entered it.

The task finished, Yvon seated himself on a bench before the door of the house. As soon as he saw the giant coming, he lolled back in his seat, crossed his legs, and began to sing one of his native airs.

"Have you cleaned the stable?" asked the giant, with a frown.

"Every thing is ready, master," answered Yvon, without troubling himself to move.

"I am going to see for myself," howled the giant. He entered the stable grumbling, found every thing in order, and came out furious.

"You have seen my Finette," cried he; "this trick did not come from your own head."

"What is myfinette?" asked Yvon, opening his mouth and shutting his eyes. "Is it one of the animals that you have in this country? Show it to me, master."

"Hold your tongue, fool," replied the giant; "you will see her sooner than you will want to."

The next morning the giant gathered his sheep together to lead them to the pasture; but, before setting out, he ordered Yvon to go in the course of the day in search of his horse, which was turned out to graze on the mountain. "After that," said he, bursting into a laugh, "you can rest all day long. You see that I am a good master. Do your task; and, above all things, don't prowl about the house, or I will cut off your head." ·

Yvon winked his eye as the giant left. "Yes, you are a good master," said he, between his teeth. "I understand your tricks; but, in spite of your threats, I shall go into the house, and talk with your Finette. It remains to be seen whether she will not be more mine than yours."

He ran to the young girl's room. "Hurrah!" cried he; "I have nothing to do all day but to go to the mountain after a horse."

"Very well," said Finette; "how will you set to work to ride him?"

"A fine question," returned Yvon. "As if it was a difficult thing to ride a horse! I fancy that I have ridden worse ones than this."

"It is not so easy as you think," replied Finette; "but I will tell you what to do. Take the bit that hangs behind the stable-door, and, when the animal rushes toward you breathing fire and smoke from his nostrils, force it straight between his teeth; he will instantly become as gentle as a lamb, and you can do what you please with him."

"I will obey," said Yvon; upon which he sat down by the side of Finette, and began to talk with her. They talked of every thing; but, however far their fancy strayed, they always came back to the point that they were promised to each other, and that they must escape from the giant. Time passes quickly in this kind of talk. The evening drew nigh. Yvon had forgotten the horse and the mountain, and Finette was obliged to send him away, advising him to bring back the animal before his master's arrival.

Yvon took down the bit that was hidden behind the stable-door, and hastened to the mountain, when lo! a horse almost as large as an elephant rushed toward him at full gallop,

breathing fire and smoke from his nostrils. Yvon firmly
awaited the huge animal, and, the moment he opened his enormous jaws, thrust between them the bit ; when lo ! the horse
instantly became as gentle as a lamb. Yvon made him kneel
down, sprang on his back, and tranquilly returned home.

His task finished, Yvon seated himself on the bench before
the door of the house. As soon as he saw the giant coming,
he lolled back in his seat, crossed his legs, and began to sing
one of his native airs.

"Have you brought back the horse?" asked the giant, with
a frown.

"Yes, master," answered Yvon, without taking the trouble
to move. "He is a fine animal, and does you credit. He is

gentle, well trained, and as quiet as a lamb. He is feeding yonder in the stable."

"I am going to see for myself," howled the giant. He entered the stable grumbling, found every thing in order, and came out furious.

"You have seen my Finette," said he; "this trick did not come from your own head."

"Oh, master," returned Yvon, opening his mouth and shutting his eyes, "it is the same story over again. What is this myfinette? Once for all, show me this monster."

"Hold your tongue, fool," returned the giant; "you will see her sooner than you will want to."

The third day at dawn the giant gathered his sheep together to lead them to the pasture; but, before setting out, he said to Yvon,

"To-day you must go to the bottomless pit to collect my rent. After that," continued he, bursting into a laugh, "you may rest all day long. You see that I am a good master."

"A good master, so be it," murmured Yvon, "but the task is none the less hard. I will go and see my Finette, as the giant says; I have great need of her help to get through to-day's business."

When Finette had learned what was the task of the day, "Well," said she, "how will you go to work to do it?"

"I don't know," said Yvon, sadly; "I have never been to the bottomless pit, and, even if I knew the way there, I should not know what to ask for. Tell me what to do."

"Do you see that great rock yonder?" said Finette; "that is one of the gates of the bottomless pit. Take this stick, knock three times on the stone, and a demon will come out all streaming with flames, who will ask you how much you want. Take care to answer, 'No more than I can carry.'"

"I will obey," said Yvon; upon which he took a seat by

the side of Finette, and began to talk with her. He would
have been there till this time if the young girl had not sent
him to the great rock, when the evening drew nigh, to execute
the giant's commands.

On reaching the spot pointed out to him, Yvon found a
great block of granite. He struck it three times with the
stick, when lo ! the rock opened, and a demon came forth all
streaming with flames.

"What do you want?" he cried.

"I have come for the giant's rent," answered Yvon, calmly.

"How much do you want?"

"I never want any more than I can carry," replied the
Breton.

"It is well for you that you do not," returned the man
in flames. "Enter this cavern, and you will find what you
want."

Yvon entered, and opened his eyes wide. Every where he
saw nothing but gold, silver, diamonds, carbuncles, and emeralds. They were as numerous as the sands on the sea-shore.
The young Kerver filled a sack, threw it across his shoulder,
and tranquilly returned home.

His task finished, our Breton seated himself on the bench
before the door of the house. As soon as he saw the giant
coming, he lolled back in his seat, crossed his legs, and began
to sing one of his native airs.

"Have you been to the bottomless pit to collect my rent?"
asked the giant, with a frown.

"Yes, master," answered Yvon, without taking the trouble
to stir. "The sack is there right before your eyes ; you can
count it."

"I am going to see for myself," howled the giant. He untied the strings of the sack, which was so full that the gold
and silver rolled in all directions.

"You have seen my Finette," he cried; "this trick did not come from your own head."

"Don't you know but one song," said Yvon, opening his mouth and shutting his eyes. "It is the old story, myfinette, myfinette. Once for all, show me this thing."

"Well, well," roared the giant with fury, "wait till to-morrow, and you shall make her acquaintance."

"Thank you, master," said Yvon. "It is very good of you; but I see from your face that you are laughing at me."

III.

THE next morning the giant went out without giving Yvon any orders, which troubled Finette. At noon he returned without his flock, complaining of the heat and fatigue, and said to the young girl,

"You will find a child, my servant, at the door. Cut his throat, put him into the great pot to boil, and call me when the broth is ready." Saying this, he stretched himself on the bed to take a nap, and was soon snoring so loud that it seemed like thunder shaking the mountains.

Finette prepared a log of wood, took a large knife, and called Yvon. She pricked his little finger; three drops of blood fell on the log.

"That is enough," said Finette; "now help me to fill the pot."

They threw into it all that they could find—old clothes, old shoes, old carpets, and every thing else. Finette then took Yvon by the hand, and led him through the three ante-chambers, where she ran in a mould three bullets of gold, two bullets of silver, and one bullet of copper, after which they quitted the house and ran toward the sea.

"*On—the Kerver!*" cried Yvon, as soon as he saw himself

in the country. "Explain yourself, dear Finette ; what farce are we playing now?"

"Let us run—let us run!" she cried ; "if we do not quit this wretched island before night, it is all over with us."

"*On—the Kerver!*" replied Yvon, laughing, "and down with the giant!"

When he had snored a full hour, the giant stretched his limbs, half opened one eye, and cried, "Is it ready?"

"It is just beginning to boil," answered the first drop of blood on the log.

The giant turned over, and snored louder than ever for an hour or two longer. Then he stretched his limbs, half opened one eye, and cried out, "Do you hear me? Is it almost ready?"

"It is half done," answered the second drop of blood on the log.

The giant turned over, and slept an hour longer. Then he yawned, stretched his great limbs, and cried out impatiently,

"Isn't it ready yet?"

"It is ready now," answered the third drop of blood on the log.

The giant sat up in bed, rubbed his eyes, and looked around to see who had spoken ; but it was in vain to·look ; he saw nobody.

"Finette," howled he, "why isn't the table set?"

There was no answer. The giant, furious, sprang out of bed, seized a ladle, which looked like a caldron with a pitch-fork for a handle, and plunged it into the pot to taste the soup.

"Finette!" howled he, "you haven't salted it. What sort of a soup is this? I see neither meat nor vegetables."

No ; but, in return, he saw his carpet, which had not quite all boiled to pieces. At this sight he fell into such a fit of rage that he could not keep his feet.

"Villains!" said he, "you have played a fine trick on me; but you shall pay for it."

He rushed out with a stick in his hand, and strode along at such a rate that in a quarter of an hour he discovered the two fugitives still far from the sea-shore. He uttered such a cry of joy that the earth shook for twelve leagues around.

Finette stopped, trembling. Yvon clasped her to his heart.

"*On—the Kerver!*" said he; "the sea is not far off; we shall be there before our enemy."

"Here he is! here he is!" cried Finette, pointing to the giant not a hundred yards off; "we are lost if this charm does not save us."

She took the copper bullet and threw it on the ground, saying,

"Copper bullet, save us, pray,
Stop the giant on his way."

And behold, the earth cracked apart with a terrific noise, and an enormous fissure, a bottomless pit, stopped the giant just as he was stretching out his hand to seize his prey.

"Let us fly!" cried Finette, grasping the arm of Yvon, who was gazing at the giant with a swaggering air, defying him to come on.

The giant ran backward and forward along the abyss like a bear in his cage, seeking a passage every where and finding none; then, with a furious jerk, he tore up an immense oak by the roots, and flung it across the gap. The branches of the oak nearly crushed the children as it fell. The giant seated himself astride the huge tree, which bent under his weight, and crept slowly along, suspended between heaven and earth, entangled as he was among the branches. When he reached the other side, Yvon and Finette were already on the shore, with the sea rolling before them.

Alas! there was neither bark nor ship. The fugitives were

lost. Yvon, always brave, picked up stones to attack the giant, and to sell his life dearly. Finette, trembling with fear, threw one of the silver bullets into the sea, saying,

> " Silver bullet, bright and pliant,
> Save us from this frightful giant."

Scarcely had she spoken the magic words when a beautiful ship rose from the waves like a swan spreading its white wings. Yvon and Finette plunged into the sea; a rope was thrown them by an invisible hand; and when the furious giant reached the shore, the ship was receding rapidly at full sail, leaving behind it a long furrow of shining foam.

Giants do not like the water. This fact is certified to by old Homer, who knew Polyphemus; and the same observation will be found in all natural histories worthy of the name. Finette's master resembled Polyphemus. He roared with rage when he saw his slaves about to escape him. He ran hesitatingly along the shore; he flung huge masses of rock after the vessel, which happily fell by the side of it, and only made great black holes in the water; and, finally, mad with anger, he plunged head foremost into the sea, and began to swim after the ship with frightful speed. At each stroke he advanced forty feet, blowing like a whale, and like a whale cleaving the waves. By degrees he gained on his enemies; one more effort would bring him within reach of the rudder, and already he was stretching out his arm to seize it, when Finette threw the second silver bullet into the sea, and cried, in tears,

> "Silver bullet, bright and pliant,
> Save us from this frightful giant."

Suddenly from the midst of the foam darted forth a gigantic sword-fish, with a sword at least twenty feet in length. It rushed straight toward the giant, who scarcely had time to dive, chased him under the water, pursued him on the top of the waves, followed him closely whichever way he turned, and forced him to flee as fast as he could to his island, where he finally landed with the greatest difficulty, and fell upon the shore dripping, worn out, and conquered.

"*On—the Kerver!*" cried Yvon; "we are saved."

"Not yet," said Finette, trembling. "The giant has a witch for a godmother; I fear that she will revenge on me the insult offered to her godson. My art tells me, my dear Yvon, that if you quit me a single instant until you give me your name in the chapel of the Kervers, I have every thing to dread."

"By the unicorn of my ancestors," cried Yvon, "you have the heart of a hare and not of a hero! Am I not here? Am I going to abandon you? Do you believe that Providence has saved us from the fangs of that monster to wreck us in port?"

He laughed so gayly that Finette laughed in turn at the terror that had seized her.

IV.

THE rest of the voyage passed off admirably. An invisible hand seemed to impel the ship onward. Twenty days after their departure the boat landed Yvon and Finette near Kerver Castle. Once on shore, Yvon turned to thank the crew. No one was there. Both boat and ship had vanished under the waves, leaving no trace behind but a gull on the wing.

Yvon recognized the spot where he had so often gathered shells and chased the crabs to their holes when a child. Half an hour's walk would bring him in sight of the towers of the old castle. His heart beat; he looked tenderly at Finette, and saw, for the first time, that her dress was fantastic, and unworthy of a woman about to enter the noble house of Kerver.

"My dear child," said he, "the baron, my father, is a noble lord, accustomed to be treated with respect. I can not introduce you to him in this gipsy dress; neither is it fitting that you should enter our great castle on foot like a peasant. Wait for me a few moments, and I will bring you a horse and one of my sister's dresses. I wish you to be received like a lady of high degree. I wish my father himself to meet you on your arrival, and hold it an honor to give you his hand."

"Yvon, Yvon," cried Finette, "do not quit me, I beg you. Once returned to your castle, I know that you will forget me."

"Forget you!" exclaimed Yvon. "If any one else were to offer me such an insult, I would teach him with my sword to suspect a Kerver. Forget you, my Finette! you do not know the fidelity of a Breton."

That the Bretons are faithful, no one doubts; but that they are still more headstrong is a justice that none will deny them. It was useless for poor Finette to plead in her most loving tones ; she was forced to yield. She resigned herself with a heavy heart, and said to Yvon,

"Go without me, then, to your castle, but only stay long enough to speak to your friends ; then go straight to the stable, and return as soon as possible. You will be surrounded by people ; act as if you saw no one, and, above all, do not eat or drink any thing whatever. Should you take only a glass of water, evil would come upon us both."

Yvon promised and swore all that Finette asked, but he smiled in his heart at this feminine weakness. He was sure of himself; and he thought with pride how different a Breton was from those fickle Frenchmen, whose words, they say, are borne away by the first breath of the wind.

On entering the old castle he could scarcely recognize its dark walls. All the windows were festooned with leaves and flowers within and without ; the court-yard was strewn with fragrant grass ; on one side were spread tables groaning under their weight; on the other, musicians, mounted on casks, were playing merry airs. The vassals, dressed in their holiday attire, were singing and dancing, and dancing and singing. It was a great day of rejoicing at the castle. The baron himself was smiling. It is true that he had just married his fifth daughter to the Knight of Kervalec. This marriage added another quartering to the illustrious escutcheon of the Kervers.

Yvon, recognized and welcomed by all the crowd, was instantly surrounded by his relatives, who embraced him and shook him by the hand. Where had he been ? Where did he come from ? Had he conquered a kingdom, a duchy, or a barony? Had he brought the bride the jewels of some queen? Had the fairies protected him ? How many rivals had he overthrown ? All these questions were showered upon him without reply. Yvon respectfully kissed his father's hand, hastened to his sisters' chamber, took two of their finest dresses, went to the stable, saddled a pony, mounted a beautiful Spanish jennet, and was about to quit the castle, when he found his relatives, friends, squires, and vassals all standing in his way, their glasses in their hands, ready to drink their young lord's health and his safe return.

Yvon gracefully thanked them, bowed, and made his way by degrees through the crowd, when, just as he was about to cross the draw-bridge, a fair-haired lady, with a haughty and disdainful air, a stranger to him, a sister of the bridegroom, perhaps, approached him, holding a pomegranate in her hand.

"My handsome knight," said she, with a singular smile, "you surely will not refuse a lady's first request. Taste this pomegranate, I entreat you. If you are neither hungry nor thirsty after so long a journey, I suppose at least that you have not forgotten the laws of politeness."

Yvon dared not refuse this appeal. He was very wrong. Scarcely had he tasted the pomegranate when he looked round him like a man waking from a dream.

"What am I doing on this horse?" thought he. "What means this pony that I am leading? Is not my place in my father's house at my sister's wedding? Why should I quit the castle?"

He threw the bridle to one of the grooms, leaped lightly to the ground, and offered his hand to the fair-haired lady, who accepted him as her attendant on the spot, and gave him her bouquet to hold as a special mark of favor.

Before the evening was over there was another betrothed couple in the castle. Yvon had pledged his faith to the unknown lady, and Finette was forgotten.

V.

Poor Finette, seated on the sea-shore, waited all day long for Yvon, but Yvon did not come. The sun was setting in the fiery waves, when Finette rose, sighing, and took the way to the castle in her turn. She had not walked long in a steep road, bordered with thorn trees in blossom, when she found herself in front of a wretched hut, at the door of which stood an old woman about to milk her cow. Finette approached her, and, making a low courtesy, begged a shelter for the night.

The old woman looked at the stranger from head to foot. With her buskins trimmed with fur, her full red petticoat, her blue jacket edged with jet, and her diadem, Finette looked more like an Egyptian princess than a Christian. The old woman frowned, and, shaking her fist in the face of the poor forsaken girl, "Begone, witch!" she cried; "there is no room for you in this honest house."

"My good mother," said Finette, "give me only a corner of the stable."

"Oh," said the old woman, laughing, and showing the only tooth she had left, which projected from her·mouth like a bear's tusk, "so you want a corner of the stable, do you! Well, you shall have it, if you will fill my milk-pail with gold."

"It is a bargain," said Finette, quietly. She opened a leather purse which she wore at her belt, took from it a golden bullet, and threw it into the milk-pail, saying,

> "Golden bullet, precious treasure,
> Save me, if it be thy pleasure."

And behold, the pieces of gold began to dance about in the pail; they rose higher and higher, flapping about like fish in a net, while the old woman on her knees gazed with wonder at the sight.

When the pail was full the old woman rose, put her arm through the handle, and said to Finette, "Madam, all is yours, the house, the cow, and every thing else. Hurrah! I am going to the town to live like a lady with nothing to do. Oh dear, how I wish I were only sixty!" And, shaking her crutch, without looking backward, she set out on a run toward Kerver Castle.

Finette entered the house. It was a wretched hovel, dark, low, damp, bad-smelling, and full of dust and spiders' webs— a horrible refuge for a woman accustomed to living in the giant's grand castle. Without seeming troubled, Finette went to the hearth, on which a few green boughs were smoking, took another golden bullet from her purse, and threw it into the fire, saying,

> "Golden bullet, precious treasure,
> Save me, if it be thy pleasure."

The gold melted, bubbled up, and spread all over the house like running water, and behold! the whole cottage, the walls, the thatch, the wooden rocking-chair, the stool, the chest, the bed, the cow's horns, every thing, even to the spiders in their webs, was turned to gold. The house gleamed in the moonlight, among the trees, like a star in the night.

When Finette had milked the cow and drank a little new milk, she threw herself on the bed without undressing, and, worn out by the fatigue of the day, fell asleep in the midst of her tears.

Old women do not know how to hold their tongues, at least in Brittany. Finette's hostess had scarcely reached the village when she hastened to the house of the steward. He was an important personage, who had more than once made her tremble when she had driven her cow into her neighbor's pasture by mistake.   The steward listened to the old woman's story, shook his head, and said that it looked like witchcraft; then he mysteriously brought a pair of scales, weighed the guineas, which he found to be genuine and of full weight, kept as many of them as he could, and advised the owner to tell no one of this strange adventure.   "If it should come to the ears of the bailiff or the seneschal," said he, "the least that would happen to you, mother, would be to lose every one of these beautiful bright guineas.   Justice is impartial; it knows neither favor nor repugnance; it takes the whole."

The old woman thanked the steward for his advice, and promised to follow it.   She kept her word so well that she only told her story that evening to two neighbors, her dearest friends, both of whom swore on the heads of their little children to keep it secret.   The oath was a solemn one, and so well kept that at noon the next day there was not a boy of six in the village that did not point his finger at the old woman, while the very dogs seemed to bark in their language, "Here is the old woman with her guineas!"

A girl that amuses herself by filling milk-pails with gold is not to be found every day.   Even though she should be something of a witch, such a girl would none the less be a treasure in a family.   The steward, who was a bachelor, made this wise reflection that night on going to bed.   Before dawn he rose to make his rounds in the direction of the stranger's cottage.   By the first gleam of day he spied something shining in the distance like a light among the woods.   On reaching the place, he was greatly surprised to find a golden cottage instead of the wretched hut that had stood there the day before.   But, on entering the house, he was much more surprised and delighted to find a beautiful young girl, with raven hair, sitting by the window, and spinning on her distaff with the air of an empress.

Like all men, the steward did himself justice, and knew, at the bottom of his heart, that there was not a woman in the world that would not be too happy to give him her hand. Without hesitating, therefore, he declared to Finette that he had come to marry her. The young girl burst out laughing, upon which the steward flew into a passion.

"Take care!" said he, in a terrible voice; "I am the master here. No one knows who you are or whence you came. The gold that you gave the old woman has raised suspicions. There is magic in this house. If you do not accept me for a husband this very instant, I will arrest you, and before night, perhaps, a witch will be burned before Kerver Castle."

"You are very amiable," said Finette, with a charming grimace; "you have a peculiar way of paying court to ladies. Even when they have decided not to refuse, a gallant man spares their blushes."

"We Bretons are plain-spoken people," replied the steward; "we go straight to the point. Marriage or prison, which do you choose?"

"Oh!" cried Finette, laying down the distaff, "there are the firebrands falling all over the room."

"Don't trouble yourself," said the steward, "I will pick them up."

"Lay them carefully on the top of the ashes," returned Finette. "Have you the tongs?"

"Yes," said the steward, picking up the crackling coals.

"*Abracadabra!*" cried Finette, rising. "Villain, may the tongs hold you, and may you hold the tongs till sunset!"

No sooner said than done. The wicked steward stood there all day with the tongs in his hand, picking up and throwing back the burning coals that snapped in his face, and the hot ashes that flew into his eyes. It was useless for him to

shout, pray, weep, and blaspheme ; no one heard him. If Finette had staid at home, she would doubtless have taken pity on him ; but, after putting the spell upon him, she hastened to the sea-shore, where, forgetting every thing else, she watched for Yvon in vain.

The moment that the sun set, the tongs fell from the steward's hands. He did not stop to finish his errand, but ran as if the devil or justice were at his heels. He made such leaps, he uttered such groans, he was so blackened, scorched, and benumbed, that every one in the village was afraid of him, thinking that he was mad. The boldest tried to speak to him, but he fled without answering, and hid himself in his house, more ashamed than a wolf that has left his paw in the trap.

At evening, when Finette returned home in despair, instead of the steward, she found another visitor little less formidable. The bailiff had heard the story of the guineas, and had also made up his mind to marry the stranger. He was not rough, like the steward, but a fat, good-natured man, that could not speak without bursting into a laugh, showing his great yellow teeth, and puffing and blowing like an ox, though at heart he was not less obstinate or less threatening than his predecessor. Finette entreated the bailiff to leave her alone. He laughed, and hinted to her, in a good-natured way, that, by right of his office, he had the power to imprison and hang people without process of law. She clasped her hands, and begged him with tears to go. For his only answer, he took a roll of parchment from his pocket, wrote on it a contract of marriage, and declared to Finette that, should he stay all night, he would not leave the house till she had signed the promise.

"Nevertheless," said he, "if you do not like my person, I have another parchment here on which I will write an agreement to live apart ; and if my sight annoys you, you have only to shut your eyes."

"Why," said Finette, "I might decide to do as you wish if I were sure of finding a good husband in you ; but I am afraid."

"Of what, my dear child ?" asked the bailiff, smiling, and already as proud as a peacock.

"Do you think," said she, with a pettish air, "that a good husband would leave that door wide open, and not know that his wife was freezing with cold ?"

"You are right, my dear," said the bailiff; "it was very stupid in me. I will go and shut it."

"Have you hold of the knob ?" asked Finette.

"Yes, my charmer," answered the happy bailiff; "I am just shutting the door."

"*Abracadabra !*" cried Finette. "May you hold the door, villain, and may the door hold you till daybreak."

And behold, the door opened and shut, and slammed against the walls like an eagle flapping its wings. You may judge what a dance the poor captive kept up all night. Never had he tried such a waltz, and I imagine that he never wished to dance a second one of the same sort. Sometimes the door swung open with him in the street ; sometimes it flew back and crushed him against the wall. He swung backward and forward, screaming, swearing, weeping, and praying, but all in vain ; the door was deaf, and Finette asleep.

At daybreak his hands unclasped, and he fell in the road head foremost. Without waiting to finish his errand, he ran as if the Moors were after him. He did not even turn round, for fear that the door might be at his heels.   Fortunately for him, all were still asleep when he reached the village, and he could hide himself in bed without any one seeing his deplorable plight.   This was a great piece of good fortune for him, for he was covered with whitewash from head to foot, and so pale, haggard, and trembling that he might have been taken for the ghost of a miller escaped from the infernal regions.

When Finette opened her eyes, she saw by her bedside a tall man dressed in black, with a velvet cap and a sword.   It was the seneschal of the barony of Kerver.   He stood with his arms folded, gazing at Finette in a way that chilled the very marrow of her bones.

"What is your name, vassal?" said he, in a voice of thunder.

"Finette, at your service, my lord," replied she, trembling.

"Is this house and furniture yours?"

"Yes, my lord, every thing, at your service."

"I mean that it shall be at my service," returned the seneschal, sternly.   "Rise, vassal!   I do you the honor to marry you, and to take yourself, your person, and your property under my guardianship."

"My lord," returned Finette, "this is much too great an honor for a poor girl like me, a stranger, without friends or kindred."

"Be silent, vassal!" replied the seneschal.   "I am your lord and master ; I have nothing to do with your advice.   Sign this paper."

"My lord," said Finette, "I don't know how to write."

"Do you think that I do, either?" returned the seneschal, in a voice that shook the house.   "Do you take me for a clerk?   A cross—that is the signature of gentlemen."

He made a large cross on the paper, and handed the pen to Finette.

"Sign," said he. "If you are afraid to make a cross, infidel, you pass your own death sentence, and I shall take on
myself to execute it." He drew his heavy sword from the
scabbard as he spoke, and threw it on the table.

For her only answer, Finette leaped out of the window, and
ran to the stable. The seneschal pursued her thither; but,
on attempting to enter, an unexpected obstacle stopped him.
The frightened cow had backed at the sight of the young girl,
and stood in the doorway with Finette clinging to her horns,
and making of her a sort of buckler.

"You shall not escape
me, sorceress!" cried the
seneschal, and, with a grasp
like that of Hercules, he
seized the cow by the tail,
and dragged her out of the
stable.

"*Abracadabra !*" cried
Finette. "May the cow's
tail hold you, villain, and
may you hold the cow's tail
till you have both been

around the world togeth-
er."

And behold, the cow
darted off like lightning,
dragging the unhappy
seneschal after her. No-
thing stopped the two
inseparable comrades ;
they rushed over mount-
ains and valleys, crossed
marshes, rivers, quag-

mires, and brakes, glided over the seas without sinking, were
frozen in Siberia and scorched in Africa, climbed the Hima-
layas, descended Mont Blanc, and at length, after thirty-six
hours of a journey, the like of which had never been seen,
both stopped out of breath in the public square of the village.

A seneschal harnessed to a cow's tail is a sight not to be
seen every day; and all the peasants in the neighborhood
crowded together to wonder at the spectacle. But, torn as
he was by the cactuses of Barbary and the thickets of Tartary,
the seneschal had lost nothing of his haughty air. With a
threatening gesture, he dispersed the rabble, and limped to
his house to taste the repose of which he began to feel the
need.

VI.

WHILE the steward, the bailiff, and the seneschal were ex-
periencing these little unpleasantnesses, of which they did not
think it proper to boast, preparations were being made for a
great event at Kerver Castle, namely, the marriage of Yvon
and the fair-haired lady. Two days had passed in these preparations, and all the friends of the family had gathered together for twenty leagues round, when, one fine morning
Yvon and his bride, with the Baron and Baroness Kerver,
took their seats in a great carriage adorned with flowers, and
set out for the celebrated church of St. Maclou.

A hundred knights, in full armor, mounted on horses decked
with ribbons, rode on each side of the betrothed couple, each
with his vizor raised and his lance at rest in token of honor.
By the side of each baron, a squire, also on horseback, carried
the seigniorial banner. At the head of the procession rode
the seneschal, with a gilded staff in his hand. Behind the
carriage gravely walked the bailiff, followed by the vassals,

while the steward railed at the serfs, a noisy and curious rabble.

As they were crossing a brook, a league from the castle, one of the traces of the carriage broke, and they were forced to stop. The accident repaired, the coachman cracked his whip, and the horses started with such force that the new trace broke in three pieces. Six times this provoking piece of wood was replaced, and six times it broke anew, without drawing the carriage from the hole where it was wedged.

· Every one had a word of advice to offer; even the peasants, as wheelwrights and carpenters, were not the last to make a show of their knowledge. This gave the steward courage; he approached the baron, took off his cap, and, scratching his head,

"My lord," said he, "in the house that you see shining yonder among the trees, there lives a woman who does things such as nobody else can do. Only persuade her to lend you her tongs, and, in my opinion, they will hold till morning."

The baron made a sign, and ten peasants ran to the cottage of Finette, who very obligingly lent them her gold tongs. They were put in the place of the trace; the coachman cracked his whip, and off went the carriage like a feather. ·

Every one rejoiced, but the joy did not last long. A hundred steps farther, lo! the bottom of the carriage gave way; little more, and the noble Kerver family would have sunk quite out of sight. The wheelwrights and the carpenters set to work at once; they sawed planks, nailed them down fast, and in the twinkling of an eye repaired the accident. The coachman cracked his whip, and the horses started, when behold! half of the carriage was left behind; the Baroness Kerver sat motionless by the side of the bride, while Yvon and the baron were carried off at full gallop. Here was a new difficulty. Three times was the carriage mended, three times it broke anew. There was every reason to believe that it was enchanted.

Every one had a word of advice to offer. This gave the bailiff courage. He approached the baron, and said, in a low tone,

"My lord, in the house that you see shining yonder among the trees, there lives a woman who does things such as nobody else can do. Only persuade her to lend you her door for the bottom of the carriage, and, in my opinion, it will hold till morning."

The baron made a sign, and twenty peasants ran to the cottage of Finette, who very obligingly lent them her gold door. They put it in the bottom of the carriage, where it fitted as if it had been made expressly for it. The party took their seats in the carriage, the coachman cracked his whip, the church was in sight, and all the troubles of the journey seemed ended.

Not at all! Suddenly the horses stopped, and refused to draw. There were four of them. Six, eight, ten, twenty-four more were put to the carriage, but all in vain; it was impossible to stir them. The more they were whipped, the deeper the wheels sunk into the ground like the coulter of a plow.

What were they to do? To go on foot would have been a disgrace. To mount a horse, and ride to the church like simple peasants, was not the custom of the Kervers. They tried to lift the carriage, they pushed the wheels, they shook it, they pulled it, but all in vain. Meanwhile the day was declining, and the hour for the marriage had passed.

Every one had a word of advice to offer. This gave the seneschal courage. He approached the baron, alighted from his horse, raised his velvet cap, and said, ·

"My lord, in the house that you see shining yonder among the trees, there lives a woman who does things such as nobody

else can do. Only persuade her to lend you her cow to draw
the carriage, and, in my opinion, she will draw it till morning."

The baron made a sign, and thirty peasants ran to the cottage of Finette, who very obligingly lent them her golden-
horned cow.

To go to church drawn by a cow was not, perhaps, what the
ambitious bride had dreamed of, but it was better than to remain unmarried in the road. The heifer was harnessed, therefore, before the four horses, and every body looked on anxiously to see what this boasted animal would do.

But, before the coachman had time to crack his whip, lo!
the cow started off as if she were about to go around the
world anew. Horses, carriage, baron, betrothed, coachman,
all were hurried away by the furious animal. In vain the
knights spurred their horses to follow the pair ; in vain the
peasants ran at full speed, taking the cross-road and cutting
across the meadows. The carriage flew as if it had wings ; a
pigeon could not have followed it.

On reaching the door of the church, the party, a little disturbed by this rapid journey, would not have been sorry to
alight. Every thing was ready for the ceremony, and the
bridal pair had long been expected ; but, instead of stopping,
the cow redoubled her speed. Thirteen times she ran round
the church like lightning, then suddenly made her way in a
straight line across the fields to the castle, with such force that
the whole party were almost shaken to pieces before their arrival.

VII.

No more marriage was to be thought of for that day ; but
the tables were set and the dinner served, and the Baron
Kerver was too noble a knight to take leave of his brave

Bretons until they had eaten and drank according to custom —that is, from sunset till sunrise, and even a little later.

Orders were given for the guests to take their seats. Ninety-six tables were ranged in eight rows. In front of them, on a large platform covered with velvet, with a canopy in the middle, was a table larger than the rest, and loaded with fruit and flowers, to say nothing of the roast hares, and the peacocks smoking beneath their plumage. At this table the bridal pair were to have been seated in full sight, in order that nothing might be lacking to the pleasures of the feast, and that the meanest peasant might have the honor of saluting them by emptying his cup of hydromel to the honor and prosperity of the high and mighty house of Kerver.

The baron seated the hundred knights at his table, and placed their squires behind their chairs to serve them. At his right he put the bride and Yvon, but he left the seat at his left vacant, and, calling a page, "Child," said he, "run to the house of the stranger lady who obliged us only too much this morning. It was not her fault if her success exceeded her good will. Tell her that the Baron Kerver thanks her for her help, and invites her to the wedding feast of his son Lord Yvon."

On reaching the golden house, where Finette in tears was mourning for her beloved, the page bent one knee to the ground, and, in the baron's name, invited the stranger lady to the castle to do honor to the wedding of Lord Yvon.

"Thank your master for me," answered the young girl, proudly, "and tell him that if he is too noble to come to my house, I am too noble to go to his."

When the page repeated this answer to his master, the Baron Kerver struck the table such a blow that three plates flew in the air.

"By my honor," said he, "this is spoken like a lady, and,

for the first time, I own myself beaten. Quick, saddle my dun mare, and let my knights and squires prepare to attend me."

It was with this brilliant train that the baron alighted at the door of the golden cottage. He begged Finette's pardon, held the stirrup for her, and seated her behind him on his own horse, neither more nor less than a duchess in person. Through respect, he did not speak a single word to her on the way. On reaching the castle, he uncovered his head, and led her to the seat of honor that he had chosen for her.

The baron's departure had made a great excitement, and his return caused still greater surprise. Every one asked who the lady could be that the baron treated with such respect. Judging from her costume, she was a foreigner ; could she be the Duchess of Normandy or the Queen of France? The steward, the bailiff, and the seneschal were appealed to. The steward trembled, the bailiff turned pale, and the seneschal blushed, but all three were as mute as fishes. The silence of these important personages added to the general wonder.

All eyes were fixed on Finette, who felt a deadly chill at her heart, for Yvon saw, but did not know her. He cast an indifferent glance at her, then began again to talk in a tender tone to the fair-haired lady, who smiled disdainfully.

Finette, in despair, took from the purse the golden bullet, her last hope. While talking with the baron, who was charmed with her wit, she shook the little ball in her hand, and repeated, in a whisper,

> " Golden bullet, precious treasure,
> Save me, if it be thy pleasure."

And behold, the bullet grew larger and larger, until it became a goblet of chased gold, the most beautiful cup that ever graced the table of baron or king.

Finette filled the cup herself with spiced wine, and, calling the seneschal, who was cowering behind her, she said, in her gentlest tones, " My good seneschal, I entreat you to offer this goblet to Lord Yvon.   I wish to drink his health, and I am sure that he will not refuse me this pleasure."

Yvon took the goblet, which the seneschal presented to him on a salver of enamel and gold, with a careless hand, bowed to the stranger, drank the wine, and, setting the cup on the table before him, turned to the fair-haired lady who occupied all his thoughts.   The lady seemed anxious and vexed. He whispered a few words in her ear that seemed to please her, for her eyes sparkled, and she placed her hand again in his.

Finette cast down her head and began to weep.   All was over.

"Children," cried the baron, in a voice of thunder, "fill your glasses.   Let us all drink to the noble stranger who honors us with her presence.   To the noble lady of the golden cottage !"

All began to huzzah and drink.   Yvon contented himself with raising his goblet to a level with his eyes.   Suddenly he started and stood mute, his mouth open and his eyes fixed, like a man that has a vision.

It was a vision.   In the gold of the goblet Yvon saw his past life as in a mirror : the giant pursuing him ; Finette dragging him along; both embarking in the ship that saved them ; both landing on the shore of Brittany ; he quitting her for an instant ; she weeping at his departure.   Where was she ? By his side, of course.   What other woman than Finette could be by the side of Yvon ?

He turned toward the fair-haired lady, and cried out like a man treading on a serpent.   Then, staggering as if he were drunk, he rose and looked around him with haggard eyes. At the sight of Finette he clasped his trembling hands, and,

dragging himself toward her, fell on his knees and exclaimed,
" Finette, forgive me !"

To forgive is the height of happiness. Before evening,
Finette was seated by the side of Yvon, both weeping and
smiling.

And what became of the fair-haired lady? No one knows.
At the cry of Yvon she disappeared ; but it was said that a
wretched old hag was seen flying on a broomstick over the

castle walls, chased by the dogs ; and it was the common
opinion among the Kervers that the fair-haired lady was none
other than the witch, the godmother of the giant. I am not

sure enough of the fact, however, to dare warrant it. It is always prudent to believe, without proof, that a woman may be a witch, but it is never wise to say so.

What I can say on the word of an historian is that the feast, interrupted for a moment, went on gayer than ever. Early the next morning they went to the church, where, to the joy of his heart, Yvon married Finette, who was no longer afraid of evil spirits ; after which they ate, drank, and danced for thirty-six hours, without any one thinking of resting. The steward's arms were a little heavy, the bailiff rubbed his back at times, and the seneschal felt a sort of weariness in his limbs, but all three had a weight on their conscience which they could not shake off, and which made them tremble and flutter, till finally they fell on the ground and were carried off. Finette took no other vengeance on them ; her only desire was to render all happy around her, far and near, who belonged to the noble house of Kerver. Her memory still lives in Brittany ; and, among the ruins of the old castle, any one will show you the statue of the good lady, with five bullets in her hand.

THE CASTLE OF LIFE.

I.

ONCE upon a time there lived at Salerno a poor old woman, who earned her bread by fishing, and whose only comfort and stay in life was her grandson, a boy twelve years of age, whose father had been drowned in a storm, and whose mother had died of grief. Graceful, for this was the child's name, loved nobody in the world but his grandmother; he followed her to the shore every morning before daybreak to pick up the shell-fish or draw the net to the beach, longing for the time when he should be strong enough to go to sea himself, and brave the waves that had swallowed up all his kindred. He was so handsome, so well-made, and so promising, that no sooner had he entered the town with his basket of fish on his head than every one ran after him, and he sold the whole before he reached the market.

Unfortunately, the grandmother was very old; she had but one front tooth left, her head shook with age, and her eyes were dim. Every morning she found it harder to rise than the day before. Feeling that she had but a few days longer to live, at night, before Graceful wrapped himself in his blanket and lay down on the ground to sleep, she always gave him good counsels for him to follow when she was gone; she told him what fishermen to avoid, and how, by being good and industrious, prudent and resolute, he would make his way in the world, and finally have a boat and nets of his own. The poor boy paid little heed to all this wisdom. As soon as his grandmother began to put on a grave air, he threw his arms around her neck, and cried, "Grandmamma, grandmamma, don't leave me. I have hands, I am strong, I shall soon be able to work for us both ; but if you were not here at night when I came home from fishing, what would become of me ?"

·"My child," said the old woman one day to him, "I shall not leave you so much alone as you think ; when I am gone you will have two powerful protectors, whom more than one prince might envy you. A long time ago I did a favor to two great ladies, who will not forget you when the time comes to call them, which will be very soon."

"Who are these two ladies?" asked Graceful, who had never seen any women but fishermen's wives in the hut.

"They are two fairies," replied his grandmother—"two powerful fairies—the Fairy of the Woods and the Fairy of the Waters. Listen to me, my child ; I am going to intrust you with a secret—a secret which you must keep as carefully as I have done, and which will give you wealth and happiness. Ten years ago, the same year that your father died and your mother also left us, I went out one morning before daybreak to surprise the crabs asleep in the sand. As I was stooping down, hidden by a rock, I saw a kingfisher slowly floating toward the beach. The kingfisher is a sacred bird, which should always be respected ; knowing this, I let it alight, and did not stir for fear of frightening it. At the same moment I saw a beautiful green adder come from a cleft of the mountain and crawl along the sand toward the bird. When they were near each other, without either seeming surprised at the meeting, the adder coiled itself around the neck of the kingfisher, as if tenderly embracing it ; they remained thus entwined for a few moments, after which they suddenly separated, the adder to return to the rock, and the kingfisher to plunge into the waves which bore it away.

"Greatly astonished at what I had seen, I returned the

next morning at the same hour, and at the same hour the kingfisher also alighted on the sands and the adder came from its retreat. There was no doubt that they were fairies, perhaps enchanted fairies, to whom I could render a service. But what was I to do? To show myself would have been to displease them and run into danger; it was better to wait for a favorable opportunity which chance would doubtless offer. For a whole month I lay in ambush, witnessing the same spectacle every morning, when one day I saw a huge black cat arrive first at the place of meeting and hide itself behind a rock, almost under my hand. A black cat could be nothing else than an enchanter, according to what I had learned in my childhood, and I resolved to watch him. Scarcely had the kingfisher and the adder embraced each other, when behold! the cat gathered itself up and sprang upon these innocents. It was my turn to throw myself upon the wretch, who already held his victims in his murderous claws; I seized him despite his struggles, although he tore my hands in pieces, and without pity, knowing with whom I had to deal, I took the knife which I used to open shell-fish, and cut off the monster's head, claws, and tail, confidently awaiting the success of my devotion.

"I did not wait long; no sooner had I thrown the body of the animal into the sea than I saw before me two beautiful ladies, one crowned with white plumes, the other with a serpent's skin thrown like a scarf across her shoulder. They were, as I have already told you, the Fairy of the Waters and the Fairy of the Woods, who, enchanted by a wretched genie who had learned their secret, had been forced to remain a kingfisher and an adder until freed by some generous hand, and who owed me their power and freedom.

"'Ask of us what you will,' said they, 'and your request shall be instantly granted.'

"I reflected that I was old, and had suffered too much in
life to wish to begin it anew, while the day would come, my
child, when nothing would be too great for your desires ; when
you would wish to be rich, noble—a general, a marquis, a
prince, perhaps ! When that day comes, thought I, I can

give him every thing ; and a single moment of such happiness will repay me for eighty years of pain and misery. I thanked the fairies, therefore, and entreated them to keep their good will till the day when I should have need of it. The Fairy of the Waters took a small feather from her crown, and the Fairy of the Woods detached a scale from her scarf.

" ' My good woman,' said they, ' when you wish for us, place this feather and this scale in a vessel of pure water and call on us, making a wish. Should we be at the end of the world, we will be at your side in an instant, ready to pay the debt we owe you.'

" I bowed my head in token of gratitude. When I raised it all had vanished ; even the wounds and blood had disappeared from my hands, and I should have thought that I had been dreaming had not the scale of the serpent and the feather of the kingfisher remained in my hand."

"And where are these treasures, grandmamma ?" asked Graceful.

" My child, I have carefully concealed them," answered the old woman, " not wishing to show them to you till you were a man, and able to make use of them ; but, since death is about to separate us, the moment has come to give you these precious talismans. You will find at the back of the cupboard a wooden chest hidden under some rags ; in the chest is a little pasteboard box, wound about with tow ; open this box, and you will find the scale and the feather carefully wrapped in cotton. Take care not to break them ; handle them respectfully, and I will tell you what next to do."

Graceful brought the box to the poor woman, who was no longer able to quit her pallet, and she herself took from it the two articles.

" Now," said she, giving them to her grandson, " put a bowl full of water in the middle of the room ; place the scale and the feather in the water, and make a wish—wish for fortune, nobility, wit, power, whatever you please ; only, as I feel that I am dying, kiss me once more, my child, before speaking the words that will separate us forever, and receive my last blessing ; it will be another talisman to bring you happiness."

But, to the old woman's surprise, Graceful did not come near her, either to kiss her or to receive her blessing. He quickly placed the bowl in the middle of the room, threw the feather and scale into the water, and shouted at the top of his voice, "Appear, Fairy of the Waters ! I wish that my grandmother may live forever. Appear, Fairy of the Woods ! I wish that my grandmother may live forever."

And behold ! the water bubbled, bubbled, bubbled ; the bowl grew to a great basin, which the walls of the hut could scarcely hold, and from the bottom of the basin Graceful saw two beautiful young women rise, whom he knew directly from their wands to be fairies. One wore a crown of holly leaves mixed with red berries, and diamond ear-rings resembling acorns in their cups ; she was dressed in a robe of olive-green, over which a speckled skin was knotted like a scarf across the right shoulder—this was the Fairy of the Woods. As to the Fairy of the Waters, she wore a garland of reeds on her head, with a white robe trimmed with the feathers of aquatic birds, and a blue scarf, which now and then rose above her head, and fluttered like the sail of a ship. Great ladies as they were, they looked smilingly at Graceful, who had taken refuge in his grandmother's arms, and trembled with fear and admiration.

"Here we are, my child," said the Fairy of the Waters, who spoke first, as the eldest. "We have heard what you said, and your wish does you honor ; but, though we can help you in the plan which you have conceived, you alone can execute it. We can, indeed, prolong your grandmother's life for some time, but, for her to live forever, you must go to the Castle of Life, four long days' journey from here, on the coast of Sicily. There you will find the Fountain of Immortality. If you can accomplish each of these four days' journey without turning aside from the road, and, on reaching the castle, can answer three questions that will be put to you by an invisible voice, you will obtain what you desire. But, my child, reflect well before undertaking this adventure, for you will meet more than one danger on the way; and if you fail a single time to reach the end of your day's journey, you will not only miss the object of your pursuit, but you will never quit the country, from which none has ever returned."

"I will go, madam," returned Graceful.

"But you are very young, my child," said the Fairy of the Woods, "and you do not even know the way."

"No matter," replied Graceful; "I am sure, beautiful ladies, that you will not forsake me, and to save my grandmother I would go to the end of the world."

"Wait," said the Fairy of the Woods. Then, separating the lead from a broken window-pane, she placed it in the hollow of her hand.

And behold! the lead began to melt and bubble without seeming to burn the fairy, who threw the metal on the hearth, where it cooled in a thousand different forms.

"What do you see in all that?" said the fairy to Graceful.

"It seems to me, madam," said he, after looking attentively, "that I see a spaniel, with a long tail and large ears."

"Call him," said the fairy.

A barking was instantly heard, and forth from the metal sprang a black and flame-colored spaniel, which began to gambol and leap around Graceful.

"This will be your companion," said the fairy. "His name is Fido. He will show you the way; but I warn you that it is for you to direct him, and not for him to lead you. If you make him obey, he will serve you; if you obey him, he will destroy you."

"And I," said the Fairy of the Waters, "have I nothing to give you, my poor Graceful?"

Then, looking around her, the lady saw on the ground a bit of paper, which she tossed into the fire with her tiny foot. The paper caught fire, and as soon as the blaze had died away, thousands of little sparks were seen chasing each other about. The fairy watched these sparks with a curious eye; then, as the last one was about to go out, she blew upon the cinders, when, lo! the chirp of a bird was heard, and a swallow rose, which fluttered, terrified, about the room, and finally alighted on Graceful's shoulder.

"This will be your companion," said the Fairy of the Waters. "Her name is Pensive; she will show you the way; but I warn you that it is for you to direct her, and not for her to lead you. If you make her obey, she will serve you; if you obey her, she will destroy you."

"Stir the black ashes," added the good Fairy of the Waters, "and perhaps you will find something there."

Graceful obeyed. Under the ashes of the paper he found a vial of rock crystal, sparkling like a diamond. This, the fairy said, was to hold the water of immortality, which would break any vessel made by the hand of man. By the side of the vial Graceful found a dagger with a triangular blade—a very different thing from the stiletto of his father the fisherman, which he had been forbidden to touch. With this weapon he could brave the proudest enemy.

"My sister, you shall not be more generous than I," said the other fairy; then, taking a rush from the only chair in the room, she blew upon it, when, lo! the rush instantly swelled, and in less time than it takes to tell it became a beautiful musket, inlaid with mother-of-pearl. A second rush produced a cartridge-box, which Graceful slung around his body, and which became him marvelously. One would have thought him a prince setting out for the chase ; he was so handsome that his grandmother wept for joy and emotion.

The two fairies vanished ; Graceful kissed the good old woman, urging her to await his return, and knelt before her to receive her blessing. She entreated him to be patient, just, and charitable, and, above all, not to wander from the right path. "Not for my sake," added the old woman, "for I would gladly welcome death, and I regret the wish that you have made, but for your own, my child, that you may return to me, and that I may not die without your being here to close my eyes."

It was late. Graceful threw himself on the ground, too agitated, it seemed, to sleep. But slumber soon overtook him, and he slept soundly all night, while his poor grandmother watched the face of her dear child lighted by the flickering lamp, and did not weary of mournfully admiring him.

II.

EARLY in the morning, when dawn was scarcely breaking, the swallow began to twitter, and Fido to pull the blankets. "Let us go, master—let us go," said the two companions, in their language, which Graceful understood by the gift of the fairies ; "the tide is already rising on the beach, the birds are singing, the flies are humming, and the flowers are opening in the sun ; let us go ; it is time."

Graceful kissed his grandmother for the last time, and took the road to Pæstum, Pensive fluttering to the right and the left in pursuit of the flies, and Fido fawning on his young master or running before him.

They had not gone two leagues from the town when Graceful saw Fido talking with the ants, who were marching in regular troops, carrying all their provisions with them.

"Where are you going?" asked he.

"To the Castle of Life," they answered.

A little farther on Pensive encountered the grasshoppers, who had also set out on a journey, together with the bees and the butterflies; all were going to the Castle of Life, to drink of the Fountain of Immortality. They traveled in company, like people following the same road. Pensive introduced Graceful to a young butterfly, that chatted agreeably. Friendship springs up quickly in youth; in an hour the two comrades were inseparable.

To go straight forward does not suit the taste of butterflies, and Graceful's friend was constantly losing himself among the grass. Graceful, who had never been free in his life, nor had seen so many flowers and so much sunshine, followed all the windings of his companion, and troubled himself no more about the day than if it were never to end; but, after a few leagues' journey, his new friend began to be weary.

"Don't go any farther," said he to Graceful; "see how beautiful is this landscape, how fragrant these flowers, and how balmy these fields. Let us stay here; this is life."

"Let us go on," said Fido; "the day is long, and we are only at the beginning."

"Let us go on," said Pensive; "the sky is clear, and the horizon unbounded. Let us go on."

Graceful, restored to his senses, reasoned sagely with the butterfly, who fluttered constantly to the right and the left, but all in vain. "What matters it to me?" said the insect; "yesterday I was a caterpillar, to-night I shall be nothing. I will enjoy to-day." And he settled on a full-blown Pæstum rose. The perfume was so strong that the poor butterfly was suffocated. Graceful vainly endeavored to recall him to life ; then, bemoaning his fate, he fastened him with a pin to his hat like a cockade.

Toward noon the grasshoppers stopped in turn. "Let us rest," said they ; "the heat will overpower us if we struggle against the noonday sun. It is so pleasant to live in sweet repose! Come, Graceful, we will divert you, and you shall sing with us."

"Listen to them," said Pensive ; "they sing so sweetly!" But Fido would not stop ; his blood seemed on fire, and he barked so furiously that Graceful forgot the grasshoppers to follow his importunate companion.

At evening Graceful met the honey-bee loaded with booty. "Where are you going?" said he.

"I am returning home," said the bee ; "I shall not quit my hive."

"What!" rejoined Graceful ; "industrious as you are, will you do like the grasshoppers and renounce your share in immortality?"

"Your castle is too far off," returned the bee. "I have not your ambition. My daily labor suffices for me ; I care nothing for your travels ; to me work is life."

Graceful was a little moved at losing so many of his fellow-travelers on the first day ; but when he thought with what ease he had accomplished the first day's journey, his heart was filled with joy. He caressed Fido, caught the flies which Pensive took from his hand, and slept full of hope, dreaming of his grandmother and the two fairies.

III.

THE next morning, at daybreak, Pensive called his young master.

"Let us go," said he; "the tide is already rising on the shore, the birds are singing, the bees are humming, and the flowers are opening in the sun; let us go; it is time."

".Wait a moment," said Fido. "The day's journey is not long; before noon we shall be in sight of the temples of Pæstum, where we are to stop for the night."

"The ants are already on the way," returned Pensive; "the road is harder than yesterday, and the weather more uncertain; let us go."

Graceful had seen his grandmother smiling on him in his dreams, and he set out on his way with even greater ardor than the day before. The morning was glorious; on the right the blue waves broke with a gentle murmur on the strand; on the left, in the distance, the mountains were tinged with a roseate hue; the plain was covered with tall grass sprinkled with flowers; the road was lined with aloes, jujubes, and acanthuses, and before them lay a cloudless horizon. Graceful, ravished with hope and pleasure, fancied himself already at the end of his journey. Fido bounded over the fields and chased the frightened partridges; Pensive soared in the air and sported with the light. All at once Graceful saw a beautiful doe in the midst of the reeds, looking at him with languishing eyes as if she were calling him. He went toward her; she bounded forward, but only a little way. Three times she repeated the same trick, as if to allure him on.

"Let us follow her," said Fido; "I will cut off the way, and we will soon catch her."

"Where is Pensive?" said Graceful.

"What does it matter?" replied Fido; "it is the work of an instant. Trust to me—I was born for the chase—and the doe is ours."

Graceful did not let himself be bid twice. While Fido made a circuit, he ran after the doe, which paused among the trees as if to suffer herself to be caught, then bounded forward as soon as the hand of the pursuer touched her. . "Courage, master!" cried Fido, as he came upon her. But, with a toss of the head, the doe flung the dog in the air, and fled swifter than the wind.

Graceful sprung forward in pursuit. Fido, with burning eyes and distended jaws, ran and yelped as if he were mad. They crossed ditches, brakes, and hedges, unchecked by nothing. The wearied doe lost ground. Graceful redoubled his ardor, and was already stretching out his hand to seize his prey, when all at once the ground gave way beneath his feet, and he fell, with his imprudent companion, into a pit covered over with leaves. He had not recovered·from his fall when the doe, approaching the brink, cried, "You are betrayed; I am the wife of the King of the Wolves, who is coming to eat you both." Saying this, she disappeared.

"Alas! master," said Fido, "the fairy was right in advising you not to follow me. We have acted foolishly, and I have destroyed you."

"At all events," said Graceful, "we will defend our lives;" and, taking his musket, he double-loaded it, in readiness for the King of the Wolves; then, somewhat calmed, he examined the deep ditch into which he had fallen. It was too high for him to escape from it; in this hole he must await his death. Fido understood the look of his friend.

"Master," said he, "if you take me in your arms and throw me with all your might, perhaps I can reach the top; and, once there, I can help you."

Graceful had not much hope. Three times he endeavored to throw Fido, and three times the poor animal fell back; finally, at the fourth effort, he caught hold of some roots, and aided himself so well with his teeth and paws that he escaped from the tomb. He instantly threw into the ditch the boughs which he found about the edge.

"Master," said he, "plant these branches in the earth, and make yourself a ladder. Quick! quick!" he added; "I hear the howls of the King of the Wolves."

Graceful was adroit and agile. Anger redoubled his strength; in a moment he was outside. Then he secured his dagger in his belt, changed the powder in the pan of his musket, and, placing himself behind a tree, awaited the enemy with firmness.

Suddenly a frightful cry was heard, and an animal, with tusks like those of the wild boar, rushed on him with prodigious bounds. Graceful took aim and fired. The bullet hit the mark, and the animal fell back howling, but instantly sprang forward anew. "Load your musket again! make haste!" cried Fido, springing courageously in the face of the monster, and seizing his throat with his teeth.

The wolf had only to shake his head to fling the poor dog to the ground. He would have swallowed him at one mouthful had not Fido glided from his jaws, leaving one of his ears behind. It was Graceful's turn to save his companion; he boldly advanced and fired his second shot, taking aim at the shoulder. The wolf fell; but, rising, with a last effort he threw himself on the hunter, who fell under him. On receiving this terrible shock, Graceful thought himself lost; but, without losing courage, and calling the good fairies to his aid, he seized his dagger, and thrust it into the heart of the animal, which, ready to devour his enemy, straightened his limbs and died.

Graceful rose, covered with blood and froth, and seated himself, trembling, upon a fallen tree. Fido crept painfully to his feet, without daring to caress him, for he felt how much he was to blame.

"Master," said he, "what will become of us? Night is approaching, and we are so far from Pæstum!"

"We must go," said the child; and he rose; but he was so

weak that he was obliged to sit down again. A burning thirst devoured him ; he was feverish, and every thing whirled before his eyes. He thought of his grandmother, and began to weep. What was poor Graceful's remorse for having so soon forgotten such fair promises, and condemned himself to die in a country from which there was no return, and all this for the bright eyes of a doe! How sadly ended the day so well begun !

Sinister howls were soon heard ; the brothers of the King of the Wolves were calling him and coming to his aid. Graceful embraced Fido, his only friend, and forgave him the imprudence for which they were both about to pay with their lives ; then loaded his musket, offered up a prayer to the good fairies, commended his grandmother to them, and prepared to die.

"Graceful ! Graceful ! where are you?" cried a little voice that could be none other than Pensive's, and the swallow alighted on the head of his master.

"Courage !" said she ; "the wolves are still far off. There is a spring close by where you can quench your thirst and stanch your bleeding wounds, and I have found a hidden path which will lead us to Pæstum."

Graceful and Fido dragged themselves along to the brook, trembling with hope and fear ; then entered the obscure path, a little reanimated by the soft twittering of Pensive. The sun had set ; they walked in the twilight for some hours, and, when the moon rose, they were out of danger. They had still to journey over a painful and dangerous road for those who no longer had the ardor of the morning. There were marshes to cross, ditches to leap, and thickets to break through, which tore Graceful's face and hands ; but, at the thought that he could still repair his fault and save his grandmother, his heart was so light that his strength redoubled at every step with his hope. At last, after a thousand obstacles, they reached Pæstum just as the stars markèd midnight.

Graceful threw himself on the pavement of the temple of Neptune, and, after thanking Pensive, fell asleep, with Fido at his feet, wounded, bleeding, and silent.

IV.

THE sleep was not long. Graceful was up before daybreak, which seemed long in coming. On descending the steps of the temple, he saw the ants, who had raised a heap of sand, and were bringing grain from the new harvest. The whole republic was in motion. The ants were all going or coming, talking to their neighbors, and receiving or giving orders ; some were dragging wisps of straw, others were carrying bits of wood, others conveying away dead flies, and others heaping up provisions : it was a complete winter establishment.

"What!" said Graceful to the ants, "are you not going to the Castle of Life? Do you renounce immortality?"

"We have worked long enough," answered one of the laborers ; "the time for harvest has come. The road is long and the future uncertain, and we are rich. Let fools count on to-morrow, the wise man uses to-day. When a person has hoarded riches honestly, it is true philosophy to enjoy them."

Fido thought that the ant was right ; but, as he no longer dared advise, he contented himself with shaking his head as they set out. Pensive, on the contrary, said that the ant was a selfish fellow, and that, if life were made only for enjoyment, the butterfly was wiser than he. At the same time, and with a lighter wing than ever, the swallow soared upward to lead the way.

Graceful walked on in silence. Ashamed of the follies of the day before, although he still regretted the doe, he resolved that on the third day nothing should turn him aside from the road. Fido, with his mutilated ear, limped after his master, and seemed not less dreamy than he. At noon they sought for a shady place in which to rest for a few moments. The sun was less scorching than the day before. It seemed as if both country and season had changed. The road lay through meadows lately mown for the second time, or beautiful vineyards full of grapes, and was lined with great fig-trees laden with fruit, in which thousands of insects were humming; golden clouds were floating in the horizon, the air was soft and gentle, and every thing tempted to repose.

In the most beautiful of the meadows, by the side of a brook which diffused its coolness afar, Graceful saw a herd of buffaloes chewing the cud under the shade of the ashes and plane-trees. They were lazily stretched on the ground, in a circle around a large bull that seemed their chief and king. Graceful approached them, and was received with politeness. They invited him by a nod to be seated, and pointed out to him great bowls full of milk and cheese. Our traveler admired the calmness and gravity of these peaceful and powerful animals, which seemed like so many Roman senators in their curule chairs. The gold ring which they wore in their noses added still more to the majesty of their aspect. Graceful, who felt calmer and more sedate than the day before, thought, in spite of himself, how pleasant it would be to live in the midst of this peace and plenty; if happiness were any where, it must surely be found here.

Fido shared his master's opinion. It was the season of the southward migration of the quails; the ground was covered with tired birds, resting to regain strength before crossing the sea, and Fido had only to stoop down to find game worthy of a prince. Satiated with eating, he stretched himself at Graceful's feet, and slept soundly.

When the buffaloes had finished chewing their cud, Graceful, who had hitherto feared to disturb them, entered into conversation with the bull, who showed a cultivated mind and wide experience.

" Are you the masters of this rich domain?" asked he.

"No," replied the old buffalo; "we belong, with all the rest, to the Fairy Crapaudine, the Queen of the Vermilion Towers, the richest of all the fairies."

" What does she require of you?" asked Graceful.

" Nothing, except to wear this gold ring in the nose, and to pay her a tribute of milk," returned the bull, " or, at most, to give her one of our children from time to time to regale her guests. At this price we enjoy our plenty in perfect security, and we have no reason to envy any on earth, for none are so happy as we."

" Have you never heard of the Castle of Life, and the Fountain of Immortality?" asked Graceful, who, without knowing why, blushed as he put the question.

"There were some old men among our ancestors who still talked of these visions," replied the bull; "but we are wiser than our fathers; we know that there is no other happiness than to chew the cud and sleep."

Graceful rose sadly to resume his journey, and asked what were those reddish square towers which he saw in the distance.

" They are the Vermilion Towers," returned the bull; " they bar the way; and you must pass through the castle of the Fairy Crapaudine in order to continue your road. You will see the fairy, my young friend, and she will offer you hospitality and riches. Take my advice, and do like those that have gone before you, all of whom accepted the favors of our mistress, and found that they had done well to abandon their dreams in order to live happy."

"And what became of them?" asked Graceful.

"They became buffaloes like us," rejoined the bull, who, not having finished his afternoon nap, closed his eyes and fell asleep.

Graceful started and awakened Fido, who rose grumbling. He called Pensive. Pensive did not answer; she was talking with a spider that had spun a great web between the branches of an ash-tree, which was glittering in the sun, full of flies. "Why take this long journey?" said the spider to the swallow. "What is the use of changing your climate, and putting your life at the mercy of the sea, the weather, or a master? Look at me; I depend on nobody, and have every thing from myself. I am my own mistress; I enjoy my art and genius; I bring the world to me; nothing can disturb either my calculations, or a serenity which I owe to myself alone."

Graceful called Pensive three times without making her hear, so completely was she engrossed in admiration of her new friend. Every instant some giddy fly fell into the web, and each time the spider, like an attentive hostess, offered the prey to her astonished companion, when suddenly a breeze passed—a breeze so light that it did not ruffle a feather of the swallow's wing. Pensive looked for the spider; the web had been swept away by the winds, and the poor insect was clinging by one foot to the last thread, when a bird seized it and bore it away.

V.

SETTING out again on their way, they proceeded in silence to the palace of Crapaudine. Graceful was introduced with great ceremony by two beautiful greyhounds, caparisoned with purple, and wearing on their necks broad collars sparkling with rubies. After crossing a great number of halls, all full of pictures, statues, gold, and silver, and coffers overflowing with money and jewels, Graceful and his companions entered a circular temple, which was Crapaudine's drawing-room. The walls were of lapis-lazuli, and the ceiling, of sky-blue enamel, was supported by twelve chiseled pillars of massive gold, with capitals of acanthus leaves of white enamel edged with gold. A huge frog, as large as a rabbit, was seated in a velvet easy-chair. It was the fairy of the place. The charming Crapaudine was draped in a scarlet mantle covered with glittering spangles, and wore on her head a ruby diadem, whose lustre lighted up her fat cheeks mottled with green and yellow. As soon as she perceived Graceful, she extended to him her fingers, covered with rings, which the poor boy was obliged respectfully to raise to his lips as he bowed.

"My friend," said the fairy to him, in a hoarse voice, which she vainly tried to soften, "I was expecting you, and I will not be less generous to you than my sisters have been. On your way here you have seen but a small part of my riches. This palace, with its pictures, its statues, and its coffers full of gold, these vast domains, and these innumerable flocks, all may be yours if you wish ; it depends only on yourself to become the richest and happiest of men."

"What must I do for this?" asked Graceful, greatly excited.

"Less than nothing," replied the fairy ; "chop me up into little pieces and eat me. It is not a very disagreeable thing to do," added Crapaudine, looking at Graceful with eyes redder than usual.

"Can I not season you, at least?" said Graceful, who had been unable to look without envy at the beautiful gardens of the fairy.

"No, you must eat me without seasoning ; but walk about my palace, see and handle all my treasures, and reflect that, by giving me this proof of devotion, they will all be yours."

"Master," sighed Fido, in a supplicating voice, "a little courage ! we are so comfortable here !"

Pensive said nothing, but his silence was consent. As to Graceful, who remembered the buffaloes and the gold ring, he distrusted the fairy. Crapaudine perceived it.

"Do not think, my dear Graceful, that I wish to deceive you," she said. "In offering you all that I possess, I also demand of you a service which I will reward as it deserves. When you have done what I propose, I shall become a young girl, as beautiful as Venus, except that my hands and feet will remain like those of a frog, which is very little when one is rich. Ten princes, twenty marquises, and thirty counts have already begged me to marry them as I am ; when I become a woman, I will give you the preference, and we will enjoy my vast fortune together. Do not blush for your poverty ; you have about you a treasure that is worth all mine, the vial which my sister gave you." Saying this, she stretched out her slimy fingers to seize the talisman.

"Never !" cried Graceful, shrinking back, "never ! I wish neither repose nor fortune ; I wish to quit this place and to go to the Castle of Life."

"You shall never go there !" exclaimed the fairy, in a rage. The castle instantly disappeared, a circle of fire surrounded Graceful, and an invisible clock began to strike midnight. At the first stroke the child started ; at the second, without hesitating, he plunged headlong into the flames. To die for his grandmother seemed to him the only means of showing his love and repentance.

VI.

To Graceful's surprise, the flames parted without touching him, and he suddenly found himself in a new country, with his two companions by his side. This country was no longer Italy, but Russia, the end of the earth. He was wandering on a mountain covered with snow. Around him he saw nothing but great trees, coated with hoar-frost, and dripping water from all their branches ; a damp and penetrating mist chilled him to the bones ; the moist earth sunk under his feet ; and, to crown his wretchedness, it was necessary to descend a steep precipice, at the bottom of which a torrent was breaking noisily over the rocks. Graceful took his dagger and cut a branch from a tree to support his faltering steps. Fido, with his tail between his legs, barked feebly ; and Pensive, his ruffled feathers covered with icicles, clung to his master's shoulder. The poor bird was half dead, but she encouraged Graceful, and did not complain.

When, after infinite pains, he reached the foot of the mountain, Graceful found a river filled with enormous icebergs, striking against each other and whirling in the current, and this river he must cross, without bridge, without boat, and without aid.

"Master," said Fido, "I can go no farther. Accursed be the fairy that drew me from nothingness to place me in your service." Saying this, he lay down on the ground and would not stir. Graceful vainly tried to restore his courage, and called him his companion and friend. All that the poor dog could do was to answer his master's caresses for the last time by wagging his tail and licking his hands ; then his limbs stiffened, and he expired.

Graceful took Fido on his back in order to carry him to the Castle of Life, and boldly climbed one of the icebergs, still followed by Pensive. With his staff he pushed this frail bark into the middle of the current, which bore it away with frightful rapidity.

"Master," said Pensive, "do you hear the roaring of the waters? We are floating toward a whirlpool which will swallow us up! Give me a last caress, and farewell!"

"No," said Graceful; "why should the fairies have deceived us? The shore may be close by; perhaps the sun is shining behind the clouds. Mount, mount, my good Pensive; perchance above the fog you will find light, and will see the Castle of Life!"

Pensive spread his half-frozen wings, and courageously soared amidst the cold and mist. Graceful listened for a moment to the sound of his flight; then all was silent, while the iceberg pursued its furious course through the darkness. Graceful waited a long time; at last, when he felt himself alone, hope abandoned him, and he lay down to await death on the tottering iceberg. Livid flashes of lightning shot through the clouds, horrible bursts of thunder were heard, and the end of the world and of time seemed approaching. All at once, in the midst of his despair, Graceful heard the cry of the swallow, and Pensive fell at his feet. "Master, master," cried she, "you were right. I have seen the shore; the dawn is close at hand; courage!" Saying this, she convulsively spread her tired wings, and lay motionless and lifeless.

Graceful started up, placed the poor bird that had sacrificed itself for him next his heart, and, with superhuman ardor, urged the iceberg on to safety or destruction. Suddenly he heard the roaring of the breakers. He fell on his knees and closed his eyes, awaiting death.

A wave like a mountain broke over his head and cast him fainting on the shore, which no living person had touched before him.

VII.

WHEN Graceful recovered his senses, the ice, clouds, and darkness had disappeared. He was lying on the ground in the midst of a charming country, covered with trees bathed in a soft light. In front of him was a beautiful castle, from which bubbled a brook that flowed into a sea as blue, calm, and transparent as the sky. Graceful looked about him; he was alone—alone with the remains of his two companions, which the waves had washed on the shore. Exhausted with

suffering and excitement, he dragged himself to the brook, and bent over the water to refresh his parched lips, when he shrank back with affright. It was not his face that he saw in the water, but that of an old man with silvery locks who strongly resembled him. He turned round ; there was no one behind him. He again drew near the fountain ; he saw the old man, or rather, doubtless, the old man was himself. "Great fairies," he cried, "I understand you. If it is my life that you wish in exchange for that of my grandmother, I joyfully accept the sacrifice." And without troubling himself farther about his old age and wrinkles, he plunged his head into the water and drank eagerly.

On rising, he was astonished to see himself again as he was when he left home, only more beautiful, with blacker hair and brighter eyes than ever. He picked up his hat, which had fallen near the spring, and which a drop of water had touched by chance, when what was his surprise to see the butterfly that he had pinned to it fluttering its wings and seeking to fly. He gave it its liberty, and ran to the beach for Fido and Pensive, then plunged them both into the blessed fountain. Pensive flew upward with a joyful cry, and disappeared amid the turrets of the castle. Fido, shaking the water from both ears, ran to the kennels of the palace, where he was met by magnificent watch-dogs, which, instead of barking and growling at the new-comer, welcomed him joyfully like an old friend. Graceful had at last found the fountain of immortality, or rather the brook that flowed from it—a brook already greatly weakened, and which only gave two or three hundred years of life to those that drank of it ; but nothing prevented them from drinking anew.

Graceful filled his vial with this life-giving water, and approached the palace. His heart beat, for a last trial remained. So near success, he feared the more to fail. He mounted the steps of the castle. All was closed and silent ; no one was there to receive the traveler. When he had reached the last step and was about to knock at the door, a voice, rather gentle than harsh, stopped him.

"Have you loved?" said the invisible voice.

"Yes," answered Graceful ; "I have loved my grandmother better than any one in the world."

The door opened a little way.

"Have you suffered for her whom you have loved?" resumed the voice.

"I have suffered," replied Graceful ; "much through my own fault, doubtless, but a little for her whom I wished to save."

The door opened half way, and the child caught a glimpse of woods, waters, and a sky more beautiful than any thing of which he had ever dreamed.

"Have you always done your duty?" said the voice, in a harsher tone.

"Alas ! no," replied Graceful, falling on his knees ; "but when I have failed I have been punished by my remorse even more than by the hard trials through which I have passed. Forgive me, and punish me as I deserve, if I have not yet expiated all my faults ; but save her whom I love—save my grandmother."

The door instantly opened wide, though Graceful saw no one. Intoxicated with joy, he entered a court-yard surrounded with arbors embowered in foliage, with a fountain in the midst, spouting from a tuft of flowers larger, more beautiful, and more fragrant than any he had seen on earth. By the side of the spring stood a woman dressed in white, of noble bearing, and seemingly not more than forty years old. She advanced to meet Graceful, and smiled on him so sweetly that the child felt himself touched to the heart, and his eyes filled with tears.

"Don't you know me?" said the woman.

"Oh, grandmother! is it you?" he exclaimed. "How came you in the Castle of Life?"

"My child," said she, pressing him to her heart, "He who brought me here is an enchanter more powerful than the fairies of the woods and the waters. I shall never more return to Salerno. I shall receive my reward here for the little good I have done by tasting a happiness which time will not destroy."

"And me, grandmother!" cried Graceful, "what will become of me? After seeing you here, how can I return to suffer alone?"

"My dear child," she replied, "no one can live on earth after he has caught a glimpse of the celestial delights of this abode. You have lived, my dear Graceful; life has nothing more to teach you. You have passed in four days through the desert where I languished eighty years, and henceforth nothing can separate us."

The door closed, and from that time nothing was heard of Graceful or his grandmother. It was in vain that search was made for the palace and enchanted fountain; they were never more discovered on earth. But if we understood the language of the stars, if we felt what their gentle rays tell us every evening, we should long ago have learned from them where to look for the Castle of Life and the Fountain of Immortality.

DESTINY.

A DALMATIAN TALE.

ONCE upon a time there were two brothers, who lived together in one family. One did every thing, while the other was an idle fellow, who troubled himself about nothing but eating and drinking. The harvests were always magnificent; they had cows, horses, sheep, pigs, bees, and every thing else in plenty.

The elder brother, who did every thing, said to himself one day, "Why should I work for this idler? It is better for us to separate; I will work for myself alone, and he can do as he likes." He said to his brother, therefore,

"Brother, it is not just for me to do every thing, while you trouble yourself about nothing but eating and drinking; we must separate."

His brother tried to dissuade him from his plan, saying,

"Brother, don't do this, we are so well off as we are. You have every thing in your own hands; what is mine is yours; and you know that I am always satisfied with what you do or order done."

The elder, however, persisted in his resolution till the younger was forced to yield. "Since it must be so," said he, "I am not angry; divide the property as you like."

The division made, each took his share. The idler hired a drover for his cattle, a groom for his horses, a shepherd for his sheep, a goatherd for his goats, a swineherd for his hogs, and a keeper for his bees, and said to them all, "I intrust my property to you : may God have you in his keeping." And he continued to stay at home with no more care than before.

The elder, on the contrary, labored for himself as he had done for the common good ; he kept his own flocks, and had an eye to every thing ; yet, in spite of all this, he found bad luck and misfortune every where ; every thing went wrong with him, until at last he was so poor that he had not even a pair of shoes, but was forced to go barefoot. He said to himself, " I will go to my brother's house, and see how affairs are prospering with him."

His road lay through a pasture in which a flock of sheep was feeding. On approaching them he saw that they had no shepherd. A beautiful young girl was seated near them, with her distaff, spinning gold thread.

He saluted the young girl, and asked her to whom the flock belonged.

" To him to whom I belong belong also these sheep," answered she.

" And who are you ?" said he.

" I am your brother's fortune ?" she replied.

" And where is my fortune ?" he exclaimed, seized with anger and envy.

" Ah ! she is far from you," said the young girl.

" Can I find her ?" asked he.

" You can," she replied, " if you only look yonder."

On hearing these words, and seeing that the sheep were the finest that could be imagined, he had no wish to see the other flocks, but went straight to his brother, who, as soon as he saw him, burst into tears, moved with pity.

" Where have you been so long ?" asked he. And, seeing him clothed in rags and barefooted, he gave him a pair of shoes and some money.

After staying three days in his brother's house, the poor man set out for home. No sooner had he reached his house than he threw a bag across his shoulder, with a piece of bread in it, took a staff in his hand, and set out to seek his fortune.

After walking for some time he found himself in a great forest, where he saw a wretched old hag asleep under a tree. He gave her a blow on the back with his staff to awaken her. She moved with difficulty, and, half opening her bleared eyes, said to him, "Thank God that I was asleep, for if I had been awake you would not have had those shoes."

"Who are you, then," asked he, "that would have prevented my having these shoes?"

"I am your fortune," answered the old woman.

"What! are you my fortune?" cried he, striking his breast. "May God exterminate you! Who gave you to me?"

"It was Destiny," replied the old woman.

"Where is Destiny?" he asked.

"Go and find him," said the old woman, lying down to sleep again.

He set out in search of Destiny. After a long, long journey, at length he reached a wood, where he found a hermit, of whom he asked the way to the abode of Destiny.

"Go straight up yonder mountain, and you will find his castle," answered the hermit; "but when you find him, take care not to speak to him, but only do all that you see him do."

The traveler thanked the hermit, and took his way to the mountain. When he reached the abode of Destiny, he saw a magnificent palace full of servants constantly bustling about and doing nothing. As to Destiny, he was supping at a table bountifully served. When the stranger saw this, he also sat down at the table and supped with the master of the house. After supper Destiny went to bed, and his guest did the same.

At midnight a terrible noise was heard in the castle, and a

voice cried, " Destiny, Destiny, such a number of souls have come into the world this night ; give them something according to thy good pleasure."

And behold ! Destiny rose, and opened a golden chest filled with shining guineas, which he scattered by handfuls about the room, saying, " Such as I am to-day, such shalt thou be all thy life !"

At daybreak the beautiful castle had vanished, and in its place stood an ordinary house, in which, however, nothing was wanting. When evening came, Destiny sat down to supper. His guest did the same, but no one spoke a word. Supper over, they went to bed. At midnight a terrible noise was heard, and a voice cried, " Destiny, Destiny, such a number of souls have come into the world this night ; give them something according to thy good pleasure."

And behold ! Destiny rose, and opened a silver chest, but this time there were no guineas in it, but only silver coin, with a few small pieces of gold, which Destiny scattered on the floor, saying, " Such as I am to-day, such shalt thou be all thy life !"

At daybreak this house had also disappeared, and a smaller one stood in its place. The same thing happened every night, and every morning the house was smaller, until finally there was nothing but a wretched hut. Destiny now took a spade and began to dig the ground. His guest did the same, and both worked all day. When night came, Destiny took a crust of bread, and, breaking it in two, gave half to his companion. This was all their supper. When they had eaten it they went to bed.

At midnight a terrible noise was heard, and a voice cried out, " Destiny, Destiny, such a number of souls have come into the world this night ; give them something according to thy good pleasure."

And behold! Destiny rose, and opened a wooden chest filled with pebbles mixed with a few copper coins, which he scattered on the ground, saying, "Such as I am to-day, such shalt thou be all thy life!"

When morning dawned the cabin was changed into a splendid palace, as on the first day. Then, for the first time, Destiny spoke to his guest. "Why did you come here?" asked he.

The poor man told him the whole story of his wretchedness, and how he had come to ask Destiny himself why he had given him such a bad fortune.

"You saw what I was the first night, when I scattered guineas, and what followed," replied Destiny. "Such as I am on the night that a man is born, such will that man be all his life. You were born on a night of poverty; you will always be poor. Your brother, on the contrary, came into the world on a lucky night; he will always be fortunate. But, since you have taken so much trouble to find me, I will tell you how to help yourself. Your brother has a daughter by the name of Miliza, who is as fortunate as her father. Take her for your wife when you return home, but be careful always to say that all that you have belongs to her."

The poor man thanked Destiny again and again, and set out for home. As soon as he arrived, he went straight to his brother's house and said,

"Brother, give me Miliza for a wife; you see that I am all alone in the world."

"I am willing," answered his brother; "Miliza is yours."

The bridegroom carried Miliza to his house. He soon became very rich, but he always took good care to say, "All that I have belongs to Miliza."

One day, however, as he was admiring his wheat, which was the most beautiful that ever was seen, a stranger passed by and asked, "Whose wheat is this?"

"It is mine," answered he, without thinking. But scarcely had he spoken, when behold! the wheat took fire, and the flames spread all over the field. Without stopping to put it out, he ran after the traveler, crying, " Stop, sir, I was mistaken ; it belongs to Miliza, my brother's daughter."

The fire went out at once of its own accord. He had learned a good lesson which he never forgot, and from that time thenceforth he was fortunate, thanks to Miliza.

THE TWELVE MONTHS.

A BOHEMIAN TALE.

THERE was once a woman who was left a widow with two children. The elder, who was only her step-daughter, was named Dobrunka; the younger, who was as wicked as her mother, was called Katinka. The mother worshiped her daughter, but she hated Dobrunka, simply because she was as beautiful as her sister was ugly. Dobrunka did not even know that she was pretty, and she could not understand why her step-mother flew into a rage at the mere sight of her. The poor child was obliged to do all the work of the house; she had to sweep, cook, wash, sew, spin, weave, cut the grass, and take care of the cow, while Katinka lived like a princess, that is to say, did nothing.

Dobrunka worked with a good will, and took reproaches and blows with the gentleness of a lamb; but nothing soothed her step-mother, for every day added to the beauty of the elder sister and the ugliness of the younger. "They are growing up," thought the mother, "and suitors will soon appear, who will refuse my daughter when they see this hateful Dobrunka, who grows beautiful on purpose to spite me. I must get rid of her, cost what it may."

One day in the middle of January, Katinka took a fancy for some violets. She called Dobrunka, and said, "Go to the forest and bring me a bunch of violets, that I may put them in my bosom and enjoy their fragrance."

"Oh, sister, what an idea!" answered Dobrunka; "as if there were any violets under the snow!"

"Hold your tongue, stupid fool," returned her sister, "and do as I bid you. If you do not go to the forest and bring me back a bunch of violets, I will beat you to a jelly." Upon this, the mother took Dobrunka by the arm, put her out of the door, and drew the bolt on her.

The poor girl went to the forest weeping bitterly. Every thing was covered with snow ; there was not even a foot-path. She lost her way, and wandered about till, famishing with hunger and perishing with cold, she entreated God to take her from this wretched life.

All at once she saw a light in the distance. She went on, climbing higher and higher, until at last she reached the top of a huge rock, upon which a great fire was built. Around the fire were twelve stones, and on each stone sat a motionless figure, wrapped in a large mantle, his head covered with a hood which fell over his eyes. Three of these mantles were white like the snow, three were green like the grass of the meadows, three were golden like the sheaves of ripe wheat, and three were purple like the grapes of the vine. These twelve figures, gazing at the fire in silence, were the Twelve Months of the year.

Dobrunka knew January by his long white beard. He was the only one that had a staff in his hand. The poor girl was terribly frightened. She drew near, saying, in a timid voice, " My good sirs, please to let me warm myself by your fire ; I am freezing with cold."

January nodded his head. "Why have you come here, my child ?" he asked. "What are you looking for ?"

" I am looking for violets," replied Dobrunka.

" This is not the season for them ; there are no violets in the time of snow," said January, in his gruff voice.

" I know it," replied Dobrunka, sadly ; " but my sister and mother will beat me to a jelly if I do not bring them some, My good sirs, please to tell me where I can find them."

Old January rose, and, turning to a young man in a green mantle, put his staff in his hand, and said to him, " Brother March, this is your business."

March rose in turn, and stirred the fire with the staff, when behold! the flames rose, the snow melted, the buds put forth on the trees, the grass turned green under the bushes, the flowers peeped through the verdure, and the violets opened— it was spring.

"Make haste, my child, and gather your violets," said March.

Dobrunka gathered a large bouquet, thanked the Twelve Months, and joyfully ran home. You can imagine the astonishment of Katinka and the step-mother. The fragrance of the violets filled the whole house.

"Where did you find these fine things?" asked Katinka, in a disdainful voice.

"Up yonder, on the mountain," answered her sister. "It looked like a great blue carpet under the bushes."

Katinka put the bouquet in her bosom, and did not even thank the poor child.

The next morning the wicked sister, as she sat idling by the stove, took a fancy for some strawberries.

"Go to the forest and bring me some strawberries," said she to Dobrunka.

"Oh, sister, what an idea! as if there were any strawberries under the snow!"

"Hold your tongue, stupid fool, and do as I bid you. If you don't go to the forest and bring me back a basket of strawberries, I will beat you to a jelly."

The mother took Dobrunka by the arm, put her out of the door, and drew the bolt on her.

The poor girl returned to the forest, looking with all her eyes for the light that she had seen the day before. She was fortunate enough to spy it, and she reached the fire trembling and almost frozen.

The Twelve Months were in their places, motionless and silent.

"My good sirs," said Dobrunka, "please to let me warm myself by your fire ; I am almost frozen with cold."

"Why have you returned?" asked January. "What are you looking for?"

"I am looking for strawberries," answered she.

"This is not the season for them," returned January, in his gruff voice ; "there are no strawberries under the snow."

"I know it," replied Dobrunka, sadly ; "but my mother and sister will beat me to a jelly if I do not bring them some. My good sirs, please to tell me where I can find them."

Old January rose, and, turning to a man in a golden mantle, he put his staff in his hand, saying, "Brother June, this is your business."

June rose in turn, and stirred the fire with the staff, when behold ! the flames rose, the snow melted, the earth grew green, the trees were covered with leaves, the birds sang, and the flowers opened — it was summer. Thousands of little white stars enameled the turf, then turned to red strawberries, looking, in their green cups, like rubies set in emeralds.

"Make haste, my child, and gather your strawberries," said June.

Dobrunka filled her apron, thanked the Twelve Months, and joyfully ran home. You may imagine the astonishment of Katinka and the step-mother. The fragrance of the strawberries filled the whole house.

"Where did you find these fine things?" asked Katinka, in a disdainful voice.

"Up yonder on the mountain," answered her sister ; "there were so many of them that they looked like blood poured on the ground.

Katinka and her mother devoured the strawberries without even thanking the poor child.

The third day the wicked sister took a fancy for some red apples. The same threats, the same insults, and the same violence followed. Dobrunka ran to the mountain, and was fortunate enough to find the Twelve Months warming themselves, motionless and silent.

"You here again, my child?" said old January, making room for her by the fire. Dobrunka told him, with tears, how, if she did not bring home some red apples, her mother and sister would beat her to death.

Old January repeated the ceremonies of the day before. "Brother September," said he to a gray-bearded man in a purple mantle, "this is your business."

September rose and stirred the fire with the staff, when behold! the flames ascended, the snow melted, and the trees put forth a few yellow leaves, which fell one by one before the wind — it was autumn. The only flowers were a few late pinks, daisies, and immortelles. Dobrunka saw but one thing, an apple-tree with its rosy fruit.

"Make haste, my child; shake the tree," said September.

She shook it, and an apple fell; she shook it again, and a second apple followed.

"Make haste, Dobrunka, make haste home!" cried September, in an imperious voice.

The good child thanked the Twelve Months, and joyfully ran home. You may imagine the astonishment of Katinka and the step-mother.

"Green apples in January! Where did you get these apples?" asked Katinka.

"Up yonder on the mountain; there is a tree there that is as red with them as a cherry-tree in July."

"Why did you bring only two? You ate the rest on the way."

"Oh, sister, I did not touch them; I was only permitted to shake the tree twice, and but two apples fell."

"Begone, you fool!" cried Katinka, striking her sister, who ran away crying.

The wicked girl tasted one of the apples; she had never eaten any thing so delicious in her life, neither had her mother. How they regretted not having any more!

"Mother," said Katinka, "give me my fur cloak. I will go to the forest and find the tree, and, whether I am permitted or not, I will shake it so hard that all the apples will be ours."

The mother tried to stop her. A spoiled child listens to nothing. Katinka wrapped herself in her fur cloak, drew the hood over her head, and hastened to the forest.

Every thing was covered with snow; there was not even a foot-path. Katinka lost her way, but she pushed on, spurred by pride and covetousness. She spied a light in the distance. She climbed and climbed till she reached the place, and found the Twelve Months each seated on his stone, motionless and silent. Without asking their permission, she approached the fire.

"Why have you come here? What do you want? Where are you going?" asked old January, gruffly.

"What matters it to you, old fool?" answered Katinka. "It is none of your business where I came from or whither I am going." She plunged into the forest. January frowned, and raised his staff above his head. In the twinkling of an eye the sky was overcast, the fire went out, the snow fell, and the wind blew. Katinka could not see the way before her. She lost herself, and vainly tried to retrace her steps. The snow fell and the wind blew. She called her mother, she cursed her sister, she cursed God. The snow fell and the wind blew. Katinka froze, her limbs stiffened, and she fell motionless. The snow still fell and the wind still blew.

The mother went without ceasing from the window to the door, and from the door to the window. The hours passed, and Katinka did not return.

"I must go and look for my daughter," said she. "The child has forgotten herself with those hateful apples." She took her fur cloak and hood, and hastened to the mountain. Every thing was covered with snow; there was not even a foot-path. She plunged into the forest, calling her daughter. The snow fell and the wind blew. She walked on with feverish anxiety, shouting at the top of her voice. The snow still fell and the wind still blew.

Dobrunka waited through the evening and the night, but no one returned. In the morning she took her wheel and spun a whole distaff full; there was still no news. "What can have happened?" said the good girl, weeping. The sun was shining through an icy mist, and the ground was covered with snow. Dobrunka prayed for her mother and sister. They did not return; and it was not till spring that a shepherd found the two corpses in the forest.

Dobrunka remained the sole mistress of the house, the cow, and the garden, to say nothing of a piece of meadow adjoining the house. But when a good and pretty girl has a field under her window, the next thing that follows is a young farmer, who offers her his heart and hand. Dobrunka was soon married. The Twelve Months did not abandon their child. More than once, when the north wind blew fearfully and the windows shook in their frames, old January stopped up all the crevices of the house with snow, so that the cold might not enter this peaceful abode.

Dobrunka lived to a good old age, always virtuous and happy, having, according to the proverb, winter at the door, summer in the barn, autumn in the cellar, and spring in the heart.

F

SSWANDA, THE PIPER.

SSWANDA, the Piper, was a jolly companion. Like every true musician, he was born with an unquenchable thirst; besides, he was madly fond of play, and would have risked his soul at strajak, the favorite game at cards in Bohemia. When he had earned a little money, he would throw aside his pipes, and drink and play with the first comer till he returned to his home as light in pocket as when he had left it. But he was always so merry, witty, and good-natured that not a drinker ever left the table while the piper was there, and his name still lives in Bohemia as the prince of good fellows.

One day there was a festival at Mokran, and no merry-making was ever complete without the piper. Sswanda, after blowing his pipe till midnight and earning twenty zwanzigers, determined to amuse himself on his own account. Neither prayers nor promises could persuade him to go on with his music; he was determined to drink his fill and to shuffle the cards at his ease; but, for the first time in his life, he found no one to play with him.

Sswanda was not the man to quit the inn so long as he had a kreutzer in his pocket, and on that day he had many of them. By dint of talking, laughing, and drinking, he took one of those fixed ideas which are not uncommon among those who look too often in the bottom of their glass, and determined to play at any price; but all his neighbors refused his challenge. Furious at finding no partner, he rose with an unsteady step, paid for what he had drank, and left the inn.

"I will go to Drazic," said he; "the schoolmaster and the bailiff there are honest people who are not afraid of play, and I shall find partners. Hurrah!"

The night was clear, and the moon shone like a fish's eye. On reaching a cross-road, Sswanda raised his eyes by chance, and stopped mute and motionless. A flock of ravens were croaking over his head, and in front of him rose four posts, standing like pillars, and connected at the top by cross-beams, from each of which swung a half-devoured corpse. It was a robbers' gallows, a spectacle by no means amusing to a less stoical spirit than that of Sswanda.

He had not recovered from the first shudder when suddenly there appeared before him a man dressed in black, with pale and hollow cheeks, and eyes that glittered like carbuncles.

"Where are you going so late, friend Piper?" asked he, in a soft voice.

" To Drazic, Mr. Black Coat," answered the intrepid Sswanda.

" Would you like to earn something by your music ?"

" I am tired of blowing," returned Sswanda. " I have some silver in my pocket, and wish to amuse myself."

" Who talks to you of silver? It is with gold that we pay."

Saying this, the stranger flashed before his eyes a handful of shining ducats. The piper was the son of a thrifty mother ; he knew not how to resist such an invitation, and followed the black man and his gold.

How the time passed he never could remember. It is true that his head was a little heavy. The only thing that he recollected was that the black man warned him to accept whatever was offered him, whether gold or wine, but never to return thanks except by saying " Good luck, brother !"

Without knowing how he had entered, he found himself in a dark room where three men, dressed in black like his guide, were playing at strajak by no other light than their glittering eyes. On the table were piles of gold, and a jug from which each one drank in his turn.

" Brothers," said the black man, " I bring you friend Sswanda, whom you have long known by reputation. I thought to please you on this feast-day by giving you a little music."

" A good idea !" said one of the players. Then, taking the jug, he handed it to Sswanda, saying, " Here, piper, drink and play."

Sswanda had some scruples ; but, after all, it is impossible to have charcoal without putting your fingers into the ashes. The wine, though rather warm, was not bad. He replaced the jug on the table, and, raising his hat, said, "Good luck, brother !" as he had been advised.

He began to play, and never had his music produced such an effect. Each note made the players leap for joy. Their eyes shot forth flames ; they moved about uneasily in their chairs ; they staked the ducats by handfuls ; they shouted and burst into loud fits of laughter without stirring a muscle of their pallid faces. The jug passed from hand to hand, always full, though replenished by no one.

As soon as Sswanda finished an air, they handed him the jug, from which he never failed to drink deeply, and threw handfuls of gold into his hat. " Good luck, brother !" he repeated, astounded at his fortune—" good luck !"

The feast lasted a long time. At last, the piper having struck up a polka, the black men, in a transport of mirth, quitted the table, and danced and waltzed with an ardor and frenzy which ill accorded with their icy faces. One of the dancers gathered up all the gold that was heaped on the table, and, pouring it into Sswanda's hat, " Here," said he, " take this for the pleasure that you have given us."

" God bless you, my good lords !" said the dazzled piper. Scarcely had he spoken when men, room, and cards vanished.

In the morning a peasant on his way to the fields heard the sound of a pipe as he approached the cross-road. " It is Sswanda," said he. But where was the piper ? Seated on a corner of the gallows, he was blowing with all his might, while the corpses of the robbers danced in the wind to his music.

" Halloo, comrade !" cried the peasant, " how long have you been playing the cuckoo up there ?"

Sswanda started, dropped his pipe, opened his eyes, and glided, bewildered, down the gallows. His first thought, however, was for his ducats. He rummaged his pockets, and turned his hat inside out, but all in vain ; there was not even a kreutzer !

" My friend," said the peasant, making the sign of the cross, " God has punished you by giving you the devil for a partner ; you love cards too well."

"You are right," said Sswanda, trembling; "I will never touch them again in my life."

He kept his word; and, to thank Heaven for having preserved him from such peril, he took the fatal pipe to which the devil had danced, and suspended it as a votive offering in the church of Strakonic, his birth-place, where it may be seen to this day. The pipe of Strakonic has become a proverb, and it is even said that its sound is heard every year at the day and hour when Sswanda played for Satan and his friends.

THE GOLD BREAD.

A HUNGARIAN TALE.

ONCE upon a time there was a widow who had a beautiful daughter. The mother was modest and humble ; the daughter, Marienka, was pride itself. She had suitors from all sides, but none satisfied her ; the more they tried to please her, the more she disdained them.

One night, when the poor mother could not sleep, she took her beads and began to pray for her dear child, who gave her more than one care. Marienka was asleep by her side. As the mother gazed lovingly at her beautiful daughter, Marienka laughed in her sleep.

"What a beautiful dream she must have to laugh in this way !" said the mother. Then she finished her prayer, hung her beads on the wall, laid her head on the same pillow with her daughter, and fell asleep.

"My dear child," said she in the morning, "what did you dream last night that you laughed so ?"

"What did I dream, mamma ? I dreamed that a nobleman came here for me in a copper coach, and that he put a ring on my finger set with a stone that sparkled like the stars. And when I entered the church, the people had eyes for no one but the blessed Virgin and me."

"My daughter, my daughter, that was a proud dream !" said the mother, shaking her head. But Marienka went out singing.

The same day a wagon entered the yard. A handsome

young farmer in good circumstances came to ask Marienka to share a peasant's bread with him. The mother was pleased with the suitor, but the proud Marienka refused him, saying, "Though you should come in a copper coach, and put a ring on my finger set with a stone that sparkled like the stars, I would not have you for a husband." And the farmer went away storming at Marienka's pride.

The next night the mother waked, took her beads, and prayed still more earnestly for her daughter, when behold! Marienka laughed again as she was sleeping.

"I wonder what she is dreaming," said the mother, who prayed, unable to sleep.

"My dear child," she said the next morning, "what did you dream last night that you laughed aloud?"

"What did I dream, mamma? I dreamed that a nobleman came here for me in a silver coach, and that he offered me a golden diadem. And when I entered the church, the people looked at me more than they did at the blessed Virgin."

"Hush! you are blaspheming. Pray, my daughter, pray that you may not fall into temptation."

But Marienka ran away to escape her mother's sermon.

The same day a carriage entered the yard. A young lord came to entreat Marienka to share a nobleman's bread with him.

"It is a great honor," said the mother ; but vanity is blind.

"Though you should come in a silver coach," said Marienka to the new suitor, "and should offer me a golden diadem, I would not have you for a husband."

"Take care, my child," said the poor mother ; "pride is a device of the Evil One."

"Mothers never know what they are saying," thought Marienka, and she went out shrugging her shoulders.

The third night the mother could not sleep for anxiety. As

she lay awake, praying for her daughter, behold! Marienka burst into a loud fit of laughter.

"Oh!" said the mother, "what can the unhappy child be dreaming now?" And she continued to pray till daylight.

"My dear child," said she in the morning, "what did you dream last night?"

"You will be angry again if I tell you," answered Marienka.

"No, no," replied the mother; "tell me."

"I dreamed that a noble lord, with a great train of attendants, came to ask me in marriage. He was in a golden coach, and he brought me a dress of gold lace. And when I entered the church, the people looked at nobody but me."

The mother clasped her hands. Marienka, half dressed, sprang from the bed and ran into the next room, to avoid a lecture that was tiresome to her.

The same day three coaches entered the yard, one of copper, one of silver, and one of gold; the first drawn by two horses, the second by four, and the third by eight, all caparisoned with gold and pearls. From the copper and silver coaches alighted pages dressed in scarlet breeches and green jackets and cloaks, while from the golden coach stepped a handsome nobleman all dressed in gold. He entered the house, and, bending one knee on the ground, asked the mother for her daughter's hand.

"What an honor!" thought the mother.

"My dream has come to pass," said Marienka. "You see, mother, that, as usual, I was right and you were wrong."

She ran to her chamber, tied the betrothal knot, and offered it smilingly as a pledge of her faith to the handsome lord, who, on his side, put a ring on her finger set with a stone that sparkled like the stars, and presented her with a golden diadem and a dress of gold lace.

The proud girl ran to her room to dress for the ceremony,

while the mother, still anxious, said to the bridegroom, "My good sir, what bread do you offer my daughter?"

"Among us," said he, "the bread is of copper, silver, and gold: she can take her choice."

"What does this mean?" thought the mother. But Marienka had no anxiety; she returned as beautiful as the sun, took her lover's arm, and set out for the church without asking her mother's blessing. The poor woman was left to pray

alone on the threshold; and when Marienka returned and entered the carriage, she did not even turn round to look at her mother or to bid her a last farewell.

The eight horses set off at a gallop, and did not stop till they reached a huge rock, in which there was a hole as large as the gate of a city. The horses plunged into the darkness, the earth trembled, and the rock cracked and crumbled. Marienka seized her husband's hand.

"Don't be alarmed, my fair one; in a moment it will be light."

All at once a thousand lights waved in the air. The dwarfs of the mountain, each with a torch in his hand, came to salute their lord, the King of the Mines. Marienka learned for the first time her husband's name. Whether he was a spirit of good or of evil, at least he was so rich that she did not regret her choice.

They emerged from the darkness, and advanced through bleached forests and mountains that raised their pale and gloomy summits to the skies. Firs, beeches, birches, oaks, rocks, all were of lead. At the end of the forest stretched a vast meadow, the grass of which was of silver; and at the bottom of the meadow was a castle of gold, inlaid with diamonds and rubies. The carriage stopped before the door, and the King of the Mines offered his hand to his bride, saying, "My fair one, all that you see is yours."

Marienka was delighted. But it is impossible to make so long a journey without being hungry; and it was with pleasure, therefore, that she saw the mountain dwarfs bring in a table, every thing on which glittered with gold, silver, and precious stones. The dishes were marvelous—side-dishes of emeralds, and roasts of gold on silver salvers. Every one ate heartily except the bride, who begged her husband for a little bread.

"Bring the copper bread," said the King of the Mines.

Marienka could not eat it.

"Bring the silver bread," said he.

Marienka could not eat it.

" Bring the gold bread," said he, at length.

Marienka could not eat it.

" My fair one," said the King of the Mines, " I am very sorry; but what can I offer you? We have no other bread."

The bride burst into tears. Her husband laughed aloud: his heart was of metal, like his kingdom.

" Weep, if you like," he cried; " it will do you no good. What you wished for you possess: eat the bread that you have chosen."

It was thus that the rich Marienka lived in her castle, dying of hunger, and seeking in vain for a root to allay the torture that was consuming her. God had humbled her by granting her prayer.

Three days in the year, the Rogation Days, when the ground half opens to receive the fruitful rain sent by the Lord, Marienka returns to the earth. Dressed in rags, pale and wrinkled, she begs from door to door, too happy when any one throws her a few crusts, and when she receives as alms from the poor what she lacks in her palace of gold—a little bread and a little pity.

THE STORY OF THE NOSES.

A BOHEMIAN TALE.

AT Dewitz, in the neighborhood of Prague, there once lived a rich and whimsical old farmer, who had a beautiful daughter. The students of Prague, of whom there were at that time twenty-five thousand, often walked in the direction of Dewitz, and more than one of them offered to follow the plow in hopes of becoming the son-in-law of the farmer. The first condition that the cunning peasant set on each new servant was this : " I engage you," he would say, " for a year, that is, till the cuckoo sings the return of spring ; but if, from now till then, you say once that you are not satisfied, I will cut off the end of your nose. I give you the same right over me," he added, laughing. And he did as he said. Prague was full of students with the end of their nose glued on, which did not prevent an ugly scar, and, still less, bad jokes. To return from the farm disfigured and ridiculed was well calculated to cool the warmest passion.

A young man by the name of Coranda, somewhat ungainly in manner, but cool, adroit, and cunning, which are not bad aids in making one's fortune, took it in his head to try the adventure. The farmer received him with his usual good nature, and, the bargain made, sent him to the field to work. At breakfast time the other servants were called, but good care was taken to forget Coranda. At dinner it was the same. Coranda gave himself no trouble about it. He went to the house, and, while the farmer's wife was feeding the chickens, unhooked an enormous ham from the kitchen rafters, took a huge loaf from the cupboard, and went back to the fields to dine and take a nap.

"Are you satisfied?" cried the farmer, when he returned at night.

"Perfectly satisfied," said Coranda; "I have dined better than you have."

At that instant the farmer's wife came rushing in, crying that her ham was gone. Coranda laughed, and the farmer turned pale.

"Are you not satisfied?" asked Coranda.

"A ham is only a ham," answered his master. "Such a trifle does not trouble me." But after that time he took good care not to leave the student fasting.

Sunday came. The farmer and his wife seated themselves in the wagon to go to church, saying to Coranda, "It is your business to cook the dinner. Cut up the piece of meat you see yonder, with onions, carrots, leeks, and parsley, and boil them all together in the great pot over the kitchen fire."

"Very well," answered Coranda.

There was a little pet dog at the farm-house by the name of Parsley. Coranda killed him, skinned him, cut him up with the meat and vegetables, and put the whole to boil over the kitchen fire. When the farmer's wife returned, she called her favorite; but, alas! she saw nothing but a bloody skin hanging by the window.

"What have you done?" said she to Coranda.

"What you ordered me, mistress. I have boiled the meat, onions, carrots, and leeks, and parsley in the bargain."

"Wicked wretch!" cried the farmer, "had you the heart to kill the innocent creature that was the joy of the house?"

"Are you not satisfied?" said Coranda, taking his knife from his pocket.

"I did not not say that," returned the farmer. "A dead dog is nothing but a dead dog." But he sighed.

A few days after, the farmer and his wife went to market. Fearing their terrible servant, they said to him, "Stay at home, and do exactly what you see others do."

"Very well," said Coranda.

There was an old shed in the yard, the roof of which was falling to pieces. The carpenters came to repair it, and began, as usual, by tearing down the roof. Coranda took a lad-der and mounted the roof of the house, which was quite new. Shingles, lath, nails, and tiles, he tore off every thing, and scattered them all to the winds. When the farmer returned, the house was open to the sky.

"Villain!" said he, "what new trick have you played me?"

"I have obeyed you, master," answered Coranda. "You told me to do exactly what I saw others do. Are you not satisfied?" And he took out his knife.

"Satisfied!" returned the farmer; "why

should I not be satisfied? A few shingles more or less will not ruin me." But he sighed.

Night come, the farmer and his wife said to each other that it was high time to get rid of this incarnate demon. As is always the case with sensible people, they never did any thing without consulting their daughter, it being the custom in Bohemia to think that children always have more wit than their parents.

"Father," said Helen, "I will hide in the great pear-tree early in the morning, and call like the cuckoo. You can tell Coranda that the year is up, since the cuckoo is singing; pay him, and send him away."

Early in the morning the plaintive cry of the cuckoo was heard through the fields. The farmer seemed surprised. "Well, my boy, spring is come," said he. "Do you hear the cuckoo singing yonder? I will pay you, and we will part good friends."

"A cuckoo!" said Coranda; "that is a bird which I have always wanted to see."

He ran to the tree and shook it with all his might, when behold! a young girl fell from the branches, fortunately more frightened than hurt.

"Villain!" cried the farmer.

"Are you not satisfied?" said Coranda, opening his knife.

"Wretch! you kill my daughter, and you think that I ought to be satisfied! I am furious. Begone, if you would not die by my hand!"

"I will go when I have cut off your nose," said Coranda. "I have kept my word, do you keep yours."

"Stop!" cried the farmer, putting his hand before his face; "you will surely let me redeem my nose?"

"It depends on what you offer," said Coranda.

"Will you take ten sheep for it?"

"No."

"Ten cows?"

" No ; I would rather cut off your nose."   And he sharpened his knife on the door-step.

" Father," said Helen, " the fault was mine ; it belongs to me to repair it.   Coranda, will you take my hand instead of my father's nose ?"

" Yes," replied Coranda.

" I make one condition," said the young girl.   " We will make the same bargain ; the first one of us that is not satisfied after marriage shall have his nose cut off by the other."

" Good," replied Coranda.   " I would rather it was the tongue ; but that will come next."

Never was a finer wedding seen at Prague, and never was there a happier household.   Coranda and the beautiful Helen were a model pair.   The husband and wife were never heard to complain of each other ; they loved with drawn swords, and, thanks to their ingenious bargain, kept for long years both their love and their noses.

THE THREE CITRONS.

A NEAPOLITAN TALE.

ONCE upon a time there lived a king who was called the King of the Vermilion Towers. He had but one son, whom he loved as the apple of his eye, and who was the only hope of a royal line about to become extinct. The old king's whole ambition was to marry this illustrious prince—to find him a princess at once handsome, noble, young, and rich. He could think of nothing but this wished-for marriage.

Unhappily, among all the virtues in which the heir to a crown is never lacking, Carlino, for that was the young prince's name, had the trifling fault of being shyer than a deer. He shook his head and fled to the woods at the mere sound of a woman's name, to the great grief of his father, who was in despair at seeing his family about to die out. But his grief was in vain : nothing touched the heart of Carlino. The tears of a father, the prayers of a whole people, the interest of the state, nothing could melt this stony heart. Twenty preachers had wasted their eloquence and thirty senators their Latin in reasoning with him. To be stubborn is one of the privileges of royalty, as Carlino had known from his birth, and he would have thought himself dishonored by being second to a mule in obstinacy.

But more things often happen in an hour than in a hundred years, and no one can say with safety, "This is a road that I shall never travel." One morning at breakfast, as Carlino, instead of listening to his father's sermon, was amusing himself by watching the flies buzzing in the air, he forgot that he had a knife in his hand, and pricked his finger in a gesture of impatience. The blood gushed forth and fell into a plate of cream that had just been handed to him, where it made a curious mixture of white and red. Either by chance or by the punishment of Heaven, the prince was instantly seized with the maddest caprice that could be imagined.

"Sir," said he to his father, "if I do not soon find a woman as white and red as this cream dyed with my blood, I am lost. This wonder must exist somewhere. I love her; I am dying for her; I must have her; I will have her. To a resolute heart nothing is impossible. If you would have me live, let me go in search of her, or before to-morrow I shall be dead of loneliness."

The poor King of the Vermilion Towers was thunder-struck at this folly. It seemed to him that his palace was crumbling over his head; he turned red and pale by turns, stammered, wept, and finally cried, in a voice broken with sobs,

"Oh, my child, the staff of my old age, my heart's blood, the life of my soul, what an idea have you taken into your head! Have you lost your reason? Yesterday you almost made me die of sorrow by refusing to marry; to-day you are about to drive me from the world by another piece of folly. Whither would you go, unhappy boy? Why leave your home, where you have been born and bred? Do you know to what danger and suffering the traveler exposes himself? Drive away these perilous fancies, and stay with me, my child, if you would not deprive me of life and destroy your kingdom and house at one blow."

All these words, and others equally wise, had no more effect than an official harangue. Carlino, his eye fixed and his brow bent, listened to nothing but his passion. All that was said

to him went in at one ear and out at the other ; it was eloquence cast to the winds.

When the old king, worn out with prayers and tears, perceived that it was easier to melt a leaden weather-cock on its
steeple than a spoiled child in pursuit of his whim, he heaved
a deep sigh and determined to let Carlino go ; and giving
him counsels to which he scarcely listened, several bags filled
with guineas, which were rather better received than the counsels, and two trusty servants, the good king clasped his rebel-
lious son to his heart and bade him adieu, then mounted to
the top of the great tower.to follow the ungrateful boy with
his eyes as far as he could see.   When Carlino at last disappeared in the distance, the poor monarch thought that his
heart was breaking : he buried his face in his hands and wept,
not like a child, but like a father.   The tears of a child are
like the summer rain, large drops that are soon dried up ; the
tears of a father are like the autumnal rain, which falls slowly
and soaks into the ground.

While the king wept, Carlino, mounted on a fine horse,
rode on gayly, his plume waving in the wind, like a hero
about to conquer the world. To find what he sought was not
an easy task, however, and his journey lasted more than one
day. He crossed mountains and valleys, traversed kingdoms,
duchies, earldoms, and baronies, and visited cities, villages,
castles, and cottages, gazing at all the women, and gazed at
by them in turn ; but all in vain : the treasure that he sought
was not to be found in old Europe.

At the end of four months he reached Marseilles, resolved
to embark for the Indies. At the sight of the raging sea,
however, his brave and faithful servants were seized with an
epidemic, called by the physicians stay-at-homeativeness in
Hebrew, and the headache in the feet in Latin. To the great
regret of these honest people, they were forced to quit their

good master and remain quietly on shore, wrapped in their warm blankets, while Carlino, embarked on a frail bark, braved the winds and waves.

Nothing can stop a heart hurried away by passion. The prince roamed over Egypt, India, and China, going from province to province, from city to city, from house to house, and from cabin to cabin, every where seeking the original of the fair image that was engraved on his heart, but in vain. He saw women of all colors and shades, brown, blonde, olive, sandy, white, yellow, red, and black, but he did not see her whom he loved.

Always seeking and never finding, Carlino at last reached the end of the world. There was nothing more before him but the ocean and the sky. His hopes were at an end; his dream had vanished. As he was walking despairingly up and down the sea-shore, he spied an old man warming himself in the sun. The prince asked him if there was nothing beyond these waves that stretched as far as the eye could reach.

"No," said the old man; "no one has ever discovered any thing in this shoreless ocean, or, at least, those who have ventured on it have never returned to tell the story. I remember, however, having heard the old men among us say, when I was a child," he added, "that their fathers had told them that yonder, a long, long way off, far beyond the horizon, was the Island of the Fates; but woe to the imprudent man who approaches these merciless fairies; he is struck with death at their sight."

"What does that matter?" cried Carlino; "I would face death itself to gain my wishes."

A bark lay by the strand. The prince sprang on board and unfurled the sail. The wind, which blew off the shore, hurried forward the frail craft, the land disappeared, and Carlino found himself in the midst of the ocean. In vain he gazed about him; there was nothing but the sea—the sea every where; in vain the bark bounded over the foaming waves with the speed of lightning, like a steed with mane floating on the wind; there was nothing but the sea—the sea every where. Billows followed billows, the hours passed one after another, the day declined, and the solitude and silence seemed to deepen around Carlino, when all at once he uttered a cry; he saw a black speck in the distance. At the same instant the bark, shooting ahead like an arrow, struck upon the sand at the foot of huge rocks, which raised their dark summits, notched and worn by time, to the skies. Fate had thrown Carlino upon that strand from which none had ever returned.

To climb this wall was not an easy matter; there was neither road nor path; and when Carlino, after long efforts, with torn hands and wearied limbs, at last succeeded in reaching a level spot, what he found was not calculated to reassure him. He saw nothing but glaciers piled upon each other—black, damp rocks rising from the midst of the snows—not a tree, not a blade of grass, not a bit of moss: it was the picture of winter and death. The only sign of life in this desert was a wretched hovel, the roof of which was loaded with great stones in order to resist the fury of the winds. The prince approached the hut, and was about to enter it, when he stopped short, struck with surprise and terror at the spectacle which presented itself.

At the end of the room was a great web of cloth, on which were pictured all the conditions of life. There were kings, soldiers, farmers, and shepherds, with ladies richly dressed, and peasant women spinning by their side. At the bottom boys and girls were dancing gayly, holding each other by the hand. Before the web walked the mistress of the house—an old woman, if the name woman can be given to a skeleton with bones scarcely hidden by a skin yellower and more transparent than wax. Like a spider ready to pounce upon its prey, the old woman, armed with a great pair of shears, peered at all the figures with a jealous eye, then suddenly fell upon the web and cut it at random, when lo! a piercing wail rose from it that would have moved a heart of stone. The tears of children, the sobs of mothers, the despair of lovers, the last murmurs of old age, all human sorrow seemed mingled in this wail. At the sound the old woman burst into a loud laugh, and her hideous face lighted up with ferocious delight while an invisible hand mended the web, eternally destroyed and eternally repaired.

The hag, again opening her shears, was already approaching the web anew, when she saw the shadow of Carlino.

"Fly, unhappy man," cried she, without turning round; "I know what brings you here, but I can-do nothing for you. Go to my sister; perhaps she will give you what you desire. She is Life—I am Death."

Carlino did not wait for a second bidding. He rushed onward, too happy to escape this scene of horror.

The landscape soon changed. Carlino found himself in a fertile valley. On every side were harvests, blossoming fields, vines loaded with grapes, and olive-trees full of fruit. In the thick shade of a fig-tree, by a running spring, sat a blind woman unrolling the last gold and silver thread from a spindle. Around her lay several distaffs, full of different kinds of materials ready for spinning—flax, hemp, wool, silk, and others.

When she had finished her task, the fairy stretched out her trembling hand at random, took the first distaff that came, and began to spin.

Carlino bowed respectfully to the lady, and began with emotion to tell her the story of his pilgrimage, when the fairy stopped him at the first word.

"My child," said she, "I can do nothing for you. I am only a poor blind woman that does not even know herself what she is doing. This distaff, which I have taken at random, decides the fate of all who are born while I am spinning it. Riches or poverty, happiness or misfortune, are attached to this thread that I can not see. The slave of destiny, I can create nothing. Go to my other sister ; perhaps she will give you what you desire. She is Birth ; I am Life."

"Thanks, madam," answered Carlino ; and, with a light heart, he ran to find the youngest of the Fates. He soon discovered her, fresh and smiling as the spring. Every thing about her was taking root and germinating : the corn was bursting through the earth and putting forth its green blades from the brown furrows ; the orange-blossoms were opening ; the buds on the trees were unfolding their pink scales ; the chickens, scarcely feathered, were running round the anxious hen, and the lambs were clinging to their mother. It was the first smile of life.

The fairy received the prince with kindness. After listening to him without laughing at his folly, she asked him to sup with her, and at dessert gave him three citrons, and a beautiful knife with a mother-of-pearl handle.

"Carlino," said she, "you can now return to your father's house : the prize is gained ; you have found what you have been seeking. Go, then, and when you have reached your kingdom, stop at the first fountain that you see, and cut one of these citrons. A fairy will come forth, who will ask you for a drink. Give her the water quickly, or she will slip through your fingers like quicksilver. If the second escapes you in the same way, have an eye to the last ; give her a drink instantly, and you will have a wife according to your heart."

Intoxicated with joy, the prince kissed again and again the charming hand that crowned his wishes. He was more happy than wise, and little deserved to succeed ; but fairies have their caprices, and Fortune is always a fairy.

It was a long distance from the end of the world to the kingdom of the Vermilion Towers. Carlino experienced more than one storm and braved more than one danger on his way across land and sea, but at last, after a long voyage and a thousand trials, he reached his father's country with his three citrons, which he had treasured like the apple of his eye.

He was not more than two hours' journey from the royal castle when he entered a dense forest, where he had hunted many a time. A transparent fountain, bordered with wild flowers and shaded by the trembling leaves of the aspen, invited the traveler to repose. Carlino seated himself on a carpet of verdure enameled with daisies, and, taking his knife, cut one of the citrons.

All at once, a young girl as white as milk and as red as a strawberry darted past him like lightning. "Give me a drink !" said she, pausing an instant.

"How beautiful she is !" cried the prince, so ravished by her charms that he forgot the advice of the Fate. He paid dearly for it : in a second the fairy had disappeared. Carlino smote his breast in despair, and stood as astonished as a child that sees the running water slip through his fingers.

He tried to calm himself, and cut the next citron with a trembling hand ; but the second fairy was even more beautiful and more fleeting than her sister. While Carlino admired her, wonder-struck, in the twinkling of an eye she took flight.

This time the prince burst into tears, and wept so bitterly that he seemed a part of the fountain. He sobbed, tore his hair, and called down all the maledictions of heaven on his head.

G

"Fool that I am!" he cried; "twice I have let her escape as though my hands were tied. Fool that I am, I deserve my fate. When I should have run like a greyhound, I stood still like a post. A fine piece of business! But all is not lost: the third time conquers. I will try the magic knife once more, and if it deceives me this time I will use it on myself."

He cut·the last citron. The third fairy darted forth, and said, like her companions, "Give me a drink!" But the prince had learned a lesson. He instantly gave her the water, when lo! a beautiful, slender young girl, as white as milk, with cheeks like roses, stood before him, looking like a freshly-opened rose-bud. She was a marvel of beauty such as the world had never seen, as fresh as a lily and as graceful as a swan: her hair was of brighter gold than the sun, her clear blue eyes revealed the depths of her heart, her rosy lips seemed made only to comfort and charm; in a word, from head to foot she was the most enchanting creature that had ever descended from heaven to earth. It is a great pity that we have no likeness of her.

At the sight of his bride the prince almost lost his reason from joy and surprise. He could not understand how this miracle of freshness and beauty had sprung from the bitter rind of a citron.

"Am I asleep?" he cried. "Am I dreaming? If I am the sport of a delusion, for pity's sake do not awaken me."

The fairy's smile soon reassured him. She accepted his hand, and was the first to ask to repair to the good King of the Vermilion Towers, who would be so happy to bless his children.

"My love," answered Carlino, "I am as impatient as you to see my father and to prove to him that I was right; but we can not enter the castle arm in arm like two peasants. You must go like a princess ; you must be received like a queen. Wait for me by this fountain ; I will run to the palace, and return in two hours with a dress and equipage worthy of you." Saying this, he tenderly kissed her hand and left her.

The young girl was afraid on finding herself alone ; the cry of a raven, the rustling of the trees, a dead branch broken by the wind, every thing frightened her. She looked tremblingly about her, and saw an old oak by the side of the fountain whose huge trunk offered her a shelter. She climbed the tree and hid herself in it all but her lovely face, which, encircled by the foliage, was reflected in the transparent fountain as in a clear mirror.

Now there was a negress, by the name of Lucy, who lived in the neighborhood, and who was sent every day by her mistress to the fountain for water. Lucy came, as usual, with her pitcher on her shoulder, and, just as she was about to fill it, she spied the image of the fairy in the spring. The fool, who had never seen herself, thought that the face was her own. "Poor Lucy!" she cried. "What! you, so fresh and beautiful, are forced by your mistress to carry water like a beast of burden ! No, never !" And, in her vanity, she dashed the pitcher to the ground and returned home.

When her mistress asked her why she had broken the pitcher, the slave shrugged her shoulders and said, "The pitcher that goes often to the well is soon broken." Upon this, her mistress gave her a little wooden cask, and ordered her to go back immediately and fill it at the fountain.

The negress ran to the spring, and, gazing lovingly at the beautiful image in the water, sighed and said, "No, I am not an ape, as I am so often told ; I am more beautiful than my mistress. Mules may carry casks—not I !" She dashed the cask on the ground, broke it in a thousand pieces, and returned to her mistress, grumbling.

"Where is the cask?" asked her mistress, who was waiting impatiently for the water.

"A mule ran against me and knocked it down, and it is all broken to pieces."

At these words her mistress lost patience. Seizing a broom, she gave the negress one of those lessons that are not soon forgotten; then, taking down a leathern bottle that was hanging on the wall,

"Run, wretched ape," she said; "and if you do not instantly bring this back to me full of water, I will beat you within an inch of your life."

The negress took to her heels in terror, and filled the bottle obediently; but when it was filled she stopped to look once more in the fountain; and seeing the lovely face reflected there, "No!" she cried, in a burst of anger—"no, I will not be a water-carrier; no, I was not made to serve my mistress like a dog."

Saying this, she took from her hair the great pin that held it, and pierced the bottle through and through. The water spouted out in every direction. At the sight the fairy in the tree burst into a fit of laughter. The negress looked up, saw the beautiful stranger, and understood the whole.

"Oh!" said she to herself, "so you are the cause of my beating; no matter, you shall pay me well for it." Then, raising her voice, she called, in her sweetest tones, "What are you doing up there, lovely lady?"

The fairy, who was as good as she was beautiful, tried to comfort the slave by talking with her. The acquaintance was soon made; an innocent soul is unsuspicious in friendship. The fairy, without distrust, told the negress all that had happened to her and the prince, why she was alone in the forest, and how she was every instant expecting Carlino with a grand equipage to conduct his bride to the King of the Ver

milion Towers, and to marry her there in the presence of all the court.

On hearing this story, the wicked and envious negress conceived an abominable idea. "Madam," said she, "if the prince is coming with all his suite, you must be ready to meet him. Your hair is all in disorder ; let me come to you, and I will comb it."

"With pleasure," answered the fairy, with a gracious smile, as she stretched out a little white hand, which looked, in Lucy's great black paw, like a crystal mirror in an ebony frame.

No sooner had she climbed the tree than the wicked slave

untied the fairy's hair and began to comb it; then, all at once, taking her great hair-pin, she pierced her to the brain. Feeling herself wounded, the fairy cried, "Palomba! Palomba!" when she instantly turned to a wood-pigeon, and flew away. The horrible negress took her victim's place, and stretched out her neck among the foliage, looking like a statue of jet in a niche of emerald.

Meanwhile the prince, mounted on a magnificent horse, was riding thither at full speed, followed by a long cavalcade. Poor Carlino was astonished to find a crow where he had left a swan. He almost lost his reason, his voice was choked with tears, and he gazed in all directions, hoping to see his bride among the foliage. But the negress, putting on a suffering air, said to him, casting down her eyes, "Look no farther, my prince; a wicked fairy has made me her victim, and a wretched fate has changed your lily to charcoal."

Though he cursed the fairies who had played on his credulity, Carlino, like a true prince, would not break his word. He gallantly gave his hand to Lucy, and helped her to descend from the tree, all the while heaving sighs that would have melted a heart of stone. When the negress was dressed like a princess, and covered with lace and diamonds that adorned her as the stars adorn the night, by rendering the darkness still more visible, Carlino seated her at his right hand, in a magnificent carriage lined with plate glass and drawn by six white horses, and took his way to the palace, as happy as·a criminal with the rope about his neck.

The old king came to meet them a league from the castle. The wonderful stories of his son had turned his brain. In spite of etiquette and against the remonstrances of his courtiers, he hastened to admire the incomparable beauty of his daughter-in-law. "Upon my word," he exclaimed at the sight of a crow instead of the dove that had been promised him—

"upon my word, this is too much. I knew that my son was mad, but I did not know that he was blind. Is this the spotless lily that he has been to the end of the world to seek? Is this the rose fresher than the morning dew, the miracle of beauty that has come from the rind of a citron? Does he think that I will bear this new insult to my gray hairs? Does he think that I will leave to mulatto children the empire of the Vermilion Towers, the glorious inheritance of my ancestors? This baboon shall never enter my palace."

The prince fell at his father's feet and tried to move him. The prime minister, a man of great experience, remonstrated with his master that, at court, black often becomes white and white black in the space of twenty-four hours; and that there was no reason to be astonished at such a very natural metamorphosis. What was the King of the Vermilion Towers to do? He was a king and a father, and by this double title always accustomed to do the will of others: he yielded and consented with a bad grace to this strange union. The court gazette announced to the whole kingdom the happy choice that the prince had made, and ordered the people to rejoice.

The wedding was postponed for a week ; it was impossible to make the preparations for the ceremony in less time than this.

The negress was lodged in a magnificent suite of apartments ; countesses disputed with each other the honor of putting on her slippers ; and duchesses obtained, not without difficulty, the glorious privilege of handing her her nightgown. The town and castle were adorned with flags of all colors ; walls were thrown down, yews were planted, walks were graveled, old speeches were furbished up, stale compliments were newly framed, and poems and sonnets that had done duty every where were patched up anew. There was but one idea in the kingdom—that of thankfulness to the prince for having chosen a wife so worthy of him.

The kitchen was not forgotten. Three hundred scullions, a hundred cooks, and fifty stewards set to work, under the su-

perintendence of the famous Bouchibus, the chief of the royal kitchens. Pigs were killed, sheep cut up, capons larded, pigeons plucked, and turkeys spitted : it was a universal massacre. It is impossible to have a feast worthy of the name without the help of the poultry-yard.

In the midst of this bustle a beautiful wood-pigeon, with blue wings, perched on one of the kitchen windows, and cooed in a plaintive voice,

> " Bouchibus, tell me, for you must know, sure,
> What has Carlino to do with the Moor?"

The great Bouchibus was at first too busy with public affairs to attend to the cooing of a pigeon ; but, after a while, he began to be astonished at understanding the language of birds, and thought it his duty to inform his new mistress of the wonder. The negress did not disdain to go to the kitchen. As soon as she heard the song, with a cry of affright, she ordered Bouchibus to catch the pigeon and make a stew of it.

No sooner said than done. The poor bird suffered itself to be caught without resistance. In an instant Bouchibus, armed with his great knife, cut off its head and threw it into the garden. Three drops of blood fell on the ground ; and three days after there sprang from the earth a beautiful citron-tree, which grew so fast that before night it was in blossom.

The prince, while taking the air in his balcony, chanced to spy a citron-tree which he had never seen before. He called the cook, and asked him who had planted this beautiful tree. The story of Bouchibus perplexed him greatly. He at once commanded, under penalty of death, that no one should touch the citron-tree, and that the greatest care should be taken of it.

The next morning, as soon as he awoke, the prince hastened to the garden. There were already three citrons on the tree—three citrons exactly like those which the Fáte had given him. Carlino gathered them, hastened to his apartments, and shut himself up under lock and key. With a trembling hand he filled a golden cup, set with rubies, which had belonged to his mother, with water, and opened the magic knife, which had never left him.

He cut a citron, and the first fairy came forth. Carlino scarcely glanced at her, and suffered her to take flight. It was the same with the second; but as soon as the third appeared, he gave her the cup, from which she drank with a smile, and stood before him more beautiful and graceful than ever.

The fairy then told Carlino all that she had suffered from the wicked negress. The prince, beside himself with mingled joy and anger, laughed and wept, sang and raved. The king, hearing the noise, ran to see what was the matter, and you may judge of his surprise. He danced about like a madman, with his crown on his head and his sceptre in his hand. All at once he stopped short, bent his brow, which was a sign that a thought had struck him, threw a large veil over the princess which covered her from head to foot, and, taking her by the hand, led her to the dining-room.

It was the hour for breakfast. The ministers and courtiers were ranged round a long table, magnificently served, waiting for the entrance of the royal family to be seated. The king called the guests one after another, and, raising the veil as each approached the fairy, asked,

"What shall be done to the person who sought to destroy this marvel of beauty?"

And each one, wonder-struck, answered in his own way. Some said that the author of such a crime deserved a hempen cravat; others thought that the wretch should be thrown into the water with a stone to his neck. Beheading seemed to the old minister too mild a punishment for such a villain; he

was in favor of flaying him alive, and all present applauded
his humanity.

When the negress's turn came, she approached without sus-

picion, and did not recognize the fairy. "Sire," said she, "a
monster capable of injuring this charming creature deserves
to be roasted alive in an oven, and to have his ashes thrown
to the winds."

"You have pronounced your own sentence," cried the King
of the Vermilion Towers. "Wretch, behold your victim, and
prepare to die. Let a funeral pile be built in the square in
front of the castle. I will give my good people the pleasure
of seeing a witch burn ; it will occupy them for an hour or
two."

"Sire," said the young fairy, taking the king's hand, "your
majesty surely will not refuse me a wedding gift?"

"No, indeed, my child," replied the old king. "Ask what
you will ; should it be my crown, I will gladly give it to you."

"Sire," continued the fairy, "grant me this wretched creature's pardon. An ignorant and miserable slave, life has

taught her nothing but hatred and malice ; let me render her happy, and teach her that the only happiness on earth consists in loving others."

"My daughter," said the king, "it is very evident that you are a fairy ; you know nothing of human justice. Among us, we do not reform the wicked, we kill them ; it is sooner done. But I have given my word ; tame this serpent at your own risk and peril ; I am willing."

The fairy raised the negress, who kissed her hands, weeping ; then they all sat down to the table. The king was so happy that he ate enough for four. As to Carlino, who kept his eyes fixed on his bride, he cut his thumb five or six times in a fit of absent-mindedness, which each time put him in the best humor imaginable. Every thing gives us pleasure when the heart is happy.

When the old king died, full of years and honor, Carlino and his lovely wife ascended the throne in turn. For half a century, if history is to be believed, they neither raised the taxes, shed a drop of blood, nor caused a tear to fall ; and although more than a thousand years have passed since then, the good people of the Vermilion Towers still sigh at the mention of this distant age, and little children are not the only ones to ask when the fairies will reign again.

STORY OF COQUERICO.

A SPANISH TALE.

ONCE upon a time there was a handsome hen who lived like a great lady in the poultry-yard of a rich farmer, surrounded by a numerous family which clucked about her, and none of which clamored more loudly or picked up the corn faster with his beak than a poor little deformed and crippled chicken. This was precisely the one that the mother loved best. It is the way with all mothers; the weakest and most unsightly are always their favorites. This misshapen creature had but one eye, one wing, and one leg in good condition; it might have been thought that Solomon had executed his memorable sentence on Coquerico, for that was the name of the wretched chicken, and cut him in two with his famous sword. When a person is one-eyed, lame, and one-armed, he may reasonably be expected to be modest; but our Castilian ragamuffin was prouder than his father, the best spurred, most elegant, bravest, and most gallant cock to be seen from Burgos to Madrid. He thought himself a phœnix of grace and beauty, and passed the best part of the day in admiring himself in the brook. If one of his brothers ran against him by accident, he abused him, called him envious and jealous, and risked his only remaining eye in battle; if the hens clucked on seeing him, he said it was to hide their spite because he did not condescend to look at them.

One day, when he was more puffed up with vanity than usual, he resolved no longer to remain in such a narrow sphere, but to go out into the world, where he would be better appreciated.

"My lady mother," said he, "I am tired of Spain; I am going to Rome to see the pope and cardinals."

"What are you thinking of, my poor child!" cried his mother. "Who has put such a folly into your head? Never has one of our family been known to quit his country, and, for this reason, we are the honor of our race, and are proud of our genealogy. Where will you find a poultry-yard like this—mulberry-trees to shade you, a whitewashed hen-roost, a magnificent dunghill, worms and corn every where, brothers that love you, and three great dogs to guard you from the foxes? Do you not think that at Rome itself you will regret the ease and plenty of such a life?"

Coquerico shrugged his crippled wing in token of disdain. "You are a simple woman, my good mother," said he; "every thing is accounted worthy of admiration by him who has never quitted his dunghill. But I have wit enough to see that my brothers have no ideas, and that my cousins are nothing but rustics. My genius is stifling in this hole; I wish to roam the world and seek my fortune."

"But, my son, have you never looked in the brook?" resumed the poor hen. "Don't you know that you lack an eye, a leg, and a wing? To make your fortune, you need the eyes of a fox, the legs of a spider, and the wings of a vulture. Once outside of these walls, you are lost."

"My good mother," replied Coquerico, "when a hen hatches a duck, she is always frightened on seeing it run to the water. You know me no better. It is my nature to succeed by my wit and talent. I must have a public capable of appreciating the charms of my person; my place is not among inferior people."

"My son," said the hen, seeing all her counsels useless,

"my son, listen at least to your mother's last words. If you go to Rome, take care to avoid St. Peter's Church ; thc saint, it is said, dislikes cocks, especially when they crow. Shun, moreover, certain personages called cooks and scullions ; you will know them by their paper caps, their tucked-up sleeves, and the great knives which they wear at their sides. They are licensed assassins, who track our steps without pity, and cut our throats without giving us time to cry mercy. And now, my child," she added, raising her claw, "receive my blessing. May St. James, the patron saint of pilgrims, protect thee !"

Coquerico pretended not to see the tear that trembled in his mother's eye, nor did he trouble himself any more about his father, who bristled his plumage and seemed about to call him back. Without caring for those whom he left behind, he glided through the half-open door, and, once outside, flapped his only wing and crowed three times, to celebrate his freedom—"Cock-a-doodle-doo !"

As he half flew, half hopped over the fields, he came to the bed of a brook which had been dried up by the sun. In the middle of the sands, however, still trickled a tiny thread of water, so small that it was choked by a couple of dead leaves that had fallen into it.

"My friend," exclaimed the streamlet at the sight of our traveler, "my friend, you see my weakness ; I have not even the strength to carry away these leaves which obstruct my passage, much less to make a circuit, so completely am I exhausted. With a stroke of your beak you can restore me to life. I am not an ingrate ; if you oblige me, you may count on my gratitude the first rainy day, when the water from heaven shall have restored my strength."

"You are jesting?" said Coquerico. "Do I look like one whose business it is to sweep the brooks? Apply to those of your own sort." And, with his sound leg, he leaped across the streamlet.

"You will remember me when you least expect it," murmured the brook, but with so feeble a voice that it was lost on the proud cock.

A little farther on, Coquerico saw the wind lying breathless on the ground.

"Dear Coquerico, come to my aid," it cried ; "here on earth we should help each other. You see to what I am reduced by the heat of the day ; I, who in former times uprooted the olive-trees and lashed the waves to frenzy, lie here well-nigh slain by the dog star. I suffered myself to be lulled to sleep by the perfume of the roses with which I was playing ; and lo! here I am, stretched almost lifeless upon the ground. If you will raise me a couple of inches with your beak and fan me a little with your wing, I shall have the strength to mount to yonder white clouds which I see in the distance, where I shall receive aid enough from my family to keep me alive till I gain fresh strength from the next whirlwind."

"My lord," answered the spiteful Coquerico, "your excellency has more than once amused himself by playing tricks at my expense. It is not a week since your lordship glided like a traitor behind me, and diverted himself by opening my tail like a fan and covering me with confusion in the face of nations. Have patience, therefore, my worthy friend ; mockers always have their turn ; it does them good to repent, and to learn to respect those whose birth, wit, and beauty should screen them from the jests of a fool." And Coquerico, bristling his plumage, crowed three times in his shrillest voice and proudly strutted onward.

A little farther on he came to a newly-mown field, where the farmers had piled up the weeds in order to burn them. Coquerico approached a smoking heap, hoping to find some

stray kernels of corn, and saw a little flame which was char-
ring the green stalks without being able to set them on fire.

"My good friend," cried the flame to the new-comer, "you
are just in time to save my life; I am dying for want of air.
I can not imagine what has become of my cousin, the wind,
who cares for nothing but his own amusement. Bring me a
few dry straws to rekindle my strength, and you will not have
obliged an ingrate."

"Wait a moment," said Coquerico, "and I will serve you
as you deserve, insolent fellow that dares ask my help!" And
behold! he leaped on the heap of dried weeds, and trampled
it down till he smothered both flame and smoke; after which
he exultingly shouted three times "Cock-a-doodle-doo!" and
flapped his wings, as if he had done a great deed.

Proudly strutting onward and crowing, Coquerico at last
arrived at Rome, the place to which all roads lead. Scarcely
had he reached the city when he hastened to the great church
of St. Peter. Grand and beautiful as it was, he did not stop
to admire it, but, planting himself in front of the main entrance, where he looked like a fly among the great columns,
he raised himself on tip-toe and began to shout "Cock-a-doodle-doo!" only to enrage the saint and disobey his mother.

He had not yet ended his song when one of the pope's
guard, who chanced to hear him, laid hands on the insolent
wretch who dared thus to insult the saint, and carried him
home in order to roast him for supper.

"Quick!" said he to his wife on entering the house, "give
me some boiling water; here is a sinner to be punished."

"Pardon, pardon, Madam Water!" cried Coquerico. "Oh,
good and gentle water, the best and purest thing in the world,
do not scald me, I pray you!"

"Did you have pity on me when I implored your aid, ungrateful wretch?" answered the water, boiling with indignation.

And with a single gush it inundated him from head to foot, and left not a bit of down on his body.

The unhappy Coquerico stripped of all his feathers, the soldier took him and laid him on the gridiron.

"Oh, fire, do not burn me!" cried he, in an agony of terror. "Oh, beautiful and brilliant fire, the brother of the sun and the cousin of the diamond, spare an unhappy creature; restrain thy ardor, and soften thy flame; do not roast me!"

"Did you have pity on me when I implored your aid, ungrateful wretch?" answered the fire, and, fiercely blazing with anger, in an instant it burnt Coquerico to a coal.

The soldier, seeing his roast chicken in this deplorable condition, took him by the leg and threw him out of the window. The wind bore the unhappy fowl to a dunghill, where it left him for a moment.

"Oh, wind," murmured Coquerico, who still breathed, "oh, kindly zephyr, protecting breeze, behold me cured of my vain follies ; let me rest on the paternal dunghill."

"Let you rest !" roared the wind. "Wait, and I will teach you how I treat ingrates." And with one blast it sent him so high in the air that, as he fell back, he was transfixed by a steeple.

There St. Peter was awaiting him. With his own hand he nailed him to the highest steeple in Rome, where he is still shown to travelers. However high placed he may be, all despise him because he turns with the slightest wind ; black, dried up, stripped of his feathers, and beaten by the rain, he is no longer called Coquerico, but Weathercock ; and thus expiates, and must expiate eternally, his disobedience, vanity, and wickedness.

KING BIZARRE AND PRINCE CHARMING;
OR, THE ART OF GOVERNING MEN.

A TALE OF ALL NATIONS.

I.

KING BIZARRE AND PRINCE CHARMING.

IN the kingdom of Wild Oats, a happy country, a land blessed of heaven, where the men are always right and the women never wrong, there lived long ago a king who thought of nothing but the happiness of his kingdom, and who, it is said, never was dull for lack of amusement. Whether he was beloved by his people is doubtful ; it is certain that the courtiers had little esteem and less love for their prince. For this reason, they had given him the surname of King Bizarre, the only title by which he is known in history, as is seen in the *Great Chronicles of the Kingdoms and Principalities of the World which have never existed*, a learned masterpiece which has immortalized the erudition and criticism of the reverend father, Doctor Melchisedec de Mentiras y Necedad.

Left a widower after a year's marriage, Bizarre had fixed his whole affections on his son and heir, who was the most beautiful child imaginable. His complexion was as fresh as a rose ; his beautiful fair hair fell in golden curls on his shoulders ; add to this clear blue eyes, a straight nose, a small mouth, and a dimpled chin, and you have the portrait of a cherub. At twelve years of age this young marvel danced enchantingly, rode like a riding-master, and fenced to perfection. No one could have helped being won by his smile and the truly royal manner in which he saluted the crowd in passing when he was in good humor. For this reason, the voice of the people, which is never mistaken, had christened him Prince Charming, and this name always clung to him.

Charming was as beautiful as the day; but the sun itself, it is said, has spots, and princes do not disdain to resemble the sun. The child dazzled the court with his fine mien; but there were shadows here and there which did not escape the piercing eye of love or envy. Supple, agile, and adroit in all kinds of bodily exercises, Charming had an indolent mind. He lacked application, and had taken a fancy that he ought to know every thing without studying. It is true that governesses, courtiers, and servants had continually repeated to him that work was not made for kings, and that a prince always knows enough when he lavishes on poets, writers, and artists, with a prodigal and disdainful hand, a little of the money which the people are too happy to offer him.

These maxims tickled Charming's pride; and at twelve years of age, the beautiful child, with precocious firmness, had steadily refused to learn the alphabet. Three teachers, chosen from the most able and patient instructors, a priest, a philosopher, and a colonel, had attempted in turn to bend his youthful obstinacy; but the priest had wasted his philosophy, the philosopher his tactics, and the colonel his Latin. Left master of the field of battle, Charming listened to nothing but his caprice, and lived lawless and unconstrained. As stubborn as a mule, as irascible as a turkey-cock, as dainty as a cat, and as idle as an adder, but an accomplished prince withal, he was the pride of the beautiful country of Wild Oats, and the hope and love of a people that esteemed nothing in their kings but grace and beauty.

II.

PAZZA.

NOTWITHSTANDING he had been brought up at court, King Bizarre was a man of sense. Charming's ignorance was far from pleasing to him, and he often asked himself with anxiety what would become of his kingdom in the hands of a prince whom the basest of flatterers might easily deceive. But what was he to do, what means could he employ with a child that a worshiped wife had bequeathed to him in dying? Rather than see his son weep, Bizarre would have given him his crown; his affection rendered him powerless. Love is not blind, whatever the poets may say; alas! it would be too happy not to see a jot. It is the torment of him who loves to become, despite himself, the slave and accomplice of the ingrate who feels himself beloved.

Every day, after the council, the king went to spend the evening with the Countess of Castro, an old lady who had dandled him on her knees when an infant, and who alone could recall to him the sweet memories of his childhood and youth. She was very ugly, and something of a witch, it is said; but the world is so wicked that we must never believe more than half its scandal. The countess had large features and luxuriant gray hair, and it was easy to see that she had been beautiful in former times.

One day, when Charming had been more unreasonable than usual, the king entered the countess's house with an anxious air, and, seating himself before the card-table, began to play a game of Patience. It was his way of diverting his thoughts and forgetting for a few hours the cares of royalty. Scarcely had he ranged sixteen cards in a square when he heaved a deep sigh.

"Countess," he cried, "you see before you the most wretched of fathers and kings. Despite his natural grace, Charming is every day becoming more willful and vicious. Must I leave such an heir after me, and intrust the happiness of my people to a crowned fool?"

"That is the way with Nature," replied the countess; "she always distributes her gifts with an impartial hand. Stupidity and beauty go hand in hand, and wit and ugliness are seldom separated. I have an example of this in my own family. A few days ago a great-grand-niece was sent to me, a child under ten years old, that has no other relative: she is as tawny as a frog, as scraggy as a spider, yet, withal, as cunning as an ape, and as learned as a book. Judge for yourself, sire; here is my little monster coming to salute you."

Bizarre turned his head and saw a child that answered in every respect to the countess's description. With a high, round forehead, black, wild-looking eyes, rough hair turned back in the Chinese fashion, dull, brown skin, great white teeth, red hands, and long arms, she was any thing but a beauty. But the chrysalis gives birth to the butterfly: wait a few years, and you will see what pretty women come from these frightful little girls of ten.

The little monster approached the king, and courtesied to him with so serious an air that Bizarre could not help laughing, though he felt little like it.

"Who are you?" asked he, chucking the child under the chin.

"Sire," she answered, gravely, "I am Donna Dolores Rosario Coral Concha Balthazara Melchiora Gaspara y Todos Santos, the daughter of the noble knight Don Pasquale Bartolomeo Francesco de Asiz y—"

"Enough," said the king; "I did not ask for your genealogy; we are witnessing neither your baptism nor marriage. What are you commonly called?"

"Sire," replied she, "I am called Pazza."[*]

"And why are you called Pazza?"

"Because it is not my name."

"That is strange," said the king.

"No, it is natural," replied the child. "My aunt pretends that I am too giddy for any saint to wish to own me for her god-daughter, and that is why she has given me a name that can offend no one in Paradise."

"Well answered, my child. I see that you are not an ordinary girl. The saints in Paradise are not always treated with such consideration. Since you know so much, tell me what is a wise man?"

"A wise man, sire, is one who knows what he says when he speaks, and what he does when he acts."

"Upon my word," exclaimed the king, "if my wise men were what you fancy them, I would make the Academy of Sciences my council of state, and would give it my kingdom to govern. What is an ignorant man?"

"Sire," returned Pazza, "there are three kinds of ignorant men: he who knows nothing, he who talks of what he does not know, and he who will learn nothing; all three are fit for nothing but to be burned or hung."

"That is a proverb; do you know what proverbs are called?"

"Yes, sire; they are called the wisdom of nations."

"And why are they called so?"

"Because they are mad; they say whatever you please; they are of all colors, to suit all tastes. Proverbs are like bells, which answer yes or no according to the humor of their listener."

---

[*] That is to say, Madcap, in Italian. It appears that a very mixed language is spoken in the kingdom of Wild Oats.

Upon which, springing with both feet from the ground, Pazza caught a fly that was buzzing about the king's nose ; then, leaving Bizarre astonished, she took her doll, and, seating herself on the ground, began to rock it in her arms.

"Well, sire," the countess said, "what do you think of this child?"

" She has too much wit," answered the king ; "she will not live long."

" Ah ! sire," exclaimed Pazza, "you are not complimentary to my aunt ; she is considerably older than I am."

" Hush, gipsy!" said the old lady, smiling ; "don't you know that nobody lectures kings?"

"Countess," said Bizarre, "an idea has just struck me, which is so strange that I hardly dare tell it to you ; yet I have a violent wish to carry it out. I can do nothing with my son ; reason has no power with the stubborn child ; who knows whether folly would not be more successful? If I thought so, I would make Pazza Charming's teacher. The intractable boy, who rejects all masters, might be defenseless before a child. The only objection is that no one will be of my opinion ; I shall have every body against me."

" Bah !" said the countess ; "every body is so stupid that it is a proof that you are right that you think differently."

H

III.

THE FIRST LESSON.

IN this manner Pazza was intrusted with the instruction of the young prince. There was no official appointment; it was not announced in the court gazette that the king, with his usual wisdom, had found an unparalleled genius at the first attempt, to whom he had confided the heart and mind of his child; but the very next morning Charming was sent to the countess's house, and was permitted to play with Pazza.

The two children, left alone together, gazed at each other in silence. Pazza, being the bolder, was the first to speak.

"What is your name?" asked she.

"Those who know me call me Your Highness," answered Charming, in a piqued tone; "those who do not know me call me simply My Lord, and every body says Sir to me; etiquette requires it."

"What is etiquette?" asked Pazza.

"I don't know," replied Charming. "When I want to jump, shout, and roll on the ground, I am told that it is contrary to etiquette; then I keep still, and yawn for lack of amusement—that is etiquette."

"Since we are here to amuse ourselves," resumed Pazza, "there is no etiquette needed; speak to me as if I were your sister, and I will speak to you as if you were my brother. I will not call you My Lord."

"But you don't know me," said Charming.

"What does that matter?" returned Pazza; "I will love you, that is better. They say that you dance beautifully; teach me to dance, will you?"

The ice was broken; Charming took the young girl by the

waist, and in less than half an hour taught her the last new polka.

"How well you dance!" said he. "You have caught the step directly."

"It is because you are a good teacher," she replied. "Now it is my turn to teach you something."

She took a beautiful picture-book, and showed him fine buildings, fishes, statesmen, parrots, scholars, curious animals, and flowers, all of which greatly amused Charming.

"See," said Pazza, "here is the explanation of all the pictures; read it."

"I don't know how to read," replied Charming.

"I will teach you; I will be your little tutor."

"No," replied the stubborn prince, "I do not wish to read. My masters tire me."

"Very well; but I am not a master. See, here is an A, a beautiful great A; say A."

"No," returned Charming, frowning, "I will never say A."

"Not to please me?"

"No, never.   Enough of this; I do not like people to differ from me."

"Sir," said Pazza, "a polite man never refuses ladies any thing."

"I would refuse the devil in petticoats," replied the young prince, tossing his head.   "I am tired of you; let me alone. I don't love you any longer; call me My Lord."

"My Lord Charming, or my charming lord," said Pazza, flushed with anger, "you shall read, or I will know the reason why."

"I won't read."

"Will you not?   One—two—three!"

"No! no! no!"

Pazza raised her hand, and lo! the king's son received a box on the ear.   Pazza had been told that she was witty to the ends of her fingers, and had been stupid enough to believe it; it is never right to jest with children.

At this first lesson in reading, Charming turned pale and trembled; the blood mounted to his cheeks, his eyes filled with tears, and he gazed at his young teacher with a look that made her start; then all at once, with a great effort, he regained his self-possession, and said, in a tremulous voice, "Pazza, that is A."   And the same day, and at one sitting, he learned all the letters of the alphabet; at the end of the week he spelt readily, and before the month was ended he read with ease.

King Bizarre was delighted.   He kissed Pazza on both cheeks; he insisted on having her always with him or his son, and made this child his friend and counselor, to the great disdain of all the courtiers.   Charming, still gloomy and silent, learned all that his young Mentor could teach him, then returned to his former preceptors, whom he astonished by his intelligence and docility. He soon knew his grammar so well that the priest asked himself one day whether, by chance, these definitions, which he had never understood, had not a meaning. Charming none the less astonished the philosopher, who taught him every evening the opposite of what the priest had taught him in the morning. But, of all his masters, the one to whom he listened with the least repugnance was the colonel. It is true that Bayonet, for that was the colonel's name, was a skillful strategist, and that he could say, like the ancient poet, with a slight variation, "I am a man, and nothing that pertains to the art of dispatching poor human beings is indifferent to me." It was he that initiated Charming into the mysteries of button gaiters and shoulder-straps; it was he that taught his pupil that the noblest study for a prince is the drilling of battalions, and that the ground-work of statesmanship is to have reviews in order to make war, and to make war in order to have reviews.

This was not perhaps altogether according to Bizarre's idea of the art of government; but he thought he could correct any errors in the future, and, besides, he was so rejoiced at Charming's progress that he was unwilling in any way to meddle with the admirable work of an education so long considered hopeless.

"My child," he often said, "never forget that you owe every thing to Pazza." As the king spoke thus, Pazza gazed tenderly at the young man. Despite all her wit, she was foolish enough to love him. Charming contented himself with coldly answering that gratitude was a princely virtue, and that Pazza should some day learn that her pupil had forgotten nothing.

IV.

PAZZA'S WEDDING.

WHEN Prince Charming had attained his seventeenth year, he went one morning in search of King Bizarre, whose health was declining, and who was very desirous of seeing his son married before his death.

"Father," said he, "I have long reflected on your wise words. You gave me life, but Pazza has done still more in awakening my mind and soul. I see but one way of paying the debt of my heart; that is, to marry the woman to whom I am indebted for what I am. I come to ask you for Pazza's hand."

"My dear child," answered Bizarre, "this step does you credit. Pazza is not of royal blood; she is not the one whom, in different circumstances, I should have chosen for your wife; but her virtues, her merit, and, above all, the service which she has rendered us, make me forget idle prejudices. Pazza has the soul of a queen; she shall mount the throne with you. In the country of Wild Oats, wit and humor are held in sufficient estimation to win you forgiveness for what fools call a misalliance, and what I call a princely marriage. Happy is he who can choose an intelligent wife, capable of understanding and loving him! To-morrow your betrothal shall be celebrated, and in two years your marriage shall take place.

The marriage occurred more speedily than the king had foreseen. Fifteen months after these memorable words, Bizarre expired of languor and exhaustion. He had taken the vocation of king in earnest; he fell a victim to royalty. The old countess and Pazza wept their friend and benefactor, but they were the only mourners. Without being a bad son, Charming was engrossed with the cares of the empire; and the court expected every thing from the new reign, and thought no more about the old king, whose eyes were closed in death.

After honoring his father's memory by magnificent obsequies, the young prince, thenceforth wholly devoted to love, celebrated his marriage with a splendor that charmed the good people of Wild Oats. The taxes were doubled, but who could regret money so nobly employed? Men came from a hundred leagues round to gaze at the new king, and Pazza, whose growing beauty and air of goodness fascinated all hearts, was not less admired. There were interminable dinners, harangues longer than the dinners, and poems more tedious than the harangues. In a word, it was an incomparable festival, which was talked of for six months after.

Evening come, Charming took the hand of his graceful, timid, and blushing bride, and with cold politeness led her through the corridors of the old castle. All at once Pazza was frightened to find herself in a gloomy dungeon, with grated windows, and huge bars and locks.

"What is this?" asked she; "it looks like a prison."

"Yes," said the prince, with a terrible look, "it is a prison which you will quit only for the grave."

"My dear, you frighten me," said Pazza, smiling. "Am I a criminal without knowing it? Have I deserved your displeasure, that you threaten me with a dungeon?"

"You have a short memory," replied Charming. "An insult is written on sand to the giver; it is inscribed on marble and bronze to the receiver."

"Charming," returned the poor child, beginning to be afraid, "you are repeating something from those speeches that tired me so much. Can you find nothing better to say to me today?"

"Wretch!" cried the king, "you no longer remember the box

on the ear that you gave me seven years ago, but I have not forgotten it. Know that if I have wished you for my wife, it has been only to have your life in my hands, and to make you slowly expiate your crime of high treason."

"My dear," said Pazza, with a pettish manner, "you may put on your Bluebeard airs, but you will not frighten me, I assure you. I know you, Charming, and I warn you that if you do not put an end to this bad jest, I will not only give you one box on the ear, but three, before I forgive you. Make haste and let me go out, or I vow that I will keep my word."

"Vow it then, madam," cried the prince, furious at not intimidating his victim. "I accept your vow. I vow too, on my side, that I will never acknowledge you as my wife till I have been base enough to receive three times an insult which nothing but blood can wash out. He laughs well that laughs last. Here, Rachimburg!"

At this terrible name, a jailer with a bushy beard and

threatening mien entered the room, pushed the queen on a wretched truckle-bed, and shut and double-locked the iron door.

If Pazza wept, it was so quietly that no one heard her. Tired of the silence, Charming departed, with rage in his heart, resolving that his rigor should break the pride that braved him. Vengeance, it is said, is the delight of kings.

Two hours later the countess received a note by a sure hand acquainting her with the sad fate of her niece. How this note reached her is known to me, but I will not betray the secret. If a charitable jailer is found by chance, he should be treated with consideration ; the species is rare, and is daily becoming rarer.

V.

A TERRIBLE EVENT.

THE next morning the court gazette announced that the queen had been seized with a raging fit of madness on the very night of her wedding, and that there was little hope of saving her. There was scarcely a courtier, indeed, that had not observed the princess's restless air on the evening before, and no one was surprised at her malady. All pitied the king, who received with a gloomy and constrained mien the expressions of affection which were lavished on him. He was doubtless weighed down with grief, but this grief appeared very much lightened after the visit of the countess.

The good lady was very sad, and had a great desire to see her poor child, but she was so old, and found herself so weak and sensitive, that she entreated the king to spare her a heart-rending spectacle. She threw herself into the arms of Charming, who tenderly embraced her, and withdrew, saying that she placed all her hope and trust in the love of the king and the talent of the chief physician of the court.

She had scarcely left the room when the physician whispered a few words in Charming's ear which called to his face a smile quickly repressed. The countess pacified, there was nothing more to fear ; the vengeance was sure.

Doctor Wieduwillst was a great physician. Born in the country of Dreams, he had early quitted his native land to seek his fortune in the kingdom of Wild Oats. He was too able a man not to find it. In the five years that he had spent in the celebrated University of Lugenmaulberg, the medical theory had changed twenty-five times, and, thanks to this solid education, the doctor had a firmness of principle which nothing could shake. He had the frankness and bluntness of a soldier, it was said : he swore at times, even with ladies ; a rudeness which left him at liberty always to be of the same mind with the stronger, and to demand a fee for having no opinion. The queen had fallen into his incorruptible hands.

She had been imprisoned for three days, and the town was already beginning to talk of something else, when one morning Rachimburg abruptly entered the king's apartments with a distracted air, and threw himself trembling at his feet.

"Sire," said he, "I bring you my head. The queen has disappeared."

"What do you tell me !" exclaimed the king, turning pale ; "the thing is impossible ; the dungeon is barred on all sides."

"Yes," said the jailer, "the thing is impossible, that is certain ; the bars are in their places, the walls are whole, and neither the locks nor the bolts have been disturbed ; but there are witches in the world that pass through walls without moving a stone, and who knows but what the prisoner is one of them ? Was it ever known whence she came ?"

The king sent in search of the doctor. He was a strong-minded man, and had little faith in witches. He sounded the walls, shook the bars, and cross-examined the jailer, but all to no purpose. Trusty men were sent every where through the town, and spies were set on the countess, whom the doctor suspected, but all in vain, and after a week the search was abandoned. Rachimburg lost his place as jailer, but as he possessed the royal secret, as he was needed, and as he thirsted to avenge himself, he was made the warden of the royal castle. Furious at his bad luck, he exercised his supervision with such strictness that in less than three days he arrested Wieduwillst himself half a dozen times, and disarmed all suspicion.

At the end of a week some fishermen brought to the court the robe and mantle of the queen. The waves had cast on the shore these sad relics, covered with sand and sea-foam. That the poor mad woman had drowned herself, no one doubted on seeing the grief of the king and the tears of the countess. The council was assembled. It decided with a unanimous voice that the queen was legally dead, and that the king was legally a widower, and, for the interest of the people, entreated his majesty to abridge a painful mourning, and to marry again as soon as possible, in order to strengthen the dynasty. This decision was transmitted to the king by Wieduwillst, the chief physician to the king and president of the royal council, who made so touching a speech that the whole court burst into tears, and Charming threw himself into the doctor's arms, calling him his cruel friend.

It is unnecessary to say that the funeral of a queen so much lamented was magnificent. In the kingdom of Wild Oats every thing serves as a pretext for ceremony. The pageant was worthy of admiration, but the most admirable thing in it was the attitude of the young girls of the court. Every one looked at Charming, who was handsomer than ever in his mourning dress ; every one wept with one eye in honor of the princess, and smiled with the other to attract the king. Ah ! had photography only been invented, what portraits would antiquity have transmitted to us—what models for our painters! The passions still existed among these good people; their mobile faces were animated by love, hatred, and anger; to-day we are all so virtuous and prudent that we all wear the same dress, the same hat, and the same expression. Civilization is the triumph of morality and the ruin of art.

After the description of the funeral ceremonies, which, according to etiquette, filled six columns, the court gazette laid down rules for the full and the second mourning, blue and pink, which are the mourning colors in the kingdom of Wild Oats. The court was required to be in deep affliction for three weeks, and to be comforted by degrees during the three weeks following; but carnival occurring during the period of the second mourning, and respect being had for trade, it was determined to give a masked ball at the palace. Tailors and dress-makers immediately set to work, invitations were solicited by great and small, and men began to intrigue as if the fate of the monarchy had been in question.

It was in this solemn manner that they mourned for poor Pazza.

VI.

THE MASKED BALL.

THE great day so impatiently expected at length arrived. For six weeks the good people of Wild Oats had been in a fever of excitement. Nothing more was heard of ministers, senators, generals, magistrates, princesses, duchesses, and citizens; for twenty leagues round, clowns, harlequins, punchinellos, gipsies, Columbines, and Follies alone were to be seen. Politics were silenced, or, rather, the nation was divided into two great parties, the conservatives that went to the ball, and the opposition that staid at home.

If the official gazette is to be believed, the festival outshone in splendor all others past and to come. The ball was held in the midst of the gardens, in a rotunda magnificently decorated. A winding walk, shaded by elms and dimly lighted by alabaster lamps, led to a hall resplendent with gold, verdure, flowers, and light. An orchestra, half concealed in the foliage, breathed forth music, by turns plaintive and gay. Add to this the richness of the costumes, the brilliancy of the diamonds, the piquancy of the masks, and the charm of intrigue, and you will see that it would have needed the soul of an ancient Stoic to resist the intoxication of pleasure.

Yet Prince Charming was not amused. Concealed under a blue domino, with his face entirely masked, he had addressed himself to the most elegant and sprightly women, and had lavishly displayed his wit and grace, yet he had met with nothing but indifference and coldness. They scarcely listened to him, answered with a yawn, and hastened to quit him. All eyes were fixed on a black domino with pink rosettes that moved carelessly among the dancers, receiving with the air of a sultan the compliments and smiles that every one lavished on him. This domino was the Lord Wieduwillst, a great friend of the prince, but still more the friend of his own pleasure. In an unguarded moment the doctor had said that morning by chance, under the seal of secrecy, and to two ladies only, that the prince would wear pink rosettes in his black domino. Was it his fault if the ladies had been indiscreet or the prince had changed his mind?

While the doctor was enjoying, despite himself, indeed, his unexpected triumph, Charming seated himself in a corner of the hall and buried his face in his hands. Alone in the midst of the crowd, he abandoned himself to reflection, and the image of Pazza rose before him. He had no reproaches to make himself; his vengeance was just, yet he felt an indescribable remorse. Poor Pazza! no doubt she had been guilty; but at least she loved him, she understood him, she listened to him, her eyes sparkling with joy. How different from all those fools who had not recognized a prince under a domino at the first moment by his wit!

He rose suddenly to quit the hall, when he perceived, a little way off, a mask that had also left the crowd and seemed lost in contemplation. A half-open domino disclosed a gipsy's dress and a pair of slippers with buckles, containing a foot smaller than that of Cinderella.

The king approached the stranger, and saw through the velvet mask a pair of large black eyes, the melancholy glance of which surprised and charmed him.

"Fair mask," said he, "your place is not here. Why are you not among the eager and curious crowd that is pressing around the prince to dispute his smile and heart? Do you not know that there is a crown to be gained there?"

"I make no such pretensions," answered the domino, in a grave, sweet voice. "In this game of chance one runs the risk of taking the servant for the king. I am too proud to expose myself to such a hazard."

"But if I show you the prince?"

"What could I say to him?" replied the stranger. "I could not blame him without offense, or praise him without flattery."

"You think much evil of him, then?"

"No, a little evil and much good; but what does it matter?" And, opening her fan, the domino relapsed into her reverie.

This indifference surprised Charming. He addressed her with warmth, she replied coldly; he prayed her so urgently to listen to him that she finally consented to do so, not in the ball-room, where the heat was overpowering and the curiosity indiscreet, but in the long elm-walk, where a few promenaders were seeking silence and fresh air.

The night was advancing, and the gipsy had already spoken several times of retiring, to the great regret of the prince, who vainly entreated her to unmask. The stranger made no reply.

"You drive me to despair," cried he, inspired with strange respect and admiration for this mysterious figure. "Why this cruel silence?"

"Because I know you, my lord," replied the stranger, with emotion. "Your voice, which goes to the heart, your language, your grace, all tell me who you are. Let me go, Prince Charming."

"No, madam," cried the prince, delighted at so much wit, "you alone have recognized me, you alone have understood me, to you belong my heart and kingdom. Throw off that suspicious mask; this very instant we will return to the ball-room, and I will present to the ignorant crowd the woman whom I have had the happiness not to displease. Say but one word, and all my people shall be at your feet."

"My lord," replied the stranger, sadly, "permit me to refuse an offer which does me honor, and the memory of which I shall always preserve. I am ambitious, I own; the time has been when I should have been proud to share your throne and name; but, before all things, I am a woman, and place all my happiness in love. I will not have a divided heart, should my rival be only a memory; I am jealous even of the past."

"I have never loved in my life," cried the prince, with a vehemence that made the stranger start. "There is a mystery concerning my marriage which I can reveal only to my wife; but I swear to you that I have never given away my heart; I love now for the first time."

"Show me your hand," said the gipsy, approaching the lamp, "and let me see whether you have told the truth."

Charming extended his hand with assurance ; the gipsy studied the lines and sighed.

"You are right, my lord," said she, "you have never loved. But this does not appease my jealousy. Another woman has loved you before me. These sacred bonds are not broken by death ; the queen still loves you—you belong to her. To accept a heart which is no longer at your disposal would be sacrilegious and criminal in me. Farewell."

"Madam," said the king, with an ill-assured voice, "you do not know what you make me suffer. There are things which I would gladly bury in eternal silence, but which you force me to reveal. The queen never loved me ; ambition alone dictated her conduct."

"That is not so," said the stranger, letting go the prince's hand. "The queen loved you."

"No, madam," replied Charming ; "my father and I were the victims of a detestable intrigue."

"Enough !" said the stranger, whose hands trembled and whose fingers worked in a strange manner. "Respect the dead ; do not slander them."

"Madam," said the prince, "I assure you, and none ever doubted my word, that the queen never loved me. She was a wicked woman."

"Ah !" said the domino.

"Willful, violent, and jealous."

"If she was jealous, she loved you," interrupted the mask. "Seek for proofs which have at least a shadow of probability ; do not accuse a heart which was wholly yours."

"So far from loving me," said the king, excitedly, "the very night of my marriage she dared tell me to my face that she had married me only for my crown."

" That is not true," said the gipsy, raising her hand.

" I swear it," replied Charming.

" You lie !" cried the stranger.   And lo ! a box on the ear blinded the prince ; the blow was repeated, and the stranger fled.

The king stepped back furious, and sought the hilt of his sword ; but men do not go to balls armed as for war ; for his sole weapon he found a knot of ribbons.   He ran after his enemy, but which way had she fled ?   Charming lost himself twenty times in the labyrinth ; he met none but peaceful dominos walking in couples, and scarcely glancing at him as he passed.   Breathless, distracted, and desperate, he returned to the ball-room, where he doubted not that the stranger had taken refuge ; but how was he to find her ?

A brilliant idea crossed the prince's mind ; he would order all to unmask, and would doubtless see the gipsy, confounded by the king's presence and betrayed by her own agitation. He instantly leaped on a chair, and exclaimed in a loud voice that caused every one to start,

" Ladies and gentlemen, day is approaching and pleasure is languishing ; let us revive mirth by a new caprice.   Off with the masks !   I set the example ; let all who love me follow it."

He threw off his domino, raised his mask, and appeared in the richest and most elegant Spanish costume ever worn by prince.   There was a general outcry ; all eyes were at first turned toward the king, then toward the black domino with pink rosettes, who retreated as fast as possible with a modesty that was not affected.   All unmasked.   The ladies gathered round the king, who, it was remarked, had the most violent fancy for the gipsy costume.   Young or old, all the gipsies received his homage ; he took them by the hand, and gazed at them with an air which made all the other masks ready to burst with envy, then made a sign to the orchestra ; the dance recommenced, and the prince disappeared.

He hastened again to the elm-walk in search of the traitress who had insulted him, doubtless led by vengeance. His blood boiled in his veins ; he wandered at random, suddenly stopping short, looking, listening, and spying in all directions. At the faintest gleam of light through the foliage he sprang forward like a madman, laughing and weeping at the same time as though distracted.

At the turn of an alley he met Rachimburg advancing toward him trembling, with an air of terror.

"Sire," murmured he, in a mysterious voice, "has your majesty seen it?"

"What?" asked the king.

"The spectre ; it passed close by me. I am a lost man ; I shall die to-morrow."

"What spectre?" said Charming. "What fool's tale are you telling me?"

"A spectre—a domino with flashing eyes, that threw me on my knees and boxed my ears twice."

"It is she!" cried the king ; "it is she! Why did you let her go?"

"Your majesty, I had not my pike ; but if ever I see her again, I will knock her down."

"Do no such thing!" returned the king. "If ever she returns, do not frighten her ; follow her and discover her retreat. But where is she? which way did she go? Lead me ; if I find her your fortune is made."

"Sire," said the honest porter, looking at the moon, "if the spectre is any where, it must be up yonder ; I saw it, as plainly as I see your majesty, dissolving in mist. But, before taking flight, it gave me a message for your majesty."

"What? Speak quickly!"

"Sire, its words were terrible; I shall never dare repeat them to your majesty."

"Speak, I order you."

"Sire, the spectre said, in a sepulchral voice, ' Tell the king that if he marries again he is a dead man. The loved one will return.' "

"Here," said the prince, whose eyes shone with a strange lustre, "take my purse. Henceforth I attach you to my person ; I appoint you my first attendant, counting on your devotion and prudence. Let this affair remain a secret between us."

"That makes two," murmured Rachimburg, as he departed with a firm tread, like a man that neither suffers himself to be cast down by fear or dazzled by good fortune. He was a strong-minded man.

The next morning the court gazette contained the following lines, in the form of a letter without signature, in the unofficial part of the paper :

"A rumor has been spread that the king is thinking of marrying again. The king knows what he owes to his people, and is always ready to sacrifice himself for the happiness of his subjects. But the people of Wild Oats have too much delicacy not to respect a recent affliction. The king's whole thoughts are fixed on his beloved wife ; he hopes the consolation from time that is at present refused him."

This note threw the court and town in agitation. The young girls thought the scruples of the prince exaggerated ; more than one mother shrugged her shoulders, and said that the king had vulgar prejudices worthy only of the common people ; but at night there was strife in every well-ordered household. There was not a wife of any pretensions to aristocratic birth that did not quarrel with her unworthy spouse, and force him to admit that there was but one heart capable of love, and but one faithful husband in the whole kingdom, namely, Prince Charming.

VII.

TWO CONSULTATIONS.

AFTER so much excitement, the king was seized with a cruel fit of tedium. To divert himself, he attempted every kind of pleasure ; he hunted, he presided over his council, he went to the play and the opera, he received all the state corporations with their wives, he read a Carthaginian novel, and reviewed the troops half a score of times ; but all in vain : an inexorable memory, an ever-present image left him no rest or peace. The gipsy pursued him even in his dreams ; he saw her, he talked to her, and she listened to him ; but, by some unaccountable fatality, as·soon as she raised her mask, Pazza's pale, sad face always appeared.

The doctor was the only confidant to whom Charming could avow his remorse, but at this word Wieduwillst burst into laughter.

"The effect of habit, sire," he said. "Gain time, multiply impressions, and all will be effaced."·

To procure the prince excitement and to drive away sorrow by a bold diversion, the doctor supped every evening alone with his majesty, and poured out intoxication and forgetfulness with a liberal hand. Wieduwillst did not spare himself, but wine had little effect on his strong brain ; he would have defied Bacchus and Silenus together with Charming. While the prince, by turn noisy and silent, plunged into the extremes of joy and sadness, always restless and never happy, Wieduwillst, calm and smiling, directed his thoughts, and, through pure goodness of soul, took upon himself all the fatigue and care of the government.

Three decrees had already placed in his hands the police, the courts, and the finances. The doctor well understood all the advantages of centralization. The way in which he administered the taxes relieved him from all personal anxiety for the future. The courts punished those who clamored too loudly ; the police silenced those who whispered too much. Nevertheless, in spite of the ability of these political schemes, the people, always ungrateful, did not appreciate their happiness. The inhabitants of Wild Oats delight in complaining ; the pleasure was spoiled for them. King Bizarre's name was in all hearts, and every one regretted the good old times when they shouted over the roof-tops that they were gagged.

The doctor was ambitious ; he was born for a prime minister. Every morning some new ordinance made the people feel that the king was nothing and the minister every thing. Charming was the only one that did not perceive his nothingness. Shut up in his palace, and dying of ennui, his sole companion was a page placed near him by the prime minister on Rachimburg's recommendation. Frolicsome, chattering, and indiscreet, a good musician and capital card-player, Tonto, for that was the page's name, amused the king by his pranks ; he pleased the prime minister no less, but by other virtues. Devoted to his benefactor, the good-natured page innocently repeated to him the most trifling words of the prince—an easy task, moreover, as the king was constantly dreaming and never spoke.

It is a fine thing to have the advantages of power ; but appetite comes by eating even with ministers. The ambitious doctor began to desire both the honors and lustre of royalty. Charming's best friend did not once think of dethroning him ; nations sometimes have foolish prejudices and cling to old habits, but nothing was easier than to frighten a sick prince, and send him afar off in search of a cure that would be long

in coming, while in his absence the doctor would reign as his
proxy.

Charming was young ; he still clung to life, and, moreover,
how could he resist the tender solicitude of the good doctor?
The three most renowned physicians of the faculty met one

evening in consultation at the palace—long Tristram, fat Jocundus, and little Guilleret, three celebrated men—three gen-
iuses who had made their fortune, each with one idea, which
had been the reason why they had never had any more.

After the king had been cross-questioned, looked at, handled, auscultated, and turned round again and again, Tristram
spoke first, in a rude voice,

"Sire," said he, "you must be bled like a peasant, and live
without any exertion whatever. Your disease is a deficiency
of blood, a constitutional atony. Nothing but a journey to the
Clear Waters can cure you. Go quickly, or you are a dead
man. You have my opinion."

"Sire," said fat Jocundus, "I fully share the admirable opinion of my dear professional brother. You are suffering from superabundant vitality. Your disease is a constitutional plethora. Go, drink the Clear Waters, and you will be a well man again. You have my opinion."

"Sire," said little Guilleret, "the diagnostic of my masters fills me with admiration. I bow before their learning. Like them, I believe that you are suffering from disorder of the sympathetic nerves. Your disease is a constitutional nervousness. Drink the Clear Waters. Go quickly, or you are a dead man. You have my opinion."

A unanimous opinion was drawn up and immediately carried to the court gazette by Tonto; and the three doctors rose, bowed to the minister and the king, shook hands with each other, and went down stairs quarreling or laughing, I know not which; the chronicle is almost illegible, owing to a large blot in this place.

After the three physicians had gone, Wieduwillst read the opinion, reflected deeply, and looked at the king. Charming, who had supped a little better this evening even than usual, had not once listened to the doctors, but sat gazing around him with bloodshot eyes.

"Sire," said he, "it is the unanimous opinion of these gentlemen that, if you wish to be cured, you must go to the Clear Waters and abandon the affairs of state. Such a resolution appears to me unworthy of your royal majesty. A great prince should sacrifice himself for his people, and—"

"Enough," said the king; "spare me this worn-out moralizing, and come to the conclusion. You wish me to go, my good friend; you are dying for me to do so, for my own interest, of course. Draw up a decree placing the regency in your hands, and I will sign it."

"Sire, the decree is here, in your portfolio; a good minister always has papers drawn up to suit whatever circumstances may arise. He never knows what may happen."

Charming took the pen, carelessly signed the decree without reading it, and handed it to the minister, who approached to receive it with a smile ; then, seized with a new caprice, he drew back the paper and read it.

"What!" said he, "no statement of reasons ; nothing to assure my people of the kindness I bear them! Doctor, you are too modest ; to-morrow this decree shall be in the gazette, with a statement from the hand of your friend and master. Good-night ; these gentlemen have tired me."

The doctor went out with a light step, erect brow, and sparkling eye, prouder and more insolent than ever. Charming sunk again into his reverie, thinking that, in spite of all, he was not the most unhappy of princes, since Heaven had given him such a friend.

All at once the strangest little doctor that had ever been seen in a castle entered the king's apartment unannounced. He wore a wig with long white curls, his snow-white beard fell on his breast, and his eyes were so bright and youthful that it seemed as though they must have come into the world sixty years after the rest of his body.

"Where are those knaves?" cried he, with a shrill voice, rapping on the floor with his cane. "Where are those ignorant fellows, those pedants, those ill-bred men that did not wait for me? Ah! so you are the patient," said he to the stupefied king. "That is good ; put out your tongue. Quick! I am in a hurry."

"Who are you?" asked the king.

"I am Doctor Truth, the greatest doctor in the world, as you will soon see, in spite of my modesty. Ask Wieduwillst, my pupil, who sent for me from the Land of Dreams. I cure every body, even those who are not ill. Put out your tongue ;

that's right. Where is the opinion? Very well. Atony—
asinis! Plethora—*asini!* Nervousness—*asinorum!* Drink
the Clear Waters—*asininum!* Do you know what is your disease? It is vexation, and even worse."

"Do you see that?" said Charming, terrified.

"Yes, my son, it is written on your tongue. But I will cure
you: it shall be done by to-morrow noon."

"To-morrow!" said the king. "All my treasures—"

"Silence, my son. What portfolio is that?—the minister's?
Good. Sign these three papers for me."

"They are blank decrees," said the king. "What do you
wish to do with them?"

"They are my ordinances. Sign. Well done, my son; be
obedient, and to-morrow noon you shall be as gay as a lark.
First ordinance: If you would live at peace, appear at peace;
I suppress six regiments. Second ordinance: A penny in a
peasant's pocket is worth twenty in the king's treasury; I
suppress one fourth of the taxes. Third ordinance: Liberty
is like the sunshine—it is the happiness and fortune of the
poor; I throw open the political prisons and demolish the
debtors' prisons. You are laughing, my son; it is a good sign
when a patient laughs at his doctor."

"Yes," said Charming, "I am laughing to think of Wieduwillst's face to-morrow on reading these ordinances in the
court gazette. Enough of these follies, buffoon doctor; give
me back the papers and put an end to this farce."

"What is this?" said the little man, taking up the decree of
the regency. "God forgive me! it is an abdication. What
are you thinking of, Prince Charming? What! the inheritance bequeathed to you by your fathers, the people intrusted
to you by God, your name, your honor, will you throw all these
at the feet of an adventurer? Will you let yourself be de-

I

throned and duped by a deceiver? Impossible! It does not suit me; I oppose it. Do you hear?"

"What insolent fellow addresses his prince in this way?"

"Politeness is not in words. Charming, are you mad? are you dreaming? Are you wholly without heart?"

"This is too much!" cried the king. "Begone, wretch, or I will throw you out of the window."

"Begone!" said the little doctor, in a shrill voice. "No, not till I have destroyed this mad and stupid document. See, I tear your abdication in pieces and trample it under foot!"

Charming seized the madman and called his guards. No one answered. The little man struggled with wonderful strength. With his foot he threw the lamp on the ground; but the king, despite the darkness, kept fast hold of the sorcerer, who felt his strength failing.

"Let me go!" murmured he; "for Heaven's sake let me go! You know not what you are doing. You are breaking my arm."

His words and prayers were useless. Suddenly a shower of blows, dealt by a strong hand, fell on the king's ears. Charming let go his hold in surprise, and turned to attack his invisible enemy. He found nothing but empty space, and, staggering in the darkness, cried loudly for the help that did not come. Such a thing could not have happened in a minister's house; kings are always worse guarded.

VIII.

THE END OF A DREAM.

At last a door opened, and Rachimburg entered, according to etiquette, to undress the king. The faithful servant appeared greatly vexed to find him without a light, groping along the wall.

"Where is that infernal doctor?" asked Charming, foaming with rage.

"It is more than an hour, sire, since his excellency quitted the palace?"

"Who is talking of Wieduwillst?" cried the king. "Which way did the villain go that just insulted me?"

Rachimburg looked at the prince with a contrite air, and raised his eyes to heaven, sighing.

"A man went out of the door that leads to your rooms," said Charming. "How did he enter, and where has he fled?"

"Sire," said Rachimburg, "I have neither quitted my post nor seen any one."

"I tell you that a man was in this room a moment ago."

"Sire, your majesty is never mistaken; if a man was in this room he is here still, unless he has flown through the window, or your majesty has been dreaming."

"Fool, do I look like a man that has been dreaming? Did I overturn this lamp? did I tear these papers?"

"Sire, I am nothing but a worm of the earth; God forbid that I should contradict my sovereign. Your majesty does not hire me to give him the lie. But this year strange dreams are an epidemic. No one knows·what he may do or suffer in his sleep. Only just now I was overtaken with sleep in spite of myself, and if I were not sure that I was dreaming, I should declare that an invisible hand boxed my ears twice, at which I awakened with a start."

"It was the spectre!" said the king.

"Your majesty is right," replied Rachimburg; "I am nothing but a simpleton; it was the spectre."

"And I did not know her!" resumed Charming. "Nevertheless, it was her voice and air. What does this mean? Is it a new insult? Is it a warning from heaven? Does some danger threaten me? No matter, I will remain in my kingdom. My friend, not a word of all this : take this purse, and keep the secret."

"That makes the third," murmured the faithful Rachimburg, as he undressed the king with a zeal and address which several times made his majesty smile.

So many emotions one after another banished sleep ; it was daybreak before the prince dozed, and broad daylight before he awoke. In the first moment between sleeping and waking Charming fancied that he heard a strange noise—bells ringing, cannon firing, and three or four bands of music playing each a different air. He was not mistaken ; it was an infernal hubbub. The king rang : Rachimburg entered, carrying a bouquet of flowers.

"Sire," said he, "will his majesty permit the humblest of his servants to be the first to express to him the universal joy? Your people are intoxicated with love and gratitude. The taxes lessened, the prisons opened, the army reduced! Sire, you are the greatest prince in the world ; never has earth seen a ruler like you. Show yourself at the balcony ; answer these cries of 'Hurrah for the king!' Smile on the people that bless you."

Rachimburg could not finish ; tears choked his voice. He attempted to wipe his eyes, but, in his excitement, he took the gazette from his pocket instead of a handkerchief, and began to kiss it like a madman.

Charming took the journal, and vainly attempted, while dressing, to collect his ideas. By what chance had these insane ordinances found their way into the official journal? Who had sent them? Why did not Wieduwillst make his appearance? The prince wished to reflect, consult, and question ; but the people were under the windows, and their majesties were too impatient to wait.

As soon as the king appeared in the balcony he was greeted

with shouts of enthusiasm which, despite every thing, thrilled his heart. Men tossed their caps in the air, women waved their handkerchiefs, mothers lifted up their children and made them stretch their innocent hands to heaven, and repeat, " Hurrah for the king !" The guns of the palace guards were decked with flowers, the drums beat, and the officers' swords flashed in the sun. It was a scene of delirious joy. Charming was infected by the general emotion ; he wept without exactly knowing why. At that instant the clock struck noon. The spectre was right—the prince was cured.

After the crowd it was the turn of the corporations, all of whom, the ministers at the head, came to congratulate and thank the king for having so well understood the wishes of his faithful counselors. A single person was lacking, namely, Wieduwillst. None knew where he had hidden his ignorance and spite. A mysterious note received by him that morning had occasioned his flight, yet this note contained only the words, *The king knows all !* Who had written this fatal letter ? Not the prince ; he alone, perhaps, in the palace, thought of the minister, and wondered at not seeing him by his side.

All at once Tonto entered, pale and haggard. He ran to the king, and gave him a letter which an officer had brought at full gallop. The governor of the province, General Bayonet, sent terrible news ; the six disbanded regiments had mutinied, headed by Wieduwillst. The rebels had proclaimed the downfall of the king, whom they accused of abominable crimes, especially of the murder of the queen. Numerous and well commanded, they were approaching the city, which was defended only by a few doubtful and disaffected regiments. Bayonet entreated the king to come instantly and take command ; an hour later, and all would be lost.

Hurried on by Tonto and Rachimburg, the king secretly quitted the palace, followed by a few officers. A proclamation, placarded on all the walls of the city and at every corner of the streets, declared that there was no truth in the rumors spread by a few malicious persons, and that the army had never been more devoted or faithful. Upon this there was a universal panic; stocks fell fifty per cent. in half an hour, and did not rise again till unofficial news arrived that the king had been well received at head-quarters.

•

IX.

HEROIC REMEDIES FOR GREAT EVILS.

THE news was false; the prince had been received with great coldness. It was his own fault. Sad, despondent, and abstracted, Charming had neither found a jest for the soldiers nor a word of trust for the officers. He entered the general's tent and fell into a chair. Tonto was little less disheartened.

"Sire," said Bayonet, "permit me to speak to you with the frankness of a soldier and the freedom of an old friend. The army is murmuring and hesitating; we must secure it, or all is lost. The enemy is in sight; we must attack him. Five minutes sometimes decide the fate of empires; it is so with us now. Do not wait till it is too late."

"Very well," said the king. "To horse! in an instant I will be with you."

Left alone with Tonto and Rachimburg, the king exclaimed, in despair, "My good friends, quit a master who can do no more for you. I shall not dispute my wretched life with my enemies. Betrayed in friendship and treacherously assassinated, I recognize in my misfortune the hand of an avenging God. It is in punishment for my crime. I killed the queen in my stupid vengeance; the hour has come to expiate my fault, and I am ready."

"Sire," said Tonto, trying to smile, "shake off these sad

thoughts. If the queen were here she would tell you to defend yourself. Believe me," he added, twisting his budding mustache, "I am acquainted with women! Were they dead, they would still love to avenge themselves. Besides, you did not kill the queen; and perhaps she is not so dead as you imagine."

"What do you say?" exclaimed the king; "you are losing your reason."

"I say that there are women who die expressly to enrage their husbands; why should there not be those that would rise from the dead to enrage them still more? Leave the dead, and think of the living who love you. You are a king; fight like a king, and, if necessary, fall like a king."

"Sire," said Bayonet, entering, sword in hand, "time presses."

"General, to horse!" cried Tonto; "let us go."

Bayonet quitted the room to give the needful orders. When he was gone, Charming looked at Tonto and said, "No, I will not go. I do not understand my feelings; I abhor myself. I am not afraid of death; I am going to kill myself; nevertheless, I will not fight."

"Sire," said Tonto, "in Heaven's name, summon up your courage. To horse! Great God!" he exclaimed, wringing his hands, "the prince will not listen to me; we are lost. Come!" said he, taking hold of Charming's cloak; "up, sire; to horse, unhappy prince! Save your kingdom—save your people—save all that love you. Coward! look at me; I am nothing but a child, yet I am about to die for you. Fight! do not disgrace yourself. If you do not rise I will insult you— I, your servant. You are a coward; do you hear? a coward!"

And behold, the insolent page boxed the king's ears.

"S'death!" cried Charming, drawing his sword. "Before

dying I will have the pleasure of punishing one subject, at least."

But the page had left the tent. With one bound he sprang into the saddle and galloped toward the enemy, sword in hand, crying, " The king! my friends—the king! Sound the trumpets! Forward!"

Charming, mad with anger, spurred his horse in pursuit of the page : like a bull at the sight of a red flag, he rushed forward, head downward, caring neither for death nor danger. Bayonet rushed after the king, and the army after the general. It was the finest cavalry charge ever known in history.

At the noise of the squadrons, which shook the ground like thunder, the enemy, surprised, scarcely had time to form in line of battle. One man, however, had recognized the king— the infamous Wieduwillst. Charming was alone ; wholly absorbed in his vengeance, he saw nothing but the page whom he was pursuing. The traitor threw himself on the prince, sword in hand, and would have slain him at one stroke had not Tonto, plunging his spurs into the flanks of his horse, made the animal rear and fall on Wieduwillst. The page received the blow intended for his master. He threw up his arms and fell with a loud cry ; but his fall, at least, was avenged. The king thrust his sword into the throat of the treacherous physician, and drew it forth, dripping with blood, not without pleasure. Man is decidedly the king of wild beasts.

The traitor's death decided the fate of the day. The royal army, electrified by the heroism of its leader, soon dispersed the straggling battalions. The rebels, having nothing more to hope, sued for pardon, and their prayer was granted by the happy and clement king.

An hour after quitting the camp where he had wished to die, Charming returned in triumph, bringing with him conquerors and conquered, all blended in the same ranks, the former loudly protesting their loyalty, the latter overpowering them with their enthusiasm. Nothing sharpens devotion so much as a little treason.

X.

IN WHICH WE SEE THAT IT IS WRONG TO JUDGE ACCORDING TO APPEARANCES, AND THAT TONTO WAS NOT TONTO.

THE king entered his tent to rest a moment, when the sight of Rachimburg reminded him of Tonto.

"Is the page dead?" he asked.

"No, sire," answered Rachimburg; "unfortunately for him, he is still living; he is hopeless. I ordered him carried to his aunt's, the Countess de Castro's, close by here."

"Is he the countess's nephew?" said the king. "I was never told of it."

"Your majesty has forgotten it," replied Rachimburg, quietly. "The poor child is fatally wounded in the shoulder; he can not recover. It would give him great happiness could he see your majesty before he dies."

"Very well," returned the king; "lead me to him."

On his arrival at the castle Charming was met by the countess, who conducted him to a darkened room. The page was stretched, pale and bleeding, on a couch; nevertheless, he had strength to raise his head and welcome the king.

"What a miracle!" exclaimed Charming. "This is the strangest wound that I ever saw in my life: one side of Tonto's mustache is gone!"

"Sire," said the countess, "the blade of the sword probably swept off one side. Nothing is so capricious as sword wounds, as every one knows."

"How strange!" cried the king. "On one side it is Tonto,

my page, my insolent subject, and on the other it is—no, I am not mistaken—it is you, my good angel and my savior; it is you, my poor Pazza!"

He fell on his knees and seized her hand, which lay on the coverlet.

"Sire," said Pazza, "my days are numbered, but before dying—"

"No, no, Pazza, you shall not die," cried the king, in tears.

"Before dying," she added, casting down her eyes, "I hope that your majesty will forgive me the box on the ear which I gave you this morning in indiscreet zeal—"

"Enough," said the king; "I forgive you. After all, a throne and honor were well worth—what I received."

"Alas!" said Pazza, "that is not all."

"What!" exclaimed Charming, "is there any thing more!"

"Oh, sire, what have you done?" cried the countess; "my child is dying!"

"My Pazza, you must not die!" exclaimed the king. "Speak, and be sure that I forgive in advance all you have done. Alas! it is I that have need of forgiveness."

"Sire, the little doctor who took the liberty of boxing your majesty's ears—"

"Was it you that sent him?" asked Charming, with a frown.

"No, sire, I myself was he. Ah! what would I not have done to save my king! It was I who, to save your majesty from the traitorous knaves that surrounded you, took the liberty of boxing your ears—"

"Enough," said Charming; "I forgive you, though the lesson was a harsh one."

"Alas! this is not all," said Pazza.

"What, more !" cried the king, rising.

"Oh, aunt, I am dying !" exclaimed Pazza. By dint of care, however, she was restored to life ; and, turning her languishing eyes toward the king, "Sire," said she, "the gipsy girl at the masked ball, who dared to box your ears—"

"Was yourself, Pazza?" said Charming. "Oh, I forgive you for that ; I well deserved it. How could I doubt you, who are sincerity itself ! But, now I think of it, do you remember the rash vow that you made on the night of our marriage? You have kept your promise, it is for me to keep mine. Pazza, make haste to recover, and return to the castle from which happiness fled with you."

"I have a last favor to ask of your majesty," said Pazza. "Rachimburg was the witness this morning of a scene for which I blush, and of which all must remain ignorant. I commend this faithful servant to your goodness."

"Rachimburg," said the king, "take this purse, and keep the secret under penalty of your head."

"That makes the fourth," whispered Rachimburg to himself; "my fortune is made."

In a few moments Pazza was asleep. "Do you think that she will recover?" asked Charming, anxiously, of the countess.

"Bah!" said the old lady. "No matter how ill a woman may be, happiness will bring her back from the brink of the grave. Kiss the queen, my nephew; it will do her more good than all the doctors in the world."

Charming stooped and kissed the sleeping Pazza. An angelic smile stole over her features, at the sight of which he wept like a child.

XI.

A WIFE SHOULD OBEY HER HUSBAND.

THE countess was right (women are always right—past sixty). A fortnight of happiness set Pazza on her feet again, and enabled her to make a triumphant entry into the city with the king, her husband. Her paleness, and her wounded arm, which she carried in a sling, added to her grace and beauty. Charming had eyes for no one but the queen, and the people's looks followed the king's.

They were more than an hour in reaching the castle. The magistrates had erected not less than three triumphal arches, frowning fortresses, defended each by thirty-six deputations and thirty-six speeches. The first arch, made of trellis-work, and adorned with leaves and flowers, bore the inscription,

TO THE MOST TENDER AND FAITHFUL OF HUSBANDS.

This was intrusted to the keeping of five or six thousand young girls, dressed in white, with pink ribbons, representing the spring of the year, the hope of the future, welcoming Glory and Beauty.

The second arch, more solidly built, was a frame covered with tapestry, surmounted by Justice, with her eyes bandaged and her scales in her hand.

On the pedestal of the statue was written,

TO THE FATHER OF HIS PEOPLE,
THE BEST AND WISEST OF PRINCES.

A host of priests, statesmen, and magistrates, in robes of all colors, represented Religion, Wisdom, and Virtue ; at least so said these venerable and discreet personages, who are never in error.

Last came an immense arch, a true military trophy, bearing as its motto,

TO THE BOLDEST AND MOST VALIANT OF KINGS.

Here the army awaited its general, and the queen was saluted by the majestic voice of a hundred cannon and two hundred drums—a voice before which all human eloquence falters, and which always has the last word.

I spare you a description of the dinner, which was interminable, and of sixty more speeches from the court gazette, where they had already done service two or three times, and wherein they were again deposited for the use of future generations. There is nothing so monotonous as happiness, and we must be indulgent to those who sing its praises officially. In such cases, the ablest is he who says the least.

The long evening, during which the king had lavished his most gracious smiles on those whom he despised at the bottom of his heart, was at length at an end, and Charming led Pazza, no longer to a dungeon, but to a magnificent apartment, where a new surprise awaited her. At the bottom of the room was an illuminated transparency, on which were written lines so bad that a king alone could have been the author of them. These lines, which were not published in the official gazette, have been handed down to us by one of those indiscreet persons who suffer no follies of the past to be lost. Such persons are the rag-pickers of history.

> " Ye indolent dunces, who rust in your sloth,
>   Too lazy or willful to learn ;
> Ye courtiers, who crowd round the king, nothing loth
>   By base flattery his favor to earn ;
> Ye doctors, who laugh at us cowards, and sell
>   Long words and wise oracles dear—
> Beware lest some night a mischievous sprite
>   Should give you a box on the ear.

> " And you, ye proud husbands, puffed up with conceit,
>   Who deem yourselves statesmen so wise
> That the whole world admiringly bows at your feet—
>   Who truth, love, and goodness despise—
> Beware lest some day your less frivolous wives,
>   Derided by those they held dear,
> Should start from your side, aroused by just pride,
>   And give you a box on the ear."

"What means this enigma, sire ?" asked Pazza.

"It means that I do myself justice," answered the king. "I am nothing except through you, dear Pazza ; all that I know and all that I think I owe to you. Without you I am nothing but a soulless body, fit only for follies."

"Pardon me if I contradict your majesty," said Pazza.

"Oh," returned the king, "I affect no false modesty ; I know very well that I have the clearest head of any in my council ; my ministers themselves are forced to acknowledge it, for they are always of my opinion ; but with all this there is more wisdom in your little finger than in all my royal brain. My resolution, therefore, is fixed. Let my court and people celebrate my wisdom, my goodness, and even my valor ; it is all very well, and I accept the homage. You alone have the right to laugh at it, and you will not betray me. But from this day I abandon my power to you. The king, my dear Pazza, will be only the chief of your subjects, the faithful minister of your will. You shall write the piece and I will play it ; the applause will be mine, according to custom, and I will give it back to you by force of love."

"Do not talk in this way, my dear," said Pazza.

"I know what I am saying," returned the king, warmly. "I wish you to rule ; I mean that in my empire, as in my house, nothing shall be done except by your command ; I am the master and the king ; I desire and order it."

"Sire," said Pazza, "I am your wife and servant ; it is my duty to obey."

After this, says the chronicle, they lived happily to a good old age, beloved by all their subjects ; and the people of the kingdom of Wild Oats still talk of the good old days of Prince Charming and the Princess Pazza.

ABDALLAH;

OR, THE FOUR-LEAVED CLOVER.

AN ARABIAN TALE.

I.

THE JOY OF THE HOUSE.

At Djiddah the rich, on the shores of the Red Sea, there once lived an Egyptian merchant by the name of Hadji Mansour. It was said that he had formerly been a slave of the great Ali Bey, and had served by turns, and sometimes even at the same time, the French and the Turks, the Mamelukes and Mehemet Ali, in the wars of Egypt. During the struggle each party relied on him for provisions, arms, and camels, yet after the battle he always complained of having ruined himself for the victor. It is true that at that time no one showed more zeal, and no one obtained more cheaply the spoils of the vanquished. In this honest vocation the obliging Mansour had gained great wealth, though not without some anxieties. He had been denounced by the envious as a spy, he had been bastinadoed by fanatics as a traitor, twice even he would have been hung had it not been for the charity of a pacha, who had consented, for the trifling sum of a million of piastres, to acknowledge such shining innocence. Mansour had too lofty a soul to be dismayed by these political risks ; and if he retired, when peace was made, to Djiddah, it was only because lawful commerce was thenceforth the only road that led to fortune.

In this new kind of life Mansour was neither less prudent nor less successful.   It was a common report that his house was paved with gold' and precious stones.   Little love was bestowed on the Egyptian, who was a stranger in Arabia, and who passed for one of the harshest of creditors ; but at Djiddah men dared not openly show contempt for a man who measured gold by the bushel, and as soon as Mansour appeared in the bazar, all ran to vie for the honor of holding his stirrup and kissing his hand.   The merchant received all this homage with the modesty of a man who knows the prerogatives of wealth : thirty years of avarice and cunning had brought all honest men to his feet.

One thing alone was lacking to this favorite of fortune, and disturbed his happiness : he had no children.   When he passed before the shop of a poor tradesman and saw the father surrounded by young sons, the hope and pride of the house, he sighed with regret and envy, and on his return he shut himself up in his warehouse, forgot his pipe, and, instead of telling his beads or reciting the verses of the Koran, slowly stroked his white beard, reflecting with terror in his heart that old age was approaching, and that he should leave none of his flesh and blood behind him to carry on the business after he was gone.   His only heir was the pacha, who might grow tired of waiting, in which case what would hinder him from dispatching a solitary foreigner, and laying violent hands on these dearly-bought treasures?

These thoughts and fears poisoned the life of the Egyptian. What was his joy, therefore, when one of his wives, an Abyssinian woman, announced to him that he would soon be a father !   At this news the good man wellnigh lost his reason. Twice as avaricious and covetous since he had begun to amass treasures for his child, he shut himself up to weigh and count his gold, unfolded his rich stuffs, and dug up his diamonds, pearls, and rubies ; then talked to these lifeless things as if they could understand him, and told them of the new master who would watch over and love them in turn.   When he went into the city he insisted on talking to all he met of his son, for it was a son that God owed his faithful servant, and was greatly astonished to see every one attending to his business as usual, when all the inhabitants of Djiddah should have had but one thought, namely, that God, in his justice, was about to bless the house of the shrewd and fortunate Mansour.

The Egyptian was not disappointed in his expectations ; and, that nothing might be wanting to his happiness, a son was born to him at the most favorable hour of the most auspicious month of the year.   When, on the eighth day, he was permitted to see this long-wished-for child, he tremblingly approached the palm-tree cradle, lined with cotton, where the heir of the Mansours was sleeping on a silken handkerchief embroidered with gold, and, gently raising the veil that covered it, perceived a robust infant, almost as black as his mother, already gathering the cotton about him with his tiny hands. At this sight Mansour stood dumb with admiration ; large tears trickled down his cheeks ; then, controlling his feelings with an effort, he took the babe in his arms, and, approaching his lips to its ear, "God is great," he murmured ; "there is no God but God, and Mohammed is his prophet."   More tranquil after this prayer, he gazed lovingly at his son.   "Oh, gift of God," cried he, "thou art but a week old, but, to see thy strength and grace, one would take thee for a year at least. Thy face shines like the full moon !   Say," said he, turning to the mother, "what have you named him ?"

"If God had afflicted me with a daughter," answered the Ethiopian, "I should have chosen a name for her ; but since I have had the glory of bringing a man-child into the world, to you belongs that honor.   Beware, however, of too ambitious a name, which might arouse the jealousy of the evil eye."

Mansour was reflecting, when suddenly he heard a noise in the street.   A Persian dervish was driving before him an ass laden with provisions, while a crowd of children was following the heretic, and showering him with abuse and blows. The dervish pressed forward like a man who neither feared nor sought martyrdom, stopping now and then to rail at his enemies.   "Accursed be thou, oh Omar!"* cried he, striking the ass, "and accursed be all who resemble thee!"   "Behold a new proof of my happiness!" cried Mansour.   "My child shall be called Omar; such a name will ward off the evil eye, and preserve him from all witchcraft."

As he was replacing the babe in the cradle, a Bedouin woman entered the room with an infant in her arms.   She was tall and well formed; her face was unveiled, as is the custom in the desert; and her mien was so graceful and dignified that, poorly clad as she was, she might have been taken for a sultana.

"Welcome, Halima," said Mansour.   "I have not forgotten that Yusuf, your husband, fell in my service while defending my last caravan.   The moment has come to prove that I am not ungrateful.   You know what I expect of you.   If I can not make my son a sherif or give him the green turban, I can at least cause him to be brought up like the son of a sherif, under a tent, among the noble Beni Amurs.   Admitted into your family, and nurtured with your son, my beloved Omar will learn a purer speech than mine, and will find friends among your kindred who will protect him in after years.   On my side, I shall fittingly recognize and reward your devotion. Let the friendship of our children begin from this day; from this day let them sleep in the same cradle.   To-morrow you

* *Homar*, or *Omar*, in Arabic, signifies an ass.

shall carry them away, that they may grow up together in your tribe. Omar shall be your son as Abdallah shall be mine ; may Fortune smile on both !"

" May God be their refuge against Satan, the accursed !" answered Halima, bowing her head. "We are in God's hands ; to Him we must return."

Mansour looked at her, smiling. He was a freethinker, and had little faith in God, although his name was constantly on his lips. He had lived too long, and mixed too much with men, to believe that God meddles much with the affairs of this world ; on the other hand, he had a strong belief in the devil, of whom he stood in great fear. The only action in his whole life for which he reproached himself was that of having thrown seven stones at the great devil of Jamrat at the time of his pilgrimage to Mecca, and he still feared the rancor of Satan whom he had stoned. Doubtless he was proud of having cheaply earned the noble title of hadji,* which rendered him worthy of respect in the eyes of his customers ; it was with the purest devotion that he spoke of the Caaba,† that gem of Paradise placed by Father Abraham in the holy city of Mecca, but at heart he was not easy respecting the consequences of his imprudence, and would even have surrendered the name of hadji to have been sure of the devil's forgiveness for his rashness.

II.

THE HOROSCOPE.

THE same evening, just as the moon was rising, the wise Mansour entered the room where the two children were sleeping peacefully in each other's arms, followed by a ragged der-

* Hadji, or saint, is the name given to those who have made the pilgrimage to Mecca.
† The holy house, or principal temple of Mecca.

vish, with a dirty, uncombed beard, bearing a strong resemblance to the reviled heretic of the morning. He was one of those shameless beggars who seek the fortunes of others in the stars without ever finding their own therein, and who, always pursued and hooted at, and always employed, will last as long as the malice of Satan, or the avarice and credulity of men. Halima was unwilling to leave the children with this suspicious personage, but Mansour commanded it, and she was forced to obey. Scarcely had she quitted the room when the Egyptian led the dervish to the cradle, and ordered him to draw his son's horoscope.

After attentively gazing at the child, the astrologer mounted the house-top and observed the stars ; then, taking a coal, he traced a large circle, divided into several compartments, in which he placed the planets, and at length declared that the heavens were not inauspicious. If Mars and Venus were indifferent, Mercury, on the contrary, appeared under a better aspect. This was all that he could tell for the two sequins that Mansour had given him.

The merchant led the diviner back to the chamber, and, showing him two large doubloons, "Is there no means," said he, "of knowing more? Have the stars already revealed all their secrets?"

"Art is infinite," answered the dervish, pouncing on the gold ; "I can also tell you under the influence of what sign the child is destined to live."

Drawing from his girdle a cabalistic tablet and a bronze pen, the astrologer wrote the names of the child and the mother, placing the letters in a line ; he then calculated the numerical value of the letters, and, looking at Mansour with sparkling eyes, "Happy father," he said, "your son is born under the sign of the Balance ; if he lives, he may expect every thing from fortune."

"What, if he lives!" cried Mansour. "What is it that you read on that accursed tablet? Does any danger threaten my son?"

"Yes," replied the dervish, "a danger which I can not define. His best friend will be his worst enemy."

"Ha! what was I about to do?" said the Egyptian. "Perchance this Bedouin child, whom I have placed in my son's cradle, will one day be his murderer? If I thought so, I would strangle him on the spot."

"Beware of it," returned the diviner. "If your son's life is bound up with that of this child, you would only kill them both at one blow. There is no proof that this Bedouin, destined to dwell among the tents, will one day be the best friend of the richest merchant of Djiddah. Besides, what refuge is there against destiny? Can you change what is traced by the pen of the angels? What is written is written."

"Doubtless," said the merchant; "but God—His name be exalted!—has said, in the Book of Books, 'Cast not yourselves down with your own hands into perdition.'"

"The day of death," returned the dervish, gravely, "is one of the five mysteries, the key of which God holds in his own hands. Do you remember the story of the man who was with Solomon one day when Azrael passed by the king in a visible shape? Frightened by the look cast on him by the terrible stranger, he asked who he was; and upon Solomon's acquainting him that it was the angel of death, 'He seems to want me,' said he; 'wherefore order the wind to carry me hence to India.' Which being accordingly done, the angel said to Solomon, 'I looked so earnestly at this man out of wonder, because I was commanded to take his soul in India, and found him with thee in Palestine.'

> "No man can flee from death. Do as he will,
> Falls soon or late the arm e'er raised to strike;
> The sage is he who looks it in the face,
> Nor fears nor braves the doom decreed by Fate."

With these words the astrologer bowed to take leave of Mansour, who clutched his robe.

"Have you any thing more to ask me?" said the dervish, looking attentively at the Egyptian.

"Yes," replied the merchant; "but I dare not give utterance to my thoughts. Yet you seem to me a friend, and you will pardon a father's weakness where his son's interest is concerned. A wise man like you, who reads the stars, must have carried your curiosity to great lengths. It is said that there are men who, by dint of science, have discovered the great name of God—that name which has been revealed only to the apostles and the Prophet (his name be blessed!)—that name which suffices to raise the dead and kill the living—that name which causes the world to tremble, and compels the infernal powers and Eblis* himself to obey it like a slave. Do you perchance know one of these learned men, and do you think that he would refuse to oblige a man who had not the reputation of being ungrateful?"

"You are prudence itself," returned the astrologer, in a low voice, approaching Mansour; "you may be trusted; yet words are naught but wind, and the fairest promises like dreams that take flight with the morning."

For his sole reply Mansour thrust his right arm into the dervish's long sleeve, and placed one finger in his hand.

"A purse!"† exclaimed the astrologer, in a disdainful tone; "it is the price of a camel. What madman would evoke Satan at the risk of his own life for such a trifle?"

The Egyptian stretched out a second finger, looking at the dervish, whose face wore an air of indifference; then, after a moment's silence, he heaved a deep sigh and placed a third finger in the dervish's hand.

* One of the names of Satan among the Arabs.
† A purse is about twenty-five dollars.

"Three purses!" said the astrologer; "it is the cost of an infidel slave. The soul of a Mussulman can not be bought at such a price. Let us part, Mansour, and forget the imprudent words you have spoken."

"Do not abandon me!" cried the merchant, grasping the dervish's arm with his whole hand. "Five purses are a large sum, and all that I can give. If necessary, I add to it the offer of my soul; our common peril will answer to you for my discretion."

"Give me the five purses, then," returned the magician, "and my friendship shall do the rest. I own my weakness; I have been unable to see you without being drawn to you: may this yielding not cost me too dear!"

Mansour brought the money. The dervish weighed it several times, and placed it in his girdle with the tranquillity of a resolute heart; then, taking the lamp, he walked three times round the cradle, murmuring strange words, waving the light before the child's face, and prostrating himself again and again at the four corners of the room, followed by Mansour, who trembled with fear and anxiety.

After all these ceremonies, which appeared endless to the merchant, the magician placed the lamp on a bench along the wall, and, taking a little box from his inexhaustible girdle, poured a black powder upon the burning wick. A thick smoke instantly filled the whole room, amid which Mansour fancied that he saw the infernal figure and flaming eyes of an Afrite.* The dervish seized him by the arm, and both threw themselves on the carpet, their faces buried in their hands.

"Speak," said the dervish, in a breathless voice, "speak, but do not lift your head as you value your life. Make three wishes: Eblis is here, and will grant your prayer."

"I wish that my son may be rich all his life," murmured Mansour.

* One of the infernal genii.

"So be it!" returned a strange voice, which seemed to come from the other end of the room, though Mansour had seen the apparition before him.

"I wish that my son may always have good health," continued the Egyptian, "for, without health, of what use is fortune?"

"So be it!" returned the voice.

There was a moment's silence. Mansour hesitated as to his third wish. "Shall I wish for wit?" thought he. "No, he is my son, and he will inherit his father's cunning." The dervish's prediction suddenly recurred to his memory. "Threatened by his best friend," thought he, "there is but one means of safety for him, namely, to love no one, and to think of himself alone. Besides, anxiety for others spoils our own life, and those we oblige are always ungrateful. I wish that my son may love no one but himself," said he, at length.

K

"So be it!" returned the voice, with a terrible cry, which frightened the Egyptian so much that he remained motionless till the dervish pulled the skirt of his robe and commanded him to rise. At the same moment a jet of flame shot from the lamp, and the whole room seemed in a blaze. Mansour, terrified at his own rashness, rushed to the door to assure himself that he was still alive and that nothing had changed in the house.

While the dervish was putting on his cloak and sandals like a man whom habit hardens against fear, a woman rushed to the cradle of the infants. It was Halima, who had remained near the room during the enchantment, and whose terror had been heightened by Mansour's sudden departure. Her first care was to wet her finger with her lips and pass it over the forehead of the children, repeating a formula to ward off the evil eye. The serenity of the dervish reassured her; she blamed herself for having suspected this pious personage of magic, who wore on his face the blissful tranquillity of sanctity, and, respectfully approaching him, she kissed the hem of his robe. "Holy man," said she, "my son is an orphan, and I am a poor woman; I can offer you nothing but gratitude, but—"

"Well, well," exclaimed the astrologer, "I know in advance what you would ask of me—that your son should be rich, is it not? For this, what need have you of my aid? Make him a merchant, and let him steal like old Mansour; make him a bashaw, and let him pillage his brethren; make him a dervish, and let him flatter and lie: all the vices lead to fortune when they are joined with the vilest of all—avarice. This is the secret of life. Adieu."

"This is not what I wish," said the astonished Halima; "you do wrong to deride me in this way. My son will be an honest man, like his father; and what I wish is that he may be happy here on earth."

"Virtuous and happy!" cried the dervish, with a sardonic laugh; "and you address yourself to me! My good woman, what you want is the four-leaved clover, which none has seen since Adam. Let your son seek it; if he finds it, be sure that he will lack for nothing."

"What is the four-leaved clover?" cried the anxious mother; but the magician had disappeared, never more to return. Man or demon, none has since beheld him. Halima, full of emotion, bent over the cradle and gazed at her son, who seemed to smile on her in his sleep. "Rest in peace," said she, "and rely on my love. I know not what this talisman is of which the dervish speaks, but, child of my soul! we will seek it together, and something tells me that you will find it. Satan is cunning and man is weak, but God rules the heart of his faithful and does what he will."

III.

THE EDUCATION.

In choosing the Bedouin woman to whom to intrust Omar, Mansour had given a new proof of his usual prudence. From the first day Halima showed her nursling all a mother's affection, and tended him more carefully than her own offspring. When she was forced to leave her tent, the cherished child that she carried on her shoulder was always Et Tagir, or the little merchant, as Omar was called among the Beni Amurs. Yet what a difference was there between the two brothers! Tall, slender, supple, and agile, with his clear eyes and brilliant complexion, Abdallah would have filled any father's heart with pride; while the son of Mansour, with his swarthy skin, thick neck, and round paunch, was only an Egyptian astray in the desert. What mattered it to the Bedouin woman? Had she not nourished them both with the same milk? Who knows even whether, like a true mother, she had not a secret weakness for the child which had the most need of her love?

As he grew, Abdallah soon showed all the nobleness of his race. On seeing him with the Egyptian, one would have said that he already felt himself the master of the tent, and was proud of exercising the rites of hospitality. Although but six months older than Omar, he made himself his brother's guardian and protector, and his greatest pleasure was to amuse, serve, and defend him. In all the games and feasts, he insisted on giving the little merchant the best place ; and whenever a quarrel arose, it was always he, and he alone, that fought, adroit, strong, and hardy, like a son of the desert.

Omar willingly remained in the background, as if he already understood the advantage to be derived from an uncalculating friendship. As indolent as a dweller in cities, he seldom quitted the tent. The Bedouin ran between the legs of the mares, wrestled with the colts, and climbed the camels without making them kneel ; the Egyptian, his legs crossed on a mat, passed the greater part of the day in sleeping, and felt naught but disdain for the noisy exploits which made the joy of Abdallah. When he mixed with other children, it was only to play merchant with them. The son of Mansour had singular skill in bartering a date for a citron, a citron for an orange, and an orange for a piece of coral or some other toy. At ten years of age, Omar had already found that the best use of a rosary was to aid in counting. He was not, however, ungrateful ; he loved his brother after his fashion. He showered innumerable caresses on Abdallah, who seldom returned home without bringing bananas, pomegranates, apricots, or some other fruit that had been given him by the women of the neighborhood, who were charmed with his grace and sprightliness. By dint of tenderness, Omar always secured what he wished ; but he was not better pleased with the success of his cunning than was his brother in letting himself be despoiled by the one he loved. Each of us is born with his destiny clinging about his neck like a heavy collar, and hurrying him onward ; a fox nurtured by a lioness will always be a fox, and a merchant's son will never make a Bedouin.

At the age of ten, thanks to Halima, Abdallah's education was finished ; he knew all that a Beni Amur needed to know. The son of Yusuf could recite the genealogy of his family and tribe ; he knew the pedigree, name, surname, coat, and brand of all the horses ; he could read in the stars the hour of the night, and the shadows told him the time of the day. No one knew better how to make the camels kneel ; no one chanted to them in a more melodious voice those sweet songs which shorten their way and make them quicken their pace, despite fatigue and heat. Already even he handled the gun and brandished the lance and sabre as if he had been in half a score of caravans. Halima contemplated his youthful courage with tears of joy, happy to see. that the child whom she had brought into the world would some day be the honor of his people and the delight of his tribe.

Halima was a true Mussulman ; she knew that wisdom, strength, and consolation are in God alone. The children were scarcely seven years old when she had already taught them to recite the five prayers and make the ablutions. In the morning, as soon as a faint light illumined the east ; at noon, when the sun turned ; in the afternoon, when the shadows began to lengthen ; at even, when the sun set in the horizon ; and, lastly, at night, when darkness covered the earth,' Omar and Abdallah stretched the carpet of prayer upon the ground, and, turning toward Mecca, repeated the holy words which comprise all religion, "There is no god but God, and Mohammed is his prophet." The prayer ended, Halima loved to repeat to the children the precepts of Ayesha—precepts which she made the rule of her life. "Sons of my soul!" she would say to them, "listen to what Ayesha, the beloved spouse of the Prophet, the peerless virgin, and the mother of the faithful, replied to a Mussulman who asked her counsel. Remember these holy maxims; they are the legacy of the Prophet himself, and the pearl of truth.

"Acknowledge that there is but one God alone; remain steadfast in the faith; instruct yourself; bridle your tongue; repress your wrath; forbear to do evil; associate with the good; screen the faults of your neighbor; relieve the poor by your alms; and expect your reward in eternity."

The two children were thus brought up, surrounded with the same love, and a love so tender and equal that the two brothers never suspected that they were not of the same blood. One day, however, an old man entered the tent, armed with a tablet of wood, painted white, on which elegant characters were traced in black. The sheik enjoyed great renown in the tribe; it was said that he had formerly studied at Cairo in El Azar, that splendid mosque, the fountain of light, which is the joy of the faithful and the despair of infidels. He was so learned that he could read the Koran, and copy with a reed the ninety-nine names of God, and the Fát-háh.* To the great astonishment of the Bedouin, the old man, after talking in a low tone to Halima, who put a purse in his hand, turned his sole attention to the son of Mansour, caressed him with paternal tenderness, seated him by his side, put the tablet in his hands, and, after teaching him how to sway the head and body to aid the memory, made him chant the whole alphabet after him. Omar took so lively an interest in his lesson that on the very first day he learned the numerical value of all the letters. The sheik embraced him anew, promising him that, if he went on in this way, he would soon be more

* The first chapter of the Koran, and the usual prayer of the Mussulmen.

learned than his master, and quitted the tent without even looking at Abdallah.

The poor boy's heart swelled at the sight of this lesson of his brother's, by which he would have gladly profited. He was spared a second trial. The next morning he was sent to the fields to tend his mother's sheep. He was not alone ; he had been placed in the care of a maternal uncle, a one-eyed and crippled old shepherd, but a man of good counsel. Hafiz, for this was the name of Halima's brother, was a brave soldier and a pious Mussulman, who had seen much and suffered much. The companion of Yusuf, Abdallah's father, and wounded by his side, he was the last prop of an almost extinct family, and, alone and childless as he was, he loved his nephew as his own son.

It was he that had opposed the plan of making Abdallah a scholar. "Would you know more than the Prophet, whom may God protect and bless !" said he to the young Bedouin. "What would you read—the Koran? But is it on vile rags or your own heart that its sacred words should be engraved? Strange books — what is the use? Is not every thing contained in the Koran? Is it not for rash spirits who seek the truth elsewhere that it is written, 'The likeness of those who take other patrons besides God is as the likeness of the spider, which maketh herself a house? but the weakest of all houses, surely, is the house of the spider, if they knew this.' Those whose minds are swallowed up in books are like asses laden with foreign wealth, which serves only to weigh them down. Man was not born to amass the thoughts of others, but to act for himself. Go forward, my son, with an upright heart and in the fear of the Lord. At the age of strength God will give thee wisdom and knowledge as to the son of Jacob. It is thus that he rewards the just, for he himself has said it."

These words kindled Abdallah's heart. Every day, when the noontide heat confined them within the tent, Hafiz recited to the son of Yusuf a few verses of the holy book, and made him repeat them after him in turn. In this way, by degrees, he taught him the whole Koran, beginning, after the *Fät-häh*, with the short chapters *On Men*, *The Daybreak*, and *The Unity of God*, and ending with the long and beautiful teachings contained in the chapters *On Women*, *The Family of Imran*, and *The Cow*. The child was like the sands of the desert, which drink up the rain-drops without losing a single one; he never wearied of chanting this rhythmic prose, as superior to poetry as the Word of God is to that of men. Day and night he repeated these precepts in which eloquence and wisdom are strung together like pearls in a necklace. Whenever a good Mussulman wished to give a feast to his comrades or to pay honors to the tomb of a friend, the lame shepherd and his disciple were called upon to recite the whole Koran or one of its thirty sections. Seated on the ground around the master and pupil, the Beni Amurs greedily drank in the divine words. "God is great!" they exclaimed. "Gabriel himself was not more beautiful than this young man when he deposited the eternal revelation in the heart of the Prophet."

Hafiz not only taught his nephew the text of the Koran, but also repeated to him the words of the Prophet which have been handed down to us by his friends. He taught him the four great duties enjoined by God on all who would be saved —the five daily prayers, the giving of one fortieth in alms, the fast of Ramadan, and the pilgrimage to Mecca; and held up to his detestation the seven great sins—those sins which beget seven hundred others, and which destroy the soul—idolatry, that crime which God, according to his explicit declaration, never pardons; murder; the charge of adultery falsely brought against an honest woman; wrong done to orphans; usury;

flight in an expedition against the infidels, and disobedience to parents. "Oh, my son," he exclaimed, at the close of each lesson, "thou who, by the decree of God, hast been placed among the number of those who have received the Scriptures, daily repeat that divine promise which is our whole strength and comfort here below: 'Whoever obeyeth God and the apostle, they shall be with those unto whom God has been gracious, of the prophets, and the sincere, and the martyrs, and the righteous, and these are most excellent company. This is bounty from God, and from God nothing is hidden.'"

In order not to weary Abdallah, Hafiz often interspersed his teachings with the stories of some of those innumerable prophets to whose keeping God confided the truth while awaiting the coming of Mohammed. Sometimes it was Adam, our first father, to whom God in his goodness taught the name of every living thing on earth. By the command of the Lord, these creatures, born of fire, adored man, born of the dust of the earth. A single one refused, the ungrateful Eblis, urged by his pride to destruction. Unhappily, Adam and Eve suffered themselves to be tempted by the enemy, and ate of the forbidden fruit. To punish their disobedience, God drove them from Paradise. Adam was flung upon the island of Serendib, where his footprint may still be seen, and Eve fell at Djiddah, where she was doomed to live two centuries in solitude. God, however, at last took pity on the unhappy couple, and Gabriel again reunited them on Mount Arafat, near that miraculous spot where Abraham and Ishmael were to found the holy Caaba.

At another time the cripple would tell how God showed Abraham the kingdom of the heavens and the earth, that he might know true science. Reared in the faith of his fathers, the son of Azer worshipped the stars. When the night overshadowed him, he saw a star and cried, "This is my Lord!"

but when it set he said, "I like not gods which set."   And when he saw the moon rising he cried, "This is my Lord ;" but when he saw it set he said, "Verily, if my Lord direct me not, I shall become as one of the people who go astray." And when he saw the sun rising he said, "This is my Lord ; this is the greatest ;" but when he saw it set he said, "Oh, my people, verily I am clear of your idolatrous worship."   The son of Azer understood that the stars scattered through the heavens revealed a higher hand, as the footprints on the sand tell of the traveler that has gone before.

Like a true Mussulman, Abraham had no sooner found the true faith than he broke all the idols of his people except Baal, on whose neck he hung the axe with which he had demolished them.   When the furious Chaldeans asked who had treated their gods in such a manner, "It is Baal," said Abraham ; "ask him, and see what he will answer you."   "An idol can not speak," cried the Chaldeans ; and they said, "Thou art an unbeliever !"   But who can enlighten those who have eyes, yet see not!   They are blinded by the very light of truth.   Furious at having been discomfited by a child, Nimrod, the King of the Chaldeans, ordered Abraham to be thrown into a fiery furnace.   Vain cruelty ! the Lord Eternal holds the power of life and death.   By the command of God, the fire consumed none but the unbelievers.   For Abraham, the funeral pile turned to a verdant meadow, and the flames that surrounded him to a cool and refreshing breeze.   It is thus that the Lord lifts up the just and humbles the proud.

Who could exhaust the sacred stories which have been handed down to us by the Koran and tradition !   They are more numerous and more beautiful than the stars in a summer sky.   Hafiz told them as he had received them from his fathers, and Abdallah repeated them with the like ardor and faith. Sometimes it was of David, the blacksmith king, to whom God taught the art of fabricating coats of mail to protect the faithful; sometimes it was of Solomon, under whose dominion the Lord placed the winds, the birds, and the genii. Or it was of Balkis, the Queen of Sheba, when, seated on her throne of gold and silver, set with precious stones, she received Solomon's letter, brought her by a bird, kissed the seal, at which Satan trembled, and became a Mussulman at the voice of the wisest of kings. Or it was of the sleeping companions in the cavern, who awaited the reign of truth three hundred and nine years, with their faithful dog, El Rakim, crouched at their feet. Or it was of the sacred camel brought forth from the rock at the prayer of Saleh, to confound the unbelief of the Talmudites. When did God tire of working miracles to succor the faithful?

Of all these marvelous stories, to which the Bedouins never tired of listening, the one which Halima oftenest asked of her son was that of Job, that faithful servant who turned to God in the midst of his anguish. In vain his wife, weary of seeing him suffer, consented to worship Eblis to regain their lost happiness. Job refused assistance from this accursed hand. If he raised his body, eaten by worms, on the dunghill, it was to lift to the Lord that touching prayer which won pardon from God for the wretched sufferer: "Verily evil hath afflicted me, but thou art the most merciful of those who show mercy"—beautiful words, which one of the faithful alone could utter.

Hafiz was one of the faithful, but he was also a Bedouin, proud of his race—a soldier who loved the fray of battle. "Think, my son," he would often say to Abdallah, "think of the privileges which the Prophet has won for us, and which we must defend to the death. To render our life easy God has given us gardens, living springs of water, innumerable cattle, the dourah,* and the palm-tree; to render it glorious, he has given us a noble pedigree, a country that has never been conquered, and a liberty that no master has ever polluted. We are the kings of the desert. Our turbans are our diadems, our tents are our palaces, our sabres are our ramparts, and God's own word is our law. Your father fell like a martyr on the field of battle. Among your ancestors, for one who by chance has breathed his last under a tent, three have fallen in the desert, their lance in their hand. They point you the way; they understood the divine saying, 'Let them therefore fight for the religion of God who part with the present life for that which is to come; for whosoever fighteth for the religion of God, whether he be slain or be victorious, we will surely give him a great reward. The provision of this life is but small; but the future shall be better for him who feareth God.'"

Have you seen the war-horse pawing the earth and snuffing the wind at the sound of the trumpet? Such was Abdallah when Hafiz talked to him of battle; his heart throbbed, his eyes grew dim, and his face flushed. "Oh God!" he cried, "grant that it may soon be my time; permit me to crush the infidel, and make me worthy of the people from which I have sprung!"

The child of the desert was beautiful indeed in his long blue robe, confined at the waist by a leather thong passed half a score of times around his body. His thick brown hair shaded his face, and fell in curls upon his neck from under his hood. His eyes sparkled with a softer light than the planets that twinkle in the heavens, as, holding in his hand a shining lance, wound round with silver thread, he walked slowly, with the grace of a child and the dignity of a man, speaking

---

* The sorgho, the principal cereal of the East Indians and the Arabs, which they use like maize and rice.

only when necessary and never laughing.   When he returned from the pasture, carrying the young lambs in the skirt of his robe, while the sheep followed him bleating and rubbing their heads against his hand, the shepherds, his companions, stopped to see him pass, and he seemed like Joseph adored by the eleven stars.   And at evening, when he raised the stone from the common well with a strength above his age and watered the flocks, the women forgot to fill their pitchers, and cried, " He is as handsome as his father !" to which the men responded, " And he will also be as brave."

IV.

THE RECOGNITION.

Time had rolled onward since the day that Halima had carried the son of the wealthy Mansour to her tent.   Omar was fifteen years old, and was still unacquainted with the secret of his birth.   The rude jests of his companions had more than once made him feel that he was not a Beni Amur, and that the blood in his veins was not so pure as that of Abdallah ; but, although he was called Omar, the little merchant, no one in the tribe knew who was the Egyptian's father, and he himself believed that he was an orphan, adopted by Halima's goodness, and destined to live in the desert.

One evening, as the brothers were returning from the fields, they were surprised to see several richly-caparisoned camels at the door of the tent, together with a mule covered with a rich carpet and held by a negro dressed in white.

"Whose mule is this," said Omar, "and what has it brought ?"

" It is your father's," answered the slave, who easily recognized Mansour's son by his features ; "we have come for you from Djiddah."

"Who is my father ?" asked the Egyptian, greatly moved.

"Your father," returned the negro, "is the rich Mansour, the syndic of the Djiddah merchants, and the sultan of the sons of Egypt. There is not a bale of goods, great or small, that comes into the harbor or goes out of the three city gates that is not first offered to him for his disposal. At Yambo, Suez, Khartoom, and Cairo, your father's warehouses are kept by his numerous slaves; and so great is his fortune that his servants never consult him about any business involving less than a hundred thousand piastres."

"Oh, my father, where are you?" cried the young man, rushing into the tent. "Praised be God, who has given me a father so worthy of my love!" And he threw himself into Mansour's arms with an ardor that delighted the old merchant and called forth a sigh from Halima.

Early the next morning they set out for Djiddah, to the great sorrow of the Bedouin woman, who could not bear to separate from the child whom she alone had cherished for so many years. "Adieù, my son, and dearer than my son," said she, covering him with tears and caresses. Omar was more courageous; he quitted his mother with the joy of a captive who at once regains freedom and fortune. Abdallah accompanied his brother to the city by the wish of Mansour. To show the Bedouin how far the consideration attached to wealth in a city like Djiddah raised a merchant above the shepherds of the desert, and to make him feel that his mother and he should esteem themselves too happy in having loved and served Omar for fifteen years, was Mansour's fashion of paying his debt of gratitude. The rich leave their folly and vanity only beyond the tomb.

No sooner had they reached Djiddah than Omar broke forth into transports of joy. He was an exile returning to his native land. Every thing charmed him : the narrow streets, with their great stone houses ; the port, where the

ships were unloading casks of sugar, sacks of coffee, and bales
of cotton ; and the motley crowd that was thronging toward
the bazar. Turks, Syrians, Greeks, Arabs, Persians, East Indians, blacks of every shade ; Jews, pilgrims, dervishes, beggars ; Nile merchants mounted on beautifully-caparisoned
mules ; donkey-drivers leading women enveloped in great
black mantles, and looking like phantoms of which naught
was visible but the eyes ; camel-drivers shouting to the crowd
to open a passage ; Arnauts with an audacious and threatening air, proud of their Damascus weapons and flowing fusta-
nella ; peaceful smokers seated with crossed legs at the doors
of the coffee-houses ; slaves led to market—all this was to
Omar a Paradise more enchanting than any of which he had
ever dreamed. In such an abode, what could not be bought
and what could not be sold ? Had he not learned the price
of all manner of things from his father on the road ? Did he
not already know how to rate the integrity of a cadi, the scruples of a sheik, and even the conscience of a pacha ?

At the end of a narrow and gloomy alley stood the house
of Mansour. There was nothing about the building calculated to attract attention ; the ground floor was bare and unin-
viting, and furnished only with a few rush mats along the whitewashed walls ; but on ascending to the next story, which was
carefully closed, and furnished with blinds that defied both
the sun and curiosity, magnificent rooms met the eye, covered
with Turkey carpets, and surrounded with velvet divans embroidered with silver. The travelers were scarcely seated
when a chased silver salver was brought them, loaded with jel-
lied fruits. While one slave poured rose-water on Abdallah's
bronzed hands, and presented him a napkin fringed with gold,
another burned incense before old Mansour, who stroked his
beard and clothes to impregnate them with the fragrant smoke ;
coffee was then served in tiny porcelain cups, set in stands

of gold filigree-work, after which exquisite sherbets, prepared from the extract of violets and the juice of pomegranates expressed through the rind, were offered them. Lastly, three little negroes, dressed in scarlet and covered with bracelets and necklaces, lighted long jasmine pipes and presented one to each guest, then all three seated themselves on the ground, attentive and silent.

They smoked long without speaking. Mansour was enjoying the delight which he saw in his son and the admiration which he supposed in the Arab. But the Bedouin's face did not change ; amid all this luxury he was as grave and tranquil as if in the midst of his flocks. What are the luxuries of this world to him who expects the lasting rewards which God has in store for the faithful !

"Well, my son," said old Mansour at last, turning toward Abdallah, "are you content with your journey ?"

"Father," replied the young man, "I thank you for your hospitality. Your heart is even richer than your treasure."

"Well, well," returned the merchant ; "but what I want to know is what you think of Djiddah? Would you like to stay with us ?"

"No. The city is tainted ; the air is pestilential, the water impure. Then those idle dervishes, displaying to all eyes their impudence and their covetousness, and those slaves who stand there to deprive us of the use of our hands, and who spy out our passions to serve them ! Huzza for the desert ! Our terrible winds are sweeter to me than the hot, heavy air of this prison. Among the tents there are none but men. Each one rights himself, lance in hand. The dog that begs through cowardice is thrust out ; the haughty, who know not how to respect those better than themselves, are humbled."

"Your words are golden, my son," said Mansour, running his fingers through his long beard ; "a Wahabite could not be

more austere. I thought like you when I was a child and recited my nurse's lessons. Stay with us for a time ; become a
merchant ; when you see how fortune invests the vilest of men
with authority, youth, and virtue, how the powerful of the day,
the women, and even the saints fall down and worship the
metal which you despise, you will change your mind, and prefer even the unsavory odor of cities. It is beautiful to live
like the lark, free in space ; but sooner or later all are snared
like it. The douro is the king of the world, and the day
comes when the bravest, like the wisest, is the servant of the
richest."

"I know," returned Abdallah, proudly, "that nothing satis-
fies the sons of Adam ; the dust of the grave alone has power to fill their bellies ; but in the desert, at least, an ounce of
honor is worth more than a hundred weight of gold. With
God's aid, I will live like my ancestors. He who desires
naught will always be free. Farewell, therefore, Mansour ;
farewell, my brother. To-day our roads part ; may that which
you take lead you to the end which all the faithful should desire !"

"Farewell, my good Abdallah," answered Omar. "Each
of us follows his destiny. What is written is written : you were
born to dwell among the tents, and I to be a merchant. Farewell ; I shall never forget the friendship of my childhood ; if
ever I am in need of a stout arm, be sure that I shall have re-
course to you."

"Thanks, my brother," cried the Bedouin ; and, taking Omar
in his arms, he pressed him tenderly to his heart, without re-
straining or hiding his tears.

Omar tranquilly received these proofs of friendship, and
when Abdallah, with drooping head and dejected mien, had
quitted the house after more than once looking back, "Say,"
said he to his father, "what can you have been thinking of, to

leave me so long with that Bedouin? Suppose you had died, and I had appeared to claim your inheritance, the old men of the city would have said, 'We have known Mansour all our lives, and have never heard of his having either son or daughter,' and then who would have been your heir if not the pacha? Carry me quickly to the bazar, introduce me to all your friends, the merchants, and, above all, make me your partner, and give me a warehouse of my own. I feel an uncontrollable desire to handle gold. I have already learned to calculate among the tents, and know how to treat men in order to gain much and risk little. You shall not blush for your son."

"My child," cried Mansour, raising his trembling hands to heaven, "wisdom speaks through your mouth; but the day is too far advanced to go out, and, besides, your dress is not suitable. To-morrow we will go to the bazar; to-morrow all Djiddah shall know my glory and happiness."

All night Omar dreamed of gold and silver; all night Mansour tossed on his bed, unable to close his eyes : he saw himself born anew in a son shrewder, more cunning, more covetous, and more avaricious than himself. "Ah!" he exclaimed, in his joy, "I am the happiest of fathers. The dervish did not deceive me : if my son escapes the peril that threatens him, who knows where the wealth of my house will stop?"

Madman, thou forgettest that if gold is a blessing to him that gives it, it is a poison to him that hoards it. He who harbors avarice in his heart harbors there the enemy of mankind, and woe to him who chooses Satan for a companion!

V.

THE NEW SOLOMON.

THE next morning at daybreak Mansour led his son to the bath, and dressed him in a style befitting his new condition. A silken robe, striped with bright colors, and confined round the waist by a Cashmere girdle, a flowing caftan of the finest and softest cloth, and a white embroidered cap, round which was twisted a muslin turban — such was the elegant costume brought by the most fashionable tailor of Djiddah. In this dress the features of the Egyptian seemed harsher and his complexion more swarthy than ever. The tailor, however, thought otherwise ; he did nothing but praise the beauty and grace of Omar, and pity the ladies of the city who should look with indifference on his countenance, more beautiful than the moon at its full. When nothing more remained of the Bedouin of the day before, breakfast was served and sherbet brought in ; then, after sundry counsels from old Mansour, Omar, mounted on a mule, and modestly falling behind his father, took the way with him to the bazar.

The Egyptian led his son to a shop which was narrow, like all in the market, but crowded with precious articles. Shawls from India, satins and brocades from China, carpets from Bassora, yataghans in their chased silver scabbards, pipes mounted with amber and adorned with rubies, rosaries of black coral, necklaces of sequins and pearls, all that could seduce women, all that could ruin men, was found in this warehouse of perdition. A stone bench ran before the shop. Mansour seated himself on the cushions and lighted his pipe ; Omar took his beads and began to recite his prayers, without looking at the crowd.

As soon as the merchants perceived the syndic, they rose

in a body, and went to repeat the Fát-háh, and to wish him good-morning. Every one looked with surprise at the new-comer, and asked his neighbor in a whisper who the stranger could be—whether a relative of the Egyptian, or a young slave richly dressed in order to draw customers. Mansour called to the sheik, and, pointing to Omar, "This is my son," said he—"my partner and successor."

"Your son!" exclaimed the sheik. "Who ever heard that the rich Mansour had an heir?"

"I wished to deceive the evil eye," replied the old man; "this is why I have had my son brought up at a distance and in secret. I did not intend to present him to you till his beard was grown; but I was getting old; I became impatient; and to-day, with your permission, I shall place him in the bazar to learn of you the art of buying and selling."

"Mansour is always wise," replied the merchants, as they vied with each other in congratulating the happy father of such a son. "May the Lord," they exclaimed, "preserve both root and branch!"

In the midst of these wishes, which tickled the Egyptian's pride, the sheik took up the conversation. "Among us," said he to Mansour, "when a son or daughter is born, even the poor man invites his friends to rejoice with him; have you forgotten us?"

"Honor me with a visit this evening," replied the old man; "you shall be welcome."

An hour after, a messenger, carrying a huge bouquet, went through the market offering a flower to each merchant, with the words, "Recite the Fát-háh for the Prophet." The prayer ended, "Mansour entreats you," added the messenger, "to take coffee with him this evening at his house."

"Mansour is the prince of the generous," returned the invited guest; "with the blessing of God, we will pay our respects this evening to the syndic."

At the appointed time, the Egyptian and his son received the merchants in the little garden, where a splendid feast awaited the guests. Lambs stuffed with almonds and pistachio nuts, rice with saffron, cream sauces flavored with pepper, rose jellies, pastry of all kinds, nothing was spared to honor guests of such consequence. For the first time Mansour desired that the poor should partake of his joy, and ordered the remains of the feast, with some small silver coin, to be distributed among them before the door, which was enough to fill the street with huzzahs and blessings, and to cause the name of the generous Omar and the rich Mansour to resound from one end of Djiddah to the other.

Coffee served and the pipes lighted, the sheik took Omar by the hand : "Behold our friend's son," said he to the merchants, "who desires to enter our honorable company. I beseech each one to recite the Fát-háh for the Prophet."

While the prayer was being three times repeated, the sheik wound a shawl round Omar's waist, tying a knot after each Fát-háh. The ceremony finished, the young man kissed the hand of the sheik and the other spectators, beginning with the eldest. His eyes sparkled with joy. He was a Djiddah merchant; he was rich; the world was opening before him.

The rest of the evening was passed in conversation, all bearing upon trade. Omar did not open his lips ; he stood near the elders of the party, who did not weary of talking to a young man who listened with such attention and respect. They told him how a good salesman should always ask four times the value of the article haggled for, and should never lose his coolness, which is the secret of the trade. Trading is like trout-fishing ; it is necessary to draw on the customer and give him line till, wearied and dazzled, he at length knows

no longer how to defend himself. To toy with a rosary, offer
coffee or a pipe, talk of indifferent things, preserve an unmoved countenance, and yet kindle desire in the soul of the
purchaser, is a difficult act, not to be learned in a day. "But,"
they added, caressing Omar, "you are in a good school, my
son ; neither Jew nor even Armenian can overreach the wise
Mansour."

"Is commerce nothing more than this?" said the young
man in his heart ; "in that case I have no need of these people. To think only and always of one's self, and to make
use of the passions or weaknesses of others to strip fools of
the wealth they dote on—I have known this from my birth ;
I did nothing else in the desert ; my masters will be shrewd,
indeed, if, before six months are past, I do not give them a
lesson."

A few days after, Mansour repaired to the cadi on account
of a suit, the issue of which troubled him but little. A private
conversation with the judge had given him hopes of the justice
of his cause. The old man asked his son to accompany him,
in order to accustom him early to deal with the law. The cadi
was seated in the court-yard of the mosque. He was a fat,
good-looking man, who never thought, and talked little, which,
added to his large turban and his air of perpetual astonishment, gave him a great reputation for justice and gravity.
The spectators were numerous ; the principal merchants were
seated on the ground on carpets, forming a semicircle around
the magistrate. Mansour took his seat a little way from the
sheik, and Omar placed himself between the two, his curiosity strongly excited to see how the law was obeyed, and how
it was trifled with in case of need.

The first case called was that of a young Banian, as
yellow as an orange, with loose-flowing robes and an effem-
inate air, who had lately landed from India, and who com-

plained of having been cheated by one of Mansour's rivals.

"Having found a casket full of diamonds among the effects bequeathed to me by my father at Delhi," said the young man, "I set out for Egypt in order to live there in opulence on the proceeds of their sale. I was obliged by bad weather to put in at Djiddah, where I was retained by the pleasures of the city, and soon found myself in want of money. I was assured that, if I wished to dispose of my diamonds, I should find a good market here. I went to the bazar, and inquired for a dealer in precious stones. The richest, I was told, was Mansour, the most honest was Ali the jeweler. I applied to the latter. As soon as he learned the object of my visit, he welcomed me like a son, and, refusing to talk of business at the bazar, carried me home with him. For several days he treated me in the most generous manner, gained my confidence by every kind of attention, and advanced me all the money I needed. One day, after dinner, when I was not quite sober, he asked me for the casket, examined the diamonds one by one, and said, with feigned pity, 'My child, these stones are of little value in Arabia and Egypt. The rocks of our desert furnish them by thousands; my coffers are full of them.' To prove the truth of what he said, he opened a box, and, taking therefrom a diamond thrice as large as any of mine, gave it to the slave that was with me.

"'What will become of me!' I cried. 'I have no other fortune; I thought myself rich, and here I am poor, a stranger, and far from my family and country.'

"'My child,' replied the treacherous jeweler, 'I conceived a friendship for you at first sight. A Mussulman never forsakes his friends in trouble. Leave this casket with me, and, to oblige you, I will give you a price for it such as no one else would offer. Choose whatever you wish in Djiddah—gold, silver, or coral—and in two hours I promise to give you an equal weight of what you have chosen in exchange for your Indian stones.'

"On returning home, night brought reflection. I made inquiries, and soon learned that Ali had been fooling me. What he had given to the slave was nothing but a bit of crystal. Diamonds are scarcer at Djiddah than in India, and are worth ten times their weight in gold. I demanded my casket. Ali refused to restore it. Venerable magistrate, my sole hope is in your justice. I entreat you to espouse the cause of a stranger, and may the wretch who has ruined me drink boiling water for all eternity!"

It was Ali's turn to speak. "Illustrious servant of God," said he to the cadi, "this young man's story is true in but one particular, namely, that we have made a bargain, and that I am ready to keep it. All the rest is of his own invention. What matters it what I gave the slave; could a sensible man have seen in it any thing else than a jest? Did I force the stranger to leave his casket in my hands? Was it my fault if want of money made him accept my conditions? Why does he accuse me of treachery? Have I broken my word, and has he kept his?"

"Young man," said the cadi to the Banian, "have you witnesses to prove that Ali deceived you as to the value of your merchandise? If not, I shall put the accused on his oath, as the law decrees."

A Koran was brought. Ali placed his right hand on the sacred book, and repeated three times, "In the name of God the Omnipotent, and by the word of God that is contained in this book, I swear that I have not deceived this stranger. I swear it here to-day," he added, turning toward the assembly, "as I shall swear it on the judgment-day before God as cadi, with the angels for witnesses."

"Wretch," said the Banian, "thou art among those whose feet go down to destruction. Thou hast thrown away thy soul."

"That may be," whispered the sheik to Omar, "but he has gained a huge fortune. This Ali is a shrewd knave."

"He is no ordinary man," added Mansour. "This may be called a game well played."

Omar smiled, and, while Ali was enjoying the success of his ruse, he approached the stranger, who burst into tears.

"Do you wish me to help you to gain the suit?" asked he.

"Yes," cried the East Indian; "confound this wretch, and you may ask of me what you will. But you are only a child; you can do nothing."

"I only ask you to have confidence in me for a few moments," returned the Egyptian. "Accept Ali's bargain; let me choose in your stead, and fear nothing."

"What can I fear after having lost all?" murmured the stranger, letting his head fall again on his bosom like a man bereft of all hope. Nevertheless, he turned to the cadi, and, bowing respectfully, "Oh, my lord and master," said he, "thy slave implores a last favor of thy mercy; let the bargain be consummated, since the law decrees it, but permit this young man to choose in my stead what I shall receive in payment."

A profound silence ensued. Omar rose, and, bowing to the cadi, "Ali," said he to the jeweler, "you have doubtless brought the casket, and can tell us the weight thereof?"

"Here it is," said the merchant; "it weighs twenty pounds. Choose what you will, I repeat; if the thing asked for is to be found in Djiddah, you shall have it within two hours, otherwise the bargain is null and void. All know that my word is sacred, and that I never break it."

"What we desire," said Omar, raising his voice, "is ants' wings, half male and half female. You have two hours in which to furnish the twenty pounds you have promised us."

"This is absurd," cried the jeweler; "it is impossible. I should need half a score of persons and six months' labor to satisfy this foolish demand. It is trifling with justice to introduce these childish caprices into this place."

"Are there any winged ants in Djiddah?" asked the cadi.

"Of course," answered the merchants, laughing; "they are one of the plagues of Egypt. Our houses are full of them, and it would be doing us a great service to rid us of them."

"Then Ali must keep his promise or give back the casket," said the cadi. "This young man was mad to sell his diamonds weight for weight; he is mad to exact such a payment. So much the better for Ali the first time; so much the worse for him the second. Justice has not two weights and measures. Every bargain holds good before the law. Either furnish twenty pounds of ants' wings, or restore the casket to the Banian."

"A righteous judgment," shouted the spectators, wonder-struck at such equity.

The stranger, beside himself with joy, embraced Omar, calling him his savior and master; nor did he stop there: taking from the casket three diamonds of the finest water, as large as nightingale's eggs, he forced them on Omar, who put them in his girdle, respectfully kissed the Banian's right hand, and seated himself by his father, his gravity unmoved by the gaze of the assembly.

"Well done, my friend," said Mansour; "but Ali is a novice; had he not neglected the cadi he would have gained his suit. It is my turn now; mark me well, and profit by the lesson I shall give you. Stop, young man!" he cried to the East Indian, who was carrying off the diamonds, "we have an account to settle. I entreat the illustrious cadi to keep this casket for a moment; there may be those here who have a better right to it than either this stranger or the prudent Ali."

There was universal surprise among the spectators, and all listened to the new claimant.

"The day before yesterday," said Mansour, "a veiled lady entered my shop in the bazar and asked to look at some necklaces. Nothing that I showed her pleased her taste, and she was about to leave the shop, when she spied a sealed box in a corner, and entreated me to open it. This box contained a set of topazes which were no longer at my disposal, having been already sold to the Pacha of Egypt. I told the lady this, but she insisted on at least seeing the gift destined for a sultana. A woman's wish is a thing not easily thwarted. There are three kinds of obstinacy that are irresistible—that of princes, of children, and of women. I was so weak as to yield. The stranger looked at the necklace, tried it on, and declared that she would have it at any price. On my refusal, she quitted the bazar, loading me with threats and maledictions. An hour after, this young man entered my shop, and, bursting into tears, kissed my hand and entreated me to sell him the necklace, saying that his own life and that of the lady depended on it. 'Ask of me what you will, my father,' said he, 'but I must have these gems or die.' I have a weakness for young men, and, though I knew the danger of disappointing my master the pacha, I was unable to resist his supplications. 'Take the topazes,' said I to the stranger, 'but promise to give whatever I may ask in exchange.' 'My head itself, if you will, for you have saved my life,' he replied, as he carried off the necklace. We were without witnesses," added Mansour, turning to the Banian, "but is not my story true?"

"Yes," said the young man, "and I beg your pardon for not having satisfied you sooner: you know the cause. Now that I have recovered my fortune, thanks to your son, ask of me what you desire."

"What I desire," said Mansour, nodding to the pacha, who was gazing fixedly at a palm-tree, "what I desire is this casket with all its contents. It is not too much for a man who risks his life by disobeying the pacha. Illustrious magistrate, your excellency has declared that all bargains hold good before the law : this young man has promised to give me what I please ; now I declare that nothing pleases me but these diamonds."

The cadi raised his head and looked about the assembly as if to interrogate the faces, then stroked his beard and relapsed into his meditations.

"Ali is defeated," said the sheik to Omar, with a smile. "The fox is not yet born more cunning than the worthy Mansour."

"I am lost!" cried the Banian. "Oh, Omar, have you saved me only to cast me down from the highest pinnacle of joy to the depths of despair? Persuade your father to spare me, that I may owe my life to you a second time."

"Well, my son," said Mansour, "doubtless you are shrewd, but this will teach you that your father knows rather more than you do. The cadi is about to decide : try whether you can dictate his decree."

"It is mere child's play," answered Omar, shrugging his shoulders ; "but, since you desire it, my father, you shall lose your suit." He rose, and, taking a piastre from his girdle, put it into the hand of the Banian, who laid it before the judge.

"Illustrious cadi," said he, "this young man is ready to fulfill his engagement. This is what he offers Mansour—a piastre. In itself, this coin is of little value ;* but examine it closely, and you will see that it is stamped with the likeness

* About four cents.

of the sultan, our glorious master.   May God destroy and confound all who disobey his highness !   It is this precious likeness that we offer you," added Omar, turning to Mansour ; "if
it pleases you, you are paid ; to dare to say that it displeases
you is an insult to the pacha, a crime punishable by death ;
and I am sure that our worthy cadi will not become your accomplice—he who always has been and always will be the
faithful servant of all the sultans."

When Omar had finished speaking, all eyes turned toward
the cadi, who, more impenetrable than ever, stroked his face
and waited for the old man to come to his aid.   Mansour
was agitated and embarrassed.   The silence of the cadi and
the assembly terrified him, and he cast a supplicating glance
toward his son.

"My father," said Omar, "permit this young man to thank
you for the lesson of prudence which you have given him by
frightening him a little.   He knows well that it was you who
sent me to his aid, and that all this is a farce.   None is deceived by hearing the son oppose the father, and who has
ever doubted Mansour's experience and generosity ?"

"No one," interrupted the cadi, starting up like a man suddenly awakened from a dream, "and I least of all ; and this
is why I have permitted you to speak, my young Solomon.   I
wished to honor in you the wisdom of your father ; but another time avoid meddling with his highness's name ; it is not
safe to sport with the lion's paws.   The matter is settled.   The
necklace is worth a hundred thousand piastres, is it not, Mansour?   This madcap shall give you, therefore, a hundred thousand piastres, and all parties will be satisfied."

Despite his modesty, Omar could not escape the gratitude
of the East Indian or the praises of the merchants.   The
former tried to force the casket into his hands ; and it was
impossible to prevent him from seizing the bridle of the mule

that carried Omar, and accompanying to his door him whom
he styled the most generous and wisest of men. The merchants, on their side, heaped congratulations on Mansour;
and the celebrated case which called forth the wisdom of him
whom the sagacious cadi styled the new Solomon is still talked of at Djiddah.

Once at home, Mansour broke forth into reproaches. "I
can not understand you, my son," said he. "I had a fortune
in my hands, and you have snatched it from me. Is this your
idea of business? Is this the respect that you show your
father?"

"Have patience, my father," replied Omar, coldly. "To-
day I have made myself a reputation for prudence and prob-
ity. It is a noise that will be lasting, a first impression that
will never be effaced. Reputation is a jewel which nothing
can replace; it is ten thousand times more valuable capital
than your diamonds. All distrust Mansour's cunning, but all
will confide, like this foreigner, in Omar's honesty and integrity. The bait is thrown, the trout will not be long in coming."

Mansour stood confounded. He had desired a son that
should be worthy of himself; he began to fear that Eblis had
granted his prayer too literally. He admired Omar indeed;
such calculation at so tender an age could not but delight a
man whose whole life had been one of calculation. But—
it must be confessed to the old man's shame—this precocious
experience chilled his heart, and, to tell the truth, he stood
appalled before this sage of fifteen.

VI.

VIRTUE REWARDED.

NOTHING was wanting to Mansour's happiness; during the five remaining years of his life the merchant could fully enjoy the education and success of his son. He saw all his trade pass into Omar's hands; the wealth of his house became enormous, and, as is always the case, public esteem increased in proportion to wealth. How could Omar help succeeding? He had every thing in his favor; an abundance of money, few passions, and no scruples. None had ever combined to such a degree what constitutes genius in business—love of gold and contempt of men. Mansour could therefore breathe his last in peace. His life had been long, disease had spared his old age, his dreams were realized, and he was sure of leaving an heir behind him who would keep and increase the fortune accumulated with such difficulty; yet it is affirmed that the Egyptian died with his heart filled with rage, crying out that no one loved him, execrating his folly, and trembling at the sight of his treasures, as if the gold, heated in the infernal fire, already lay a burning weight on his breast and brow.

Omar heard of his father's death with complete resignation. Business had called him away from his dying bed; business was his consolation. His courage was worthy of admiration; at the mere sight of a piastre, he dried up his tears and stifled his sorrow.

Left alone with so noble an inheritance, the son of Mansour set no bounds to his desires. Nothing escaped his schemes; it seemed as if from within his little house in Djiddah, like the spider in his web, he drew all the wealth of the world into his invisible net. Rice and sugar from India;

gum and coffee from Yemen ; ivory, gold dust, and slaves from Abyssinia ; corn from Egypt ; tissues from Syria ; ships and caravans—all came to Omar. Yet never did man welcome good fortune more modestly. To see him in the street in his rusty clothes and scanty turban, his eyes cast down, telling his wooden beads with his fingers, he would not have been thought worth twenty thousand piastres. Nothing betrayed the rich man in his conversation ; he was familiar with his inferiors, free and easy with his equals, cringing toward those from whom he hoped for any thing, and respectful toward those who had it in their power to do him an injury. According to him, it was a great mistake to attribute to him a large fortune ; all this merchandise was not his property, but consignments from foreign correspondents who had confidence in him—a confidence which must have cost him dear, for he constantly complained of losing money. If he bought the handsomest slaves, the richest perfumes, the choicest tobacco, and the rarest stuffs, it was always for some pacha or foreign trader. It was whispered that these treasures never left the Egyptian's house—who can silence men's tongues ?— but nothing certain was known. Omar had no friends, transacted his business at the bazar, and received no visits. Whether he was poor or rich, a sage or an egotist, humble or hypocritical, was the secret of Satan.

His prudence was on a par with his modesty. Beginning with the pacha and ending with the collector of customs, there was not an officer at Djiddah, great or small, with whose pipe-bearer, groom, or favorite slave Omar was not acquainted. He was not fond of giving, and often repeated the maxim of the Koran that prodigals are the brethren of Satan, but he knew how to open his hand at the right time, and no one ever repented a service rendered this honest man. Pachas pass away quickly at Djiddah ; the hand of the Turk is heavy, and the richest merchants were often forced to pay a ransom. The son of Mansour alone escaped these loans, which are never repaid. Within a week, by one means or another, he was the friend, it was even said the banker, of the new governor, and the storm which had threatened him always burst on other heads than his, so that he was an object of astonishment and envy to all his brethren.

The day came, however, when his star paled. A pacha, who had made a fortune in three months in rather too obvious a manner, was recalled to Constantinople, and his successor received orders to be an honest man, the government being anxious to please the Franks, of whom, unhappily, it stood in need, and who were raising a great outcry. Turk as he was, the new pacha understood how to give satisfaction in high places. The day after his arrival, he went in disguise to buy provisions of the chief butcher and baker in Djiddah. The mohtesib, or inspector of the market, was forewarned, and was ready in the street, with his clerks and great scales, to weigh what the pacha had just bought. The twelve pounds of bread fell short two ounces, and the huge quarter of mutton one ounce. The crime was a flagrant one, and the offenders were speedily brought to justice. The pacha overwhelmed the wretches who fattened on the sweat of the people with abuse and reproaches, and, in his just anger, refused to listen to their defense, but ordered them to be instantly stripped, bound, and bastinadoed, after which, by express command, the baker was nailed by the ear to his shop door, and the butcher was fastened to one of the windows of the great mosque, after having his nose pierced with an iron wire, from which the ounce of meat which he had stolen was suspended. The populace heaped every species of outrage upon the two unfortunates ; God was glorified throughout the whole city, the pacha was styled the friend of the people, the lover of

justice, and the new Haroun Al-Raschid ; and the story of this virtuous deed, after rejoicing the sultan, spread to the West, to the confusion and despair of the infidels.

The same evening several of the merchants freighted a ship for Egypt, having suddenly learned that their presence was needed at Cairo.   Omar, instead of giving way to terror, calmly stroked his beard.   "Virtue is a kind of merchandise not in the market," thought he ; "when it is needed, therefore, it must be bought dear."   Whereupon he repaired to the bazar, chanced to meet the pacha's secretary, made him sit down beside him, and offered him a pipe by mistake that had been designed for the sultan.

"It is always bad policy to do justice to the people," said Omar to the secretary ; "once led into bad habits, they grow exacting.   It is a death-blow to large speculations."   The secretary gazed at his magnificent pipe, and thought Omar a man of sense.

Alas ! the Egyptian had judged but too rightly.   The first market-day grain was found to have risen two piastres an ardeb.* The populace became excited ; two men especially talked with extreme vehemence—the butcher whose nose had been slit and the one-eared baker. The cheats of yesterday had become the heroes of to-day ; they were pitied as victims, and the more they clamored, the more they were admired.

From word to deed there is but a step among the populace. The mob was already attempting to burst open Omar's house when the chief of the police, surrounded by soldiers, came to summon the merchant before the pacha. Omar received the officer with an emotion that may be easily understood, and fervently glued his lips to his hand ; but the chief of the police hastily withdrew it, and thrust it clenched into his girdle, as if polluted by the kiss of a criminal. Nevertheless, he neither abused nor maltreated the son of Mansour, to the great displeasure of the populace, which loves justice, and is not sorry to see a man accused of crime treated as though convicted of it, especially when he is rich ; on the contrary, the chief of the police more than once urged the prisoner to rely on the equity of the governor.

"What is written is written," replied the Egyptian, telling his beads one by one.

The doors of the palace were open, and the people thronged into the court-yard, where the pacha sat, grave and impassive, calming the turbulent passions around him by his presence. The two accusers were brought forward ; the governor commanded them to speak without fear. "Justice for all is my duty," said he, aloud ; "rich or poor, no plunderer shall find grace in my sight."

"God is great and the pacha is just," cried the crowd ; whereupon four merchants, quaking with fear, were thrust before the tribunal, all of whom kissed the Koran, and swore

* About five bushels.

that Omar had bought from them all the corn imported from Egypt.

"Death! death!" cried the people. The pacha made a sign that the accused should be heard, and silence ensued.

"Oh, my lord and master," cried Omar, prostrating his forehead on the earth, "your slave places his head in your hands. God loves those who show mercy; the meaner the culprit, the more noble is it not to crush him. Solomon himself spared the ant. It is true that I have bought a few cargoes of corn in the harbor of Djiddah, as any honest merchant may do; but all here, except my enemies, know that the purchase was made for my master the sultan. This corn is designed for the troops posted by your highness on the road to Mecca for the protection of the pilgrims; so, at least, I was told by your highness's secretary, when he gave me the money in your name, which a poor man like me was not able to advance. May my master pardon me for delaying so long to send him the thousand ardebs of corn that he ordered: the chief of the police will tell your highness that force alone has prevented me from obeying him."

"What do you mean by a thousand ardebs of corn?" asked the governor, fiercely.

"Forgive me, my lord," returned Omar, in an agitated voice, "I am so much troubled that it is difficult for me to reckon correctly. I believe that it was fifteen hundred," he added, gazing at the contracted features of the pacha, "if not, indeed, two thousand."

"It was three thousand," said the secretary, handing a paper to the governor. "Here is the order given to this man, in my own hand-writing, under the seal of your highness."

"And has the merchant received the money?" asked the pacha, in a softened tone.

"Yes, your excellency," replied Omar, bowing anew. "The

chief of the police, here present, will tell you that he transmitted this order to me, and your highness's secretary advanced me yesterday the two hundred thousand piastres which I needed for the purchase. I am therefore responsible to the pacha for two hundred thousand piastres or three thousand ardebs of corn."

"Then what is all this noise about?" exclaimed the pacha, looking savagely at the two frightened accusers. "Is this the respect you pay my master the sultan? Are the soldiers who protect the holy pilgrims to die of famine in the desert? Seize these two knaves, and give each of them thirty strokes of the bastinado. Justice for all, and no grace for false witnesses. To accuse an innocent man is to rob him of more than life."

"Well said," cried the multitude; "the pacha is right."

The sentence pronounced, the butcher was seized by four soldiers, who did not scruple to do justice in their own cause. A running noose was passed round the prisoner's ankles and fastened to a stake, after which one of the Arnauts, armed with a stick, beat the soles of his feet with all his might. The butcher was a hero in his way; he counted the strokes one by one, and, the punishment being ended, was carried off by his friends, casting furious glances at Omar. The slit-eared man was less resolute; at every blow he uttered Allâh! with a groan that might have melted a heart of stone. At the twelfth stroke Omar kissed the ground before the pacha and entreated pardon for the culprit, which was graciously granted. This was not all; he slipped a douro into the wounded man's hand before all the people, and declared that he had thirty ardebs of corn left, which should be divided among the poor, then returned home amid the blessings of those very persons who, an hour before, were ready to tear him to pieces. Praises or threats, he received both with the same humility or the same indifference. "Allah be praised!" said he, on entering his house. "The pacha drove rather a hard bargain, but now I have him in my hands."

Tranquil in this respect, the son of Mansour resumed his ingenious schemes. Thanks to him, the wealth of Djiddah increased daily. One morning, on waking, the slave-dealers learned with joy that the price of their merchandise had doubled. Unfortunately, they had sold all they had the day before to Omar, to fill an order from Egypt. The next month it was rice, then tobacco, wax, coffee, sugar, and gold dust. Every thing rose in value; but Omar's correspondents were always the ones that profited by this sudden rise. In this manner Djiddah became an opulent market, so wealthy, indeed, that the poor could no longer live there, though the rich acquired fortunes by buying the good graces of the Egyptian.

As to him, seated every day at his counter, more honeyed than ever to those of whom he had need, he passed the hours in counting on his beads the millions of piastres that he accumulated in all directions. He said to himself in his heart that, despised as he was, he was the master of men, and that, should he need the assistance of the sultan, he was rich enough to buy him and his seraglio in the bargain.

Men do not grow rich with impunity. It is as impossible to hide fortune as smoke. Despite all his humility, Omar received an invitation from the grand sherif of Mecca to repair to Taif for an important service, which he alone, it was said, could render the descendant of the Prophet. The merchant was less elated by the honor than dismayed at the service which might be asked of him. "The rich have two kinds of foes," said he, "the small and the great. The first are like the ants, that empty the house grain by grain; the second like the lion, the king of robbers, that flays us with one stroke of his paw. But, with patience and cunning, it is easier to shake off the lion than the ant. Let us see what the sherif desires; if he wishes to deceive me, I will not be duped by him; if he wishes to be paid, he shall give me the worth of the money."

It was with this respect for the Commander of the Faithful that Omar took the way to Taif. The sight of the desert soon changed the current of his thoughts. The tents and the clumps of palm-trees scattered amid the sands recalled his childhood, and for the first time his brother Abdallah recurred to his memory. "Who knows," he thought, "whether by chance I may not need him?"

VII.

BARSIM.

WHILE the son of Mansour abandoned himself to the love of gain as if he were to live forever, Abdallah grew in piety, wisdom, and virtue. He had adopted his father's calling, and guided the caravans between Yambo, Medina, and Mecca. As ardent as the young horse that flings his mane to the wind, and as prudent as a graybeard, he had gained the confidence of the principal merchants, and, despite his youth, it was he that was recommended by preference to the pilgrims when they thronged from all parts of the world in the sacred month to march seven times round the holy Caaba, encamp on Mount Arafat, and offer sacrifices in the valley of the Mina. These journeys were not without peril. The Bedouin had more than once risked his life to protect those under his keeping, but he had fought so well that all on his route were beginning to respect and fear him. The aged Hafiz never quitted his pupil; crippled as he was, he always found means to be useful. Wherever there are men, there are always stout arms and resolute hearts, but not always a faithful friend and wise counselor.

This life, interspersed with repose and alarm, peace and danger, was delightful to the son of Yusuf. To live a brave man, and die like a soldier in case of need, as his father had done, was Abdallah's sole ambition. His wishes went no farther. Nevertheless, a cloud overshadowed the serenity of his soul. Halima had told him of the dervish, and the child of the desert thought continually of the mysterious plant which had the gift of bestowing happiness and virtue.

Hafiz, to whom Abdallah first opened his heart, saw in this thought nothing but a wile of Satan. "What is the use of troubling yourself?" he said. "God tells us how to please him in the Koran ; he has but one law ; do what he bids, and have no farther anxiety ; our business is only with the present moment."

These words failed to appease the curiosity of Abdallah. Hafiz had told him so many marvels which he did not doubt, why should he not believe the story of this talisman to be true, and why might not one of the faithful discover it ? "We dwellers among the tents are unlearned," thought the Bedouin ; "what hinders me from questioning the pilgrims ? God has dispersed the truth abroad throughout the earth ; who knows whether some hadji of the East or West may not know the secret which I am seeking ? The dervish did not answer my mother at random ; and, with God's help, I will find the right path."

A short time after, Abdallah guided to Mecca a caravan of pilgrims from Egypt. At the head of the troop was a physician who talked constantly, laughed without ceasing, and doubted every thing—a Frank, it was said, who had abjured his errors to enter the service of the pacha. Abdallah resolved to question him. As they passed a meadow, he gathered a sprig of clover in blossom, and presenting it to the stranger, "Is this plant known in your country?" said he.

"Certainly," answered the physician. "It is what you call *barsim*, and we *trifolium*. It is the Alexandrian trefoil, family leguminosæ, calyx tubular, corolla persistent, petals divided into three segments or foliolæ, and sometimes into four or even five, though this is an exception, or, as we say, a monstrosity."

"Is there no species of clover, then, in your country that always has four leaves ?"

"No, my young scholar, neither in my country nor any where else. Why do you ask ?"

Abdallah gave him his confidence, whereupon he burst out laughing. "My child," said he, "the dervish was fooling your mother. She asked what was impossible of him, and he promised her what was impossible."

"Why should not God create a four-leaved clover if he wished ?" asked the Bedouin, wounded by the stranger's disdainful smile.

"Why, young man ? Because the carth produced all the plants on one day by virtue of a germinating power which was then exhausted. Since the time of King Solomon there has been nothing new under the sun."

"And if God wished to work a miracle, is His power exhausted ?" said Hafiz, who had approached the travelers ; "He who drew the seven heavens and the seven earths from the smoke in the space of two days, and set them five hundred days' march from each other—He who ordered the night to envelop the day—He who planted life every where, could He not add a new blade of grass to the millions of plants which he has created for the food and pleasure of man ?"

"Certainly," replied the physician, in a mocking tone ; "I am too good a Mussulman to pretend the contrary. God might also send his thunderbolt to light my pipe that has just gone out, but he does not wish to do it ; on the contrary, he

wishes me to ask you for a little fire." With these words he
began to puff his pipe and to whistle a foreign air.

"Accursed be unbelievers!" cried the cripple. "Come,
my son, leave this miscreant, whose breath is death. If it is
in punishment for our sins that God has given the Franks the
knowledge that makes their power, it is also to chastise these
dogs, and hurry them faster toward the bottomless pit. Madmen, who, to deny God, make use of his very power, and the
perpetual miracle of his goodness! Begone, infidel!" he added, raising his hand to heaven as if to call down its thunders
on the head of the renegade; "begone, ingrate, who turnest
thy back upon the Lord! God beholds the innermost recesses
of thy soul; thou wilt die in despair, and wilt feed forever on
the tree of hell, with its bitter fruit and poisoned thorns."

At the other end of the caravan walked a Persian, with a
white beard and a tall sheepskin hat, the poorest and most
aged of the band, as well as the most despised, for he was of
a heretical nation. The old man seemed unconscious of his
poverty, age, and solitude. He spoke to no one, ate little, and
smoked all day long. Perched on a lean camel, he passed
his whole time in turning in his fingers the ninety-nine beads
of his rosary, lifting his trembling head meanwhile toward
heaven, and murmuring mysterious words. The poor man's
gentleness and piety had touched Abdallah's heart. Too
young as yet to know hatred, it was with the heretic that the
son of Yusuf sought a refuge from the unbeliever.

The animated face and sparkling eyes of the young guide
touched the heart of the dervish, who welcomed the confidence that he divined with a kindly smile. "My son," said
he, "God give thee the wit of Plato, the knowledge of Aris-
totle, the star of Alexander, and the happiness of Cosroes!"

"My father, thou speakest well," cried Abdallah; "it is
knowledge that I need; not the knowledge of a heathen, but

that of a true Mussulman, to whom faith opens the treasure of truth."

"Speak, my son," returned the old man; "perchance I can serve thee. Truth is like the pearl : he alone possesses it who has plunged into the depths of life and torn his hands on the rocks of time. What thou seekest I perhaps have found. Who knows whether I may not be able to give thee the light which thou enviest, and which is now valueless to my dim eyes ?"

Won by such kindliness, Abdallah poured out his soul before the dervish, who listened in silence. The confidence ended, the old man for his sole answer drew a lock of white wool from the mat on which he was sitting, and cast it to the wind ; then, swaying his body like a drunken man, and fixing a strange gaze on Abdallah, he improvised the following lines :

> "Tulip with dark corolla, charming cypress,
>   Young man, with eyes more black and soft than night,
>   Seest thou yon white speck fluttering in the breeze?
>   Thus pass our days—a dream that soon is told !
>   The desert rain less speedily dries up,
>   The falling rose less quickly fades away;
>   All cheats or fails us, and the noblest life
>   Is but the long sigh of a last adieu.
> God alone is true ; God alone is great ; God alone is God !
>   Would'st thou, my child, that in the sacred book
>   Thy guardian angel should inscribe thy name?
>   Flee the intoxicating joys of sense.
>   God loves a heart unsullied by the world ;
>   The body is naught but a sepulchre :
>   Happy the man who breaks its deadening bonds,
>   To plunge into the depths of boundless love !
>   To live in God is death ; to die in God is life !"

"Thy words inflame my heart," said Abdallah ; "but thou dost not answer me."

"What, my son !" cried the mystic, "dost thou not understand me? The four-leaved clover does not exist on earth; thou must seek it elsewhere. The four-leaved clover is a symbol—it is the impossible, the ineffable, the infinite! Wouldst thou possess it? I will reveal to thee the secret. Stifle thy senses; become blind, mute, and deaf; quit the city of existence; be like a traveler in the kingdom of nothingness; plunge into ecstatic rapture; and when nothing more causes your heart to beat, when you have encircled your brow with the glorious crown of death, then, my son, thou wilt find eternal love, and be swallowed up in it like a drop of water in the vast ocean. This is life! When nothing was yet in being, love existed; when nothing more remains, love will endure; it is the first and the last; it is God and man; it is the Creator and the creature; it is the heights above and the depths below; it is every thing."

"Old man," said the Bedouin, affrighted, "age has weakened thy reason; thou dost not feel that thou art blaspheming. God alone existed before the world had being, God alone will remain when the heavens shall have crushed the earth in their fall. He is the first and the last, the manifest and the hidden; he is mighty and wise; he knoweth all things, and is able to do all things."

The old man did not hear; he seemed in a dream; his lips moved, his eyes were fixed and sightless; a vision carried far from the earth this victim of the delusions of Satan. Abdallah returned mournfully to Hafiz and related to him this new disappointment.

"My child," said the cripple, "flee these madmen who intoxicate themselves with visions like others with opium or hasheesh. They are idolaters who worship themselves. Poor fools! does the eye create the light? does the mind of man create the truth? Woe to him who draws from his brain a world lighter and more hollow than a bubble; woe to him who sets man on the throne of God! As soon as he enters the city of dreams he is lost; God is effaced, faith evaporates, the will becomes lifeless, and the soul is stifled ; it is the reign of darkness and death."

VIII.

THE JEW.

YOUTH is the season of hope and desire.   Despite his discomfiture, Abdallah did not tire of questioning the pilgrims whom he guided to Mecca, still relying on a happy chance ; but Persia, Syria, Egypt, Turkey, and India were mute ; no one had heard of the four-leaved clover.   Hafiz condemned a curiosity which he thought guilty, while Halima consoled her son by making him believe that she still hoped with him.

One day, when Abdallah had retired to his tent more melancholy than usual, and was debating in his own mind whether he would not do well to quit his tribe and go to foreign lands in search of the talisman that evaded his grasp, a Jew entered the inclosure to ask hospitality.   He was a little old man, dressed in rags, so thin that his girdle seemed to cut him in two.   Leaning on a staff, he slowly dragged along his feet, wrapped in bloody rags, as he raised his head from time to time, and looked around as if imploring pity.   His wrinkled brow, his inflamed eyelids, his thin lips, which scarcely covered his toothless gums, his disordered beard, which fell to his waist, every thing about him bespoke want and suffering.   The stranger perceived Abdallah, and stretched out his trembling hand to him, murmuring in a weak voice, " Oh, master of the tent, behold a guest of God !"

Wholly absorbed in his thoughts, the son of Yusuf heard nothing.   The old man had already thrice repeated his prayer when, unhappily, he turned his head toward a neighboring tent, where a negress was nursing her child.   At the sight of the Jew the woman hid her babe to preserve it from the evil eye, and, rushing from her tent, cried, " Begone, thou wretch worthy to be stoned ! Hast thou come here to bring misfortune ? May as many curses light on thee as there are hairs in thy beard !" And, calling the dogs, she set them on the wretched man, who tried to flee ; but his foot caught in his robe and he fell, uttering lamentable cries, too weak to drive off the enemies that were tearing him.

His shrieks roused Abdallah. To rush to the Jew, punish the dogs, and threaten the slave was the work of an instant. He picked up the Jew, took him in his arms, and carried him into the tent ; a moment after he was washing his feet and hands, and binding up his wounds, while Halima brought him dates and milk.

"I bless thee, my son," said the old man, in tears. "The blessing of the meanest of mankind is never contemptible in the sight of the Lord. May God remove far from thee jealousy, sadness, and pride, and grant thee wisdom, patience, and peace, the gifts that he has promised to the generous of heart like thee !"

At evening, Hafiz, Abdallah, and the Jew talked long together round their frugal repast, although the cripple could not conceal his repugnance to the son of Israel. Abdallah, on the contrary, listened to the old man with interest, for the stranger was a great traveler, and told them of his journeyings. He was acquainted with Muscat, Hindostan, and Persia ; he had visited the country of the Franks and crossed the deserts of Africa ; he had now come from Egypt through Soudan, and was returning to Jerusalem by the way of Syria.

" But the object of my search is not wealth, my dear host," said the Jew ; " more than once have I seen it on the roadside and passed it by. Poverty befits the children of Abraham, say our sages, as do scarlet trappings the snow-white steed. What I have pursued for half a century over deserts and seas, through fatigue and misery, is the Word of God, the sacred tradition. That unwritten word, which God gave to Moses on Mount Sinai, was confided by Moses to the keeping of Joshua ; Joshua transmitted it to the seventy elders, the elders to the prophets, and the prophets to the synagogue. After the destruction of Jerusalem, our masters collected it in the Talmud, but how far were they from possessing it entire ! To punish the sins of our fathers, God broke asunder the truth, and scattered the fragments to the four winds of heaven. Happy is he who can gather together these dispersed shreds —happy is he who can discover a ray of the divine splendor ! The children of the age may despise and hate him ; their insults are to his soul like the rain to the earth : in bursting it asunder, they purify and refresh it."

"And are you this man, my father?" said Abdallah, so deeply moved by the words of his guest that he quite forgot that he was talking with an infidel. "Have you discovered this treasure ? Do you possess the whole truth?"

"I am but a worm of the earth," replied the Jew ; "but from my childhood up I have questioned the masters, and entreated them to repeat to me the secrets of the law ; I have sought in the Cabala for the wealth that is thought valueless in the marts of the world, and I have endeavored to decipher that language of numbers which is the key to all truth. How far I have succeeded God alone can judge ; to Him be the praise ! One thing is certain, namely, that the angel Razriel initiated Adam into the mysteries of the creation ; and who dare say that this revelation is lost? If there lives a man who has lifted a corner of the veil, he has nothing more to hope or fear on earth ; he has had his day, and is ready for death."

"My father," asked the young Bedouin, trembling, "has

your science told you of a sacred plant which at once bestows virtue and happiness?"

"Certainly," replied the old man, smiling; "it is treated of in the Zohar, with many other marvels."

"It is the four-leaved clover, is it not?"

"Perchance," returned the Jew, with a frown; "but how did this name reach your ears?"

When the son of Yusuf had finished his story, the old man gazed at him tenderly. "My son," said he, "the poor often repay hospitality better than the rich, for God himself holds the purse-strings. The secret which thou art seeking I long ago discovered in the recesses of Persia; and, since God has led my steps to thy tent, it is doubtless because he has chosen me to bring thee the truth. Listen, therefore, and let what I am about to tell thee be engraven on thy heart."

Hafiz and Abdallah drew near the old man, who related the following tale in a low and mysterious voice:

"You know that when God drove our first father Adam from Paradise, he permitted him to carry with him upon earth the date-tree to serve as his nourishment, and the camel, which was moulded of the same clay as himself, and which could not exist without him."

"That is true," exclaimed the cripple. "When my young camels come into the world, they would die of hunger if I did not hold their head to their mother's breast; the camel is made for us as we are for the camel."

"When the flaming sword drove the first criminals before it, Adam cast a look of despair at the abode which he was forced to forsake, and, to carry with him a last memento, broke off a branch of myrtle. The angel let him alone; he remembered that by God's command he had formerly worshiped the mortal whom now he pitied."

"True!" said Hafiz. "It was the same branch of myrtle

that Shoaib long after gave to his son-in-law Moses ; it was the staff with which the prophet tended his flocks, and with which he afterward wrought his miracles in Egypt."

" Eve also paused in tears before those flowers and trees which she had loved so well ; but the sword was pitiless, and she was forced to proceed. Just as she was about to go out, she hastily snatched one of the plants of Paradise. The angel shut his eyes as he had done with Adam. What the plant was Eve knew not ; she had clutched it in her flight, and had instantly closed her hand. She would have been wise had she carried it away in the same manner ; but curiosity once more prevailed over prudence, and, before crossing the fatal threshold, our mother opened her hand to see what she had gathered. It was the four-leaved clover, the most brilliant of all the flowers of Paradise. One leaf was red like copper, another white like silver, the third yellow like gold, and the fourth glittering like diamond. Eve paused to look at her treasure, when the fiery sword touched her ; she started, her hand trembled, and the diamond leaf fell within the gates of Paradise, while the other three leaves, swept away by the wind, were scattered over the earth ; where they fell, God alone knows."

" What !" exclaimed the young man, " have they never since been seen ?"

" Not that I know of ; and it is even possible that the story is only an allegory, concealing some profound truth."

" No, no," said Abdallah, " that is not so. Try to remember, my father ; perchance you will recall something more. I must have this plant at any price ; I wish it, and, with God's aid, I will have it."

The old man buried his face in his hands, and long remained absorbed in contemplation. Abdallah and Hafiz scarcely dared breathe for fear of disturbing his revery.

M

"My efforts are in vain ; I can recall nothing to memory," said he, at last ; "perhaps my book will give me some information."   He took from his girdle a yellow manuscript volume, with a black, greasy cover, turned the pages slowly, carefully examined the squares, circles, and alphabets mixed with figures, beginning some with *aleph* and others with *thau*, the last letter of the Hebrew alphabet.   "Here are four lines which are repeated in Soudan, and which may interest you," said he, at last, "but their meaning escapes me :

> "'There is a mysterious herb
>   That grows hidden from human eyes ;
>   Seek it not upon earth,
>   'Twill be found above in the skies.'

"Patience, patience," he added, seeing Abdallah's emotion, "the words have more than one meaning ; the ignorant seek to fish up truth from the surface, the wise pursue it to the remotest depths, where they attain it, thanks to the most powerful of instruments, the sacred decade of the Sephiroth.   Do you not remember the saying of one of our masters, the Rabbi Halaphta, the son of Dozza?

> "'Seek not heaven in yonder azure depths,
>   Where glows the burning sun and pales the moon ;
>   For heaven, my son, lies hid in thine own soul,
>   And Paradise is naught but a pure heart.'

"Yes," he continued, raising his voice, "I discern a light that guides me.   Since God has permitted us to meet, he has doubtless decreed that you shall find what you desire ; but beware of outstripping his will by a vain and guilty curiosity. Follow his law, execute his commands, create a heaven in your soul, and some day, perchance, when you least expect it, you will find the desired reward.   This, at least, is all that my science can tell you."

"Well spoken, old man," said Hafiz, laying his hand on

Abdallah's shoulder.   "Nephew," he added, "God is master of the hour ; wait and obey."

IX.

THE WELL OF ZOBEYDE.

THE night was a sweet one to Abdallah.   He saw the mysterious plant more than once in his dreams, and, as soon as he awakened, he sought to retain the friend who had given him hope, but the Jew obstinately refused his entreaty.

"No, my son," said he, "one night in thy tent is enough. The first day a man is a guest, the second a burden, the third a pest.   Thou hast nothing more to tell me, and I have nothing more to teach thee ; it is time for us to part.   Let me thank thee once more, and pray God in thy behalf.   If we have no longer the same keblah,* at least we are both the children of Abraham, and both worship the same God."

The only favor that Abdallah could obtain was for the Jew to mount a camel, and permit his two friends to accompany him a day's journey on his way.   Hafiz had taken a fancy to the stranger, and Abdallah hoped to gain some new light on the subject nearest his heart ; but the sight of the desert awakened new ideas in the old man's mind, and he thought no more of the stories of the past night.

"If I am not mistaken," said he to Hafiz, "we shall find on our way the well dug in olden times by the Sultan Zobeyde in his pilgrimage to Mecca."

"Yes," replied the cripple, "it is Haroun Al-Raschid's monument in our country.   To the calif and his pious wife we owe our finest gardens."

"A glorious monument," exclaimed the Jew, "and one that

---

* The point of the horizon toward which men turn their faces in prayer ; the Mohammedans turn toward Mecca, the Jews toward Jerusalem.

will endure when what men call glory, that is, blood uselessly shed and money foolishly spent, shall be forgotten."

"Spoken like one of the children of Israel," rejoined Hafiz. "You are a shop-keeping people. A Bedouin reasons in a different fashion. War to him is the best thing of all that earth affords. He who has not looked death in the face knows not whether he is a man. It is noble to strike with the front to the foe ; it is glorious to overthrow an enemy and avenge those we love. Are you not of the same mind, my nephew?"

"You are right, my uncle ; but battle is not pleasure without alloy. I remember the time when, closely pressed by a Bedouin who held a pistol to my head, I plunged my sword into his breast. He fell ; my joy was extreme, but it was of short duration. As I looked on his dim eyes, and his lips covered with the foam of death, I thought in spite of myself that he had a mother who, however proud she might be of having given birth to a brave man, must thenceforth remain lonely and desolate, as my mother would have been had her son been killed instead. And this man was a Mussulman— that is, a brother ! Perhaps you are right," added the young man, turning to the Jew. "War doubtless is noble ; but to fight the desert, like the calif, and force the wilderness to give way before fertility and abundance—this is great indeed ! Happy they who lived in the days of Zobeyde the Good !"

"Why not imitate those you admire?" asked the old man in a low tone, as if wishing to be heard by Abdallah alone.

"Explain yourself," said the Bedouin ; "I do not understand you."

"Nor I neither," said the cripple.

"It is because the eyes of youth are not yet open, and those of old age are blinded by habit. Why is this clump of acacias in this spot, when all around it is barren ? Why do these sheep browse on grass which is almost green here when the sands of the desert have dominion every where else? Why do these birds flutter in and out among the sheep, and pick up the still sprouting earth with their beaks? You see this daily, and because you see it daily you do not reflect on it. Men are made thus ; they would admire the sun did it not return every morning."

"You are right," said Abdallah, thoughtfully : "there is water in this spot ; perhaps one of the wells formerly dug by the calif."

"How can you be certain?" asked Hafiz.

"You would not ask the question," returned the Jew, "if, like me, you had grown old on the Talmud. Hearken to the words of one of our masters, and know that all knowledge is contained in our law. 'The words of the law before the coming of Solomon were like unto a well, whose cool water lies far below the surface of the earth, so that none can drink thereof. Seeing this, the wise man fastens one rope to another and one thread to another, then draws and drinks. It was thus that Solomon passed from allegory to allegory, and from speech to speech, till he had fathomed the words of the law.'"

"Whoever finds this spring will find a treasure," said the shepherd. "Stay with us, stranger, and we will seek it together : you shall aid us with your science, and we will share with you."

"No," replied the Jew. "He who weds Science weds poverty. I have lived too happily for half a century with Study to be divorced from her now. Wealth is an imperious mistress ; she requires the whole heart and life of man. Leave her to the young."

The sun was going down on the horizon. The old man dismounted from his camel and thanked his two companions, whom he tenderly embraced, insisting that they should go no farther. "Be not concerned about me," he said; "he has nothing to fear who has poverty for his baggage, old age for his escort, and God for his companion." And, waving his hand for the last time, he resolutely plunged into the desert.

X.

THE COPPER LEAF.

IT was not a difficult matter to purchase the spot of ground where the piercing eye of the pilgrim had divined a spring; a few feddans* of half-barren sand are of little value in the desert, and twenty douros that Halima had formerly received from Mansour, and had kept carefully in an old vase, sufficed to crown Abdallah's wishes. Hafiz, who was always prudent, gave out that he intended to build there a shelter for his flock, and immediately set to work to bring sufficient boughs thither to conceal from all eyes the mysterious work about to be undertaken.

Wherever there are women and children there are curiosity and gossip. It was soon a common rumor among the tribe that Hafiz and his nephew passed the nights in digging for treasure; and when, at nightfall, as the shepherds led their flocks to water, they spied the two friends covered with sand, they did not spare their taunts and jeers. "What is that?" they asked; "jackals hiding in their den, dervishes hollowing out their cell, or old men building their tomb?" "No," was the answer, "magicians digging a path to the bottomless pit." "Let them be patient," cried others; "they will find their way there only too soon." And the laughter and ridicule went on: no bit has yet been found to curb the mouth of the envious and ignorant.

* The feddan is a little less than our acre.

Abdallah and his uncle continued to dig with ardor for more than a month with but little progress; the sand caved in, and the night destroyed the labor of the day. Halima was the first to lose patience. She accused her brother of having yielded too easily to the folly of a child. By degrees Hafiz grew discouraged, acknowledged the justice of his sister's reproaches, and abandoned the undertaking. "God has punished me for my weakness," said he. "It was a great mistake to listen to the wretched impostor who amused himself with our credulity. Could any thing else have been expected from those eternal foes of the Prophet and the truth?"

Abdallah, left alone, did not suffer himself to be cast down by misfortune. "God is my witness," he repeated, "that I am laboring for my people, and not for myself alone. If I fail, what matters my pains? if I succeed, what matters the time?" He passed another whole month in propping up the inside of the well with wood, and, having secured his work, began to dig anew.

On the fifteenth day of the third month, Hafiz, urged by Halima, determined to make a last effort with that headstrong nephew who continued to cherish a foolish hope after his uncle had set him the example of wisdom and resignation. To preach to Abdallah was not an easy task; the well was already thirty cubits deep, and the workman was at the bottom. Hafiz threw himself on the ground, and, putting his mouth to the edge of the hole, shouted, "You headstrong child, more stubborn than a mule, have you sworn to bury yourself in this accursed well?"

"Since you are there, uncle," answered Abdallah, in a voice which seemed to come from the bottomless pit, "will you be kind enough to draw up the pannier and empty it, to save time?"

"Unhappy boy," cried Hafiz, in a tone more of anger than

pity, "have you forgotten the lessons which I gave you in your childhood? Have you so little respect for your mother and me that you persist in afflicting us? Have you forgotten the beautiful saying of the Koran, 'Whoso is preserved from the covetousness of his own soul, he shall surely prosper?' Do you think—"

"Father! father!" cried Abdallah, "I feel moisture; the water is coming; I hear it. Help! draw up the pannier, or I am lost."

Hafiz sprang to the rope, and well it was for him that he did so, for, despite all his haste, he brought up his nephew covered with mud, senseless, and half drowned. The water was rushing and boiling up in the well. Abdallah soon came to himself, and listened with delight to the rushing of the water; his heart beat violently, and Hafiz's eyes filled with tears. Suddenly the noise ceased. Hafiz lighted a handful of dry grass and threw it into the well, and, less than ten paces from the surface, he saw the water, smooth and glittering as steel. To lower a jug and draw it up again was the work of an instant. The water was sweet. Abdallah fell on his knees and bowed his head to the earth. His uncle followed his example, then rose, embraced his nephew, and entreated his pardon.

Within an hour, despite the heat of the day, the two Bedouins had fixed a windlass by the side of the spring, furnished with earthen buckets and turned by two oxen, and the groaning sakiah poured the water upon the yellow grass, and restored to the earth the freshness of spring.

At nightfall, instead of going to the watering-place, the shepherds stopped with their flocks at the spring, and the scoffers of the night before glorified Abdallah. "We foresaw it," said the elders. "Happy the mother of such a son!" exclaimed the matrons. "Happy the wife of such a brave and handsome youth !" thought the maidens. And all added, " Blessed be the servant of God and his children's children !"

When the tribe was assembled together, the son of Yusuf filled a jug with water as cool as that of the well of Zemzem,* and, resting it on his arm, offered it first to his mother, and then to each of the others in turn. He himself was the last to drink. As he lifted the vessel to drain it to the bottom he felt something cold strike his lips. It was a bit of metal that had been swept along by the spring.

"What is this, my uncle?" asked he of Hafiz. "Does copper thus lie hidden in the bowels of the earth?"

"Oh, my son, preserve it ; it is the choicest of treasures," cried the old man. "God has sent you the reward of your courage and labor. Do you not see that it is a clover leaf? The earth itself has opened to bring you from its depths this flower of Paradise. All that the honest son of Israel told us is true. Hope, my child, hope ! Praise God the Only, the Incomparable, and the All-powerful ! He alone is great !"

XI.

THE GARDENS OF IREM.

VERDANT gardens watered by living springs, branches laden with fruit, palm-trees, pomegranates, eternal shade—such is the paradise which the Book of Truth promises the faithful. Abdallah received a foretaste of this paradise on earth. His garden in a few years was the most beautiful spot imaginable —a shady and peaceful retreat, the delight of the eye and the heart. White clematis twined round the acacias and olive-trees, hedges of myrtle surrounded the dourah, barley, and melon-beds with perpetual verdure, and the cool water, flow-

---

* A sacred well within the walls of the temple at Mecca; the same, according to tradition, which gushed forth in the desert at the command of the angel to quench the thirst of Hagar and Ishmael.

ing through numerous trenches, bathed the foot of the young orange-trees. Grapes, bananas, apricots, and pomegranates abounded in their season, and flowers blossomed all the year round. In this happy abode, where sadness never came, the rose, the jasmine, the mint, the gray-eyed narcissus, and the wormwood with its azure blossoms, seemed to smile on the passer-by, and delighted him with their gentle fragrance when his eye was weary of admiring their beauty. What thicket escapes the piercing eye of the bird? These friends of the fruits and flowers hastened thither from every quarter of the horizon. One would have said that they knew the hand that fed them. In the morning, when Abdallah quitted his tent to spread the carpet of prayer on the dew-bespangled grass, the sparrows welcomed him with joyful cries, the turtle-doves cooed more tenderly than ever from under the broad fig-leaves, the bees alighted on his head, and the butterflies fluttered around him ; flowers, birds, humming insects, and murmuring waters, all things living seemed to render him thanks, all lifted up Abdallah's soul toward Him who had given him peace and plenty.

It was not for himself that the son of Yusuf had desired the wealth which he shared with his friends. He dug a deep basin at the bottom of the garden into which the water flowed and remained cool during the summer droughts. The birds, fluttering about it, attracted the caravans from afar. "What water is that?" said the camel-drivers. "During all the years that we have traveled over the desert we have never seen this cistern. Have we mistaken our road? We filled our skins for seven days, and here we find water on the third day's march? Are these the gardens of Irem* which we are per-

---

* Sheddad, the king of Ad, having heard of Paradise and its delights, undertook to build a palace and garden which should rival it in magnificence. A terrible voice from heaven destroyed this monument of pride, or, rather, rendered it invisible, for a certain

mitted to behold? Has God forgiven the presumptuous monarch who undertook to create a paradise in the midst of the desert?" "No," answered Halima, "these are not the gardens of Irem. What you behold is the work of labor and prayer. God has blessed my son Abdallah." And the well was called the Well of the Benediction.

XII.

THE TWO BROTHERS.

THREE things are the delight of the eye, says the proverb —running water, verdure, and beauty. Halima felt what was lacking in this well-watered and verdant garden. Again and again she repeated to her son that a man should not suffer his father's name to perish, but Abdallah turned a deaf ear to her. He had no thought of marriage; his mind was elsewhere. He looked continually at the tiny copper leaf, and continually asked himself by what deed of valor or goodness he could please God and obtain the only boon that he desired. Man's heart has not room for two passions at the same time.

One evening, when old Hafiz had visited his sister, and was using all his eloquence to persuade this wild colt to submit to the bridle, a gun fired at a distance announced the arrival of a caravan. Abdallah rose instantly to meet the strangers, leaving Halima in despair and poor Hafiz confounded. He soon returned, bringing with him a man still in his youth, but already fat and corpulent. The stranger bowed to Hafiz and Halima, gazed at them earnestly, then, fixing his small eyes on the Bedouin, "Is not this the tribe of the Beni Amurs," he

Ibn Kelabah pretended to have seen them during the reign of the Calif Moyawiah. The gardens of Irem are as celebrated among the Arabs as the Tower of Babel among the Hebrews.

asked, " and am I not in the tent of Abdallah, the son of Yusuf?"

" It is Abdallah that has the honor of welcoming you," answered the young man; "all that is here belongs to your lordship."

"What!" cried the new-comer, "have ten years' absence so changed me that I am a stranger in this dwelling? Has Abdallah forgotten his brother? Has my mother but one son?"

The meeting was a joyful one after so long a separation. Abdallah embraced Omar again and again, and Halima kissed first one and then the other, while Hafiz whispered to himself that man is a wicked animal. To suspect the son of Mansour of ingratitude was a crime, but how often had this crime been committed by the old shepherd.

The repast finished and the pipes brought, Omar took up the conversation. "How delighted I am to see you," said he, tenderly clasping his brother's hand, "and the more so that I come to do you a service."

" Speak, brother!" said the son of Yusuf. "Having nothing to hope or fear except from God, I know not what service you can render me; but danger often draws near us without our knowledge, and nothing is quicker than the eye of a friend."

"It is not danger, but fortune that is in question," returned the son of Mansour. "Behold what brought me hither. I come from Taif, whither I had been summoned by the grand sherif. 'Omar,' said he to me, 'I know you to be the richest and most prudent merchant of Djiddah; you are known throughout the desert, where there is not a tribe that does not respect your name, or is not ready, at the sight of your signet, to furnish camels to transport your merchandise, or brave men to defend it. For this reason, I have conceived a high esteem for you, and it is to give you a proof of it that I have summoned you hither.'

"I bowed respectfully and awaited the pleasure of the sherif, who stroked his beard a long time before proceeding. 'The Pacha of Egypt,' said he at last, in a hesitating manner —'the Pacha of Egypt, who prizes my friendship as I prize his, has sent me a slave who will be the gem of my harem, and whom, through respect for the hand that chose her, I can receive only as a wife. The pacha does me an honor which I accept with gratitude, though I am old, and at my age, having already a wife whom I love, it would have been wiser not to risk the peace of my household. But this slave has not yet arrived, and it is to conduct her hither that I need your prudence and skill. She can not land at Djiddah, which is under Turkish rule, and must therefore go to Yambo, in my dominions. The way is long from Yambo to Taif, and the wandering hordes and haughty tribes of the desert do not always respect my name. It does not suit me to make war on them at present, neither is it fitting that I should expose myself to insult. I am in need, therefore, of a wise and sagacious man to go to Yambo for me as if on his own behalf. You can easily make the journey, and no one will be surprised at it. What is more natural than that you should go to meet a valuable cargo, and who would attack you, a simple merchant, in a country where you have so many friends and resources?'

"Thus spoke the sherif. I sought to decline the dangerous favor, but was met with a terrible look. The displeasure of a prince is like the roar of the lion ; to incense him is to rush into his jaws. I resigned myself to what I could not help. 'Commander of the Faithful,' I replied, 'it is true that God has blessed my efforts, and that I have a few friends in the desert. It is for thee to command ; speak, and I obey.'"

"That is well," said Abdallah; "there is peril to brave and glory to win."

"It is for this reason that I have come to thee," resumed the son of Mansour. "With whom should I share this noble enterprise if not with thee, my brother, the bravest of the brave—if not with the wise and prudent Hafiz—if not with thy bold comrades? The Bedouins on the road have never seen me—they only know my name; and, besides, instead of defending my caravan, they might plunder it, as they have done more than once; but if thou art there with thy followers, they will think twice before attacking it. To thee, therefore, it belongs to conduct the affair—to thee will revert all the honor thereof. Thou seest that I speak with perfect frankness. As for me, I am only a merchant; thou art a man of thought and action. It is said in the desert that I am rich and fond of money—a reputation which is a peril rather than an aid; thou, on the contrary, art respected and dreaded. The name of the son of Yusuf is a power—his presence is worth an army. Without thee I can do nothing; with thee I am sure of succeeding in an adventure in which my head is at stake. Am I wrong in relying on thee?"

"No," said Abdallah; "we are links of one chain; woe to him who breaks it! We will set out to-morrow, and, happen what may, thou shalt find me by thy side. A brother is born for evil days."

XIII.

THE CARAVAN.

THE same evening every thing was in readiness for departure—the skins filled, the provisions prepared, the bundles of hay counted, and the harness examined. Abdallah chose the surest camels and the most experienced drivers. Nor was this all : he engaged twelve young men, brave companions, of tried courage, who laughed at fatigue and war. Who would not have been proud of following the son of Yusuf? His glance commanded respect, his words went to the heart. With sabre always drawn and hand always open, he was the boldest of leaders and the tenderest of friends. Beside him men were as tranquil as the hawk in the cloud or death in the tomb. On his part, Hafiz passed a sleepless night. To clean the guns, try the powder, run the bullets, and sharpen the sabres and daggers, was work to his taste, a pleasure that he yielded to no one.

As soon as the stars began to pale the caravan set out on its way, with Abdallah at the head by the side of Omar, and Hafiz in the rear, watching every thing, and throwing out timely words of fault-finding or praise. The camels walked slowly in single file, accompanied by their leaders chanting the songs of the desert. In the midst of the band proudly marched a magnificent dromedary, with a slender head, of the Oman breed, covered with gold, silver, and shining plumes, and bearing a litter hung with velvet and brocade, the equipage of the new favorite. The silver-pommeled saddles, Damascus blades, and black burnous embroidered with gold, of twelve riders mounted on fine horses, glittered in the first beams of the sun. Next came Abdallah's mare, led by a servant. Nothing could be imagined more beautiful than this mare, the glory of the tribe, and the despair and envy of all the Bedouins : she was called Hamama, the Dove, because she was as snowy, gentle, and fleet as this queen of the forests.

Abdallah, dressed like a simple camel-driver, and armed with a long iron-headed staff, walked on foot by the side of Omar, who was seated tranquilly on his mule. They were among friends, and had nothing to fear, so that the brothers could talk at length of the past. When the sun darted its vertical rays. on their heads, and the scorching air enervated man and beast, the son of Yusuf took his place by the side of the first camel-driver, and, in a grave and solemn voice, chanted one of those hymns of the desert which beguile the lonely way, to the praise of God.

> God alone is great!
> Who maketh the earth to tremble?
> Who launcheth the thunderbolt through the burning air?
> Who giveth the sands to the fury of the simoom?
> Who causeth the torrent to gush forth from its arid bed?
> His name? hearest thou it not in the whirlwind?
> God alone is great!
>
> God alone is great!
> Who calleth the storm from the depths of the sea?
> Who causeth the rain and clouds to give way before the sun?
> Who forceth the hungry wave to lick the strand?
> His name? the wind murmureth it in its flight to the dying wave:
> God alone is great!

Oh the power of the divine name! At the sound of these praises the very brutes forgot their fatigue and marched with a firm tread; the camel-drivers raised their heads; all refreshed themselves with these words as at a running brook. It is the strength of the soul that gives energy to the body, and for the soul there is no strength but in God.

Thus passed the first day. The next day some precautions were taken; Hafiz went in advance as a scout; they set out as soon as the moon had risen, marched in silence, and stopped earlier than the day before, but saw no one. The succeeding days also passed quietly, and on the evening of the ninth day's march they saw at last the walls and towers of Yambo.

XIV.

CAFOUR.

THE caravan made a short stay in the city; the brig that brought the slave had arrived the night before, and Omar was in haste to return in peace to Djiddah. The camels rested, they took the way to the desert.

They received the sultana at the water's edge. A flat-boat put off from the ship with two women wrapped in habarahs, or large mantles of black taffeta, and their faces shrouded, all but the eyes, in bourkos, or white muslin veils that fell to the feet. Omar received the strangers with a respectful bow, and led them to the equipage that awaited them. The dromedary knelt down at the voice of Abdallah. One of the women slowly mounted the palanquin and seated herself, gracefully drawing the folds of her robe about her; the other approached with equal gravi- ty, but, suddenly snatching off her mantle and veil, she threw them over Omar's head, twisting the muslin around his face, and almost smothering him; then, putting one foot on the camel's neck, she leaped on his back like a cat, grimacing like an ape at the astonished Bedouins, and shouting with laughter.

"Cafour, you shall be whipped," cried the veiled lady, who had much ado to preserve her gravity; but Cafour did not believe her mistress's threats, and continued to laugh and grimace at Omar as soon as his head emerged from the coverings. The son of Mansour at last threw off the heap of silk under which he had been buried, and raised his head angrily toward the creature that had insulted him; but what was his astonishment to see a smile on the faces of the grave Bedouins and Abdallah himself. All shrugged their shoulders as they pointed to his enemy. He looked, and saw a little negro girl of surpassing ugliness. A round flat face, with small eyes, the whites of which were scarcely visible, a flat nose sunken below the cheeks, wide nostrils, from which hung a silver ring that fell below the mouth, enormous lips, teeth as white as those of a young dog, and a chin tattooed blue—such was the charming face of the damsel. To add to her ugliness, she was loaded with jewels like an idol. On the crown of her head was a plume of parrot's feathers. The thick wool that covered her head was parted in little tresses ornamented with sequins; her ears were pierced like a sieve, and hung with rings of every shape and size; a broad necklace of blue enamel encircled her neck, and her arm was covered from the wrist to the elbow with seven or eight bracelets of coral, amber, and filigree work; lastly, she wore on each ankle a prodigious silver band. Such was Cafour, the delight of her mistress, the beautiful Leila.

Full license is given fools, the favorites of God, whose soul is in heaven while their body drags on the earth. The whole caravan, therefore, except Omar, who still bore her a grudge, took a liking to the poor negress. It was but too evident that she had not her reason; she talked and laughed continually; her tongue spared nobody, and her judgments were insane. For instance, she gazed long at the son of Mansour, who, half reclining on his mule, marched by the side of the litter, surrounded by his slaves, slowly smoking Persian tobacco in his jasmine pipe. One of the servants having filled the pipe too full, he dealt him a box on the ear. "Mistress," cried Cafour, "do you see that old man buried in a cushion, with his feet in slippers? He is a Jew, mistress; beware of him; he would beat us for a douro, and sell us for a sequin." Leila laughed, while Omar flew into a passion and threatened the negress. To style a man who counted his piastres by millions an old man and a Jew was indeed the act of an idiot. What person in his right mind would have dared to talk thus?

It was soon the turn of Abdallah, who was reviewing the caravan.   He had put on his war-dress, and every one admired the grace of the young chief.   His white burnous floated in long folds ; his Damascus pistols and silver-hilted cangiar glittered in his belt ; and a red and yellow silk turban overshadowed his eyes, and added to the fierceness of his glance. How beautiful he was !   All hearts went out toward him, and his very mare seemed proud of carrying such a master.   Hamama tossed her serpentine head and reed-like ears ; her dilated nostrils breathed forth fire ; on seeing her start, vault, stop short, and bound forward, it seemed as if she and her rider were but one.   As the son of Yusuf paused near the litter, a camel-driver could not help saying to Cafour, "Look, child ; do you see such beauty among your coarse Egyptians or in your Maghreb ?"

"Look, mistress," cried the negress, leaning over the camel's neck ; "see these fine clothes, elegant air, tapering fingers, and cast-down eyes !   Pretty bird, why don't you look at us ?" said she to Abdallah.   "Oh, I know ; it is a woman in disguise— the virgin of the tribe.   Driver, tell him to come up here ; he belongs here with us."

"Silence, infidel !" exclaimed Abdallah, losing his patience. "Must you have a ring through your lips to stop your serpent's tongue ?"

"It is a woman," said Cafour, laughing loudly; "a man does not avenge himself by insults.   Come, women are made to love each other.   You are handsome, and so am I, but my mistress is the handsomest of the three.   Look !"

The eye is quicker than the thought.   Abdallah raised his eyes to the litter.   Cafour playfully laid hold of her mistress's veil, the frightened Leila drew back, the string broke, and the bourko fell.   Leila uttered a cry and covered her face with one hand, while with the other she boxed the ears of the negress, who began to cry. The whole passed like a flash of lightning.

"How beautiful she is!" thought the son of Mansour. "I must have her."

"Glory to Him who created her, and created her so perfect!" murmured the son of Yusuf.

Who can tell the pain and pleasure that a moment can contain? Who can tell how this fleeting vision entered and filled Abdallah's soul? The caravan went on, but the Bedouin remained motionless. Leila had hidden herself in her veil, yet a woman stood smiling before the son of Yusuf. He closed his eyes, yet, despite himself, he saw a brow as white as ivory, cheeks as blooming as the tulip, and tresses blacker than ebony falling on a gazelle-like neck, like the date-branch laden with golden fruit. A pair of lips like a thread of scarlet parted to call him ; a pair of large eyes gazed at him—eyes surrounded with a bluish ring, and sparkling with a lustre softer than that of the violet moist with dew. Abdallah felt his heart escaping him ; he buried his face in his hands and burst into tears.

The caravan continued its march, and old Hafiz, who brought up the rear, soon found himself by the side of his nephew. Astonished at the silence and inaction of the young chief, he approached him, and, touching his arm, "Something new has happened, has there not?" he asked.

Abdallah started, and, recovering himself like a man aroused from a dream, "Yes, my father," he answered in a dejected tone.

"The enemy is at hand !" cried Hafiz, with sparkling eyes ; "you have seen him ! Glory to God, our guns are about to speak !"

"No one threatens us ; the danger is not there."

"What is the matter then, my son?" said the old man, anxiously. "Are you sick? have you a fever? You know that I am skilled in the art of healing."

"That is not it: at our first halt I will tell you all."

"You frighten me," said Hafiz; "if it is neither danger nor sickness that disturbs you, some evil passion must be troubling your soul! Take care, my son; with God's aid the foe is defeated, and with God's aid sickness is cured: there is but one enemy against which there is no defense, and that enemy is our own heart."

XV.

THE SULTAN OF CANDAHAR.

WHEN the caravan halted, Abdallah took his uncle aside. Hafiz seated himself on his carpet and began to smoke, without uttering a word. The young chief, wrapped in his cloak, stretched himself on the ground, and long remained motionless. Suddenly he started up, and, kissing the old man's hand, "My uncle," said he, "I implore the protection of God. What God wills must come; there is no strength nor power but in Him." And, in an agitated voice, he related the vision which had troubled him.

"Oh, my son," said the shepherd, with a sigh, "thou art punished for not hearkening to our words. Happy is he who chooses a virtuous and obedient wife from among his tribe, with the sole desire of perpetuating the name of his father. Woe to him who suffers his soul to be taken in the snares of a strange woman! Can any thing good come out of Egypt? All the women there, since Joseph's time, have been dissolute and treacherous, worthy daughters of Zuleika!"* ⌐ ____

"Treachery had naught to do with it, my uncle; it was wholly the work of chance."

* The name given by the Arabs to Potiphar's wife.

"Do not believe it, my nephew; there is no such thing as chance with these cunning fishers for men's hearts, who spread their nets every where."

"She loves me, then!" exclaimed the youth, starting up; "but no, my uncle, you are mistaken. In two days we shall be at Taif; in two days we shall be separated forever, yet I feel that I shall always love her!"

"Yes, you will love her, but she will forget you for the first jewel from the hand of her new master. Your heart serves her as a plaything; when the whim of the moment has passed, she will break it without remorse. Have your forgotten what the Koran says of that imperfect and capricious being who is brought up among ornaments and jewels? 'The reason of women is folly, and their religion love. Like the flowers, they are the delight of the eyes and the joy of the senses, but they are poisoned blossoms; woe to him who draws near them; he will soon have a winding-sheet for his raiment!' Believe in my experience; I have seen more families destroyed by women than by war. The more generous a man is, the greater is his danger. Do you not know the story of the Sultan of Candahar, who was a true believer, though he lived in the days of ignorance before the coming of Mohammed, and a sage, though he sat on a throne? He undertook to gather together all the maxims of human prudence, in order to leave to his children an inheritance worthy of him. With this end, the philosophers of the Indies had written a library, which he took with him every where, and which ten camels scarce sufficed to carry. 'Reduce all this science to first principles,' said he. It was done, and but a camel's load remained. This was still too much. A number of aged Brahmins, chosen by the king, reduced this abridgment of long experience first to ten volumes, then to five, and then to a single one, which was offered to the sultan in a box of velvet and gold. The prince had reigned long, and life had few secrets from him. He took the book, and began to blot out all that was self-evident and therefore unnecessary. 'What is the danger that threatens my sons?' thought he; 'not avarice, for that is the malady of the old; nor ambition, for that is the virtue of princes. I will strike out all this. But at last he came to a more violent passion. He was so forcibly struck by the truth of an adage that he threw the book into the fire, and bequeathed this maxim alone to his children, calling it the key to the treasure of life: 'All women are false—above all, the one that loves thee!' Such was the adage. Wouldst thou, my son, be more prudent than this infidel, more enlightened than Solomon, or wiser than the Prophet? No; believe me, the beauty of woman is like the scabbard of the sabre—a glittering covering that hides death. Do not go to meet thy destruction. Think of God, preserve thyself for thy old and true friends, and, if more is needed to move thee, have pity on thy mother and old Hafiz."

"Thou art right," said Abdallah, sadly, as he stretched himself on the ground, with his burnous for a pillow. For the first time he did not believe his uncle's words; for the first time, too, the four-leaved clover was forgotten.

XVI.

THE ATTACK.

NIGHT is an antidote to fatigue and a poison to sorrow. The son of Yusuf rose with a mind more diseased than the night before. Struck with incurable madness, he no longer felt himself the master of his will or his movements; it was the delirium of fever, the dejection of despair. Despite himself, the fatal litter attracted him; he hastened to it, then turned and fled, pursued by those terrible yet charming eyes.

If he saw from afar a horseman approaching the palanquin—
if the son of Mansour turned toward the two women, he spurred on his horse as if about to attack an enemy, then suddenly paused, daring neither to draw back nor advance. The
whole morning he tortured his horse. Panting and covered
with foam, Hamama bounded forward under the spur which
tore her sides, astonished at not understanding her master
and sharing his madness.

The shepherd cast withering glances toward the litter.
Leila had thrown herself back in the corner, and covered her
head with her veil, and no one was to be seen but Cafour,
spiritless and mute as a wet bird. More tranquil in this respect, Hafiz turned to look for his nephew, and saw him wandering at random in the desert. Every thing about him betrayed a diseased mind. Hafiz spurred his horse toward
Abdallah. "Cheer up, my nephew!" he cried. "Courage!
We are men in order to suffer; we are Mussulmen in order
to submit to fate."

"I am stifling," answered the youth; "I am conquered by
the malady that is preying upon me. Any thing—any thing,
my uncle, rather than what I suffer! Let danger come—let
the enemy draw near; I wish to fight and to die!"

"Mad wishes and guilty words," replied the old man, sternly. "God is the master of life and death. Beware lest he
grant thy prayer; it is sufficient punishment that God should
give us what we ask him in our folly. What is that?" he
added, leaping from his horse, and carefully examining the
ground. "These are the prints of horses' feet; there are no
camels among them. An armed band has passed this way.
The marks are fresh; the enemy is not far off. Do you not
feel that your passion is destroying us? You, our leader, have
noticed nothing; you are leading us to death."

The two companions looked about them, but saw nothing

but the desert. They were passing through a desolate country. The road wound among prodigious blocks of reddish
granite, strewed over the sands like crumbling ruins. The
earth was full of gaping crevices, the beds of dried-up tor-
rents and deep caves—graves open for the traveler. There
was not a bird in the air, not a gazelle in the distance, not
a black speck in the horizon; with a steel-like sky above
their heads, and the silence of death around them, attacked
there, their only hope was in their sabres and God.

Hafiz ran to the head of the caravan. Each one fell in
line and was as silent as in a night-march; naught was to be
heard but the crackling of the sand under the feet of the
camels. After an hour's march—an hour which seemed interminable—they reached a hill which it was necessary to
turn. Hafiz went in advance; he ascended the hill, and,
leaving his horse half way from the top, crept on his belly
among the rocks. After gazing long, he noiselessly descended, put his horse to the gallop, and reached Abdallah's side,
his face as calm as at his departure. "There are white tents
in the distance," said he. "They are not Bedouins, but Arnauts from Djiddah. They are numerous, and are awaiting
us; we have been betrayed. No matter; we will sell our
skin more dearly than they will care to buy it. Forward, my
son, and do your duty." And, calling six of the bravest of
the company, Hafiz loaded his gun and again took the way to
the height.

Abdallah had just reached the head of the column when a
white smoke appeared from a rock, a bullet whizzed through
the air, and a camel fell. Great confusion instantly prevailed
in the caravan; the camels fell back, rushing against and
overthrowing each other; the drivers fled to the rear, and the
horsemen rushed to the front. It seemed like a forest shaken
by the wind. The moans of the camels and neighing of the

horses mingled with the shouts of the men. In the disorder, a handful of robbers, whose red vests, white drawers, and broad girdles easily showed them to be Arnauts, fell upon the litter and hurried it away with shouts of joy. It was in vain that Abdallah and his friends attempted to charge on them; the sharp-shooters in ambush felled them on the way. Thrice Abdallah spurred his horse against his invisible foe; thrice he was forced to return, his comrades falling around him.

Abdallah trembled with rage; by his side, and not less excited, was Omar, rending his clothes—Omar, whose passion made him forget all prudence, and who thought of nothing but the treasure that was snatched from him. "Forward, my brother!" he cried. Both were reining up their horses for a last effort, when several musket-shots followed each other rapidly. The Arnauts had forgotten old Hafiz, who suddenly came upon them from above, and shot them down without pity.

The road clear, the brothers rushed forward, followed by Hafiz. "Gently, my son," cried he to Abdallah; "spare your horse; we have time."

"Where is Leila, my uncle? They are carrying her off; she is lost."

"Old fool," said Omar, "do you think that these robbers will wait for us? Twenty douros to him who brings down the dromedary!"

One of the Bedouins raised his gun, and, taking aim, fired, at the risk of killing the two women. The shot struck the shoulder of the animal, which fell with his precious burden.

"Well done, young man," said Hafiz, sarcastically, to the Bedouin. "The Arnauts will thank you; you have rid them of the only obstacle to their flight. Now the sultana is lost."

Hafiz had judged but too rightly. The robbers surrounded the litter and tore from it a woman wrapped in a mantle,

in whom Abdallah recognized Leila; then, by the command of
a magnificently-dressed chief, a man took her behind him and
set off at full gallop. At this sight the son of Yusuf darted
upon the enemy like an eagle from the clouds. "Dog! son
of a dog!" he cried, "show your face, if you are a man! Is it
to fly the better that you have so fine a horse?" And he fired
his pistol at him.

"Wait, son of a Jew!" said the captain, turning round, "my
sabre is thirsting for your blood."

"Forward, children of powder!" cried old Hafiz. "Charge,
my sons; death before disgrace! Charge! Bullets do not
kill. What is to be will be, according to God's will."

Abdallah and the Arnaut rushed upon each other at full
speed. The captain advanced with a pistol in one hand and
a sword in the other. Abdallah had nothing but a dagger,
which he held in his hand as he leaned forward, almost concealed by the mare's neck. The Arnaut fired and missed.
The horses met with a violent shock, and the riders engaged
hand to hand. But Abdallah had the strength and rage of a
lion; he seized his rival around the waist, shook him with a
terrible grasp, and plunged his dagger into his breast. The
blood spouted forth like wine from a pierced skin, and the
Arnaut bounded up and reeled in his saddle. Abdallah
snatched him from his horse and threw him on the ground
as if to trample on him. "There is one that will drink no
more," said Hafiz, leaping on the body to despoil it.

The fall of the captain, the swords of the Bedouins, who fell
on the enemy like bees robbed of their honey, and the cries
of the camel-drivers, who rushed thither with their guns, soon
decided the day. The Arnaut troop disappeared amid dust
and smoke, the bravest remaining in the rear and firing their
pistols to protect a retreat which it was not dared to molest.
The victory was dearly bought; more than one was wounded.

"Well, my brother," said Omar, with flashing eyes, "shall we stand here while these robbers are carrying off our property?"

"Forward, my friends!" cried Abdallah. "One more effort; we must have the sultana."

"She is here, my lord, she is here," answered several voices.

Abdallah turned abruptly and saw Leila, who had just been extricated from the litter, covered with dust and blood, with pale face and disheveled hair, yet more beautiful than ever despite this disorder. "Save me!" she cried, stretching out her arms, "save me! my only hope is in you."

"Who was it, then, that those knaves carried off?" asked Hafiz.

"It was Cafour," said Leila; "she had put on my mantle and wrapped me in her burnous."

"Well played," said a Bedouin, laughing; "those sons of dogs have taken an ape for a woman."

"Let us begone quickly," cried the son of Mansour, feasting his eyes on Leila. "Let us begone; the day is ours. Come, madam, do not mourn for the slave," said he to Leila. "For two hundred douros I can buy just such another at Djiddah, which I shall be happy to offer you."

"Let us go," echoed the camel-drivers; "the band is large, and will return to attack us during the night."

Hafiz looked at Abdallah. "What!" said the young man, moved with pity, "shall we leave the negress in the hands of these wretches?"

"What is written is written," replied Omar, who had lost all desire to fight. "Is it wise, my brother, to risk your life and that of these brave Mussulmen for a heathen whom we can replace in two days? We must go; we are expected at Taif. Are you about to quit us when we are in need of you?"

"Abdallah," said the young woman, raising her beautiful eyes to him, "do not abandon me!"

The son of Yusuf placed his hand on his heart, which he felt faltering. "No, no," he exclaimed; "it shall not be said that a Bedouin forfeits his word. If a sack of coffee had been intrusted to me, I would not leave it in the hands of these robbers, and shall I abandon to them one of God's creatures? Are there any men here? Who will come with me?" There was silence, and one of the Beni Amurs stepped forth.

"There are six of us wounded, and the sultana is saved," said he. "We have kept our engagement."

"Come, my child," said Hafiz, ironically, "I see that we are the only two here that have madness in our veins. Let us go. With God's aid, we will recover the child."

"Adieu, my brother," said Abdallah, embracing Omar; "take good care of the stranger. If you do not see me in two days, tell the sherif that I have done my duty, and my mother not to weep for me." And, without turning his head, the son of Yusuf took the way to the desert, accompanied by Hafiz, who unclasped his burnous, and threw over his shoulders a camel-driver's cloak. "We need the skin of the fox instead of the lion," said he, laughing.

Omar followed them with his eyes, and when he saw them disappear, "If they do not return," thought he, "it will be no great matter. I shall make a better bargain with the sherif than with that youth. It is not easy to dazzle or deceive these madcaps who never reason. Hurrah for men that calculate! they are always to be bought, and through their wisdom we get them at half price."

As he went on, Abdallah heard behind him the shouts of the camel-drivers and the noise of the moving caravan. He was quitting all that he loved for a strange child. More than once he was inclined to look back, but he dared not brave his uncle, who, his eyes fixed upon him, seemed to read the depths of his heart. When the last sound died away in the distance, Abdallah paused in spite of himself. His horse turned round, snuffing the wind, and anxious to rejoin its friends. Hafiz laid his hand on the young man's shoulder: "My son," said he, "your road lies before you."

XVIII.

AFTER an hour's march they came in sight of the Arnaut tents, until then hidden by a rising ground. The camp was in the midst of a small tract of brushwood, where the cattle had been turned out to browse. "Let us stop here," said Hafiz, approaching a rock illumined by the setting sun; "we have six hours before us."

The horses tethered, the old man set to work to pick up the dead branches, and tie them in small bundles, with cartouches and cotton inside. When he had finished his task, he took from a bag a piece of dried meat and a handful of dates; and, having eaten them, lighted his pipe, and began to smoke tranquilly. "Now, my nephew," said he, "I am going to sleep. Lovers do not need repose, but old men are not like lovers. Wake me when the Great Bear and her cubs are yonder in the horizon." A few moments after he was asleep, while Abdallah, his face buried in his hands, mused on her whom he had saved, and was never more to behold.

Hafiz awakened of his own accord just before the time appointed, and looked tenderly at his young companion. "Well, my child," said he, "you wished for danger that you might forget your folly, and God has granted your prayer. Have courage; two friends that cling together will come out safe from the fire."

On nearing the camp, the Bedouins glided among the bri

ers and bushes. By creeping on their hands and knees between the horses' legs, they assured themselves that it was defenseless. No sentinels had been posted except at a distant point; all were asleep; the fires had gone out, and only one tent was lighted. They noiselessly crept toward it; being in the shade, they could see without being seen. "Listen," said Hafiz; "perhaps we shall learn what has become of the child."

Three men, better dressed than soldiers, were seated on carpets, smoking long pipes, around a table* on which coffee was served. A lamp in the middle dimly lighted their faces. All three were talking warmly.

"A bad day's work!" said one of the officers. "Who would have thought that the captain would have let himself be killed by a camel-driver!"

"My dear Hassan," answered the youngest of the party, "what is one man's misfortune is another's good luck. Since the captain is dead, the command belongs to us."

"Very well, my dear Mohammed," returned Hassan; "but which of us three shall be chief?"

"I will sell my chance," said the one who had not yet spoken, and who stood with his back to Abdallah. "It is said that the woman we have taken is a relative of the Pacha of Egypt. Give me the sultana, and I will return to Epirus to live at my ease. A graybeard like me cares little for a woman, but the sherif will think differently. To him the prisoner will be well worth five thousand douros."

"Done," said Hassan. "Kara Shitan, I surrender to you my share of the prize."

"But I do not," said Mohammed; "I am twenty-five, and do not sell women. The idea of marrying a sultana pleases

---

* These tables, called kursi, are a species of benches from fifteen to eighteen inches high.

me. I should not be sorry to be the pacha's cousin. My share of the command for the princess. I have time enough to become captain."

"We can arrange it," said the graybeard; "the sword to one, the woman to another, and the money to me."

"So be it," said Hassan. "I will give two thousand douros."

"But what will Mohammed give?"

"Mohammed will promise any thing you like," replied the young man, laughing. "He who has nothing but hope in his purse does not stop to haggle."

"You have a black mare; I will take her."

"Old Jew," cried Mohammed, "dare to touch my mare and I will break your head."

"Then you shall not have the sultana," returned the graybeard.

"Who will hinder me?"

"A man that fears you little," cried Kara Shitan; and, going to the end of the tent, he touched the curtain that divided it in two. "The sultana is here; take her if you can," he said.

Mohammed drew his dagger. Hassan threw himself between the rivals, opposing prayers and counsels to threats and insults, without succeeding in imposing silence on the opponents.

"We have them," whispered Hafiz in Abdallah's ear. "I am going to draw them from the tent; take the child, go with the horses, and wait for me at the Red Rocks till daybreak."

The old man crept to his bundles of sticks, and slipped them here and there under the most distant tents, lighting the end of a match which projected from each. Manwhile Hassan had pacified the two chiefs by dint of persuasions and promises. Kara Shitan delightedly thrust in his girdle a magnificent sabre, which Mohammed eyed with regret. "Well," said he, "since I have bought the sultana, give her to me."

"It is just," said the graybeard. He called the stranger, the curtain rose, and a veiled woman came forth, wrapped in an Egyptian mantle. The young Arnaut approached her, and said, in a softened voice, "Madam, war has its rights; you no longer belong to the sherif, but to me; I have bought you with my gold; if necessary, I would have bought you with my blood."

"It is a dear bargain," said a mocking voice which made Abdallah start.

"Beauty is above all price," said Mohammed. "What treasure could pay for your charms?"

"Two purses would be enough," replied the veiled lady.

"Madam, that was not the opinion of the sherif. I am sure that the Commander of the Faithful would give half his wealth to be in my place, with the beautiful Egyptian by his side."

"If the caravan is still on its way, the beautiful Egyptian will be at Taif to-morrow," returned the stranger.

"Who are you, then?" asked Mohammed. For the answer, the veil fell, and showed the ebony face and white teeth of Cafour. The negress made so strange a figure that the old Arnaut could not help bursting into a laugh, which raised to its height the fury of his companion.

"Woe to him who has trifled with me!" cried Mohammed, looking at Kara Shitan; "he shall pay me sooner or later. As for you, dog, you shall carry it no farther." And, blind with rage, he drew a pistol and fired at the child. The negress staggered, uttering a cry of pain and terror. At the same instant a shot was heard, and Mohammed reeled and fell. Abdallah was in the tent with a pistol in his hand.

"To arms!" cried the chiefs, putting their hand to their belt. Swifter than lightning, Cafour overturned the table and lamp

with her foot, and Abdallah felt a little hand grasp his and draw him to the back of the tent. To enter the women's apartments and lift a corner of the canvas was an easy thing for Cafour, who seemed to see in the dark. Once outside, Abdallah took the child in his arms and fled to the desert.

The voice of the chiefs had roused the whole band, but on rushing into the tent they could find no one. "To horse!" cried Hassan; "dead or alive, the traitor shall not escape us."

All at once a burning torch fell in the midst of the brush. The frightened horses rushed into the plain, and at the same time the cry of fire was raised. The conflagration spread in every direction, while at a distance shots were fired at the sentinels. "Come, my children," said the captain, "it is an attack; the enemy is at hand. Forward!"

Hassan had his ear to the ground. "Allah is great; Abdallah is saved!" he exclaimed, when he heard the enemy coming toward him. He plunged into a thicket and waited for the Arnauts to pass; then, leaping upon a stray horse, he galloped into the desert, without troubling himself about the balls that whistled round him.

XVIII.

THE SILVER LEAF.

ABDALLAH ran with his burden to the rock where he had tethered the horses. He seated Cafour before him on the saddle, and gave full rein to Hamama, who flew over the ground, followed by the horse of Hafiz. An hour passed before the son of Yusuf dared stop to listen. Becoming more tranquil in proportion as he advanced, he at last slackened his speed, and tried to steer his course in the darkness toward the place where he was to meet his uncle.

During this rapid flight Cafour had remained mute and motionless, pressed close to Abdallah. When she understood that the danger was passed, she called him her savior. "Were you too a prisoner?" she whispered.

"No, thank God," answered Abdallah.

"Then why did you come among the tents of your enemies?"

"Why?" said the son of Yusuf, smiling; "to save you, of course."

The answer surprised Cafour. She mused for some time. "Why did you wish to save me?" she said.

"Because you had been confided to my keeping."

"Keep me always, Abdallah; no one will protect me like you."

"I am not your master," answered the young chief; "you belong to Leila."

Cafour sighed and said no more. On reaching the Red Rocks, Abdallah lifted her from the saddle. She uttered a cry, which she instantly smothered. "It is nothing, master; I am wounded," she whispered, and she stretched out her bleeding arm. The ball had grazed the shoulder, tearing the flesh. Abdallah examined the wound by the light of the stars, then sponged and bandaged it, while Cafour looked at him with astonishment.

"Since I do not belong to you, why do you bind up my wound?" she asked.

"Silence, heathen! you know not the words of the Book of Truth: 'Serve God, and associate no creature with him; show kindness unto parents, and relations, and orphans, and the poor, and your neighbor who is of kin to you, and also your neighbor who is a stranger, and to your familiar companion, and the traveler, and the captives whom your right hands shall possess; for God loveth neither pride, nor vanity, nor avarice.'"

"That is beautiful," said Cafour; "it was a great God who said it."

"Hush, and go to sleep," interrupted the young man; "the road will be long to-morrow, and you need rest." As he spoke, Abdallah took the child on his lap, and, wrapping her in his burnous, supported her head with his arm. Cafour soon fell asleep. At first she tossed about and talked in her sleep, while her heart beat so loudly that Abdallah could hear it. By degrees she grew calmer, her limbs relaxed, and she slept so sweetly that she could hardly be heard to breathe. The soldier gently rocked the young girl whom the fate of war had given him for a day, thinking, as he gazed on her, of his mother and all that she had suffered for him. He remained thus through the night, enjoying a peace to which he had before been a stranger. A deep silence reigned around him on the earth; not a breath of wind or a sound was stirring; in the heavens all was motionless save that luminous army which for centuries has obeyed the command of the Eternal. This repose of all things refreshed Abdallah's soul, and he forgot both the dangers of the day and the anxiety of the morrow.

A faint streak of light in the horizon had scarcely announced the dawn, when the cry of a jackal was heard in the distance. The sound was thrice repeated. Abdallah echoed it. His cry was answered, and a panting horse bounded to the rock—Hafiz was safe.

"Well, nephew," said he, laughing, "the trick has succeeded; they are smoked out like so many rats. Forward! we must not make them wait for us at Taif."

A red light streaked the east. Abdallah spread the carpet of prayer, and the two comrades, with their faces turned toward Mecca, thanked the All-Powerful who had rescued them from peril.

"Abdallah," said Cafour, falling on her knees before her savior, "you are my god; I will worship no other."

"Silence, heathen!" cried the son of Yusuf. "There is but one God, who has no associate—the Eternal, the Incomparable; it is he whom you must worship and adore."

"Then your God shall be my God," said Cafour. "I will not have a god that leaves me to be murdered."

"Your god," said Abdallah, "is deaf, dumb, and blind; it is some piece of wood rotting in the Maghreb."

"No," interrupted the child, "my god was with me, and did not help me. Here," she added, taking from her hair a tuft of feathers, "take it; break it in pieces; I want it no longer."

"Is that bunch of feathers your god?" said Hafiz, smiling.

"Yes," replied the child, "it is the god my mother gave me when she sold me. It is pretty; look at it." And, pulling out and breaking the feathers while she loaded them with reproaches, she took from the bunch a thin piece of silver, which she gave to Abdallah.

"My uncle," cried the latter, in a transport of joy, "see what has come to us from the Maghreb! God has sent us the clover-leaf. You have saved me, my uncle. Glory and gratitude to God!"

And the two friends, intoxicated with joy, embraced the child, who, not understanding their caresses, gazed at them with tears in her eyes, astonished and happy at feeling herself beloved.

XIX.

THE SECRET.

WHEN the two friends at last perceived the caravan winding like a huge serpent in the distance, night was approaching; the last beams of the sun shone on the white houses of Taif, gleaming amid the gardens like eglantines in a thicket. They were quitting the empire of the sands; the peril was overcome and the journey finished. At the sight of Taif, Abdallah was seized with bitter sorrow. Restless, troubled, bereft of his reason, one thought filled his soul—Leila was lost to him. The Bedouins received their companions with cries of joy. Omar embraced his brother with the greatest tenderness. Abdallah remained cold to all these caresses; his only emotion was on parting with Cafour. The poor girl threw herself into her savior's arms, and nothing could tear her from them, until at last Abdallah was forced harshly to command her to return to her mistress. She departed in tears. The son of Yusuf fixed a longing gaze on her; he had broken the last link that bound him to Leila.

Cafour was approaching the litter when Omar called to her,

showing her two articles which he held in his hand. "Come hither, child of Satan," he said, in a half-jeering, half-threatening tone; "what is the difference betwen this whip and this necklace of five strings of pearls?"

"The same difference that there is between your brother and you," answered the negress. "One is as beautiful as the rainbow; the other is fit for nothing but to kindle the fires of the pit."

"You have your father's wit," returned Omar, calmly; "it will not be hard, therefore, for you to choose. Do you want the necklace?"

"Yes, indeed," said the negress, with sparkling eyes. "What am I to do for it?"

"Very little. In an hour you will be in the harem; every one will wish to see you, and nothing will be easier than for you to gain admittance to the sherif's wife, the Sultana Fatima. Repeat to her, word for word, what I shall tell you, and the necklace is yours."

"Give it to me," said Cafour, stretching out her hand; "I am listening."

"While you are amusing the sultana with your ape's face and kittenish grimaces, whisper to her, 'Mistress, I have a message to you from a friend. "Moon of May," he says, "a new moon is approaching. If you do not wish her to disturb the serenity of your nights, keep the sun in the sign of Gemini. Importune, urge, and command. Take for your motto, Love is like madness; every thing is forgiven it." ' "

"Repeat the last sentence," said Cafour. "Good; I know it now: 'Love is like madness; every thing is forgiven it.' The sultana shall have your message. One word only: can these words do any harm to your brother?"

"None," replied the son of Mansour, suppressing a smile. "Abdallah has nothing whatever to do with it; he is threatened by no danger; and even if he were in peril, these words would insure his safety. Farewell; speak of this to no one; and if you obey me, rely on my generosity. The date is ripe, who will gather it?" he added to himself. "I am rid of the handsome Abdallah; it remains for me now to second the sultana's jealousy and add to the enemies of the sherif. The game is not without danger; but, cost what it may, Leila must quit the harem; once outside of it, she is mine."

On rejoining her mistress, Cafour was surprised to see her pale and haggard, her eyes glittering with fever. "What is the matter?" said the child. "Are you weeping when your happiness is about to begin? when you will have four slaves to wait on you, robes of velvet and satin, Cashmere scarfs, slippers embroidered with gold and pearls, enamel necklaces, diamond tiaras, and ruby and sapphire bracelets? What more can a woman desire? You were so happy at coming here on quitting Egypt, why have you changed?"

"You can not understand me—you are only a child," said Leila, in a languishing voice.

"I am no longer a child, mistress," returned the negress. "I am almost twelve years old; I am a woman; you can trust in me."

"Ah! my poor Cafour," cried the Egyptian, sighing, "if you would preserve your heart, keep your eyes shut. Why did I see that handsome young man? Had it not been for him, I should have joyfully entered the harem; now I shall be there like the dead among the living."

"Do you love Abdallah, then?" asked the child, touched by this confidence.

"Do I love him? Is it possible to see him without loving him? Is there a more beautiful face than his in Paradise? His look is so gracious, his voice so sweet, his very name is perfume! Do I love him? Awake, my soul lives for him alone; asleep, my heart wakes and languishes with love! Would to God that I had been born amid the tents, with this Bedouin for my brother, that I might cast myself into his arms with none to despise me!"

"Go with him," said Cafour. "I will tell him to carry you off."

"What are you thinking of? I am a slave; I have a master. Besides, do you think that Abdallah would ever break his word? He is taking me to the sherif; would you have him betray his faith?"

"Then tell the sherif to give you Abdallah for a husband."

"Hush, idiot. Such a request would be the death-sentence of us all."

Cafour musingly repeated to herself Omar's message; then, looking at Leila, "Mistress," said she, "if you should become Abdallah's wife, and go to dwell with him amid the tents, would you keep me with you?"

"Always, child. I love you; you shall never quit me."

"Should I be your slave and Abdallah's all my life?"

"Of course. But of what use is such a question?"

"Swear this to me," returned Cafour, in a solemn voice, "and let me alone. Do not question me; do not shake your head with disdain. What do you risk in swearing what I ask? Would you sell me or send me away?"

"No, indeed. Should it please God for me to become the wife of him whom I love like my own soul, you shall always remain with us; I swear it to you in the name of God, the clement, the merciful, the sovereign of the worlds—"

"My mistress, I am an ignorant heathen; swear it to me only by the God of Abdallah."

Talking thus, the two friends reached the harem, where numerous companions awaited them. Cafour, still laughing, leaped from the palanquin and ran toward a large room, brilliantly lighted, and filled with tables covered with silver and flowers. Leila complained of the fatigue of the journey, and retired to her chamber to weep without restraint. Useless grief, powerless remedy for an ill that could not be cured! "He who is intoxicated with wine," says the sage of Shiraz, "awakens during the night; he who is intoxicated with love awakens only on the morning of the resurrection!"

XX.

THE PATIENCE OF REYNARD.

ABDALLAH wished to set out the same evening, and Hafiz was not less impatient. It seemed to him that by fleeing to the desert, his nephew would leave anxiety and sorrow behind him. But the sherif had announced that he would receive the chiefs of the caravan the next day, and it was impossible to decline the honor.

At an early hour they repaired to the palace. The courtyard was full of Bedouins, dressed in their blue robes set off by a scarlet scarf thrown across the shoulder. All wished to shake hands with the brave Abdallah and the prudent Hafiz. Omar talked in a low voice with the old shepherd; for the first time he complained of the dangers of the road; for the first time he reproached the sherif for having exposed so many brave men to almost certain death. Hafiz approved his words, and seconded them with a warmth which delighted the son of Mansour.

The visiters were led by black slaves into a room covered with rich carpets, and surrounded with divans of green silk embroidered with gold. The walls were bare of all ornament except a beautiful Turkish sabre, set with topazes and rubies, a gift from the sultan. Omar pointed it out to Hafiz, who, while murmuring against what he called a weakness, never-

theless bowed respectfully before the Commander of the Faithful. After receiving the salutations of all the band, the sherif
clapped his hands, and pipes and coffee were instantly served.
The Bedouins seated themselves on the ground, and each
smoked in silence. Abdallah started ; among the crowd of
servants who stood awaiting their master's orders, he had just
seen Cafour, who raised her hand to her throat. Whether it
was to him or to some other that the child made the sign,
he could not guess ; no one raised his eyes, least of all
Omar.

The descendant of the Prophet seemed buried in deep reflection. He was a noble-looking old man, whose white beard,
large nose, and calm eyes gave him an air of majesty. A large
turban, a blue robe of the finest Cashmere, and a girdle of gold
and purple, in which glittered a dagger covered with precious
stones, added to his dignity. At heart, the sherif was a sage
who thought of no one but himself. Intractable toward all who
disturbed his peace, he was the gentlest of mankind when his
passions and habits were let alone. Power had not spoiled
him ; he readily listened to the truth when it did not affect
himself, and suffered without complaint the most shameless
falsehoods of his flatterers and servants. Fastidious, a great
lover of stories, and a refined poet, his only weakness—a weakness natural to his age—was the desire to be loved. Thanks
to this secret, which she had learned the very first day, the
beautiful Fatima had made her master the most obedient of
slaves ; she made him submit to all her fancies by telling him
that a woman's caprices are the proof of her love. At sixty
it is easier to believe than to quarrel, and the sherif yielded to
avoid a storm, too happy when he was rewarded with a caress.
This morning, however, there was not a cloud on the horizon.
The Commander of the Faithful seemed in excellent humor ;
he smiled as he ran his fingers through his long beard, and

looked like a man just waking from a blissful dream which he would fain retain.

The second pipe finished, the sherif took up the conversation, and in the most gracious terms thanked the Bedouins and Omar for their visit and their services. Instead of replying to this courtesy, the son of Mansour started up like a criminal struck with terror, and, prostrating himself before the descendant of the Prophet, kissed his feet.

"Son of Ali and of Hassan," said he, in a broken voice, "I know what the slave deserves who suffers his master's trust to be violated. I know my crime, and await without complaint the punishment reserved for me by your justice."

"Rise," said the sherif, kindly. "What is written is written. God sends disaster and success by turns to men, in order that he may know the believers, and choose his witnesses from among you. As to the insult offered me by those wretches, I shall choose the day and hour for reparation. Patience— with patience every thing comes in due season."

"Alas!" continued the son of Mansour, still on his knees, "the attack was nothing ; my brother Abdallah and his brave Bedouins repulsed the traitors. But we were surprised ; the slave was for a moment in the hands of the enemy ; those men without faith and honor tore off her veil, and profaned with their unworthy looks that beauty which should have been sacred from all."

"Enough!" interrupted the sherif, displeased at this tale. "The care of my honor concerns me alone. Patience !"

"Patience !" exclaimed Hafiz ; "that was what the fox said when he feigned death."

"What was it that the fox said ?" asked the sherif, looking sternly at Hafiz, who seemed moved by any other feeling than that of fear.

"There was once a fox who was growing old," said the

Bedouin, "and who abandoned the chase and all adventures in order every night to visit a poultry-yard near his hole, where he grew fat without trouble or danger. One night he forgot how the time was passing, and when he was ready to go out, he found the sun risen and every one at work. To return safely seemed impossible; so, in order not to brave certain danger, he stretched himself by the roadside and pretended to be dead, saying, 'Patience — in patience there is safety.' The first who passed by paid no attention to him. The second turned him over with his foot to be sure that he was dead. The third was a child, who amused himself by pulling out his whiskers. 'Patience!' said the fox. 'The child knows not what he is doing; he does not mean to insult me. It is better to suffer vexation than to run the risk of death.' Next came a hunter with a gun on his shoulder. 'A fox's nail is a sovereign remedy for a felon,' said he, taking out his knife. 'Patience!' said the fox; 'it is better to live with three paws than to die with four;' and he let himself be mutilated without stirring. Next came a woman with a child on her shoulder. 'This fox's teeth will make a necklace that will preserve my babe from the evil eye,' said she."

"I know the story," interrupted the sherif; "when the mother came near, the fox flew in her face."

"My story does not say so," returned Hafiz, gravely. "When once we compound with our courage, we know not where to stop. The fox let himself be robbed of his teeth, repeating 'Patience!' and lay still till a last thief tore out his heart, when he saw, but too late, that patience is the surest of dangers."

"I begin to think so," said the sherif, "since a Bedouin comes to my palace to tell me his foolish stories. A shepherd must be rude indeed not to understand my indulgence and to insult my goodness. If the caravan was attacked in a safe country traversed by all the merchants, whose fault was it except those who chose for their leader a child whom I spare through pity? A dozen armed and resolute Bedouins always cross the desert without any one daring to attack them. If the Arnauts surprised you, a snare must have been laid for you, into which you fell either through folly or treachery."

"My lord," cried the son of Mansour, raising his hands in supplication, "you speak truly; this was my fault. In choosing my brother and friend for the leader of the caravan, I ought to have remembered that at our age passion renders us blind. Chance destroyed us. At the beginning of the journey the sight of the slave troubled the young man, and made him forget his prudence."

"What do I hear?" cried the sherif, with flashing eyes. "Is this the way that I am obeyed—is this the way that I am respected? Woe to him who has trifled with me! He shall see whether I will submit to insult. Merchant, you shall be punished for your imprudence, and, young man, you shall suffer for your folly." And, calling a negro with a large sabre at his side, the Commander of the Faithful pointed to Omar and Abdallah, making a horizontal movement with his hand. It was the sentence of death.

The Bedouins looked at each other, shuddering, but no one, not even Hafiz, dared rebel against the descendant of the Prophet. Omar heard the sentence without changing countenance; he looked around him as if to implore aid, and, raising his hand, made a sign to the negress which she did not seem to comprehend. The son of Mansour frowned angrily. "Accursed be the dervish," murmured he. "Can he have told the truth? Is my confidence in the Bedouin about to plunge me into this ruin? Can I have loved this madman better than I thought?"

Abdallah raised his eyes, and proudly smiled at the execu

tioner. "Poor child," said Hafiz, embracing his nephew, "I have slain you."

"No, my father," replied the young man, calmly, "it is God that gives life and death. Be resigned, and comfort my mother. Do not pity me ; to me death is better than life." Then, turning to Omar, who still kept his eyes fixed on the negress, he gave him his hand. "My brother, pardon me," said he, "in the name of her who watched over your childhood." And, bowing respectfully to the Commander of the Faithful, he followed the executioner.

"Stop !" cried Cafour, falling at the sherif's feet. "It was my fault ; it was I that snatched off my mistress's veil. Kill me, but spare Abdallah."

"Drive off this daughter of a dog, and punish her till she is silent," said the sherif.

"Pardon !" cried the child, as a negro was carrying her off —"pardon !" and with a desperate effort she tore herself from the slave, leaving a piece of her dress in his hands. "Pity !" she murmured, clasping the knees of the sherif, who rudely repulsed her. "Pity, master ; Abdallah is innocent ; he was not the guilty one." Then, suddenly spying Omar's contracted features, she sprang up as if struck with lightning, and, stretching her hands toward the prince, "Do not be cruel," said she. "Remember that love is like madness ; every thing is forgiven it."

"Stop !" cried the sherif to the executioner. "There is something strange in this," thought he ; "it is the same sentence that Fatima repeated to me this morning, and refused to explain to me. Come here, child," said he to Cafour, in a milder tone. "Where do these words come from—do you know ?"

"Yes," said Cafour ; "they come from lips that open only for consolation and pity."

"Do you know the meaning of them?"

"Yes," replied Cafour, trembling as she spoke. "Abdallah has never heard these words, but Omar has long known the secret of them; question him; he will tell you every thing."

"Oh, my master," cried Omar, dragging himself to the sherif's feet, and speaking in a suppressed voice, "the child is right. I know these words but too well; it was they which caused my fault, and which will perhaps excuse it. When you summoned me to Taif, my errand was suspected; before I could quit your palace, a mad promise was wrung from me, which I have only too faithfully obeyed. I compromised the slave as I had been commanded. Could I resist a will protected by your love? Happy is he who can inspire such ardent passion; will not happiness render him indulgent?"

While uttering these unblushing falsehoods, the son of Mansour studied the sherif's face, which resumed its serenity. Omar soon ceased to supplicate the old man who held his life in his hands. Sure of his victory, he began to flatter him beyond measure, and, by adroit words, gradually soothed the last emotions of anger in his soul.

"Rise! I pardon you," said the sherif, at length. "I also pardon this proud Bedouin, who braves me even under the sword of the executioner. I have shown that I fear no one, and that I know how to punish those who insult me; it is enough; I keep the blood of my faithful followers for a better occasion. Young man," he added, looking at Abdallah with a kindly smile, "remember that henceforth your life belongs to me; I rely on you, as well as your friends, to avenge our common insult."

For his sole answer, the son of Yusuf took the sherif's hand and kissed it with emotion, while Hafiz burst into transports of joy and gratitude.

"Here!" said the Commander of the Faithful, calling Cafour; "come hither, daughter of night; is this all that the sultana told you."

"No," answered the negress, boldly, putting on a mysterious air. "The sultana told me that if you pardoned her her mad love, she must also have a proof of your affection."

"Speak," said the old man; "what can I refuse a poor creature that loves me to distraction?"

"The sultana fears that you will refuse her request; to grant it, she says, needs a love as great as her own."

"Speak," said the sherif; "I am dying of impatience."

"Well, then, do not give her for a rival this strange woman, dishonored by the gaze of the Bedouins and Arnauts."

"Is that all?" replied the Commander of the Faithful, smiling. "What! raise this woman to my throne, after all that has passed? Never! She shall remain a slave, and end her days in a corner of the harem."

"That is not what the sultana means; she is anxious and jealous. What she desires is that Leila should quit the palace, never more to return. 'Let my husband,' said she, 'let the beloved of my soul give me a last pledge of his love. Can he not leave this creature to those who brought her hither? It will be easy to find an honorable match for her among the Bedouins, and I shall be left alone to love the master of my life.'"

"Oh, the weakness of women!" cried the descendant of the Prophet. "The Koran is right in recommending indulgence to us who have strength and sense. This jealousy of Fatima's is madness, at which I should blush to yield, were it not my pleasure to show her that nothing is impossible either to my power or my love. Bring Leila hither, and tell the sultana that her rival shall not return to the harem. Such is my will; I mean that all shall respect it."

O

And, turning to the Bedouins, " My friends," said the sherif, in a loud voice, " I make you the judges of my conduct. What should I do with the Egyptian woman whom you have escorted hither? Through respect for myself, I can not take her as a wife ; through respect for the pacha, I can not keep her as a slave. This, therefore, is what I propose to do : if there is any one among you who is willing to marry a foreigner, I will give her to him with a fitting dowry, otherwise I will marry her to some rich merchant of Medina or Mecca."

" God is great !" cried the son of Yusuf, seizing Hafiz's arm. " We will look no farther for the four-leaved clover ; it is here ; it is mine ; I have found happiness."

" Courage, my son," said the old man ; " it is needed even to be happy. I do not think," he added, looking at the sherif, " that it will be necessary to go to Mecca to marry the stranger. If a husband only is needed, here is a young man who will yield to no one either in birth, fortune, or courage."

" My lord," said Omar, bowing low to the sherif, " I should never have had the boldness to raise my eyes to a woman confided to my charge ; but, since things have changed, and you permit it, I venture to aspire to the hand of Leila. She is a slave of the pacha ; from her childhood she has been accustomed to the ease and luxury of the harem ; on coming hither she dreamed of a fortune which has escaped her grasp ; who knows whether tent-life will not seem hard to her? Wealth is a necessity to a woman that has always lived in a palace. I entreat your lordship, therefore, to give the stranger to the one that shall offer the largest dowry ; it will be a last mark of kindness to her who owes every thing to your goodness."

" The request is just," said the sherif. " Bring the Egyptian hither. Let the suitors come forward ; I will hear their proposals."

" My uncle," murmured the son of Yusuf, " I am lost !"

"At last," said Omar, "Leila is mine!"

Cafour looked at the two brothers, and ran to the harem.

XXI.

THE AUCTION.

WHILE the slaves went in search of Leila, Hafiz approached the son of Mansour.

"Omar," said he, "listen to an old man who has dandled you on his knees. It is said that you are richer than your father; women bow before your fortune, and there is not a merchant in Egypt or Syria but would think himself honored by your alliance. Nothing fetters your desires. Abdallah, on the contrary, can never love another woman; he has given his heart to her whom he has saved. Be generous; pay to-day the debt of gratitude by making your brother and Halima happy."

"My brother is a selfish fellow," answered Omar; "I have suffered too much through him already. He knows that I wish this Egyptian woman; he knows that I will have her at any price; what does he expect to gain, therefore, by declaring himself my rival? If I should lose a hundred thousand piastres, of what advantage would it be to him? Let him give up Leila, and I will try to forget that this very day he has put my head for the second time in danger."

"It is well for you that you are a Mussulman," said Hafiz, "otherwise we would teach you before the day was over that an ounce of lead weighs more than all your gold; but you have not succeeded as you think, and, with the aid of God, we will confound your abominable selfishness."

Omar shrugged his shoulders and went to meet Leila. She had just entered, concealed from all eyes by the wrappings which enveloped her, yet it seemed to poor Abdallah that a fiery glance shot from the thick veil which he could scarce withstand. Cafour followed her mistress. What she had said to the sultana none could tell, but she had on her neck a necklace of pink coral, which certainly had not been cut for a slave. From time to time she ran to a latticed balcony which overlooked the room, and exchanged mysterious words with invisible figures. The whole harem was there, deeply interested in the fair Leila, and perhaps offering up prayers for the son of Yusuf.

Abdallah was the first to speak. "My sole fortune," said he, "is the spring which I have discovered, and the garden which I have planted. With my father's arms and my mare, these are my only possessions. All are yours, Leila, if you will accept my heart and life."

"They are not worth a hundred thousand piastres," said Omar, coldly. "Here at Taïf I have a garden of orange-trees where the sherif sometimes does me the honor to take coffee. This garden is worth more than two hundred thousand piastres; I offer it to Leila in pledge for a like sum in jewels."

"Jewels!" said Hafiz; "my nephew has those which are as rich as yours. Here is a casket which is worth all your promises."

To the general astonishment, the old shepherd, aided by Cafour, opened a tortoise-shell and mother-of-pearl casket, filled with ear-rings, bracelets, and precious stones. Abdallah could not repress a cry. Was not that ruby bracelet the one which Leila wore on her arm on the day of the attack, and was not that coral necklace one which Cafour had just snatched from her neck? He attempted to speak; a gesture of his uncle stopped him.

"Beautiful jewels which have been worn already!" said the son of Mansour, biting his lip. "I do not ask where all these

spoils of women come from, which I esteem as they deserve; but my generosity shall not be outdone. I offer three hundred thousand piastres."

"Promising is not giving," interrupted Hafiz; "something more than words is needed."

For his sole reply, Omar drew a pocket-book from his girdle, and, taking from it several papers, handed them to the sherif. "My lord," said he, "these are the orders which you sent me some months ago, and which are already filled. They are worth more than a million piastres; will your lordship refuse to be his slave's security till to-morrow to these exacting Bedouins?"

"It shall be as you desire," answered the sherif. "I will be your security for a hundred thousand piastres."

"If this sum is all that is needed," said one of the Bedouins, "we will not leave a companion in trouble, and will give a lesson to this merchant who forgets himself. Here are our sabres; we will redeem them with a hundred thousand piastres." And, taking off his yataghan, he flung it at the sherif's feet with a contemptuous glance at Omar, while Hafiz approached to do the same, and to set an example to the rest of the band.

"Take back your sabre," said the Commander of the Faithful to the Bedouin. "I will be security for you and your friends. God forbid that I should see you disarmed about me, you who are my strength and my glory. Omar," he added, "before making new promises, perhaps you would do well to reflect. Repentance often follows satisfied passion. A lost slave can be replaced, but friends lost are never found again."

"Commander of the Faithful," proudly rejoined the son of Mansour, "it was on the faith of your word that I entered into this business, and, unless you command me to stop, I will carry it through. I fear no one's displeasure but yours. And, to put an end at once to this wrangling, I offer a million piastres; it is not too large a dowry for a woman whom your lordship has honored with his protection."

"Are you rich enough to commit such follies?" said the descendant of the Prophet. "I shall remember it on the first occasion."

"Command, my lord," returned the merchant; "my fortune and life are yours."

A deep silence followed. Leila, who had remained standing, sunk upon a divan; Abdallah cast down his head; and Hafiz and his friends threatened Omar, who braved them with a disdainful air. Cafour began to gesticulate in a strange manner toward the balcony, and disappeared. All eyes were fixed on the sherif, who evidently hesitated.

"I have given my word," said he at last, slowly addressing the Bedouins; "you are witnesses that every thing has been done in an impartial manner. This merchant, your companion in the caravan, offers a million; the slave, therefore, must belong to him, if none of you offers more."

"Where could such treasures be found in the desert?" cried Hafiz. "Souls sold to Satan alone possess this infernal wealth. As for us, we have nothing but our guns and sabres ; may the day come when their value will be felt !"

" You forget Abdallah's jewels," said Omar, smiling.

" Ah! my brother," cried the son of Yusuf, "what have I done that you should treat me thus? Ought you to be the one to plunge a dagger into my breast?"

"What is this?" asked the sherif of two slaves who laid a heavy casket of chased silver at the feet of Abdallah.

" My lord, it is the treasure of the son of Yusuf," answered one of the porters, as he opened the casket and took up handfuls of the most beautiful precious stones ever seen, which at the first glance were seen to be worth more than a million.

" It is strange," thought the sherif, "how much this diamond tiara and these topaz bracelets resemble those I gave the sultana. Who has sent you?" he asked the slave.

" My lord," replied the negro, bowing, "love is like madness ; all things are forgiven it." And he went out.

Abdallah thought himself the sport of a dream. Omar turned pale with rage. "There is some snare here," murmured he ; "no matter, I will have the last word. I will give two million piastres, if necessary."

Four more slaves, heavily laden with plate, silver lamps, and chased cups, paused like the first before Abdallah, and laid this treasure at his feet. At the first glance, the sherif recognized a magnificent epergne, the ornament of his harem, which he had received as a present from the sultan, and given, not without regret, to Fatima, the day after a quarrel.

" Who can have given orders to bring all these treasures hither?" he cried.

"My lord," replied the porters, bowing, "love is like madness ; all things are forgiven it."

"Let these knaves be bastinadoed," said the Commander of the Faithful ; "I will teach them to answer me in proverbs. Who sent them ?"

"My lord, it was Cafour," replied one of the slaves, in a tremulous voice.

"Bring that child of the devil hither," said the sherif. "If she is let alone she will carry off my whole palace."

The four slaves had not quitted the room when six more entered, carrying a litter heaped with the most costly robes and the richest stuffs. At the head of the procession was Cafour, giving orders with the gravity of an imaum. The sherif called her, and, taking her by the ear, "Come here, wretch," said he ; "once for all, will you tell me the meaning of these follies ?"

"Love is like madness ; all things are forgiven it," answered Cafour, gravely.

"Do you dare to mix up the sultana with this disorder ?"

"The sultana is there," rejoined Cafour, tranquilly pointing to the balcony ; "she has seen and heard every thing ; she knows all, and," she added, lowering her voice, "she is furious."

"Furious ? and at what ?" cried the astounded sherif.

"She knows," continued Cafour, "that you regret having sacrificed Leila ; she has guessed the part played by this merchant, who is bidding in your name ; she feels that passion alone could hurry you away so far as to make you humble these brave Bedouins, who are the honor of your empire. 'Since he loves me no longer,' she said, 'I want no more of his favors ; take away from my sight the jewels which he has given me, and the robes with which I delighted in adorning myself to please him. Carry all to Abdallah ; let him contend for me to the last moment. If the master of my soul returns to me, what need have I of riches? if he abandons me, I wish to keep nothing but the memory of his love.'"

The sherif looked at the balcony somewhat ill-humoredly. He fancied that he spied through the lattice a little hand tearing a lace handkerchief in pieces, and the sound of tears and stifled sobs made him cast down his head. That instant he became conscious that the friendship of the Beni Amurs was worth more to him than the gratitude of Omar, and decided on his course.

"I will not be made an accomplice of unworthy weaknesses," said he, in a solemn voice. "I never take back a promise which I have made. I wished to secure a suitable dowry to this woman, who is under my protection ; a hundred thousand piastres is sufficient. As to deciding between the rivals, that belongs to Leila. Let her take the merchant or the Bedouin, the city or the desert, it matters little to me. I shall respect her choice, and force all others to do the same."

"Neither David nor Solomon could have judged more righteously," cried Hafiz.

The two brothers stood by the side of Leila. Abdallah gazed at her with deep tenderness, and was mute with hope and fear. Omar spoke, moved with anger and jealousy.

"Think of the future," said he ; "do not sacrifice to this man the flower of your youth and beauty. Do you know the life of women in the tents ?—a beggarly and slavish existence. Are your hands made to grind corn, milk sheep, weave cloth, and gather grass and sticks? Will this Bedouin give you the baths, jewels, and perfumes to which you are accustomed? Will he dye your eyebrows and eyelids? will he wash your tresses with orange-flower water, and dry them with musk and amber? With me, you will have women to wait on you, robes to deck you, and jewels to adorn you ; you will not be a servant, but a mistress ; each of your caprices will be a law and a pleasure to me."

Leila bowed, took the trembling hand of Abdallah, and placed it on her head. "I am my lord's slave," she said. "A stranger, I have no other refuge than he ; an orphan, I have no other family. He is my father, my mother, and my brother. Oh, my beloved," she added, in a low voice, raising her eyes, "at last I am thine, and can tell thee that thou art my joy and my life." And, smiling and weeping at the same time, she kissed the hand of her husband.

The Commander of the Faithful gazed delightedly at this spectacle, which renewed his youth. "It is rather a hard lesson for Fatima," thought he ; "but I am not sorry for having confounded the sultana ; she will be cured for some time of her incurable jealousy."

Omar was mute ; his contracted features, his threatening. eyes, every thing about him betrayed the conflict of grief and pride.

"Son of Mansour," said Hafiz, "you should marry Cafour. Your soul is as black as her skin ; you would have children worthy of their grandfather Satan."

"You are cruel, my uncle," exclaimed the son of Yusuf. "If Omar had been in my place, he would have spared us. My brother," he added, extending his hand to the Egyptian, "forgive me my happiness."

"You are shrewder than I ; I congratulate you on your success," answered Omar. And he quitted the room in despair.

"What a fine thing is youth !" said Hafiz ; "how honest ! how confiding ! what faith in virtue ! As for me, I am old, and have been in battle. When I find a wicked man under my feet, I crush him like a scorpion, that he may sting me no more."

XXII.

THE ARRIVAL.

IT is easier to retain wealth in the hand of a prodigal, or to carry water in a sieve, than to lodge patience in the heart of a lover. The day had not dawned and the bird had not quitted its nest when the son of Yusuf awakened his companions, and arranged in a long file the camels loaded with the gifts of the sherif and the sultana. He impatiently awaited his beloved, whom Fatima had kept with her all night, that she might tell her the story of her love. A woman always loves the rival that she has ceased to fear. When Cafour opened the door of the harem and showed herself, uglier and more smiling than ever, Abdallah uttered a cry of surprise and joy. Could the woman behind the child, who stretched out her hand to him, really be Leila?

It was she—a lover could not be mistaken ; yet it was no longer the Egyptian loaded with jewels, but a Bedouin who had always lived in the tents. Leila was clad in a long blue cotton robe, which was gathered around the neck and fell to the feet. Over this robe was a red woolen burnous, which covered her head. Her black tresses, arranged in numerous small braids, each ending in a coral bead, fell to her eyes, and added to the softness and brilliancy of her glance. In this simple costume, with her head uncovered and her feet bare, Leila was the queen of the desert. The delighted Bedouins saluted her as she passed, as fresh and smiling as the dawn.

They set out. A recent storm had revived nature ; the grass, wet with dew, and the freshly opened flowers, smiled on these happy hearts. Leila no longer hid herself in the back of the palanquin ; Abdallah rode beside her, talking all the way, with his hand on the side of the litter. Cafour had never been more talkative and saucy.

"Oh, Abdallah," said Leila, " if you bear so hard on the side of the litter, you will overturn it and throw us both on the ground."

"Well, let go the camel's rein, then ; don't refuse me the pleasure of holding your hand."

"Ingrate !" cried Cafour, "you have quite forgotten me. So, black Bedouin, you are carrying off the wife of the Calif Moyawiah !" And, with a joyous voice, she struck up the Bedouin girl's song :*

> "Oh, take these purple robes away,
>   Give back my cloak of camel's hair,
> And bear me from this towering pile
>   To where the black tents flap in air.
> The camel's colt, with faltering tread,
>   The dog that all but barks at me,
> Delight me more than ambling mules—
>   Than every art of minstrelsy.
> And any cousin, poor but free,
>   Might take me, fatted ass, from thee."

They went on thus the whole day, unconscious of heat or fatigue. When joy follows suffering, do we think of aught else than joy? Hafiz, besides, was there to lead the caravan, and Abdallah did not need to quit the treasure that the Bedouins were bringing back in triumph.

Night was approaching when they came in sight of the tents of the Beni Amurs. The sun was setting beneath the arch of an immense rainbow that spanned half the sky, a roseate light illumined the sands of the desert, and golden rays flashed their gleams on the summit of the granite pyramids. In the distance was heard the shrill cry of the sakiah, the

* The song of the beautiful Bedouin girl Moyawiah is renowned among the Arabs. It may be found in Burton's Personal Narrative of a Pilgrimage to El Medina and Mecca.

barking of the dogs, and the cooing of the pigeons. Suddenly a piercing shout announced the return of the travelers.

"What cry is that?" asked Leila.

"It is my mother's voice," answered Abdallah, dismounting from his horse. "You will have two to love you."

Halima soon appeared, greatly astonished at the sight of so long a caravan. "What are these?" said she, pointing to the packages; "has the son of Yusuf sold his horse and arms to turn merchant?"

"Yes, my mother," answered Abdallah; "and I bring you the rarest and choicest of wares, a daughter to respect and assist you."

Leila alighted from the litter and threw herself into the arms of Halima, who looked at her with astonishment, and asked the name of her father and tribe. She was not less surprised at the sight of Cafour, and, despite all Hafiz's speeches, returned to the tent with a sigh. She had little liking for a stranger woman. But when Abdallah came and seated himself by her side after unloading the camels, and Leila hastened with a basin of warm water to wash her husband's feet herself, "God be praised," cried Halima, "this woman will be truly a handmaid unto her husband. My house has at last found a mistress; I can die in peace." And she tenderly embraced the daughter whom God had given her in his goodness.

"What is the matter, master?" said Cafour, who was lying at Abdallah's feet, with her head resting on her preserver's lap; "has the smoke of your pipe got into your eyes? you look as if you were crying. Oh, your pipe has gone out; will you have a coal to light it?"

"Hush! hush!" said the Bedouin, stroking the negress's head as if caressing a faithful dog. The child lay down again, at the same time jerking her mistress's arm so suddenly that

Leila's forehead came in contact with Abdallah's lips. Cafour laughed at the success of her stratagem. Poor creature! to whom every thing was denied, and who found means to be happy by placing her happiness in that of others.

XXIII.

KARA SHITAN.

OMAR had returned to Djiddah with despair in his heart. It was in vain that his slaves tried to divert him; it was in vain that business and gold poured in on him from all sides; his passion consumed him. He passed whole days in his chamber, sitting cross-legged on a carpet, revolving impossible projects in his brain, and seeking for a vengeance which escaped him.

"Of what avail is my father's wish to me?" he cried. "Of what use is my health and the money that I have accumulated? am I any the less, on that account, the most unhappy of men? That wretched Bedouin, in his poverty, triumphs over me. I am lonely and desolate in the midst of my abundance. Accursed be life—accursed be my brother! The oracle has not deceived me; I am slain by my best friend." And he relapsed into his despair.

The grief of Omar was the talk of the whole city. If little love was felt for the son of Mansour, on the other hand his fortune was greatly esteemed. Was there not some service to offer or some consolation to sell him? it was asked. After such an insult, he would well reward whomsoever should avenge him on the Bedouin. Such words are not lost. It is the curse of the rich that there are those around them ready to enter the fires of hell in their behalf. The passions of the poor are flames which consume the heart, and then quickly die out; the passions of the rich are a brazier, fed by all about it, and giving forth conflagration, crime, and death.

One morning the son of Mansour received a visit from an Arnaut captain, who came, he said, on important business that would suffer no delay. Omar received him politely, and ordered pipes and coffee to be served.

" Capital coffee !" said the captain, sipping it slowly ; " as bitter as death, as black as Satan, and as hot as Hades. And what an exquisite mixture of nutmeg, cinnamon, and clove ! What a fine thing it is to be rich ! the world seems to move for you alone."

" Men are sometimes mistaken about the happiness of the rich," said Omar, sighing.

" Bah ! a rich man in sorrow is a miser who knows not how to use his gold. If he loves a woman, let him buy her ; if he wishes to be rid of a rival, let him sell his skin. Every thing can be bought here on earth ; with money, a man can have every thing."

" To whom have I the honor of speaking?" asked the son of Mansour.

" My name is Kara Shitan," replied the stranger. " I am an Arnaut chief—one of those who attacked you in the desert. By killing my friend Mohammed, your brother Abdallah made me lose five thousand douros ; pay me this sum, and I will rid you of Abdallah."

" A murder !" said Omar.

" Bah !" rejoined the captain, coldly ; " if God had not invented death, it would not be long before we should eat each other. Away with false scruples ! When an occasion offers, wisdom commands us not to let it slip. It is just to force our enemies to drink the bitter cup which they have made us taste ; we are right in striking them with the weapon with which they were the first to wound us."

"My brother !" said Omar, in a hesitating tone.

"Your brother and your enemy. What matters his death to you? you will have no hand in it. I shall kill Abdallah like a dog if I find him in the desert ; I shall avenge my own quarrel ; only, in order to avenge myself, I must have five thousand douros."

"Of what use will your vengeance be to me?" said the son of Mansour.

"I know nothing about it," replied Kara Shitan ; "I don't understand business as well as you do ; but, if I were in your place, and Abdallah should disappear, I should find no trouble in gaining possession of the beautiful Leila. The Bedouin, it is said, has no family but his mother and an old dotard ; a little courage and resolution will remove these obstacles. An abduction is an easy matter ; Leila once a widow and in your house, it will not take long to console her. What is there to fear? The sherif? At Djiddah, men laugh at the anger of the Bedouins. The pacha? He is a man like the rest of us ; he has a conscience, and we know its price."

"And the tribe—have you thought of that?"

"The tribe is nothing," said the captain. "I know that these Bedouins have as much rancor and malice as their camels ; but blood can be bought as well as other things ; money is not despised in the desert any more than any where else, and the Beni Amurs will console themselves with Abdallah's inheritance."

"Yes," returned Omar, "blood can be ransomed when the murder is involuntary. A hundred camels is the price of a man's blood ; but there is no composition for murder, and I shall suffer death."

"The desert is mute," said the captain, "and dead men tell no tales. He who finds a shriveled corpse among the sands must be shrewd indeed if he can distinguish a murder from

an accident. But we will say no more about it," added he,
rising. "What is the charming Leila, whom I have never beheld, to me? Let her love her Bedouin; let them be happy
together and laugh at the son of Mansour—it is all the same
to me. After all, Abdallah is a brave man, and I respect him;
if you had inflicted on him the outrage which you have received, he would not haggle about the price of vengeance.
Farewell."

"Stay," cried the son of Mansour; "you are right. While
Abdallah lives there is no security for me on earth; it was
predicted to me at my birth, and I feel it daily. Deliver me
from this enemy. As to the cripple, I have an account to settle with him which I will attend to myself. Leila, you will
cost me dear!"

"If you take my advice," resumed the captain, "we shall
both strike at the same time. I will entice away Abdallah,
never more to return, and you shall carry off the lady; all will
be done in two hours, and the enemy overthrown even before
he suspects the danger."

"So be it," said Omar; "but remember that I never wish
to see your face again."

"That is very natural," replied Kara Shitan. "Tell me the
day and hour, give me the five thousand douros, and rely on
my punctuality. My reputation is made; I would not fail to
keep my word for the finest horses in Arabia."

XXIV.

HOSPITALITY.

WHILE avarice and hatred were plotting Abdallah's death,
the son of Yusuf was enjoying his happiness without dreaming of a cloud in the horizon. Could he suspect that he had
an enemy when his soul was so pure and his heart so free

from bitterness? He who loves and is beloved looks on all men as his brethren. For a month he had been intoxicated with joy and tenderness, with no other care than that of admiring Leila and thanking God for having blessed his house.

In one of those hot, misty mornings which precede a storm, Abdallah was reposing in his garden in the shade of the citron-trees. Cafour carelessly lay at his feet, her eyes fixed on him like a dog watching for an order or a glance. At the back of the tent Halima was baking loaves in the ashes, while Leila, seated before a loom, was embroidering gold and silver lozenges on her husband's burnous. The son of Yusuf abandoned himself to the happiness of living surrounded by all whom he loved. The barking of the dogs roused him from his reverie. A man had stopped his camel at the garden gate, and was stretching out his hand to the young Bedouin. Leila disappeared, and Abdallah went to meet the stranger.

"Welcome," said he; "thy arrival brings us the blessing of God. The house and all it contains are thine; thou art the master thereof."

"Son of Yusuf," answered the stranger, "I will not set foot on the ground till thou hast sworn to render me the service of which I am in need."

"Speak," said Abdallah; "thou art a guest—thy word is a command."

"I am a poor merchant from Syria," resumed the stranger. "I have been to Mecca on business. Yesterday I was drawn into a quarrel in the Holy City with a Beni Motayr, and had the misfortune to kill my adversary. His family and friends are pursuing me; I have no one to defend me; if I can not reach the noble Medina, I am lost. You alone, it is said, can conduct me thither in safety; my life is in your hands—decide my fate."

"Enter my tent," replied the son of Yusuf. "In two hours we will set out."

"Remember," said the merchant, "that I trust myself to you alone."

"I alone will accompany you," returned Abdallah; "I answer for your safety on my head."

No sooner had the stranger been brought into the tent and confided to the care of Halima than the young Bedouin went out to prepare for departure. Cafour stopped him on the way. "Do you know this man?" said she.

"No; what matters it? It was God that sent him hither."

"He is not a merchant; I have seen his pistols—they are too handsome; he is a soldier. Beware of him."

"Soldier or merchant, what have I to fear from a stranger and a fugitive?" returned Abdallah. "Make haste and prepare supper; I have only time to tell Leila of the journey."

When the son of Yusuf returned to his guest, Cafour had spread the table with unleavened bread, pressed dates, boiled rice, new milk, and cold water. She bustled about him and gazed at him earnestly, trying to recall where she had seen this face, which seemed familiar to her. The stranger was perfectly calm and indifferent. In her anxiety, she determined to arouse him and break the charm that hid the danger. Seizing an earthen vase, she placed herself behind the pretended merchant, and threw it on the ground, shivering it in pieces. The stranger looked angrily around.

"The Arnaut!" cried she, looking at her master.

"Begone," said Abdallah, "and do not trouble me with your follies."

Cafour glided to a corner of the tent, and soon returned with boiling tea. The stranger was perfectly tranquil; the word Arnaut had not moved him.

"My guest," said Abdallah, "welcome to this poor table.

The journey will be long, and it is good to strengthen yourself against the fatigue to come. Satisfy your hunger."

"Excuse me," replied the merchant; "my anxiety and fatigue have given me a fever, and I have but one desire—to set out on my way."

"Salt is good for the appetite," said Cafour, and, taking a handful of salt, she thrust it into the stranger's mouth and fled to the garden.

"Wretch!" cried Abdallah, "I will chastise your insolence," as he rushed furiously after Cafour to punish her.

"Strike," said Cafour, weeping, "strike the dog that warns you, and caress the jackal that will devour you. Did you not hear the dogs howl this morning? they saw Azrael. Madman, your sins blind you; death is hovering over this house. Do you not know that merchant?"

"A guest is above suspicion," interrupted Abdallah; and, returning to the tent, he found the stranger seated in the same place, with a smile on his lips.

"The slave has given me a lesson in politeness," said he. "The beard of the guest is in the hand of the master of the tent; I will endeavor to do honor to your hospitality." He fell to eating with an excellent appetite for a sick man, talking freely, and seeking every means to be agreeable to Abdallah.

At the moment of departure, when the stranger was already mounted, Leila came out, with her face half concealed in her burnous, holding a pitcher in her hand, from which she sprinkled a few drops of water on the feet and haunches of the camel. "May God give thee a good journey," said she, "and conduct thee back in safety to those who love and watch for thee."

"Those who love me are under ground," answered the stranger; "and since I lost my mother, twenty years ago, no one has watched for me."

"Then may God give thee a wife to love thee and grow old by thy side."

"Let us go," said the stranger, abruptly; "the moments are numbered."

"My lord," said Leila to her husband, "thou bearest happiness away with thee; mayest thou soon bring it back again!"

Cafour was by Abdallah's side. "Master," said she, "don't you take your gun?"

"No, it would be an insult to him whom I accompany. Fear nothing; he whom God guards is well guarded. When my uncle returns from the fields, tell him to watch over the tent. Next to God, it is to him that I trust you."

And, taking his lance in his hand, Abdallah set out on his way, walking by the side of the stranger's camel. Halima and Leila followed the travelers with their eyes as long as they could see them, then returned to the tent. Cafour alone remained outside, with fixed gaze and trembling heart. It seemed to her that the horizon was about to open and the desert to give back the master for whom she watched. Vain hope of an anxious soul! Night fell on the earth without bringing Abdallah.

XXV.

THE GOLDEN LEAF.

No sooner had they plunged into the sands than the stranger looked around him to be certain that he was alone, and began to play with the handle of his pistol.

"I hope, my dear guest," said Abdallah, "that you will pardon the folly of that child who disturbed your repose."

"If the slave had been mine, I should have punished her severely," answered the traveler.

"We should be indulgent to those who love us," returned

Abdallah. "Cafour thought me threatened with some great danger; it was to save me from this imaginary peril that she involuntarily offended you. By forcing you to eat my salt she has made us friends for life and death. Is not this the case among you Syrians?"

"In my tribe," said the stranger, "the obligation lasts for one day. But if the second day passes without partaking of the same dish, the salt loses its virtue, and we are free to hate each other."

"Well, my guest," replied Abdallah, smiling, "you shall kill me to-morrow after I have saved your life. Until then I am in your keeping; it is your duty to protect me against all men."

"So I will," returned the stranger—then was silent. "These are strange words," thought he. "The Bedouin is right; I can not kill him while the salt of hospitality is still in my stomach —it would be a crime. I will wait till evening. When the sun sets another day will begin, and I shall have the right to do as I like."

All along the way he gazed at Abdallah, who went on with an erect head and calm brow. The Bedouin's pistols were not loaded, and if he carried a lance in his hand, it was only to aid him in walking.

"This man's confidence hampers me," said the stranger to himself. "I would gladly fell an enemy; I can not slaughter a sheep. Five thousand douros for such a task is not enough; I would rather kill that dog of an Omar for half the price."

When the sun was near setting, the merchant urged on his camel in order to prepare his weapons without being seen by Abdallah; then, hiding his arms under his burnous, he paused. "Well," thought he, "the moment has come."

As he turned round, the son of Yusuf approached him, seized the camel by the bridle, and, thrusting his lance into the ground, spread two carpets on the sand. "My brother," said he, "this is the hour of prayer. The keblah is before us, and if we have no water for our ablutions, you know that the Prophet permits us to use the sand of the desert."

"I have no time to waste here; let us go on," cried the stranger.

"Are you not a Mussulman?" said Abdallah, looking at him with a threatening air.

"There is no God but God, and Mohammed is his prophet," the merchant hastened to reply. "But the religion of a poor pilgrim like me is simpler than that of a noble Bedouin. I do not pray, because all that God does he does well; I do not wash my face, because I need the water of the desert to drink; I do not give alms, because I ask them; I do not fast in the month of Ramadan, because I famish with hunger all the year round; and I do not go on pilgrimages, because the whole earth is the house of God. This is my faith; so much the worse for those who are too nice to like it."

"You surprise me, my dear guest," resumed the son of Yusuf. "I had a different opinion of you. Do you not wear, like myself, an amulet on your arm to drive away the temptations of the evil spirit? Do you not know that it contains the two saving chapters?"

"Yes, I wear a talisman," said the stranger. "My mother gave it to me twenty years ago on her dying bed. It is the only thing that I respect; more than once it has turned aside the death that was whistling about me."

"Have you forgotten the words that make the virtue of this treasure?"

"I have never troubled myself about them; my mother chose them for me; she knew that of which I am ignorant."

"Hearken to them," said Abdallah, solemnly. "When a man lives in the midst of these sands which may overwhelm him at a breath, it is good to draw nigh by prayer to him who alone rules the danger."

And, bending toward Mecca, the son of Yusuf repeated, with emotion, the chapter of the Koran entitled the

DAYBREAK.

"In the name of the clement and merciful God,
· Say, I fly for refuge unto the Lord of the DAYBREAK ;
From the mischief of the beings whom he has created ;
From the mischief of the night when it cometh on ;
From the mischief of the envious, who beareth us envy."

"Peace be upon thee !" cried the merchant. "Are those the words which my mother left me ?" and, while listening to Abdallah, he replaced the pistols in his belt.

The son of Yusuf continued to recite the Koran :

MEN.

"In the name of the clement and merciful God,
Say, I fly for refuge unto the Lord of MEN,
The King of men,
The God of men ;
From the mischief of him who suggests evil thoughts and slyly withdraweth,
Who whispers evil into the hearts of men—
From genii and men."

"Who says this ?" asked the stranger. "Who reads thus the heart ?"

"It is God himself," replied Abdallah ; "we are his. If he wishes our destruction, our feet lead us where death awaits us. If he wishes our safety, death falls before us like a wounded lion. He saved Abraham in the midst of the flames ; he drew Jonah from the depths of the sea and the belly of the whale."

"Then do you never fear death ?"

"No. Where God commands, all precautions are vain. There are two days in our life when it is useless to arm ourselves against death—the day when God orders Azrael to strike us, and the day when he forbids him to approach us."

"May we not still fear the unknown hour that is destined to carry us away?"

"No, not if we have followed the Word of God. Your mother doubtless told you more than once what mine has often repeated to me, 'Remember that on the day of thy birth thou alone wept, while all around thee rejoiced. Live so that at thy last moment all around thee may be in tears, while thou alone hast no tears to shed; then thou wilt not fear death, whatever may be the hour of its coming.'"

"You dwellers in the desert are a strange people," murmured the stranger;. "your words are golden, but your acts are evil." And he involuntarily carried his hand to his pistol.

"We are the people of the Prophet," returned the Bedouin; "we follow his teachings. Before ever you set foot in my tent," he continued, raising his voice, "I knew you, Kara Shitan. You are my enemy; you came to my dwelling under a false name; I know not the end of your journey, and nothing would have been easier than for me to rid myself of you; but you demanded my hospitality; God placed you under my keeping, and this is why I have accompanied you, alone and unarmed. If you have evil thoughts, may God protect me; if not, give me your hand."

"May hell be my inheritance if I touch him who has spared me!" said Kara Shitan. "Here is my hand; it is that of a soldier who returns evil for evil, and good for good."

No sooner had the Arnaut uttered the words than he began to regret them. "Here I have allowed myself to be trifled with like a child," thought he. "Shall I give back the five thousand douros? No; Omar is rich enough to pay his brother's debt. Besides, have I not rid him of Abdallah? If his heart has not failed him, Leila by this time is on the way to Djiddah. If he undertakes to complain, let him come for his douros ; I have promised to kill some one—I give him the preference." At this happy thought, Kara Shitan laughed to himself, and admired his own wit.

An instant after he was seized with remorse. "It is not natural," thought he, "for me to give way to such weakness. Who now will ask my aid? I am like an old lion without teeth or claws. That young woman who spoke to me so gently, this Bedouin who trusts in me, the voice of my mother which seems to rise from the tomb—all this is magic. Accursed amulet, thou hast destroyed me !" and he snatched the talisman from his arm.

"Captain," said Abdallah, "we must plunge into the desert if you would not meet the caravan which we see yonder on the way to the noble Medina."

"No," said Kara Shitan ; "on the contrary, I shall join it ; I need you no longer. What shall I give you to show my gratitude? Here, take this talisman. You know not what you owe it ; you know not what it costs me. Farewell ; if you hear me called a coward, remember that I have been your guest and your friend."

And, urging on his camel, he rode off, leaving Abdallah surprised by these strange words, the meaning of which escaped him.

Left alone, the son of Yusuf endeavored to fasten the protecting amulet about his arm. It was a little roll of parchment, wound around with a silken thread. On one side was sewed a bit of velvet, to which something resembling a golden bee was attached. Abdallah uttered a cry of joy : he could not be mistaken ; it was the third leaf—the clover was complete. The son of Yusuf had nothing more to seek for on earth ; the diamond leaf awaited him in heaven.

With a soul overflowing with gratitude, Abdallah prostrated

himself on the earth, and, in a voice full of emotion, recited the Fát-háh :

<blockquote>
" In the name of the clement and merciful God.
Praise be to God, the Lord of the universe,
The clement and merciful,
The King of the day of judgment,
Thee alone do we worship, and of thee alone do we beg assistance.
Direct us in the right way,
In the way of those whom thou hast loaded with thy blessings,
Not of those who have incurred thy wrath, nor of those who go astray,
Amen, Lord of the angels, of the genii, and of men."
</blockquote>

The prayer finished, Abdallah turned his face homeward with a light heart and joyous tread. A new thought had entered his brain—a thought which was a new happiness in itself. Was it certain that the diamond leaf had fallen within the gates of Paradise? Did not these three leaves, reunited from different parts of the globe, cry out for their sister? Could a blessing of God remain imperfect? Why might not a new effort, a more entire devotion to the divine will, obtain the highest prize for which Abdallah's heart sighed?

Intoxicated with this hope, the son of Yusuf walked on without thinking of the length and fatigue of the journey, and the darkness alone forced him to stop. The sky was lowering, and the moon did not rise till near morning. Wrapped in his burnous, the Bedouin threw himself at the foot of a tree, and quickly fell asleep. But his thoughts did not quit the divine clover ; he saw it in his dreams : then the leaves grew and assumed a human form ; Leila, Hafiz, Halima, and poor Cafour, hand in hand, formed the mysterious plant, and enriched him with their smiles and love. "To-morrow, my loved ones, to-morrow we shall meet again !" murmured he.

"Verily, the knowledge of the hour of judgment is with God. No soul knoweth what it shall gain on the morrow, neither doth any soul know in what land it shall die ; but God is knowing, and fully acquainted with all things."

XXVI.

THE RETURN.

WHEN the son of Yusuf awakened, the moon was shedding her gentle light on the earth, and the breeze of the morning was already felt. The impatient traveler quickened his steps, and, on mounting a small rising ground, he saw the tents of his tribe in the distance by the first beams of daylight. In front of them, and nearer him, was his own dwelling; he had waited for autumn before removing from the garden he had planted, the bower in which Leila took delight.

At the sight of his people, Abdallah paused to take breath and enjoy the spectacle before his eyes. The first sounds of the morning were succeeding the calmness of the night. A few women were already on their way to the well, with their pitchers on their heads; the camels were stretching out their long necks and braying; and the sheep were bleating in their folds for the shepherd. Around Abdallah's tent all was silent; there was neither sound nor movement in the garden. "My uncle is growing old," thought the Bedouin; "there is great need of me at home. What happiness to surprise them all! Who would have thought once that a day's absence would seem so long to me!"

As he descended the hill a horse ran past him at full gallop —it was Hamama. He called her; the frightened mare fled toward the Bedouin village; for the first time she did not hear the voice of her master.

"Who has untied Hamama?" thought Abdallah. "What has frightened her? It is some new prank of Cafour's. Why haven't they kept better guard?"

He entered the garden, the gate of which was open. At the sound of his steps the dogs came out of the tent, but, instead of running to meet him, they set up a mournful howl. "God is great!" exclaimed the son of Yusuf. "Misfortune has entered my dwelling."

In a moment he felt the bitterness of death. He tried to go on, but his knees bent beneath him, and a cloud passed before his eyes. He tried to call out, but his words choked him. At last, with a desperate effort, "My uncle, my mother, Leila, Cafour, where are you?" shouted he.

There was no answer. The doves were cooing among the branches, the bees were humming around the last remaining flowers, the water was rippling over the pebbles; every thing was living in the garden—the tent was mute and lifeless. Abdallah dragged himself from one clump of trees to another; then his strength returned, and the blood mounted to his cheeks. He staggered onward like a drunken man.

The tent was empty, the furniture overturned, and a table broken; there had been a struggle. The curtain of the apartment of the women was down. Abdallah ran thither. As he entered he stumbled over a corpse—it was Hafiz. The old man was stretched on his back, his teeth shut, his mouth covered with foam, and his features contracted with rage. His hands were clenched. In the left he held a shred of blue cotton stuff—it was the robe of Leila; in the right a piece of scarlet cloth, torn doubtless from the ravisher. Brave Hafiz! the cowards had not dared attack him face to face, but had assassinated him from behind while he was defending Leila.

Abdallah fell on his knees by the side of his uncle and closed his eyes. "God grant thee mercy!" said he; "may he be as good to thee as thou wert to us!" He rose without shedding a tear, and walked with a firm step toward the village; but his limbs failed him on the way, and he was forced to lean against a palm-tree for support. Taking his pistols from his girdle, he fired them in the air. At the sound the

Bedouins ran from all sides. Men and women surrounded Abdallah, who stood pale, with frenzied eyes and trembling limbs. "Here you are," he cried, "brave warriors, Beni Amurs, kings of the desert! Oh, sons of Jews, hearts of women, cowards, the curses of God fall upon your heads!" And for the first time he wept.

A cry of rage answered his words. "He is mad," cried one of the old men; "respect him whose soul is with God. Come, my child," added he, taking Abdallah's hand, "calm yourself; what is the matter?"

"What is the matter?" cried the young man. "This night, in my absence, Hafiz has been killed, my mother has been carried off, all that I loved have been snatched from me. And you—you were asleep—you heard nothing. Curses on you. To me the misfortune; to you the outrage and in-famy!"

At the first words of Abdallah the women had rushed toward the tent, where they were heard moaning and weeping. The sheik cast down his head.

"Who would have thought of watching over your family when your uncle and brother were there to protect them?" said he.

"My brother! impossible!"

"Your brother came here last evening with six slaves," said a Bedouin. "I knew the little merchant; I helped Hafiz kill a sheep for the supper of his guests."

The son of Yusuf hid his face in his hands, then looked at his companions, and said in a faint voice, "Come and see what my brother has done, and advise me what to do."

"Advice is easy," replied the sheik. "After an outrage there is but one thought for him who has a soul—vengeance! You are a finger of our hand; whoever touches you wounds us; whoever seeks your life seeks ours. Omar has a few hours the start of us, but with God's aid we will kill him before night. Come, my brave men," he added, "saddle your horses and take a double ration of water; the weather is lowering, and the skins dry fast. Let us go."

Before mounting his horse, Abdallah wished to see his uncle once more. The women had already surrounded the corpse and commenced their lamentations. "Oh, my father, my only friend," cried the Bedouin, "you know why I leave thee. Either I will never more enter this dwelling, or thou shalt be avenged."

The Beni Amurs followed the son of Yusuf. The sheik gazed long at old Hafiz; then, raising his hand, "Accursed be he who returns to his wife till he has stricken down the enemy!" said he. "Woe to him who has insulted us; before this night we will fling his corpse to the eagles and jackals. The whole earth shall know whether the Beni Amurs are brethren who cling together, or children with whom men can trifle with impunity."

XXVII.

LEILA.

THE band set out amid the cries of the women and shouts of vengeance; once in the desert, all was silent, each making ready his arms and watching the horizon. It was not difficult to follow the caravan; the wind had not yet effaced the footprints of the camels, all of which pointed toward Djiddah. Abdallah, always in advance, counted the minutes, and called God to his aid; but, however much he strained his gaze, he saw naught but solitude. The air was burning, the heavens were heavy with the coming storm. The horses, panting and covered with sweat, advanced at a slow pace. The son of Yusuf sighed; vengeance seemed escaping him.

At length he perceived a black speck in the distance—it was the caravan. It had felt the approach of the storm, and had taken refuge near those Red Rocks known so well to Abdallah. "My friends, we have them!" cried he. "Here they are; God has delivered them into our hands. Forward!" And each one, forgetting fatigue, spurred his horse on the ravishers.

In these endless plains it is not easy to surprise an enemy that stands on his guard. Omar soon recognized his pursuers, and did not wait for them. He ranged the camels in line, and placed a few drivers behind them to feign a defense, then mounted a horse and fled with the rest of the band into the desert.

The Bedouins came up. At the first discharge, Omar's camel-drivers gave way and fled among the rocks. Before the smoke was cleared away a woman ran to meet Abdallah: it was Halima, who had been left behind and had escaped her enemies.

"Blessed be thou, my son!" she cried. "Do not stop; give chase to that negro with the red jacket; he is the assassin of Hafiz and the kidnapper of Leila. Avenge us; eye for eye, tooth for tooth, life for life! Death to traitors, death to murderers!"

At these cries Hamama rushed over the sands with the swiftness of a torrent, as if sharing in her master's passion. The Bedouins had great difficulty in keeping their companion in sight. As for Abdallah, rage made him forget danger. "Cowards!" cried he to the accomplices of Omar, "where would you flee when God pursues you?" and with drawn sabre he passed amid the bullets, his eye fixed on the negro who was carrying off Leila. The pursuer and pursued soon left the rest of the party behind. The Ethiopian, mounted on a fleet horse, sped like an arrow through the air, while Abdallah followed close behind. Hamama gained ground; vengeance was approaching. Leila, placed in front and held by a powerful arm, called her husband, writhing in the stifling embrace, and vainly struggling against the terrible rider. Suddenly she seized the bridle and gave it a jerk, which disturbed the horse, and caused him to stop for an instant. "Curses on you," cried the negro; "I am lost. Let go the bridle, or I shall be killed."

"Here, my beloved!" cried Leila, clinging to the bridle, despite threats and blows, with the energy of despair.

She was saved. The son of Yusuf fell like a thunderbolt on the ravisher, when suddenly the frightened Hamama sprang aside with a bound which would have thrown any other than her rider. A heavy mass had fallen at her feet. Abdallah heard a groan which chilled him to the heart. Without thinking of the flying enemy, he leaped to the ground and raised the unhappy Leila, pale and bleeding, with distorted features. A deep wound was gaping in her throat, and her eyes were sightless. "Leila, my love, speak to me!" cried Abdallah, clasping his wife to his heart, while he tried to stanch the gaping wound from which her life-blood was ebbing. Leila no longer heard him. He seated himself on the sand with his precious burden, and, taking Leila's hand, raised one finger in the air. "My child," said he, "repeat with me, 'There is no God but God, and Mohammed is his prophet.' Answer me, I entreat you; it is your husband—it is Abdallah that calls you."

At this name Leila started; her eyes sought him whom she loved, and her lips half opened; then her head fell on Abdallah's shoulder like the head of a dying hare on the shoulder of the hunter.

When the Beni Amurs joined the son of Yusuf, they found him motionless in the same place, holding his wife in his

arms and gazing in her face, which seemed to smile on him.
They surrounded their companion in silence, and more than
one wept.

At the sight of the corpse Halima uttered a cry of anguish,
and threw herself on her son's neck ; then, suddenly rising,
"Are we avenged?" said she. "Is Omar dead? is the negro
slain?"

"See those crows gathering yonder," said one of the Bedouins ; "there is the murderer of Hafiz. Omar has escaped
us, but the simoom is rising ; it will overtake him before he
can escape from the desert, and before an hour the sand will
serve as his winding-sheet."

"My son, summon up your courage," said Halima. "Our
enemy still lives ; leave tears to women. Leave us to bury
the dead ; go, punish the traitor ; God will go with you."

These words reanimated Abdallah. "God is great!" he
cried. "You are right, my mother ; to you the tears, and to
me the vengeance."

He rose and placed Leila in his mother's arms ; then, gazing at her pale face with infinite tenderness, "Peace be with
thee, daughter of my soul," he said, in a slow and grave voice.
"Peace be with thee, who art now in the presence of the
Lord. Receive what has been promised thee. It is God
that raises us up, it is God that casts us down ; it is God
that gives us life, it is God that sends us death. If it pleases
God, we shall soon join thee. O God, forgive him, and forgive us !"

He raised his hands to heaven, murmured the Fát-háh, and,
passing his hand over his brow, embraced his mother and
mounted his horse.

"Where are you going?" said a sheik. "Do you not see
that fiery cloud advancing? We have barely time to reach
the Red Rocks ; death is yonder."

" Farewell," answered Abdallah. " There is no more rest for me except in the shadow of death."

XXVIII.

VENGEANCE.

SCARCELY had the son of Yusuf quitted his friends when he found himself before a corpse ; it was the negro, already covered with birds of prey. "God hates the treacherous," murmured the Bedouin ; "he will deliver the son of Mansour into my hand."

The whirlwind was approaching ; the sky was of a milky white ; the rayless sun looked like a burning millstone ; and a poisonous blast dried up the saliva in the throat, and melted the marrow of the bones. A noise was heard in the distance like that of an angry sea ; whirlwinds of red dust rose from the sand, and mounted in columns to the sky, like giants with faces of fire and arms of vapor. Every where there was desolation, every where an implacable heat, and at moments a silence even more horrible than the moaning of the simoom.

Over this land, parched with drought, Hamama advanced slowly, with panting breath and palpitating sides. Her master had the tranquillity of a man that knows neither hope nor fear. He felt neither heat nor thirst ; one thought alone ruled his body and soul—to overtake the assassin and kill him.

After an hour's march he saw a horse stretched on the sand. A little farther on he heard something like a sigh. He approached the spot. A man lay in the dust perishing with thirst, and without strength to utter a cry. It was the son of Mansour. His eyes were starting from his head, his mouth was wide open, and his hands were pressed to his panting chest. Delirious with pain, he did not recognize Abdallah ;

all that he could do was to carry his fingers to his parched throat.

"Yes, you shall have water," said the Bedouin; "not in this way shall you die."

He dismounted from his horse, took a skin of water from the saddle-bow, and, after throwing away Omar's pistols and sabre, put it to the lips of the dying man. Omar drank deeply of the water which restored his life, and found himself face to face with Abdallah.

"You have saved me," murmured he; "I recognize your inexhaustible goodness. You are a brother to those who have no brothers, a life-giving dew to the unfortunate."

"Son of Mansour, you must die," said the young man.

"Pardon, my brother!" cried the merchant, recovering the consciousness of danger; "you have not saved my life to put me to death! Pardon, in the name of what is dearest to you on earth—pardon, in the name of her who nourished us both."

"Halima curses you," returned Abdallah; "you must die."

Terrified at the sinister air of the Bedouin, Omar fell on his knees. "My brother, I acknowledge my guilt," said he. "I have deserved your anger; but, however great my fault, can I not redeem it? Take all my fortune; be the richest man in Arabia."

"You have killed Hafiz—you have killed Leila; you must die," said Abdallah.

"Leila dead!" exclaimed the son of Mansour, bursting into tears; "it can not be. Her blood be on her murderer's head; I am not guilty of it. Spare me, Abdallah; have pity on me."

"As well implore the gates of the tomb," replied the son of Yusuf. "Make haste," he added, drawing his sabre. "May God give you patience to endure the affliction he sends you."

"At least, my brother," returned Omar, in a voice of emotion, "give me time for a last prayer. You would not have the angel of death seize me before I have implored the mercy of God?"

"Say your prayers," replied Abdallah.

The merchant unrolled his turban and spread it before him; then, throwing his robe over his shoulders and bowing his head, he awaited the death-blow.

"God is great!" he murmured; "there is no strength nor power but in God. To him we belong; to him we must return. O God! sovereign of the day of retribution, deliver me from the fires of hell; have pity on me."

Abdallah gazed at him, weeping. "It must be," he said to himself — "it must be;" yet his heart failed him. This wretch was his brother; he had loved him—he still loved him. When love has once entered the soul, it lodges there like the ball in the flesh; tear it out if you will, the wound still remains. In vain the son of Yusuf sought to rouse his courage ·by calling to mind the images of his slaughtered uncle and dying wife; despite himself, he could see nothing but the happy days of childhood, Halima clasping both her children to her breast, and old Hafiz taking them in his arms to tell them of his adventures in battle. The pleasures they had shared, the sorrows they had had in common, all these sweet recollections rose from the past to protect the son of Mansour. Strange to say, the victims themselves appeared to ask pardon for the assassin. "He is thy brother, and defenseless," said the old soldier. "He is thy brother," cried Leila, in tears; "do not slay him." "No, no," murmured the young man, repulsing the beloved phantoms, "it must be. Not to punish crime is to betray justice."

In spite of the trouble of the son of Mansour, Abdallah's hesitation did not escape his keen eye. Bathed in tears, he

clasped the knees of his judge.   "Oh, my brother," he said, " do not add thy iniquity to mine.   Remember what Abel said to his brother when threatened by him : ' If thou stretchest forth thine hand to slay me, I will not stretch forth my hand against thee to slay thee ; for I fear God, the lord of all creatures.' Alas! my folly has been greater than that of Cain. Thou hast a right to kill me; my life is too little to expiate the crime to which I have been led by my passions. But the forgiving God loves those who follow his example; he has promised indulgence to those who remember him; leave me to repent. He has promised a paradise whose breadth equaleth the heavens and the earth to those who bridle their anger; pardon me that God may show thee mercy, for God loveth the beneficent."

"Rise!" said Abdallah; "thy words have saved thee. Vengeance belongs to God alone. Let the Lord be thy judge; I will not dip my hands in the blood of him whom my mother has nursed."

"Wilt thou abandon me here?" said Omar, looking round him anxiously; "it would be more cruel than to slay me."

For his sole answer, Abdallah pointed to Hamama. Omar sprang on the mare, and, without turning his head, buried his spurs in her flanks and disappeared.

"Well," thought he, as he rode through the billows of sand upheaved by the wind, "if I escape the simoom, I am saved from the peril predicted me. This Abdallah is very imprudent to remain in the desert in such weather, alone, without a horse, and without water. No matter; his folly be on his own head. I will forget these accursed Bedouins, who have never brought me any thing but misfortune. The time has come at last to live for myself."

XXIX.

THE DIAMOND LEAF.

THE wicked laugheth in his heart at his success, and saith, "I am cunning, and cunning is the queen of the world." The just submitteth to whatever may befall him, and saith, lifting his hands to heaven, "O Lord, thou causeth to err whom thou pleaseth, and directeth whom thou pleaseth; thou art the mighty, and the wise; what thou doeth is well done."

Abdallah turned his steps homeward with profound sadness. His soul was still troubled; he had expelled its anger, but could not uproot its grief. Large tears trickled down his face, while he made vain efforts to check them. "Forgive me, O Lord," he cried; "be indulgent to the weakness of a heart that can not submit. The prophet has said, 'The eyes are made for tears and the flesh for affliction.' Glory to him who holdeth the dominion over all things in his hands! May he give me strength to endure what he has willed!"

He walked on thus in prayer amid the sands and the fiery whirlwinds; heat and fatigue soon forced him to stop. The blood in his veins was turned to fire; a strange disorder troubled his brain, and he was no longer the master either of his senses or thoughts. Devoured with a burning thirst, at moments both sight and hearing deserted him; then he saw in the distance gardens full of verdure and lakes bordered with flowers; the wind whistled through the trees, and a spring gushed from among the grass. At this refreshing sight, he dragged himself toward these enchanting waters. Vain illusion! gardens and running springs all vanished at his approach; there was naught about him but sand and fire. Exhausted and breathless, Abdallah felt that his last hour was approaching. "There is no god but God, and Mohammed is his prophet," he cried. "It is written that I shall never depart from this place. O Lord, come to my aid; remove far from me the horrors of death!"

He knelt and washed his face with the sand of the desert; then, drawing his sabre, began to dig his own tomb.

As he began to stir the earth, it suddenly seemed to him that the simoom had vanished. The horizon lighted up with a glow softer than the dawn, and the clouds slowly opened like the curtains of a tent. Was it the mirage? None can tell; but Abdallah stood mute with surprise and admiration. Before him bloomed a vast garden, watered by brooks flowing in all directions. Trees with trunks of gold, leaves of emerald, and fruits of topaz and ruby, covered broad lawns, enameled with strange flowers, with their luxuriant shade. Beautiful youths, clad in green satin and adorned with costly jewels, reclined on magnificent cushions and carpets, looking lovingly at each other, and drinking from silver cups that water, whiter than milk and sweeter than honey, which quencheth the thirst forever. By the side of the youths stood enchanting maidens, with large black eyes and modest mien. Created of the light, and like it transparent, their grace ravished the eyes and the heart; their face shone with a softer lustre than the moon emerging from the clouds. In this kingdom of delights and peace, these happy couples were smilingly conversing, while lovely children, eternally young, surrounded them like strings of pearl, each holding a vase more sparkling than crystal, and pouring out for the blessed that inexhaustible liquor which never intoxicates, and the taste of which is more delicious than the fragrance of the pink. In the distance was heard the angel Israfil, the most melodious of the creatures of God. The houris joined their enchanting voices to the notes of the angel, and the very trees rustled their leaves, and celebrated the divine praise with a harmony exceeding all that man has ever dreamed.

While Abdallah admired these marvels in silence, an angel descended toward him ; not the terrible Azrael, but the messenger of celestial favors, the good and lovely Gabriel. He held in his hand a tiny diamond leaf ; but, small as it was, it shed a light that illumined the whole desert. His soul intoxicated with joy, the son of Yusuf ran to meet the angel. He paused in terror ; at his feet was a vast gulf, full of fire and smoke, bridged only by an immense arch made of a blade of steel, which was finer than a hair and sharper than a razor.

The Bedouin was already seized with despair, when he felt himself supported and urged on by an invisible power. Hafiz and Leila were on either side of him. He did not see them ; he dared not turn for fear of awaking ; but he felt their presence, he heard their soothing words ; both supported and carried him along with them. "In the name of the clement and merciful God !" he cried. At these words, which are the key to Paradise, he was transported, like lightning, to the other side of the bridge. The angel was there, holding out the mysterious flower. The young man seized it. At last the four-leaved clover was his, the ardor of desire was quenched, the veil of the body was lifted, the hour of recompense had struck. Gabriel turned his eyes toward the bottom of the garden, where divine majesty was enthroned. Abdallah's glance followed that of the angel, and the eternal splendor flashed in his face. At this lustre, which no eye can endure, he fell with his face to the ground, uttering a loud cry.

This cry man's ear has never heard, man's voice has never repeated. The delirious joy of the shipwrecked mariner who escapes the fury of the waves, the delight of the bridegroom who presses his beloved for the first time to his heart, the transports of the mother who finds the son whom she has wept —all the joys of earth are naught but mourning and sorrow to the cry of happiness which rose from the soul of Abdallah.

At this voice, repeated afar by the echoes, the earth resumed the beauty of its days of innocence and blossomed with
the flowers of Paradise ; the sky, bluer than sapphire, seemed
to smile upon the earth ; then gradually silence fell on all
things, the heavens darkened, and the whirlwind regained dominion of the desert.

XXX.

THE HAPPINESS OF OMAR.

ON re-entering his house at Djiddah, the son of Mansour
experienced the joy of a criminal escaped from death ; he
shut himself up to regain his composure, and again viewed
his wealth and handled his gold ; it was his life and his power ! Did not his treasures give him the means to subjugate
men and the right to despise them ?

Nevertheless, the pleasure of Omar was not unmixed ; there
was still more than one danger in perspective. If Abdallah
reached home, might he not regret his clemency ? If he
should die in the desert, would he not have an avenger ?
Might not the sherif think himself offended ? Might not the
pacha set an extortionate price on his protection ? The son
of Mansour drove away these importunate thoughts. " Why
be terrified," thought he, " when the most imminent peril is
past, thanks to my address ? Am I at the end of my resources ? My real enemies have fallen ; shall I not overcome
the others ? Life is a treasure that diminishes daily ; what
folly to waste it in vain anxieties ! How difficult it is to be
perfectly happy here on earth !"

These reasonable fears were followed by other cares which
astonished the son of Mansour. In spite of himself, he thought
of old Hafiz whom he had murdered ; nor could he put aside

the remembrance of Leila, or of his brother dying in the desert, the victim of a generous devotion.

"Away with these foolish imaginings, that whiten the beard before the time!" cried he. "What weakness to think of such things! Can I change destiny? If old Hafiz is no more, it is because his time had come. On the day that Abdallah was born, his death was written before God. Why shall I, therefore, trouble myself? Am I not rich? I buy the conscience of others; I will buy repose for my own heart."

It was in vain for him to try; his soul was like the restless ocean, which, unable to appease its angry waves, casts up mire and foam upon the shore. "I must gain time," thought he; "these feelings are nothing but a remnant of agitation, which fools call remorse, but which is nothing but a little fatigue and feverishness. I know how to cure it; I have a wine of Shiraz which has more than once consoled me; why not seek patience and forgetfulness therein?"

He went to his harem, and called a Persian slave with an enchanting voice—a heretic who was not shocked at the use of the cup, and who poured out with infernal grace this poison accursed by all true Mussulmen.

"How pale you are, master!" said she, on seeing the discomposed features of the son of Mansour.

"It is the fatigue from a long journey," answered Omar. "Pour me some wine, and sing me one of the songs of your country, to drive away care and bring back mirth."

The slave brought two crystal cups set in gold, which she filled with a liquor as yellow as gold and as clear as amber; then, taking a tambourine, she struck it alternately with her hand and elbow, and waved it over her head, while she sang one of the perfumed odes of the Bulbul of Shiraz.

> "Pass round the flowing bowl, child,
> Filled to the brim with bright wine;

<blockquote>

All the ills and the woes of life
  Are healed in this juice divine.
Has Time writ his lines on thy brow?
  Has sleep through the night fled thine eyes?
Cast into these liquid flames
  Thy regretful cares and thy sighs.

" Away with that drinker morose,
  Who mourns for the years that are gone ;
In these wines of amber and rose
  The flowers and the spring live on.
Are the roses dead in thy bowers?
  Has the nightingale left thee alone?
Drink, drink, and the clink of the glass
  Shall be sweet as the bulbul's tone.

" Leave Fortune, the treacherous sprite,
  To the weak or the wicked throng ;
What good can she give us more,
  Since she leaves us wine and song?
The false one, lightly betrayed,
  Nightly in visions I see ;
Oh, wine, give me back the sweet dream !
  Oblivion and love are in thee."

</blockquote>

"Yes, give me oblivion," cried the son of Mansour. "I know not what is the matter with me to-day ; this wine saddens instead of diverting me. Strike your instrument louder, sing faster, make more noise, intoxicate me."

The beautiful Persian sang merrily, striking her tambourine :

<blockquote>

" Hafiz, thou squanderest life :
  ' In the wine-cup death lurks,' say the old ;
Oh sages, he envies you not,
  Nor your snowy locks nor your gold.
You may chide him, but still he will drink ;
  Day and night he will still drink deep,
For wine only can cause him to smile,
  Wine only can cause him to weep."

</blockquote>

" Curses on you !" cried Omar, raising his hand to strike the slave, who fled affrighted. "What name do you bring me? Can not the dead rest in their graves? Will they come even here to trouble my repose? After ridding myself of my enemies, shall I care for phantoms? Away with these chimeras!   I will tear out these memories from my heart; in spite of them all, I will laugh and be happy."   As he said this, he uttered a cry of terror.   Cafour stood before him.

"Where do you come from, child of the devil?" he exclaimed.   "What are you doing in my house?"

"That is what I wish to know," answered the child; "it was not by my will that your servants carried me to your harem."

"Begone! I do not wish to see you."

"I will not go till you have given me back my mistress.   I belong to Leila; I wish to serve her."

"Your mistress has no more need of your services."

"Why?" said the negress.

"Why?" replied the son of Mansour, in a broken voice. "You will know by-and-by.   Leila is in the desert; go and find her."

"No," said Cafour, "I shall stay here, and wait for Abdallah."

"Abdallah is not in my house."

"He is; I have seen his horse."

"My servants brought away the horse at the same time with you."

"No, they did not," returned Cafour; "before your servants seized me, I had let Hamama loose.   She was more fortunate than I; she escaped.   If she is here, Abdallah must be here too; if not, what have you done with your brother?"

"Away from here, insolent wretch; I will not be questioned by you.   Dread my anger; I can cause you to die under the bastinado."   His eyes glared at these words like a madman's.

"Why do you threaten me?" said Cafour, in a milder tone. "Although I am but a slave, perhaps I can serve you.   You

have some hidden trouble ; I see it in your face. This trouble
I can dispel. In my country we have spells to cure the heart.
Were sorrow or even remorse preying upon your soul, I could
draw it thence as the bezoar stone draws the venom from a
wound."

"You have this power, a child like you !" said Omar, ironically, looking at Cafour, whose eyes steadfastly met his gaze.
"Why not?" he added ; "these Maghrebi negroes are all children of Satan ; they know their father's secrets. Well, yes, I
have a sorrow ; cure me, and I will reward you."

"Have you any hasheesh in your house?" said Cafour.
"Let me mix you a drink ; I will restore your gayety."

"Do what you will," replied Omar. "You are a slave ;
you know that I am rich and generous. I have confidence
in you ; I wish at any price to enjoy life."

Cafour soon found the hasheesh leaves. She brought them
to the son of Mansour, who followed her movements with an
eager eye. She took the plant, washed it three times, and
rubbed it in her hands, muttering strange words. She then
pounded the leaves in a copper mortar, and mixed them with
spices and milk. "Here is the cup of oblivion," said she ;
" drink and fear nothing."

No sooner had Omar drank than he felt his head suddenly
grow light ; his eyes dilated, and his senses became marvelously acute, yet, strange to say, he seemed moved by the will
of Cafour. If she sang, he repeated the song ; if she laughed,
he burst into shouts of merriment ; if she was grave, he wept ;
if she threatened him, he trembled. As soon as the negress
saw him in her power, she set to work to wrest his secret from
him.

"You are satisfied," said she ; "you are avenged on your
enemies ?"

"Yes, I am satisfied." said Omar, laughing ; "I am

avenged. The beautiful Leila will no longer love her Bedouin."

" Is she dead ?" asked Cafour, in a trembling voice.

" She is dead," said Omar, weeping ; " but I did not kill her : it was the negro. Poor woman ! she would have been so well off in my harem !"

" And you no longer fear Abdallah !" said Cafour, with an exulting air.

" No, I do not fear him. I took his horse, and left him alone in the desert exposed to the simoom. He will never more quit it."

" Lost in the sands—dead, perhaps !" cried Cafour, tearing her clothes.

" How could it be helped !" said Omar, in a plaintive voice. " It was destiny. It had been predicted to me that my best friend would be my worst enemy. The dead always love you ; they harm no one."

" What friend had you to fear, you who had never loved any human being ?" cried the negress. "Hold!" she added, struck with a sudden inspiration ; " shall I show you this friend who will cause your death ?"

" No, no," exclaimed Omar, trembling like a child threatened with the rod. " Amuse me, Cafour ; do not make me sad."

" Look," said the slave, placing a mirror before his eyes. " See the assassin of Hafiz—see the murderer of Leila—see the fratricide—see the villain—see him for whom there is no more repose ! Wretch ! you have loved no one but yourself ; your selfishness has been your ruin—your selfishness will be your death."

At the sight of her contracted features and haggard eyes Omar stood terrified. A new light dawned on his soul ; he abhorred himself, and tore his beard in despair. Shame soon restored his consciousness : he looked around him, and, at the sight of Cafour possessed of his secret, he fell into a paroxysm of rage. "Wait, child of perdition!" he cried, "I will punish your insolence; I will send you to join your Abdallah."

Giddy as he was, he attempted to rise; his foot slipped; he struck against the table, and dragged the lamp with him in his fall; his clothes caught fire, and in an instant his whole body was in flames. "Die, villain!" cried Cafour; "die like a dog! Abdallah is avenged!"

The son of Mansour uttered lamentable shrieks, which reached the inmates of the harem. They ran to his aid. At the sound of their footsteps, Cafour set her foot on the face of Omar, and with a bound sprang to the outer door and disappeared.

XXXI.

TWO FRIENDS.

WHILE the slaves flew to the succor of the son of Mansour, Cafour saddled Hamama, took a skin of water and some provisions, and galloped through the narrow streets of Djiddah. The night was dark, and the storm was rumbling in the distance.

The child began to stroke the horse and talk to it, as if the brute understood the language of men. "Oh, dear Hamama," said she, "take me to your master. Together, we will save Abdallah. You know how much he loves you; no other hand has cared for you; help me to find him. Thanks to you, I will restore him to his mother; together we will weep for Leila, and I will comfort him. Do this, dear Hamama, and I will love you." She embraced the horse, and, stretching herself along the neck of the animal, gave it full rein. Hamama darted onward like an arrow, as if led by an invisible hand. As she rushed past an Arnaut post at daybreak, the frightened sentinel discharged his gun, declaring that he had seen Satan mounted on a white horse fleeter than the wind.

Thus flew Hamama, without pausing or needing to drink. A strange instinct impelled her toward her master. She went straight toward him, regardless of the beaten track, over rocks, through beds of rivers and across deep gullies, with God for a guide.

Toward midday Cafour perceived Abdallah in the distance, prostrate on the sand, as if in prayer. "Master! master!" she cried, "here I am." But neither the tread of the horse nor the cries of the child roused Abdallah from his contemplation. Hamama stopped, but he did not stir. Cafour, trembling, ran to him. He seemed asleep ; his face was beaming with ecstasy ; a heavenly smile was on his lips ; sorrow had fled that countenance which had been a prey to such suffering. "Master! master! speak to me," cried the poor slave, clasping him in her arms. He was cold ; life had quitted the mortal covering ; God had called to himself this spirit made for heaven.

"Abdallah!" cried Cafour, throwing herself on him and covering him with kisses, "Abdallah, I loved thee!" And she rendered up her soul to God.

Hamama gazed long at the two friends with anxiety, and laid her burning nostrils again and again on Cafour's cheek ; then she stretched herself on the sand, with her eyes fixed on the two bodies, to await the awakening of those who were never to wake again on earth.

Long after, some Bedouins, wandering in the desert, discovered Abdallah and Cafour in the sands, so closely embraced that it was necessary to put them both into the same coffin. Strange to say, the beasts of prey had devoured the horse, but not a vulture had alighted by day on the head of Abdallah, not a jackal had touched by night the body of Cafour.

Under the shade of the palms by the Well of the Benediction, two mounds of earth, surrounded with stones to keep off the jackals, mark the spot where the Bedouin, the Egyptian, and the negress await together the day of judgment. The fragrant jessamine, trailing from the branches of the trees, festoons the tomb, and surrounds it all the year with odorous blossoms. Here the weeping Halima mourned her children, till summoned by Azrael to join them ; and here the wearied travelers pause, before quenching their thirst at the blessed well, to recite a Fát-háh in honor of Abdallah, well named the servant of God.*

* Abdallah, in Arabic, signifies the servant of God.

THE END.